"Dodd slowly ratchets up the suspense level to the breaking point, while introducing readers to the diverse and quirky characters who live in the small town, and Virtue Falls's claustrophobic atmosphere adds to the menacing sense of danger. With this nail-biting book, RITA Award-winning Dodd shifts the dial of her writing more to the suspense side, but the novel's sexy romantic core will still please her longtime fans." —*Booklist* (starred review)

"Megatalent Dodd returns with a truly stunning work of mystery, danger, and romance. Dodd enhances this new tale with a ghostly presence. Heroine Elizabeth Banner is brilliant, prickly, and damaged by tragedy, but also utterly compelling. Dodd has always been a terrific author, but she kicks it into a whole new realm with this amazing and terrifying novel!" —*RT Book Reviews*
(2014 Paranormal Romantic Suspense nominee)

"Intense and suspenseful, with touches of romance, humor, and mysticism." —*Kirkus Reviews*

"Edge-of-the-seat suspense and fascinating premise. Couldn't put it down. My kind of thriller!"
—Iris Johansen

"Tight, edgy, and compelling, *Virtue Falls* redefines the romantic thriller. This is my favorite kind of suspense . . . I loved it. Fans of Nora Roberts will devour *Virtue Falls*."
—Jayne Ann Krentz

"Compulsively readable." —Elizabeth Lowell

ALSO BY CHRISTINA DODD

VIRTUE
FALLS

CHRISTINA

DODD

St. Martin's Paperbacks

This is a work of fiction. All of the characters, organizations, and events portrayed in this novel are either products of the author's imagination or are used fictitiously.

VIRTUE FALLS

Copyright © 2014 by Christina Dodd.
Excerpt from *Obsession Falls* copyright © 2015 by Christina Dodd.

All rights reserved.

For information address St. Martin's Press, 175 Fifth Avenue, New York, NY 10010.

Library of Congress Catalog Card Number: 2014016827

ISBN: 978-1-250-06830-9

Printed in the United States of America

St. Martin's Press hardcover edition / September 2014
St. Martin's Paperbacks edition / July 2015

St. Martin's Paperbacks are published by St. Martin's Press, 175 Fifth Avenue, New York, NY 10010.

10 9 8 7 6 5 4 3 2 1

Dear Scott, here we are at fifty books, and not one would have been possible without your belief and support.
Loving you is the best thing I've ever done.
Having you love me is the best gift I could ever have.

ACKNOWLEDGMENTS

The journey to create the world of *Virtue Falls* has been by turns difficult and dark, humorous and romantic, complex and fascinating. I couldn't have done it without the advice and support of the remarkable professionals at St. Martin's Press.

Jennifer Enderlin is unmatched in her guidance and editorial direction, and I look forward to a long, close relationship.

The art department, led by Ervin Serrano, thrilled me with the evocative *Virtue Falls* cover.

The publicity team, Anne Marie Tallberg, Stephanie Davis, Angela Craft, Jeanne-Marie Hudson, and Nick Small, have created a *Virtue Falls* publishing event, and held my hand all the way.

To everyone on the Broadway and Fifth Avenue sales teams—thank you for putting *Virtue Falls* into the eager readers' hands.

A huge thanks to managing editor Amelie Littell and Jessica Katz in production.

Blessings upon Caitlin Dareff for handling so many details so efficiently.

Thank you to Sally Richardson, St. Martin's president and publisher.

viii ACKNOWLEDGMENTS

And of course, thank you to Matthew Shear for your faith in me and this book. We miss you, Matthew, but what a wonderful publishing team you left to shape the future! Thank you so much.

Last night in San Francisco

Avery Laine served a mojito to the most morose guy in the bar. "I got home," he said, "and she had cleaned out the house. Not just the furniture and the assets. She even took the ice cube trays. What kind of woman takes the ice cube trays? We had an automatic ice maker. She made a big fuss about buying ice cube trays as backup, and two weeks later she was gone. She bought the trays to make a point? Was that necessary?" His name was Carl Lynch, but to Avery and the other servers, he was their Norm, a hung-over, grumbling basset hound of a guy and their resident barfly.

Avery nodded as if she was interested. She had been here at AskME Club for the whole four years of her employment. She had moved from newbie barmaid easily seduced by a hotshit black musician to the single bartender with a two-year-old kid at home. Like a mournful backdrop to her life, Carl had moved from one disaster to another, depressed and stressed the whole time.

Now she was the AskME's longest-time employee. Not that she wanted to do this forever, but she'd flunked out of San Jose High School, the recession had hit the city hard, and she was good at mixing drinks and serving sympathy to out-of-towners.

Darren Ferrugia proposed on a regular basis, mostly when he was drunk and mostly after his wife had called and given him hell for staying out past his curfew and spending too much on liquor. The guy had impulse control issues.

But in here, after enough liquor and a good look at her long legs bared by her short black skirt, most men did.

Shawn Hendriks came in every few months, whenever he was in San Francisco on business. He had two gin martinis, up, with a twist, and occasionally called his girlfriend in Paris. Not that Avery believed he had a girlfriend in Paris. His shiny bald head with the thin strands of dark hair arranged in a comb-over didn't inspire lust. But once she had eavesdropped and he was speaking French . . . or at least it sounded like French. Plus he never did more than look her over when he thought she wasn't paying attention, and to her, nothing said class like a guy in a nice suit who managed to keep his mouth shut and his zipper up.

Maya Flores sidled up to the bar. "Men. Who needs them? Even the good guys are crap."

"I was thinking exactly the same thing," Avery said. "What's the matter? Norm pinch your ass so hard you've got a bruise?"

Maya rubbed her butt. "Not Norm. Greasy."

"Greasy? Our boss, Greasy?" Tall, ugly, bony, forty-five-year-old Greasy?

Maya's lips peeled back from her teeth; she looked like a pit bull about to attack.

"O-kay. Greasy put the moves on you. I always knew he was a creep, but I didn't realize he . . . You're young enough to be his daughter."

"He's a pig." Maya was twenty-one, same as Avery had been when she started at AskME, but she was smarter than Avery had been; Avery would bet that Greasy was nursing bruised gonads. The thought made her smile.

"I've gotta go. Ready to take over?" Avery stripped off the band that held her blond hair away from her face and tossed it in the Tupperware box under the sink. She pulled her navy blue quilted vest out of the cupboard, slipped it on over her red silk shirt, and zipped it up to her chin. She took her cash drawer out of the register and said, "I'll deliver this to Greasy and see if he needs an ice bag."

To Avery's surprise, Maya didn't grin. "Why don't you stay until I get off? It's only another hour until last call, and that latest killing makes me nervous."

Avery knew immediately which killing; not that there weren't murders galore in the Bay Area every day, but this one . . . "It was in Santa Cruz."

"I don't care. The guy's been all up and down the coast, but he started out in San Francisco, he loves the fog, and it's a pea soup night out there."

"I've walked home in the fog lots of times. Trust me, it's a lot worse when guys can see me than when they can't." There was some truth in that.

Maya was not distracted. "How many girls has he killed now? Six? Eight?"

Avery tightened her grip on her cash drawer. "I don't know. I heard seven, but now they think he got that woman and her daughter in Marin County." Local news had been all too specific about every detail. "The FBI has informed us we officially have a serial killer in the area. Because we couldn't have figured *that* out on our own."

Maya leaned close. "I heard they're looking at a murder in San Diego, too. Last year. They found the woman's body. They thought her ex had done it, kidnapped the kid and taken him to Mexico. Now they're not so sure."

The rattle of ice interrupted them. "Hey! Who do I have to screw around here to get a drink?" Carl was well into his belligerent stage.

Maya smiled so pleasantly Avery knew Carl was in trouble. "We won't make you do that, Carl. This is mojito night?" She poured him an Irish whiskey, muddled it with lime and mint, and put it on the bar in front of him.

Too bad the mojito recipe called for rum.

As Avery headed up to Greasy's office, she heard Carl choke and spit.

She grinned. These guys never learned. *Don't mess with Maya.*

Avery found Greasy with his pants around his ankles, examining his balls.

He glared maliciously and almost spat his rage. "You girls. You think you're so goddamn smart."

"Not me. I'm not smart." She put her cash drawer on his desk, backed out the door, and muttered, "I'm not laughing, either."

When she got back down to the bar, Carl was subdued, Darren was proposing, and Shawn was rearranging his comb-over. It didn't matter; it still looked like he had a bar code on his head.

Maya picked up their conversation as if it had never been interrupted. "The press is calling him Edward Scissorhands, and he targets blondes. Like you. With kids." She flipped up her own black braid to show her that she was safe. "He stalks 'em, follows 'em, uses his scissors on 'em."

Avery lifted her hands, and dropped them helplessly. "What am I going to do? My babysitter said if I was late again, she was going to quit. Carter has night terrors. He wakes up screaming. He's only two. I can't take a chance no one will be there for him." Grace had started out so well, then disintegrated, and lately Avery had been wondering if the woman smoked weed on duty. "I have to go."

Maya didn't like it. But she couldn't argue. "Dye your hair."

Avery touched the ends of her shoulder-length blond bob. "I am. I'm going brunette tomorrow. It'll cut into my tips—but oh, well."

"So you're worried, too."

"Sure. They said he's been killing . . . for years. It wasn't until he started murdering the children that the cops figured out it was all the same guy. Tonight I've got no choices." Hadn't since the baby was born. But Carter was worth the worry and heartache. "I'm careful. I've got a cell phone."

"So did the other women."

"I carry a can of pepper spray in my hand and a brick in my purse. I know how to scream and I know how to run. No pretending to be brave for me."

"You should get a gun."

"If I shot every guy who made a pass at me on the streets—"

"The world would be a better place."

Avery laughed. "Yeah. Listen. I'll see you tomorrow night."

"Keep an eye out for Edward." Maya headed around the bar toward Shawn with his second gin martini perched on a tray.

Avery hurried to the ladies' room, opened her locker, and slipped out of her heels and into her running shoes. She pulled out her massive purse, loaded with her cell phone, baby paraphernalia, and the brick she'd picked up off the street. She slid her house keys in one front vest pocket and her can of pepper spray in the other, and headed out the back door.

Maya was right. It was pea soup out here, so thick Avery couldn't see her hand in front of her face. She sure as hell couldn't see if the serial killer stood at the end of the alley with his scissors gleaming. Avery gripped her pepper spray, pointed the nozzle away from herself, and inched toward the street.

No one was there. In fact, the street was spookily empty. Usually the area buzzed with people, with noise, with lights. But tonight even the homeless huddled under dirty blankets or disappeared into the missions. Nobody came out, not at this hour, not even when there were no reports of a serial killer.

Nobody . . . except women like her.

Damn Maya for bringing it up. Like Avery wasn't already scared to death.

She had a good mile to walk to her tiny, crappy one-room apartment. She looked overhead at the streetlight. Droplets of moisture swirled aimlessly, without wind, without volition. Malice and an evil glee filled the fog and muffled sound, so that her own footsteps seemed dull and soft.

She walked quickly toward the nearest busy corner, chilly spider webs of fog brushing her face. On the curb, under the streetlight, she stopped and teetered on the edge. A cab. No matter the expense, she needed a cab.

But no. None were out tonight. She lingered until she heard footsteps approaching.

Two guys, big like retired football players, appeared out of the mist, hanging on each other the way drunk guys do. They looked surprised to see her, then they leered, and she realized . . . she looked like a street-walker.

Shit. She was in trouble. She tightened her grip on the pepper spray.

The biggest guy staggered back a few steps, then staggered forward. "Hey, honey, you are *just* what we were looking for." And he grabbed her boob.

She sprayed her Mace, missed, and got his friend.

That guy screamed and rubbed his eyes.

She swung her weighted bag. Hit boob guy in the nuts.

He yelled and let her go.

She ran across the street, right in front of the cab she'd been wanting.

Boob guy dodged around the back. He bashed his knee on the bumper, stumbled in a circle, then came after her again.

Thank God for the fog. She hid, cowering, in the doorway of a town house.

He ran past.

She searched frantically in her purse for her cell phone. She found the brick first, then a package of wet wipes, a disposable diaper Carter had outgrown, her wallet, a hairbrush, a Ziploc of crumbled Cheerios . . . and her cell phone with a shattered glass face.

The brick had killed it.

She had no way to call the cops. No one would open a door to her. And she didn't have time to try for another cab. She had to get home before Grace left.

Avery started to cry, then forced herself to stop and concentrate on the good news—after this, even Edward Scissorhands couldn't track her. She doubled back on the other side of the street, and ran for it, sprinting into the residential area where the dark now seemed like sanctuary. The neighborhoods got crummier, the streets narrower, lined with street-level apartments sporting rusty bars over the windows . . . She was close to home.

A car cruised by, slowly, feeling its way.

Sweaty and exhausted, she hid behind garbage cans, then ran again.

When she could finally see the porch light's feeble yellow glow above her own narrow door, she slowed and drew in a relieved breath. After scaring herself witless, she'd made it again. It was two minutes after one, Grace should still be there, so even if Carter did wake, he wouldn't be—

The hair stood up on the back of Avery's neck. *What was that?*

She swung around and scanned the darkness. She could see nothing but shifting gray shadows. But she could have sworn she heard . . . something. Breathing. Heavy footsteps. Somehow, Edward Scissorhands had followed her.

How? How was it possible? She had long legs. She was in shape. Every survival instinct told her she should have outrun him . . . unless she'd made a mistake, and he hadn't been following her earlier.

The cops said he was a stalker. He had watched her for days, maybe months. He knew when she came home, and he'd been here all along, waiting . . .

Maternal instinct kicked in, strong and hard. She had to get away from her apartment, lead the killer away from her boy.

Her heart thumped as she hurried past. Sweat trickled between her breasts. She didn't want to die, but Carter, sweet and young, his brown eyes bright with trust . . . to think of him murdered in his bed . . .

Someone lunged out of the darkness, caught her arm.

She screamed and used the pepper spray. This time she nailed the bastard.

The killer fell backward, clawing at his eyes.

She started to turn and run. Then she recognized him. "Greasy?" Greasy was the killer? Yeah, that made a weird kind of sense. He was dysfunctional. He had no family. Just now in his office, he had sounded like he hated her. Hated all women. But . . . Greasy?

"What the fuck did you do that for?" he shouted. "Damn it, I paid for a cab to tell you . . . that guy with the hair, he—" Blindly he lunged at her again.

In a panic, she smacked him on the head with her purse.

Greasy hit the pavement, and he didn't come up again.

She stood over his body, breathing heavily.

She didn't know what to think. Was he dead? Was he the killer? What was he talking about, *the guy with the hair*?

Unsteadily, she traced her steps toward her apartment, and as she did, she listened. She drew out her keys, fumbled to fit one into the lock—and heard the slow snick of scissors opening and closing.

No. No. Please, God, be her imagination.

Turning, she saw a gray swirl of movement.

Somebody stood just out of sight.

Not her imagination. He was here.

Behind her, the door jerked open.

Avery stumbled. She sat down hard on the doorstep. She lost her grip on her pepper spray. The can rolled away.

The babysitter shrieked, "You're late!"

Still seated, Avery half-turned and shoved her. "Shut the door!"

"What do you mean, shut the door? You stupid bitch.

I don't have to listen to you. I quit!" Grace was crazed. So not weed, then. Coke.

Inside the apartment, Carter began to cry, frantically, desperately.

The gray swirl still stood there, waiting, a misty, man-shaped threat.

Avery got to her feet. "Shut. The. Door."

The babysitter must have heard Avery's cold, hard fear, or seen what Avery saw, because she stopped yelling, jumped back into the apartment, and slammed the door . . . leaving Avery alone. On the street. With a killer.

A hand, seemingly disembodied, thrust itself out of the fog, showing Avery the scissors, long sewing shears that opened and closed with a smooth snap.

"Who is it?" she asked. God. She sounded so calm.

He stepped out of the mist. The guy from the bar. Shawn Hendriks. The one with the nice suits, the French girlfriend, and the comb-over.

But the comb-over was gone. He had a full head of dark hair.

The guy with the hair.

Greasy hadn't come to hurt her. He'd come to warn her. Now he was bleeding and unconscious. She'd disabled the one man who could save her.

She twisted the straps of her purse in both hands, and still in that unnaturally calm voice, she said, "You've been hanging around since I was pregnant. No man stalks a woman for two years." Unless . . . unless the cops were right, and he'd been stalking other women at the same time. And killing them.

She swung her purse. She hit him, a bull's-eye on the wrist holding the scissors.

But he must have seen her in action, because with the

other hand he grabbed the straps and yanked her toward him, then spun her around.

Her fingers, entangled in the handles, broke. She screamed in pain, in alarm, in warning.

He pulled the purse away and thrust her into the wall, pressing her face to the grimy bricks.

She suffered one lucid moment knowing she had failed.

Carter was going to die.

Then Shawn spoke in her ear. "Let's cut off your pretty hair. We don't want to get blood in it."

CHAPTER ONE

Virtue Falls, Washington State
August 14
6:15 p.m.

If Elizabeth Banner noticed the interest with which the townspeople talked about her in low tones behind her back, she gave no indication. And in fact, she didn't notice. For as long as she could remember, she had always been the girl who had watched her father kill her mother with the scissors.

Although Elizabeth hadn't set foot in Virtue Falls for twenty-three years, the memory of Misty Banner's murder was still fresh in many people's minds. That made Elizabeth a local celebrity of sorts, and the news of her return swept the small community as vigorously as the tsunami those crazy scientists were always predicting.

Townsfolk speculated that Elizabeth had come back to reunite with her father, but after one brief visit to the Honor Mountain Memory Care Facility, she hadn't gone back. Instead she spent her time at the ongoing study of Pacific Rim tectonic plates and subduction zones, researching alluvial deposits.

Or something.

Which made sense—her father was Charles Banner, the man who had pioneered the study, and now here she was, a chip off the old block, a respected geologist at age twenty-seven with lots of official-sounding letters after her name.

A few nasty people in the town darkly muttered that they hoped she didn't follow in her father's footsteps in any matter beyond the sciences.

Most folks didn't think she would; Elizabeth resembled her mother, not her father, with the same white-blond hair, the same wide blue eyes, the same curvy body and a walk to make a man abandon all sense.

Every straight guy in Virtue Falls had tried to catch her attention; she stared at them blankly, and talked about igneous rocks and cataclysmic earth events until even the most determined would-be lover conceded defeat.

Her online profile said she was divorced.

Most men said they knew why; she was boring.

Perversely, most men considered the guy who had let Elizabeth Banner get away to be the biggest dumbshit in the history of the world. It didn't matter what she said. It was the way her full lips formed the words when she said them.

Now she sat at her usual table by the window at the Oceanview Café—when she first arrived, she had noted with interest that the ocean was nowhere in view from this part of town—reviewing her notes from the dig and occasionally sipping on a Fufu Berry Jones soda and wondering why she had ordered it.

She thought she had ordered a root beer. And what was a fufu berry, anyway? Something pink . . .

"Here you go, Elizabeth." The waitress slid a plate under Elizabeth's elbow. "Eat up while it's hot."

Elizabeth had finished work at the dig, gone home and showered, and changed into her brand-new Tory Burch sandals and her baby blue cotton jersey summer dress that was one size too big. She wore it like that on purpose. If she didn't, men had a tendency to stare at her boobs.

Well. Men had a tendency to stare at her boobs no matter what, but when she wore loose-fitting clothes, they were sometimes able to meet her eyes.

Rainbow wiped her hands on her apron. "Are you missing your team?"

Elizabeth paused, a fry halfway from the ketchup to her mouth. "Why would I?"

"They've been gone for three days to that conference in Tahoe, and you've been working alone at the site. Three days in that isolated canyon with no one to talk to. Don't you get lonely?"

"No." Elizabeth shook her head for emphasis. "At any rate, the team will soon be back covered with accolades for their research. Andrew is a very capable, if not brilliant, scientific leader."

"I don't know that I would tell him he's not brilliant," Rainbow said.

"He knows that, or he wouldn't lean so heavily on the intuitive suggestions of others." With great precision, Elizabeth spread mustard to the edges of the homemade bun.

"Trust me on this one, honey. There's a world of difference between knowing it and admitting it, and Andrew Marrero is already touchy about the fact he worked for your father and stands in his shadow."

Elizabeth considered that. "Yes. I have read my father's work. Charles Banner was, in fact, a gifted scientist, and I say that without prejudice of any kind. But why that would influence Marrero's opinion of himself, I do not understand."

"I know you don't, honey. But take my word for it, I'm right."

Elizabeth observed Rainbow, head tilted.

Rainbow sighed. "Okay, look. Marrero is a good-looking son-of-a-bitch. Dark hair, dark eyes, swarthy skin, the image of a Latin lover. But he's short. He says five-nine, but he's five-seven, maybe five-eight. Maybe. He's well hung, but he can't tell everybody that, so he wears lifts in his shoes. Short guys just have this attitude."

Elizabeth was fascinated with this unsuspected side of Rainbow. "You've slept with Andrew Marrero?"

"He's not my usual type, but it was interesting. I used to put him on and spin him." Rainbow's eyes half-closed in satisfied remembrance.

Elizabeth blurted, "I thought you were . . ." She stopped herself barely in time.

Rainbow's eyes snapped open. "Gay?"

So . . . not barely in time.

"Hey, when you're bi, you double your chance for a date on Saturday night." Rainbow chortled, patted Elizabeth's arm, and headed toward the lunch counter.

Elizabeth sank her teeth into the burger while she watched Rainbow charm three sunburned tourists who chattered with great excitement about their day at the beach.

Rainbow had apparently been the waitress here at the Oceanview when Elizabeth was a child. Twenty-three years later she was still the waitress, a fate Elizabeth considered worse than death. Of course, she couldn't even remember whether she'd ordered a root beer or a fufu berry soda, so that was part of it, but being around people all day filled her with horror.

She liked rocks.

She didn't like people. In her experience, most of them were spiteful, or thoughtless, or cruelly curious, and always, always impatient with her lack of interest in them.

But Rainbow interested her, because Rainbow seemed to be an entirely different species of human. For one thing, Rainbow was tall, with big bones, broad shoulders, and a head full of salt-and-pepper gray hair. She was hearty, cheerful, and she seemed honestly fascinated by her customers, tourist or local, always chatting, asking questions, giving unwanted advice.

At first Elizabeth hadn't known what to do with her; every time Rainbow came to the table she would tell Elizabeth stuff. Stuff Elizabeth didn't want to hear because it distracted her from her work.

But Rainbow never needed an invitation to talk. The first time Elizabeth came in for dinner, Rainbow told her, "A lot of people think my name is unfortunate for a woman my age. You know—I was born in sixty-eight in Haight-Ashbury, after the Summer of Love." She paused and seemed to be waiting for something.

Elizabeth belatedly picked up her cue. "Your parents were hippies?"

"Hippies? God, yes. The original hash-smoking, psychedelic-music-playing, free-love-practicing hippies." Rainbow shook her head like a disapproving mom. "Still are, for that matter. After I was born, they decided the city wasn't a good place to raise a baby, so they went into the Sierra Nevadas and learned weaving from a Native American woman who'd learned techniques from her great-grandmother. They're pretty good at it. You've probably heard of them."

"I don't think so."

"They've got one of the temporary exhibits in the

Metropolitan Museum of Art in New York. My parents are Alder and Elf Breezewing."

Elizabeth's head was spinning. "Which one is Alder and which is Elf?"

"He's Alder and she's Elf, of course. It's the Breezewing exhibit!"

Elizabeth blinked.

Rainbow put her broad hands on her broad hips. "You really don't know a damned thing about anything except rocks, do you?"

"That is not true. I also understand alluvial deposits and am studying the recently mapped ocean floor off the coast of Virtue Falls for an understanding of why tsunamis are so massive in this area." Elizabeth thought it an intelligent answer.

Rainbow stared at her as if she was speaking a foreign language. "Right. You're like your father. I'll get your dinner. I had the cook put an extra order of fries on the plate."

Elizabeth wanted to ask what she meant about her father. Had Rainbow known him when they lived here?

But Elizabeth had learned, the hard way, never to talk about Charles, so instead she asked, "I asked for mashed potatoes. Didn't I?"

"They're coming, too. You need fattening up."

Elizabeth knew for a fact she didn't need fattening up. She was curvy. Very curvy. For a girl growing up in California, land of the svelte, being built like her was a disadvantage, not to mention it was hard to find clothes. If pants fit her hips, they were loose around her waist, and she hadn't worn a button-up shirt since she was eleven and developed a C-cup. Her aunt said she was built like her mom. Her uncle said she was built like an exotic dancer. But he didn't realize she'd heard him, so she would acquit him of malice. Her uncle wasn't mean; he was overworked and didn't have time for his own kids, much less a niece who never talked much even after she recovered her power of speech.

Elizabeth realized she had a bit of a disconnect from the rest of the world caused by the knowledge that humanity could turn on her in an instant. She recognized the fact she sabotaged her own relationships, and sometimes she really tried to join in with the general populace and talk about the weather. She just never got it right. Not even with Garik.

Especially not with Garik.

Best not to think of Garik.

She bent her head to her reports again, and didn't notice when one of the town's elderly inhabitants held court in the corner, pointed her out to the tourists, and regaled them with the tale of how Elizabeth Banner had seen her father kill her mother with a pair of scissors.

CHAPTER TWO

"Virtue Falls Resort has already celebrated its hundredth birthday."

The tourists said, "Ooh."

"Built in nineteen-thirteen by John Smith Sr., this elegant four-story boutique hotel and spa perches on a rocky precipice over the Pacific Ocean, and was a profitable addition to the immense Smith fortune, which consisted of a thousand wooded acres, a sawmill, and the mountaintop mansion in which the family lived."

Margaret leaned on her cane and listened as the dozen newly arrived guests now said, "Ahh."

They stood in the great room of the resort, on the next to the last stop of the tour. Margaret had probably told this tale to resort guests at least five thousand times—and she loved it. It was her Irish blood that made her a storyteller, and her own self that made her love dealing with people.

She didn't mind that the guests craned their necks to look up at the massive rustic Douglas fir beams supporting the high knotty pine ceiling, or ran their hands over the restored early-twentieth-century furniture. She wanted them to admire the great room. More than that, she wanted to give them the feeling that they were part of the Smith family.

When that happened, they would return. Even now, she recognized one couple; Mr. and Mrs. Turner had first come as honeymooners. Now they brought their teenage son.

That was the kind of connection Margaret liked to see. She continued, "Unfortunately, World War One took the oldest Smith son into battle and he died in the fields of France. Grief killed John, Senior. Mrs. Ida Smith and her son Johnny had not been trained to manage properties, and surviving the Great Depression required more skill than the two of them could provide. By the time Mrs. Ida Smith visited Ireland in nineteen thirty-eight, the Smith fortunes were well on their way to vanishing. Luckily, Mrs. Smith met me." Margaret nodded while her guests laughed. "I was sixteen years old"—a lie, she'd been fifteen—"and Mrs. Smith brought me back to work for her. Eventually, I married her son Johnny"—he'd never had a chance, she'd married him within three months—"and we made a marvelous team."

"How long were you married?" Aurora Thompson was middle-aged and vacationing alone, with a white, un-tanned line across her wedding ring finger.

Margaret diagnosed her as recently divorced, poor dear, still wallowing in self-pity. "Not quite thirty years," Margaret said. "But no other man has ever tempted me to revisit the marital state."

"I'll bet a lot of men have tried." Josue Torres was no more than thirty, handsome as the devil and with a twinkle in his brown eyes.

"Ah, you are a charmer." Margaret smiled at him and checked for a ring. Married. Where was his wife? Why was he here? Was he one of the philandering bastards she despised? "Are you applying for the job?"

"If I were single . . ." He sighed dramatically. "But my wife is joining me tomorrow."

Margaret put her hand on her chest, and she deliberately deepened her Irish brogue as she said, "Ah, you've broken me heart." She straightened, and speaking toward Aurora, she said, "Actually, I find my life without a man of my own quite enjoyable. But then, I'm a pigheaded old woman who likes to do what she wants, and marriage is all about compromise and giving."

Aurora nodded, and the worry line between her brows lessened.

Yes, remember the bad times in your marriage and think on what your life can be now. You'll be happier. Satisfied she'd given the discarded wife something to consider, Margaret continued, "When I arrived here in Virtue Falls, the Smiths' wooded acres and the sawmill had already vanished, but we made the resort world-famous and when Mrs. Smith died in nineteen sixty-seven at the age of eighty-eight, she had the gratification of knowing we had saved the family's fortune. I had lost my dear Johnny the year before, our children were grown and gone, so I donated the family mansion, now a historical home, to the state of Washington, and moved here where I live in a suite of rooms overlooking the ocean. The view is spectacular, but as you've discovered, at Virtue Falls Resort, every view from every room is spectacular."

The guests murmured and nodded.

"Are there any questions before we move on to our last stop on the tour, the Virtue Falls deck, and enjoy a glass of wine?"

The drive up the coast at this time of year was always gorgeous, and one retired couple from the South had been lavish with praise for the scenery and the inn. Now in her warm, soft voice Mrs. Daniels said, "I noticed several prints on your walls that looked as if they had been painted by Bradley Hoff, and I know he says Virtue Falls is his inspiration. Have you met Bradley Hoff?"

"I have not only met him," Margaret said, "I've had him dine here many a time. And those are not prints—those are originals."

Mrs. Daniels turned to her husband. "I told you so."

Mr. Daniels sighed. "Yes, yes, you're right. I still don't want one of those slick paintings stuck on the wall of my office." He seemed to realize he might have offended Margaret, and said, "I hope my opinion didn't offend you, ma'am."

"Not at all. When it comes to art, individual taste rules, and the critics certainly are not kind to Bradley. But as he always says, he cries all the way to the bank."

Everyone laughed, even Mr. Daniels.

"Is he as nice as he seems to be on television?" Mrs. Turner asked.

"He is a lovely person, as is his wife, Vivian." Although Margaret found Vivian a little thin and sharp, like salad dressing with too much vinegar. But Bradley seemed devoted to Vivian, and as Margaret knew, every ass had a seat. "Vivian is his manager and is very protective of Bradley, his time, and his talents. Otherwise, I think, he would paint all the time. So they are the perfect couple."

"She was on the Atlanta morning show with him one day," Mrs. Daniels said, "and she said he has contributed a lot to Virtue Falls."

"He has indeed. You probably heard that he raised funds to rebuild the gym at the high school when it burned down. They named it the Bradley Hoff Facility." Which peeved Margaret more than a little, for over the years she had put a fortune into various causes and charities in Virtue Falls, too. In fact, right now, she was supporting the tiny public library, and no one had named even a brick after her.

But it was not Bradley's fault he had found fame as Nature's Artist, serving up pretty paintings to a grateful world, and Margaret was just a crotchety old innkeeper. And ungrateful, too, for . . . She gestured to a large Hoff on the wall behind them. "Bradley painted that here on our deck, and as a surprise for my eighty-fifth birthday, he had it framed and hung for me. I particularly like the way the ocean rises into the sky as if there's no horizon."

"With all this valuable stuff sitting around, you must have a great security system," Aurora said.

"Yes," Margaret said crisply. "I do. Any other questions?"

"I'd love to tour Mr. Hoff's studio. Is he in town?" Mrs. Daniels asked.

Mr. Daniels sagged.

"I believe he's on tour with a showing of his newest paintings, and in any case, the only person he allows in his studio is his wife." When Mr. Daniels straightened up again, Margaret smiled at him. "Bradley is a pleasant man, but in the end, he is an artist first and foremost, with an artist's quirks."

A hand waved.

She waved back at the teenager. "Yes, young man?"

"How old are you?"

"Mason Eugene Turner!" His mother looked shocked—and curious, too.

"It's all right," Margaret said in a soothing tone. "I'm at the age where I might as well brag about it. I'm ninety-one."

"Whoa." The boy grinned. "That's cool!"

The guests laughed.

"Thank you, I think so, too. It beats the alternative." Margaret looked around. "Any other questions?"

"Why did Mrs. Smith bring you back from Ireland? I mean, it was such good timing, it being right before World War Two and all." This female was in her early forties and here by herself, and she had that *I'm writing my first book* look about her.

Margaret made a mental note to avoid conversations with her. Authors always wanted to blather on about their plot.

"It was good timing, yes, and Mrs. Smith brought me back because I did her a favor." Before the female could ask what, Margaret gestured to her staff and they threw open the three sets of French doors.

The wind off the Pacific rushed in, filling the great room, chasing every other thought out of the guests' minds.

"That fresh air will bring a light to your eyes and a bloom to your cheeks," Margaret said in satisfaction.

They streamed out onto the deck, exclaiming at the view. The younger ones hurried to the railing and looked down fifty feet to the waves that battered the rocks. The older adults accepted the wool throws the staff were handing out.

Guests who had been here for days arrived to socialize and enjoy the complimentary drinks: Washington wines, a local beer, or bottled water.

Margaret took a moment, as she always did, to listen to the ocean.

It was a good life for little Maggie O'Brien of Dublin, Ireland. A very good life indeed.

And on that thought, she reached out and softly rapped her knuckles on the wooden railing.

Knock wood.

She knew better than to tempt fate.

CHAPTER THREE

Sheriff Dennis Foster shuffled through the papers on his desk.

His secretary wasn't worth much even when he was in town, and when he left to attend a law enforcement conference in Oakland, Mona apparently spent all her time doing her nails because she sure as hell didn't file the reports from his deputies, the mail, or God forbid, the alerts that came in from the FBI.

He could see the alert dangling, half off the edge of his desk. It had that distinctive FBI official letterhead . . .

When he first got into law enforcement, he had dreamed of being an FBI agent, of traveling the country fighting crime. But he was stuck in Virtue Falls, taking care of his mother, whom he loved, he really did, but she'd been sick for so long, and that voice of hers, like fingernails scraping on a blackboard.

No wonder he went to every conference he could wangle the money for.

He told himself he was in command here, and surely it was better to reign in hell than to serve in heaven.

He picked up an envelope and ripped the corner, blew into it, and pulled out a special offer from some women's fashion magazine.

How did he get on a list for a women's fashion magazine?

He flung it in the recycling bin, then thought better and shredded it. He wouldn't put it past Mona to go through the recycling and spread the rumor he wore women's underwear. Like he could get away with women's underwear in this town.

The alert still rested on the corner of his desk, waiting . . .

He remembered a time when he had eagerly reached for those alerts, scanned them to see what was happening in the wide world. He remembered a time, twenty-three years ago, when Charles Banner had brutally killed his wife and the local FBI office had wanted to take over jurisdiction—they were as bored as he was with the piddly-poop crimes that occurred along this stretch of the coast—and he had grinned at them and said, "No, boys, this one is mine." He'd been smart enough to recognize that this high-profile, media-attention-catching murder would make his name in the county and in the larger law enforcement community.

And it had. Every election day, he reminded voters he'd been the one to bring vicious Charles Banner to justice, and every election day they voted him back in. At every law enforcement conference, someone remembered Misty's murder and wanted to discuss the details, and he was happy to do so. Although as the years passed, fewer and fewer of the other officers could place the case, or his name.

It's not like he wanted another vicious murder to occur in Virtue Falls. He didn't. He just wished folks had a longer memory.

If he gave the stack of mail an accidental nudge, the alert would flutter to the floor and he wouldn't have to look at it.

But he would know it was there.

He didn't understand what he was so afraid of. Most of the alerts were a waste of paper. It was probably nothing more than a notice to watch for the drugs coming into the coast from Canada. Like he didn't know that.

He reached over, picked up the alert, and read the first line.

He groped for his chair, pulled it toward him, and sat down heavily.

There'd been another murder. Four murders, in fact. The mother. The babysitter. Some bar owner who got involved. And the child, a little boy named Carter.

In San Francisco. And it had happened when Foster had been at the conference in the Bay Area.

The attacks were getting more frequent. They were getting more vicious. It was definitely the work of a serial killer. And whoever he was—most serial killers were male—he always killed the child, too.

No reason to be afraid. No reason to be upset. No reason for Dennis Foster's hands to tremble. No reason to pace the house at night in fear and self-loathing.

Violently, he wadded up the alert and threw it at the trash can.

These murders were none of his business. They were out of his jurisdiction. They always occurred somewhere on the Pacific coast . . . while he was visiting there on business.

He knew nothing relevant. Nothing for sure. Nothing he could relate as fact.

These murders had nothing to do with him.

Nothing.

CHAPTER FOUR

Coast Guard lieutenant and current commanding officer Kateri Kwinault sat in the Virtue Falls Coast Guard office break room at the round table, and counted her poker chips. "Nobody ever said being in the Coast Guard is easy."

"It is when you're winning." Lt. JG Landon Adams, aka Landlubber, didn't like to lose.

Neither did Ens. Luis Sánchez, but he'd been stationed here longer than Adams. "She always wins."

"She cheats?" Adams sounded hopeful.

"Kateri's good. And she's lucky." Sánchez sounded sour, and resigned.

Adams had recently transferred from New York Harbor, a busy, cushy job which he managed to wrangle

(Kateri suspected) because his uncle was a New York senator.

But nothing lasts forever. After the sex scandal, his uncle got voted out and now Adams was stationed on the rugged Washington coast, in a fifty-year-old station that had been built twenty feet above sea level on Virtue Falls Harbor. Here, the kid faced the kind of culture shock only a white boy from the East could face when confronted with the realities of the wild Pacific Ocean and a society of summer tourists, leftover hippies, hostile Native Americans, and speeding Canadians, along with a determinedly egalitarian attitude, socks worn with sandals, and an outright worship of organic vegetables.

Washington State was an ongoing shock to poor dear Landlubber. He didn't like anything, including his nickname . . . which of course inspired an even more determined use of it.

Easterners really needed to climb out of their snotty little shells occasionally.

Kateri shuffled the cards and smirked at her guys.

They were bored.

She was bored.

This station was great in the winter: big storms, dangerous currents, commercial boats out fishing and crabbing, leaky foreign vessels passing by, lots of trouble, and plenty for the Coast Guard to do.

In the summer, they could usually depend on some idiot tourist to get out on the water and capsize, or on some greedy dealer to try and smuggle in his carefully tended stash of weed. But now, in the dog days of August, when the sun shone, the weather was clear and warm, and the water was like glass, duty could be dull. Kateri likened it to being a fireman. Nothing, nothing, nothing, nothing . . . and then all hell breaks loose.

So with three cutters in the harbor, eight guys on vacation, and nothing to do, they worked with sixteen Coasties on duty; a skeleton crew, but doable as long as they didn't have to take all the cutters out at the same time.

And they played poker.

"I worked at the tribe casino as a dealer. I know my cards." She looked at Adams. "But so do you, Landlubber. You're good."

"I used to think so." The guy's color was high. He really didn't like to lose.

She really didn't care. She dealt the cards and played them to win.

CHAPTER FIVE

At the Honor Mountain Memory Care Facility, Charles Banner sat in the dining room eating his dinner.

Unlike a lot of the residents, he didn't mind being confined. He'd been sent to the care facility directly from the Washington State Penitentiary in Walla Walla. After twenty-three years of prison life, he had diagnosed himself with early onset Alzheimer's, and also diagnosed the probable causes: stress caused by his repeated attempts to get a retrial; anguish at knowing his little daughter, Elizabeth, had been traumatized and needed him; and the repeated head injuries he'd suffered in beatings at the hands of other inmates.

The state had steadfastly denied him a retrial. The case was far too notorious for them to reexamine the evidence with an eye to injustice. As far as law enforcement was concerned, they had scored in a high-profile case and unless someone offered convincing evidence that his conviction was wrong, he was staying put.

Over the years, he had interested different lawyers in his case, but each came to the same conclusion: there was no conflicting convincing evidence. None.

The situation with Elizabeth was desperate; she was an intelligent, sensitive child who loved her parents, and to see her mother murdered had devastated her. Afterward, to be torn from his arms—that was nothing less than cruel. He worried about the possible psychological scars; he tried to comfort himself that her aunt and uncle would care for her.

But Misty's sister and her husband were middle-class, salt-of-the-earth people who worked, watched television, went to church, and never looked beyond the boundaries of their own narrow lives.

And Charles knew Elizabeth; she was like him. She would always be asking why. Why had her mommy died? Why couldn't she see her daddy?

What would they tell her? If he could only have had some communication with the child . . . But that wasn't allowed.

As for the prison beatings . . . Charles was, after all, an easy mark. The other prisoners mocked him. The guards, tough guys in a difficult environment, detested him. He was not only smarter than everyone else, but he had never won a fight in his life. In fact, before prison, he had never *been* in a fight.

He'd never been raped before, either.

There was a first time for everything.

Even losing his mind.

One day, he visited the prison library to study the current report on his geological study at Virtue Falls

Canyon, and he discovered notes written in the margins. He then realized those notes were accurate, they were in his handwriting, and he had no memory of making them.

He had at once gone to the prison doctor.

Not surprisingly, Dr. Walter Frownfelter accepted Charles's analysis. When Charles and Misty lived in Virtue Falls, Dr. Frownfelter had been the physician there, and when the doctor joined the penitentiary staff, Charles had been glad to have another scientist to talk to.

But that worked against his diagnosis; the warden noted they had a friendship, and that put Dr. Frownfelter's word in doubt. Getting Charles released to the care facility had taken multiple psychiatric evaluations with an ever-changing list of physicians, and hearings with highly suspicious parole board members.

Finally a criminologist examined the evidence that had convicted Charles, and she stated that, given the current tests that were not available twenty-three years ago, there could possibly be reasonable doubt about his guilt. She pointed out that Misty's body had never been found, which left the murder in limbo, and Charles's record of good behavior along with ongoing mental deterioration made him a likely candidate for release to an asylum or care center with a secure facility for dangerous patients.

So the state, with their typical lack of care and foresight, sent him back to the place where he had last lived, the town where the crime was committed: Virtue Falls.

By the time he arrived, two years after the diagnosis, his disease had advanced enough that he didn't remember a lot about his years in prison. He only knew this place was much nicer that the last place. No one beat him up. No one pushed him around. No one cared if he read books and scientific articles.

At first, the nurses kept him separate from the other patients. At night, they locked him in his room. They watched him in alarm, and when tending to his needs, always kept a strong, muscled orderly with them.

Then, sometime in that first year, something happened, because apparently they decided he was harmless. They stopped following recommended protocol, and even allowed him to sit at the nurses' station and tell them about the intricacies of the Virtue Falls geological studies. They didn't say he was boring; they said his pleasant voice relaxed them.

Most of the time, the other patients didn't fear Charles, either, but George Cook had developed a dementia that left him loud and abusive. Or maybe his dementia exacerbated an already nasty disposition. George was always after Charles, making comments about how he wished he'd thought to kill his wife with a pair of scissors so he could go to prison for a little while and then get out and live for free on the state's dole in this plush nursing home.

Whenever George was around, the women in the facility were frightened of Charles.

Whenever George was around, Charles always wished he had learned how to fight, because someone needed to teach George manners.

But Charles knew he wasn't the one to do it, so he ignored George.

Right now, Charles steadily ate the last of his dessert, even though George stood directly behind his chair and deliberately bumped it.

"Mr. Cook, I wish you would sit down." Nurse Yvonne sounded exasperated, but she made no attempt to relocate George Cook. None of the female nurses ever tried to move him on their own.

George Cook snickered. "What? You don't like to be

reminded of how your favorite patient killed his wife? With the scissors . . . stabbed her . . . took her body apart piece by piece . . . so he could loll around in prison while I worked all my life in a sawmill . . . until the goddamn Chinese took the wood and I don't have a job . . ."

"Mr. Cook, please sit down." Nurse Yvonne sounded stern.

Not that it mattered to George. "Charles Banner held the scissors just like this, ripped her throat out, because she'd been fucking around."

One of the female patients whimpered and clutched her throat.

"If he'd been a real man, she wouldn't have had to fuck another guy." George started bumping Charles's chair again. Humping it. "Stabbed her, stabbed her, stabbed Misty, stabbed her, stabbed her . . ."

Abruptly, memory clawed at Charles, and he froze.

He'd stood in the house, seen the blood, didn't understand what had happened. He'd looked at his own hands; blood covered them. In an ever-increasing panic, he looked for Misty, for Elizabeth . . .

His hand holding the fork began to tremble.

"Mr. Banner?" Nurse Yvonne's voice was concerned. "Are you all right?"

"Ooh! Look! He's going to stab me with his fork! I'm scared, so scared of the little geologist." George slammed himself into the back of Charles's chair, crushing Charles into the edge of the table. "C'mon, you coward, fight me! Stab me!"

The dining room erupted into pandemonium. Nurse Yvonne sounded the alarm. Medical personnel rushed in. Patients cried and screamed, and fled toward the doors and their rooms.

Charles's pulse accelerated until he was breathless, his heart pounding.

The blood. The blood. Misty. Elizabeth. Misty.

A woman's gentle voice called him. "Charlie, dear, I hate to interrupt you when you're eating, but would you come over here?"

At once, Charles's heart rate calmed.

The wonderful thing about the Honor Mountain Memory Care Facility was . . . Misty visited him here.

As always, the sight of her made him breathless with awe. She was as beautiful as ever, her white-blond hair styled loosely, her blue eyes gently smiling. She stood off to the side of the dining room, beckoning him toward the wall away from the windows.

Charles pushed back his chair and without a glance at George, or at the patients, or at the staff, he walked over to his beautiful wife. "Of course, my dear. What can I do for you?"

She stroked his hand. "Stay here with me for a moment, and be safe."

That was why, when the earthquake hit, and the ceiling fell in over the middle of the dining room, George Cook was knocked unconscious—and Charles didn't get a scratch on him.

CHAPTER SIX

As Rainbow put a slice of blueberry pie on the table, Elizabeth Banner looked up from her notes to say, "I ate most of the fries."

"Hm." Rainbow eyed the plate. "I don't know how you manage to drag your skinny rear all the way out to the river every day."

"It's not far."

Rainbow picked up the remains of the burger. "Two miles."

"One-point-six miles according to my pedometer." Elizabeth thought that was a reasonable answer. It was, after all, the truth. But all her precision got her was a disgusted look from Rainbow.

Conversation was too hard. Elizabeth should have kept quiet. She was good at being quiet.

After the murder, she hadn't spoken a word for a year and a half, and discovered that when you were speechless, adults thought you were also deaf and conversed freely about you, the crime, and the trauma you suffered. They also speculated about what had led to the murder, and the answer almost always came back to one simple fact—Misty Banner had been having an affair.

That's why Charles Banner killed her. He had seemed such a gentle man, but still waters run deep and his jealous rage had spread blood all over that house, him, and his four-year-old daughter, Elizabeth.

By the time Elizabeth was six, she had heard the scene described many times, so many that when she looked up the crime scene photos, it almost seemed she remembered it.

But she didn't. The psychologists (and after the murder, she had been dragged to many) called it childhood amnesia, and assured her aunt that it was normal. Most memory didn't start before the age of five, so Elizabeth's lack of recall surprised no one.

Except her aunt.

A person's first memory was usually of a traumatic event: getting lost in a store, having a finger slammed in the car door, getting bitten by the neighbor kid, and frequently those memories did predate a child's fifth year.

Aunt Sandy wanted Elizabeth to remember, because Misty's body had never been recovered, and her aunt wanted to bury her sister.

After a year and a half of silence, Elizabeth's first word had been spoken to her aunt in response to Aunt Sandy's insistence that Elizabeth had to remember the murder . . . "No!"

Her aunt had been so surprised, she had stopped nagging for almost as long as it took to drag Elizabeth to the court-ordered psychiatrist for another psych exam. Even now, when Elizabeth thought about talking to a stranger and knowing she would be written up in a prestigious medical journal as a famous head case, her skin would crawl. Garik had been the only person in the world she'd felt comfortable talking to, and that was because she felt that in his own way, he was scarred, too.

But who knew for sure? He would never tell her. He never confided in her.

Elizabeth much preferred sitting alone in this café in the town that considered her a freak than to sit at a table with Garik . . . and still be alone.

Rainbow touched Elizabeth's arm, and pointed out the café window. In a soft, indulgent voice, she said, "Look at that handsome boy. That's Mrs. Munn's dog, Keno. He's got quite an attitude."

Elizabeth looked, too. A scottie dog was crossing the street. Cute thing: black and gray, and he pranced so proudly, so happily, that the cars on the street stopped and waited for him without complaining.

Then no more prancing. He barked once, sharply and in alarm. He sat down. Just sat down. And braced himself.

Rainbow started to ask, "What do you suppose is wrong with . . . ?"

The earthquake hit, hard and fast, slamming into the land, tossing blueberry pie into Elizabeth's face.

The tourists screamed.

The building creaked as the tortured earth rolled in waves, lifting and falling. Elizabeth's chair tilted backward. She scrambled to her feet and, like the dog, braced herself as the ground undulated in great waves.

Her first thought: *This is it!*

The earthquake she'd waited for all her life. And she was here to see it, feel it, experience it.

Her second thought: *I need my stuff.*

She grabbed her bag, reached for her notebook.

"No, you don't, honey." Rainbow yanked her away from the window and pushed her toward the back of the diner.

A giant swell knocked Elizabeth to her knees. She hooked her bag over her neck and crawled toward the lunch counter, toward the sturdiest structure in a rolling world.

The cook ran out of the kitchen, holding his spatula, and stood gaping.

She caught a glimpse of the sunburned tourists, sitting bug-eyed on their bar stools and rocking as if this was the biggest carnival ride ever.

The walls groaned. Nails popped out of the Sheetrock. Behind Elizabeth, one by one, the windows exploded. Shards of safety glass sprayed the diner.

Elizabeth's excitement rose.

At least an eight on the Richter scale. Maybe an eight-point-five. Not the biggest earthquake ever . . . but it wasn't diminishing. It wasn't done.

There was a rhythm to the earth surges coming onto the coast, an increasing and glorious roll.

Behind the counter, the shelves tilted; the drinking glasses crashed backward, then forward and off, heaving themselves onto the floor like Disney-animated crockery. The coffee pot jumped off the heater and committed suicide, splashing hot liquid into the air. Sympathetic porcelain mugs followed.

Elizabeth was in awe; the floor was rippling, two feet up and then two feet down. She had read about earthquakes so violent, of course she had. But never had she thought she would have the luck to experience one.

Behind the bar, the cloudy antique mirror cracked in long, loud pops. The glass stubbornly clung to the wide gilded frame, then gave up and smashed on the floor one piece at a time.

Rainbow shouted something unintelligible, grabbed Elizabeth around the waist, picked her up, and flung her behind the counter. Elizabeth hit the floor on her hands and knees, landing hard. Pain pierced her palm.

Rainbow's raw-boned body crowded her tightly against the bar, protecting Elizabeth from the earth's tantrum.

Slowly Elizabeth lifted her wide-spread hand to her face.

Big chunk of glass. She stared at the blood welling under the shard. It hurt, and she wondered how, when the world was coming apart, this one injury could concentrate her attention on something so minor.

Rainbow shoved her farther under the counter, handling her like a linebacker with a football.

Elizabeth still couldn't properly observe the phenomenon that was the earthquake; her own injury fascinated her too much. She plucked the glass from her flesh; blood gushed, bright and red.

The earth rocked, but not from the earthquake.

No, this was Elizabeth's own, inevitable reaction to blood. A cold sweat broke out on her forehead. She could feel the color drain from her face. Leaning her head against the counter, she took long breaths, trying to gain control of the nausea.

Rainbow saw. Said, "Shit." Grabbing a bunch of napkins out of a fallen napkin holder, she pressed it to the wound. "How'd you do that? Never mind. You'll need stitches."

Elizabeth looked around. "I don't know how to find a doctor." Vaguely she knew that was stupid. More lucidly, she said, "After the quake is over, the doctors will be busy taking care of serious injuries."

"Yeah." Swaying like a drunken sailor, Rainbow crawled to a plastic file cabinet and opened a drawer. Released from its catch, the drawer slid out and crashed to the floor. Frowning fiercely, Rainbow rummaged around.

Still the earth rolled. Spray-on insulation rained down on them from the ceiling. The tourists shrieked louder, and some woman screamed, over and over, in unremitting panic.

No, wait. That was the cook. Who knew Dax Black could hit notes that high?

Rainbow crawled back with a clean bar towel and a handful of Band-Aids. She pulled the napkins away.

Blood gushed again.

Elizabeth turned her head away.

"You can be squeamish?" Rainbow muttered. "Now? When we're facing certain death?"

"Actually, most people survive an earthquake, even one of this magnitude." Elizabeth's voice sounded sensible, she noted. Even when she wanted to vomit, even when she wanted to pass out, even when she knew that, yes, there was a good chance of injury or death, she sounded sensible.

No wonder Garik had always been exasperated with her.

Rainbow wiped the skin around Elizabeth's injury, applied a bandage to hold the muscle together, wrapped the towel around the hand, and tied it tightly.

It hurt. Man, did it hurt. But Rainbow was swift, efficient, and having the wound out of sight helped Elizabeth relax.

"There," Rainbow said in satisfaction. "That'll hold you until we get a doctor."

"Yes," Elizabeth whispered. Then, louder, "Yes. Thank you." The red dots before her eyes cleared away. She could see again. Make her observations, take her notes . . .

The earth's movement slowed. For just a second, but it slowed.

The rocking picked up again. Grew more violent. Then slowed again.

"It's almost finished." Rainbow sounded relieved.

Elizabeth wanted to shout, *No! Not so soon!* She had wasted too much of the earthquake feeling queasy. Now it was over?

The cook's screaming became a whimper.

Someone was loudly saying, "Thank God. Thank God!" And putting fervent emotion into the prayer.

Cautiously, Rainbow rose to her feet.

Elizabeth joined her.

The tourists rose, too, holding onto the still-trembling counter.

Elizabeth looked around.

The earthquake had shaken the guts out of the building, leaving the diner in shambles, littered with shattered Sheetrock, dangling heating vents, and drooping electrical wires. Outside, through the broken windows, the devastation had brought down the town.

But what caught her unwilling attention was the people in the diner and on the street. All of them, every single one, were ashen-faced, with wide, shocked eyes and lips that moved, not in speech, but just . . . randomly, as if words were too difficult, as if brain function had been severed.

Elizabeth understood as she never had before. Everyone, all of them, had lived secure in the belief that the earth was stable, unchanging, eternal.

Now no one could trust the ground beneath their feet.

Yes, the earthquake was the story of destruction, but not just of things. An earthquake destroyed security. It destroyed complacency. It changed the people who lived through it.

Yet the sun shone as brightly as before, glinting off the scattered silverware and lighting the scattered chairs and tipped-over tables.

One of the tourists started laughing wildly. "Look at Bert. He has pie all over him!" She laughed and laughed, amusement spilling into hysteria.

Bert wiped at the meringue on his shirt. "I hope to hell no one's on the beach. If there's a tsunami . . ."

"Yes!" Elizabeth drew an excited breath, groped for the bag that by some miracle still hung from her shoulder. "A tsunami!"

Rainbow grabbed at her arm. "Don't!"

Elizabeth tore herself away and ran out the door.

How could she have forgotten, even for a moment?

A tsunami was coming. Was on its way.

And she had to beat it to Virtue Falls Canyon.

Her brand-new Tory Burch sandals were screwed.

CHAPTER SEVEN

Aurora Thompson joined the small group gathered around Margaret, waited for a lull in the conversation, and asked, "So the Smith family has always owned the resort?"

"Indeed it has." Although Margaret was not born a Smith, she was proud of the heritage.

"You must be getting ready to retire," Aurora said.

Margaret's smile faded. "Not at all. I figure I have another twenty good years in me before I'm ready to retire and take the long dirt nap."

Other members of the group laughed or looked shocked, depending on their sensibilities.

"Retirement doesn't necessarily mean death," Aurora said persuasively.

"Retirement to an active woman is nothing more than

sitting around playing cards and drinking prune juice—
and I doubt the attendants who watch over dotty old folks
would allow me to spike mine with my favorite Irish
whiskey." Margaret kept her voice pleasant. "No, I'll stay
on and manage my resort, thank you."

"But if the right offer came along . . ." Aurora trailed
off enticingly.

Margaret's spine snapped straight. A real estate woman.
The pathetic single woman was a real estate woman, probably sent by Margaret's own granddaughter to get dear
old Grams to give up the task to which the good Lord, old
Mrs. Smith, and Margaret's own tenacious nature had
given her.

All Margaret's kind feelings toward Aurora evapo-
rated, and in the cutting tone with which Margaret had
controlled her staff, her sons, and her dear departed husband, she said, "No offer is generous enough to force me
out of my home and away from the work which God has
given me."

Aurora was too self-absorbed to recognize the threat
to her well-being and to the comfort of her stay at the resort. In that amused and patronizing tone that adults
reserve for cute children and the elderly, Aurora said,
"Surely God allows us all a time to relax at the end of
our lives."

"When I'm at the end of my life, I will let you know."
Margaret smiled with all her teeth.

Only then did the stupid woman realize her mistake.

Luckily for Aurora, Margaret's manager watched over
her. He recognized her rage when he saw it, and swiftly
interrupted with an emergency that required Margaret's
attention.

She excused herself and followed him to the table
where the server from their featured winery poured her

a small glass of pinot noir. And although she usually didn't indulge in wine before dinner, she hung her cane on her arm and took it with thanks.

Harold kept his voice low. "They are all fools. Especially her."

"You don't even know what she was talking about." Margaret took a sip and grimaced. The floral notes were not to her taste.

"I have a good idea. She was asking questions earlier." Harold Ridley was tall and gaunt, a Vietnam vet who'd lost his leg to a grenade. He'd been unemployable, alcoholic and drug-addicted, until she'd picked him off the street and given him a chance. He'd been ready for that chance; he'd cleaned up his act and been her manager for thirty years.

"I wish . . ." She paused, startled and confused, and stared at the rocking chairs.

They were rocking by themselves.

The resort shivered, as if the old building felt a chill wind. The deck bucked beneath her feet. She stumbled against the table, dropped her glass. It shattered, sending red streamers of wine flying through the air.

What reason? Why?

Her panicked mind immediately seized on her greatest fear.

Stroke!

She couldn't get her balance. She was hallucinating. She must have suffered a stroke.

What other explanation could there be?

Yet it wasn't merely her glass that broke. The glasses on the table, the open bottles, flew into the air, creating a havoc of shards and red wine and white wine.

Someone shouted, "Earthquake!"

Margaret sagged with selfish relief. It wasn't her old

system betraying her. She wasn't yet condemned to lie in a bed, drooling and helpless, until the Grim Reaper came to take her to her reward.

This was merely an earthquake.

She—and the resort—had lived through them before . . .

The earth gave a giant shrug, rolled, and rolled again.

Harold caught Margaret's arm to steady her. Then he stumbled away, staggering on his artificial leg, driven by the power of the buckling earth.

She needed to herd her guests inside, to follow the well-rehearsed program for earthquake survival. But her staff had never rehearsed for *this*. No one had ever imagined *this*, an earthquake so massive the inn rose and fell like a ship in a storm off the North Sea, sending the staff and guests lurching, slamming against the sturdy outdoor iron furniture.

The resort groaned and complained at the unnatural stresses put on the structure, but oddly, the guests were wide-eyed, in shock, and preternaturally quiet.

And the earthquake went on. And on. Never in all of Margaret's long years on the coast had she experienced anything so violent, so extended, so terrifying.

Still holding the table, she turned and shouted, "Inside! Stay calm and get inside!"

White-faced and paralyzed with terror, the guests stared at her.

But she had already established her authority over them and the situation. She gestured.

They headed toward the open French doors.

Margaret's cane was gone, she realized, knocked from her arm by the violent rocking. She couldn't risk leaving the table. She wasn't steady enough . . . yet she didn't dare stay.

If the deck fell, it was a long way to the ocean.

Harold recognized her dilemma, but he couldn't assist her; he was in the same trouble.

Margaret aimed herself at the open door.

Josue Torres suddenly stood between her and the resort. With the same charming, unruffled smile as before, he said, "I spy a chance to hold this lovely lady in my arms. If I may . . . ?"

He didn't wait for her assent—as if she would deny him—but scooped her up and headed into the great room.

Margaret looked back and saw the wine maker take Harold's arm and help him inside.

As they stepped inside the great room, the moose head over the fireplace crashed to the floor. The narrow side table fell over, taking the tall antique Chinese vase with it. The vase exploded; water and chiseled ceramic chips flew across the room. The smell of crushed lilies filled the air. Yet the resort rocked and rolled as one piece, all four floors moving like the forecastle of a sailing ship.

Good damned thing, because the seismic retrofit of the resort had cost Margaret a fortune.

The staff shouted instructions at the guests, yet like sheep in a farm truck, the guests milled around the middle of the room in panic.

Margaret pointed Josue toward the Japanese gong bolted firmly to the wall.

The clever young man understood. As the floor rolled beneath his feet, he staggered over and stopped by the velvet-wrapped mallet.

The mallet flopped about like a dying fish, and it took Margaret two tries to grab the handle and unhook it. She slammed the mallet against the swaying gong, and above the cacophony of shattering glass and creaking timbers, the gong sounded loud and true.

Desperate for leadership, the guests turned to face her.

She shouted, "Follow the staff up the stairs!," and pointed toward the great staircase.

"No!" Aurora staggered out of the crowd. "This place is coming down around our ears. Outside!"

Stupid and spiteful, with a grudge against Margaret for cutting her down to size.

Margaret hit the gong again.

And as she did, the earthquake at last began to die.

She lifted her voice. "This building has withstood ice storms, raging winds, torrential rains, eclipses, bad portents." Margaret smiled. "It will withstand this, too. If you would please follow the staff, they'll take you up to a viewing window where you will be above the reach of the tsunami and can view its approach."

That got their attention. Most of them had not thought beyond surviving this moment.

As if to give emphasis to the need to hurry, the earthquake roared back to life, buckling and rocking.

The guests groped toward the stairs.

Josue followed, holding Margaret in his arms.

She considered telling him she could walk.

But he seemed unbothered by her weight, moving with the ease of a healthy young beast. They moved to the second floor, then the third. The breeze off the ocean swept down the corridors; the windows had been shattered.

At the third floor, the staff directed the guests toward the viewing decks, warning them to be careful of the broken glass.

"Go up to the fourth floor," Margaret told Josue, knowing full well some of the others would follow.

Three of them did: Mason Turner and his parents, who seemed willing to accept Margaret's authority. She could only hope her actions justified their faith.

As they got to the top, the last of the swaying subsided. Josue put her on her feet and offered his arm.

She took it and moved toward the door that led out to the narrow viewing platform.

He stepped back. "I don't want to go out there," he said.

Yes. This put them ninety feet over the water, and he was squeamish. It happened.

"Stand where you are. You'll be able to see." She walked to the edge and grasped the railing tightly.

Mason and his parents joined her.

"Are you sure there'll be a tsunami?" Mason asked.

"There's a fault out there." Margaret nodded toward the ocean. "It rattles us occasionally, and we always get some sloshing, a low run of water headed for the cliffs."

"This time, it won't be a low run of water, will it?" Mrs. Turner's voice trembled.

"No." In her mind's eye, Margaret could see it. "This time, the sea floor cracked and bounded up, creating underwater cliffs, triggering a tsunami. Poseidon's horses race toward shore . . ." She stopped herself.

Her guests stared at her, wide-eyed in horror and confusion.

She was in storytelling mode, and these people needed reassurance. In a return to her sensible voice, she said, "But here the cliffs drop straight down into very deep water. If the geologists are to be believed, and I hope they are, we won't see more than an impressive wave crash against the cliffs."

"Then why did we come up so high?" Mr. Turner asked.

"That's what the geologists think will happen," Margaret said. "With my guests' safety at risk, I'll not take a chance of them being wrong."

"Look." Fear forgotten, Josue joined them. "Look!"

A long, giant swell raced across the blue ocean, lifting the sparkling water north and south as far as the eye could see.

"It's a big one." Margaret crossed herself. "God help us all."

CHAPTER EIGHT

Paperwork was the bane of Dennis Foster's existence, and in the twenty-one years he'd been sheriff, the load had doubled. Worse, most of this crap had nothing to do with law enforcement. He had environmental reports. Racial integration reports. Reports to the state police, the county commissioners, every little town council in his jurisdiction, every self-righteous state senator who wanted to stick his or her nose into local law enforcement. Computers were supposed to lighten the sheriff's workload; instead the Internet made it possible for everyone and his dog to lean on him for information. He wished the whole damned world would mind its own business.

He wished he could mind his own business, and ignore that mess in San Francisco. But the details preyed on his mind, kept him awake at night, chewing at the edges of his consciousness, forcing him to make choices he didn't want to make.

When the computer screen rocked backward, he thought the lack of sleep had finally caught up with him.

Then his office chair rolled forward. He caught at his desk and stood. The chair rolled out from under him.

And he heard it, the creaking of the earth as it turned to Jell-O.

Thank God. *Thank God.* He was saved from making a decision about that vicious serial killer. He had an excuse, a good one: earthquake. The big one.

As if he could stop the shaking, Mona started shouting at him, demanding he take charge, that he do something.

God, that woman was stupid. Couldn't she hear the sound of gunfire on the street? Had some crazy fool decided the world was ending? Was he using his pistol to send people to their heavenly reward?

As Foster ran through the old town hall, the ceiling disintegrated, and chunks of white plaster turned to pellets and rained down on him. He grabbed the massive wooden front door, but no matter how hard he tried, he couldn't get it open; the quake had wedged it tightly into the frame. Then the earth shifted and the door flung itself open.

He staggered back, arms flailing, then forward, pulling his pistol. He stepped onto the high concrete steps—and discovered what he heard wasn't gunshots.

The bricks were popping off the façade of the town hall, hitting the sidewalk and exploding in puffs of red dust. Some hit the street so hard they buried themselves into the warm asphalt.

A huge crack opened in the pavement, then as the wave rolled on, the crack slammed shut like the giant's mouth. Over and over it happened, and each time, dust and water flew into the air.

One car was halted in the middle of the street. The driver sat inside clutching the steering wheel as if she could somehow control the wild motion. Behind it, another driver honked his horn, perhaps imagining that if she got out of his way, he could drive to safety.

There was no safety. Not anywhere. Not in this disaster.

Citizens Foster recognized, tourists he did not, clung to lampposts or squatted with their arms over their heads, protecting themselves from flying debris. A five-year-old stood alone on the sidewalk, face raised to the sky, crying his fear to the heavens.

Foster holstered his gun and ran out.

One whole brick smacked him in the back, knocking the air out of him. Another one, lighter and broken, struck his ear, and he felt a warm stream of blood gush down his neck.

He reached the child and scooped him up, and carried him into the middle of the street. He pointed his index finger at the honking driver.

The driver stopped that infernal noise.

But the infernal noise didn't stop. The church bell on the old Episcopal church across the street rang wildly, and when Foster looked up, the steeple toppled in slow motion into the roof.

Behind him someone yelled, and he turned to see the town hall's concrete scrollwork drop straight down onto the street. It smashed three parked cars; one was a county patrol car.

Someone else shouted to him, and he saw the woman step out of the shelter of her car.

"Give him to me," she yelled, and extended her arms to the child.

Not her kid, but she saw the child's need, and his.

He thrust the boy at her and ran toward the crushed vehicles. God knows why. Anyone inside was dead.

But no one was inside, and now people knew what to

do. They all scrambled toward the middle of the streets, falling, crawling, away from the buildings and the traffic lights that snapped up and down on wires that cracked like whips.

Other cops joined him, running through the increasing destruction.

Good men and women. They would risk their lives for the people of this county. Even while the earthquake still tore at the town with its vicious teeth, ripping the roads, the homes, the buildings, he sent them fanning out across Virtue Falls.

He knew that before the day was over, this calamity would take all his attention, all his energy, all his knowledge, and no one could blame him if for the moment he forgot the events in San Francisco and did the duty for which he was hired.

No one could blame him at all.

CHAPTER NINE

Kateri raked in the pile of chips and rose from the table. "I've got to pour me a cup of coffee. Anybody else want some?"

"No, I want liquor," Sánchez said.

"You're on duty," Kateri retorted, and grinned at him.

Sánchez was kidding. She knew that. He was responding to the first-class poker ass-whupping she had just delivered on the whole crew . . . but especially on him and Adams. Sánchez would never cause her trouble, but Adams was sulking big time.

Of course, the teasing the rest of the guys had given him hadn't helped, and as she turned away from the table and headed for the coffee pot, she wondered whether he was the kind of guy who would try to foment trouble for her, or if he'd be pulling strings to get transferred out of here.

But she wasn't expecting a physical attack, so when he slammed her in the back and knocked her to the ground, she landed hard, then rolled and came up, fists raised, instantly ready to fight—and stumbled like a drunken fool.

The earth rocked like the deck of a ship in a storm.

An attack, yes. But not an attack from Adams. An attack from the earth itself.

Kateri's mother's tribe had legends, that a giant frog monster-god crouched off the coast and when it woke and hopped up to taste the sun, the earth broke apart. They had other legends; that here on the coast, in this particular spot where the river met the harbor, the ocean would periodically rise to eat the land. Her tribe spoke of the government's stupidity in putting the Coast Guard station in Virtue Falls Harbor; the elders predicted a day of disaster.

Now it had come.

But Kateri had planned. She knew what to do.

As the ground rocked under her and cabinets fells off the wall, she shouted, "Get out there and get the people out of the harbor. If they're on their boats, send them straight out the breakwater and tell them to keep going as fast as they can over the top of the wave. Then get the cutters out of the harbor."

Like great, stupid fools, the men stared at her.

"A tsunami's on its way." She gestured widely toward the shuddering window that looked out on the blue ocean.

They understood then. Cold professionalism swiftly overcame their shock, and all the men battled the violent rocking to leap toward their gear.

All the men . . . except Adams.

He stood still, his eyes cold and unresponsive. "How do you know that?"

"That a tsunami's coming? I know." She pulled on her life vest. "This wave will be huge, and it'll lift everything in the harbor and carry it inland." She staggered as the ground fell away from her feet, then lifted again. This earthquake was a killer. Literally. "A wave like this will lift the cutters and carry them inland."

"A tsunami can't be strong enough to lift a Coast Guard cutter," Adams said.

"You dumbshit." Sánchez staggered toward the door. "Did you never see the footage of the Japanese tsunami?"

Adams watched the crew as they raced, carrying the gear they hadn't yet donned, up and down the harbor, yelling instructions to the boaters.

The fishermen were already on the move, taking their boats out through the breakwater; they knew this ocean.

The casual vacationers were running toward town; they were scared spitless.

And here Kateri was, stuck with the guy too stupid to be scared spitless.

"I need you in charge of the *Ginia*." She plunged after her men. "Do your duty, lieutenant."

Turning, she saw Adams fighting the earthquake to stand in one place.

"Stay here if you like," she said. "The tsunami's going to clear the waterfront, and after it does, I'll have your corpse court-martialed."

Finally he moved toward his gear. He didn't believe her. He made that clear by his studied reluctance. But through the window he could see the other Coasties now headed to the dock. Maybe the other guys' alarm had finally gotten through to him.

They had a skeleton crew and three cutters to steer through the narrow breakwater. They could battle through the swell if they got their boats headed straight out to sea before the first big wave started to break. If they didn't . . . the force of the water would catch the cutters and they would capsize and submerge, or be carried inland and break apart.

Grimly she ran toward the *Iron Sullivan*, the last cutter in the line.

They didn't have much time.

CHAPTER TEN

Elizabeth ran all the way from the Oceanview Café in downtown Virtue Falls to the rim of Virtue Falls Canyon. She looked, and looked again, and in a gasping prayer of thanksgiving, she sang, "Oh, God. Oh, God. Oh, God."

She'd arrived in time. The first wave hadn't yet arrived.

As she put down her bag, she trembled with excitement. Or was that an aftershock?

Beneath her feet, dirt tumbled down into the depths of the canyon.

She moved back from the rim—a little. She had a duty to geology, to her team, to her father's legacy. Not the murder part; the geology part.

She stood sandwiched between the two greatest scientific moments of her life: a magnificent earthquake, and the resulting tsunami.

Yet as she pulled out her video camera, it was the cut in her hand that kept her attention focused not on the restless, ruthless earth, but on the pain, and a glance at the bandage Rainbow had fashioned proved the blood still seeped into the white towel, turning it red.

In the big scheme of things, the cut could never be considered anything but minor. But Elizabeth moved carefully as she popped the lens cap. She took a long, calming breath.

This was the most important moment of her life. No one needed to know she had just run 1.6 miles and was still panting. No one needed to know she had cut her hand and the sight of blood made her faint. She needed to be focused in her mind and clear in her voice.

Pointing the camera to the east, upstream, she started filming. "I'm Elizabeth Banner of the Banner Geological Study outside of Virtue Falls, Washington. The date is August fifteenth, the time is 7:38 P.M. It's been approximately twenty-five minutes since the earthquake ended, and I'm here on the rim of the canyon to report on its effects on the terrain, and to watch for an incoming tsunami. When we look to the east, we're looking toward Virtue Falls, where the Virtue River drops forty feet off the granite escarpment into Virtue Falls Canyon. The river then runs seven miles before it enters the Pacific Ocean." She did a slow sweep from east to west, toward the ocean.

A quick glance showed the ocean still appeared normal, wild and churning, but that defined the Pacific. If everything the study had revealed was true, the tsunami

would arrive, and soon. The timing depended on which
fault had broken, and how far offshore it was.

"I've studied this area extensively, including the photos Charles Banner took on his first day in the canyon and
photos of the work done in the twenty-five years since.
For the past ten months, I've done hands-on work as a
member of the study. I've hiked the paths, knelt in the
dirt, examined the geological layers. As you can see, even
after this massive earthquake, most of the terrain looks
the same. The river still tumbles over the stones." She focused on the river bed, then slowly the lens lifted up the
far wall of the canyon. "The trees and brush still dig their
roots into the canyon walls. But look! Rockslides have
ripped down the walls, cleaning away vegetation and exposing new geological layers. We have to look at this
now, because when we look to the west, we see that the
canyon widens out." Slowly she walked toward the highest, westernmost point.

In the few minutes since her last glance, the ocean had
changed.

She had to swallow her excitement before she could
continue, and keep her voice level, calm and scientific.
"Here where the river meets the Pacific Ocean, trouble
is brewing." She did a long shot of the entire area.
"Frequently, before a tsunami sweeps into an area, the
ocean sucks back, exposing rocks, sandbars, the ocean
floor itself, and leaving fish and aquatic life flopping in
the air."

Elizabeth had always heard so much about the onset
of a tsunami, seen videos shot by people on the scene,
tried to imagine what it would be like to view it in person. Now she *was* viewing it, large and clear, the only
one of the team lucky enough to be a witness to the cataclysm.

She had so much at stake here, not merely the knowledge that hundreds of scientists would study every scrap of evidence in classes and conferences, and thousands of people would view her video on television. She also had a reputation to uphold, a reputation formed not by her actions but by the actions of her parents. She had to prove she wasn't Misty, beautiful and wanton. She had to prove she wasn't Charles, prey to murderous rages. If Elizabeth could remain cool under this pressure, never again would there be suspicious glances cast her way, or whispered rumors behind her back.

Of course, Garik would tell her she was kidding herself, and maybe she was.

But hey, Garik—maybe I want to prove something to myself.

In her best lecture voice, she said, "We can clearly see this is the case, and can also see why the geological evidence in Virtue Falls Canyon points to massive tsunamis which in the past have swept far up the river, filling it like a bathtub, then . . . wait. Far out to sea—is that the swell?"

Her heart began to pound so loudly she could hear it in her ears.

It was only a swell. On a normal day, she wouldn't have glanced twice.

But it was long, stretching from north to south as far as she could see, and moving fast. She took the camera away from her face and watched, glancing from the view screen to the real panorama as the swell got closer, rose higher, and higher still, and finally higher in the middle where it raced toward her.

Her excitement mounted, and she resumed her commentary. "You're witness to the fact that our theory that the shallow ocean floor at the mouth of Virtue Falls

Canyon contributes to unusually large tsunamis . . . is correct."

The wave crested and crashed, the noise unimaginable, and she filmed the forward edge as it swept up the river, ripping out giant trees by their roots and tossing them into the air. The water cut the soil out from under the rim of the canyon; giant boulders tumbled like marbles in the hands of a careless boy. As the wave churned through the channel, it grew brown, and then black.

Elizabeth raised her voice. "The roar and tumult shakes the ground, and I don't know if I'm experiencing the power of the tsunami or another earthquake. Although I'm standing on the high point, and never in geological time has the water ever reached this area around me, I know there's a first time for everything, and the danger is real."

The danger *was* real; the water could claw its way up here, sweep her away, and her body would never be recovered.

Yet she wouldn't move for the world. She had been born to bear witness to this moment. She had dreamed about it, hoped for it, imagined it. She remembered her father describing the long-ago cataclysm . . .

Charles sat next to her on a rock toasted by the sun, and pointed out to sea, and with gestures and exuberance he told the young Elizabeth about the restless earth, and how the ground that seemed stable could change in a minute, and glow red with fire or blue with ice, or tremble and break.

Elizabeth listened, eyes wide, caught up in his wonder and excitement, until Mommy slid her arms around his neck, and kissed his cheek, and said, "Enough now, Charles, she'll have nightmares."

"You won't, will you, Elizabeth?" Daddy asked.

"No!" Elizabeth said stoutly.

Daddy turned to Mommy. "See? She's my daughter through and through. Except that she's almost as pretty as you." He smiled at her, a thin, tall, tanned man with thinning hair and wrinkles around his eyes.

Mommy kissed his mouth. But she crushed the collar of his golf shirt in her fist, and her knuckles strained white against the faded blue. Lifting her head, she smiled at her little girl. "When Elizabeth is grown, she will be much prettier than I am. In the meantime, it's time to eat."

Daddy let Mommy go reluctantly, and he watched her so lovingly Elizabeth felt warm. Secure.

But Elizabeth hadn't believed Mommy. Mommy was so beautiful, with a halo of gold hair and big pretty dark blue eyes, and Elizabeth loved everything about her.

Mommy . . .

The earth-breaking, forward-grinding noise stopped. Elizabeth caught her breath.

Remarkable and startling as it had been, the memory was over.

The moment was now—and danger appeared from an unexpected source.

The long, giant, frothy wave became a whirlpool. It swirled, roaring like the open mouth of a hungry beast. It ate the sides of the canyon, climbing higher and higher, and for the first time, fear caught at her.

Run. Elizabeth, run!

Then, inexorably, the water in the middle of the canyon slipped backward toward the ocean, dragging the edges after it, ripping more of the now water-softened ground away.

Elizabeth backed away from the edge. She pretended

that her terror had been minor—certainly it had been natural—and she took up her commentary again. With a depth of fascination that marked her encounters with the natural world, she said, "The first tsunami is pulling back, but considering the magnitude of the earthquake, I expect at least three big waves."

And next time, she would know about the whirlpool, and before it threatened her, she would back away.

Garik always said she had no common sense when it came to danger.

Maybe not. Not the first time. But she learned from her mistakes.

Which was more than she could say about him.

CHAPTER ELEVEN

Over an hour later, three waves had advanced and retreated in a horrible, magnificent, destructive rhythm. The second tsunami had been the largest, cresting halfway up the canyon, sucking away debris while the earth rocked beneath Elizabeth's feet. She hated for it to be over, and yet it was, the earthquake reduced to the occasional aftershock, the waves subsiding as if weary . . . and anyway, her camera battery was almost dead. In a voice hoarse with excitement and fatigue, she said, "The sun is setting, and I believe the worst of nature's onslaught is finished. When the team returns, and we're sure it's safe, we'll return to the many sites we have studied in the Virtue Falls Canyon—it will take a GPS to locate them—

and investigate the changes the earthquake and tsunami have wrought. For now, as the sun sets, I can feel the earth living and breathing beneath my feet, and I have to wonder—what will tomorrow bring? Elizabeth Banner, signing off from Virtue Falls Canyon."

Trembling with excitement and perhaps a small residue of fear, she put the camera away in her bag, and placed it on the ground. With the light failing and the worst of the disaster behind her, she should go into town.

But her heart still raced, and the need to discover more, learn more, observe every detail of a splendid cataclysm was a drug in her veins.

One last surveillance and she would go. One last examination of the powerful, pervasive evidence that everything she and her father had worked to prove was true.

Walking to the edge of the canyon, right to the spot where the ground dropped away into its steep slope, she looked, just looked with her whole eyes and for her whole self. She hugged herself, thankful she had been in the right place at the right time, amazed at the savagery and glory of nature.

Yet the pain in her hand now prodded at her. Her focus was narrowing, returning to the smaller details of life. She wanted to remain, to savor, yet she knew she should get back to town and find a doctor.

About twenty feet down in the canyon, caught in a pile of debris, something bleached and white caught her eye.

What was that . . . down there? A bone?

She inched down the slope, peering at it. Holding on to tree trunks and grabbing at branches, she slid farther down the slope, the loose dirt falling away beneath her feet.

A femur? A human femur? Her mind leaped in scientific anticipation. Had the tsunami uncovered an archeological treasure? How cool would that be, if not only had her father's prediction of earth-shattering disaster come true, but also the cataclysm had unearthed some ancient encampment built by prehistoric man?

Something slithered in the underbrush.

She half-screamed, then clutched her chest as a garter snake rippled away. Somewhere in the back of her mind, she heard her father's voice say, *They're more afraid of you than you are of them.*

She doubted that. She was pretty calm about most of the creatures that populated the great outdoors, but snakes . . . She shuddered.

She should climb back up. She knew she should. Snakes weren't the only creatures that had been displaced by the water. All of those creatures would be confused and hostile. The tree trunks and the wild clutter of branches that was her goal had come to rest at the highest watermark. The ground in the vicinity was unstable, ready to slide into the chasm. The earth's slightest shudder could send her tumbling into the mud below. She'd slip down into the canyon until a rock or debris stopped her—or until she rolled off a newly exposed cliff face and fell all the way to the bottom.

At least the video would be safe in its bag at the top of the canyon.

Stupid thought, but that bone beckoned. She scooted closer, and closer, the bone gleaming in the gathering twilight. She stretched until her fingertips touched it, leaned farther until she was able to grasp it, brought it back and looked at it.

It didn't look that old.

Of course, it *was* old. All the flesh had been cleaned

away. But it wasn't petrified. It didn't show the cracks of extreme old age. She turned it over and over in her hands. In fact, she didn't even know if it was human. What had she been thinking, to allow her enthusiasm to lead her here?

From the rim above, a man's voice snapped, "What are you doing?"

She gasped, jumped, and dropped the bone. Grabbed for it. Caught it. Her feet skidded out from underneath her. She landed on her butt, crashed into the pile of brush, and came to an ignominious, and lucky, halt. That hurt her hand, a piercing pain that made her close her eyes long enough to gain control.

Then she looked up at the rim.

The man loomed there, a silhouette against the failing blue of the sky. He wore a broad hat. His hands rested on his belt. He carried a gun.

It was the sheriff. Dennis Foster. He glared at her as if he discovered her committing a crime.

Swift guilt rose in her. "I'm, um . . . I saw this bone." She showed him. "I thought an . . . archeological find . . ."

He still glared.

"You know. I thought that the tsunami had uncovered a site where ancient man had built his home and . . ." Her voice faltered.

Sheriff Foster had never liked her.

She was used to people not liking or trusting her. But from the first moment they'd met, he had seemed more hostile than most. He'd been the one who had brought in the evidence to convict her father. She would have thought he'd be gloating, or patronizing. But he made it clear, right from the first moment he'd spotted her at the Ocean-view Café, that he hated the sight of her.

Maybe she reminded him of Misty. Her aunt had been

like that sometimes, angry that Elizabeth looked so much like her mother.

"You're alone out here," he said. "If anything happened to you, no one would find you for a very long time."

She found his choice of words . . . menacing. "I know."

"Especially since the earthquake created real emergencies in town."

"I'm sure." She tucked the bone under her arm and started to pull herself up the steep slope to the rim. She grabbed branches and trees, used her good hand to hoist herself from one spot to another.

Sheriff Foster watched without any offer of assistance. Probably he figured that if she had managed to get herself down there, she could get herself out. But he still loomed, unmoving, impatience shimmering, and if she could have figured out a different way around, she would have taken it.

At last, she crawled, literally crawled, onto level ground.

He moved back. But not far.

She stood. She looked around and located her bag . . . behind him.

"Are you satisfied now?" He asked as if he had the right to know.

Taking the bone out from underneath her arm, she looked at it again. "Archeology is not my specialty, of course, but I think this bone is probably no more than a hundred to two hundred years old."

He barely glanced at it. "Probably it came from the whore's cemetery."

The contemptuous tone, the use of that word, the word she'd heard applied to her mother, shocked her. He wasn't being rude to *her*—but it sure seemed like it. "What are you talking about?"

"Local story goes that late in the nineteenth century, Virtue Falls sported a thriving brothel. When the whores died, the ladies of the town didn't want them resting beside them in the town cemetery, so they consecrated some ground somewhere farther up the canyon on a flat spot, and buried them there." His words were clipped, his tone was flat and cold.

"Is that true?" Elizabeth clutched one end of the bone in both her hands.

"I don't know. But it seems likely."

"Wow." She was, she realized, holding the bone like a weapon. "That's so unfeeling."

His impatience grew to something more, something close to violence. "I've barely got things under control in town, I'm running a fast perimeter check to survey damage and see if there's anyone who needs help, and you want me to concern myself with old bones?"

It took her a minute to realize that he had thought she was calling him unfeeling. "No! I meant . . . I meant it was cold of the town women to shove the prostitutes into such a lonely place."

"Oh. That." He waved a dismissive hand.

She flinched, and ducked.

Satisfaction gleamed in his eyes.

A bully. He was a bully.

But he wouldn't hurt her. After all, he was the sheriff.

Although, if he did want to hurt her, they were 1.6 miles from town, there was no one to hear her scream, and he could dispose of her body by the simple act of shoving her off the cliff and telling everybody the crazy man's daughter had fallen while filming the tsunami.

"Was anybody in town hurt?" She hoped not.

"We haven't found any bodies yet. But people are trapped in collapsed buildings. Medical personnel are hopping. You should go back to town. Get that hand stitched."

She stepped sideways and caught the strap of her bag. "How did you know my hand needs stitching?"

His impatience swelled again, and his voice was sharp and aggressive. "Because Rainbow Breezewing found me and shrieked that you were probably bleeding to death and I had to find you. Why else would I do a perimeter check now?"

"I don't know. But thank you. This was nice of you." She inched away, bag over her shoulder, still holding the bone like a club.

"Give me that damned thing!" He moved fast, grabbing the bone and twisting it out of her grasp.

She turned and ran.

Sheriff Foster was a man teetering on the edge of violence, and she wanted to be nowhere near when he fell.

CHAPTER TWELVE

Garik Jacobsen walked into his Las Vegas apartment, his home now for eight months. He flipped on the TV, flung his suit jacket on the chair, and placed the Styrofoam containers that held his dinner on the kitchen counter. As he headed for the bedroom, his stomach rumbled.

Ever since the FBI had taken his badge, he hadn't been eating regularly.

But tonight, for the first time, he knew exactly what to do, and his appetite had come back with a vengeance.

Yay for him.

The bedroom was stark: blinds at the window, a bed, a nightstand, a reading lamp. He pulled open the drawer and looked down at the pistol he wasn't supposed to own. He picked it up, weighed it in his hand, checked to see that it was properly loaded. It was. And the safety was on. Putting the pistol back, he shut the drawer.

He kicked his dress shoes in the direction of the closet. They banged, one by one, into the cheap wooden sliding door.

He worked as a security guard at Nordstrom; the tie had been loosened as soon as he left the store. The jacket had come off as soon as he got to the court-ordered therapist's office. Now it was time for T-shirt and jeans, and he donned them with the reverence of a man who wore them all too seldom.

Opening the drawer again, he picked up the pistol. He shoved it into his waistband, and headed back to the kitchen. There, he kicked a discarded pizza box aside. He flipped open the tops of his Styrofoam containers and admired the contents.

Yeah. Steak: thick, charbroiled, rare. Potatoes au gratin with enough cheese to give a cardiologist a heart attack. Green beans cooked with bacon.

He might skip the green beans. He liked them, but what was the point of eating something good for him now?

In the other container, tiramisu. In the paper cup, espresso.

Yeah.

He heated the skillet on the stove, melted a stick of butter until it was smoking, and slapped the steak in to crisp it up. He put the beans and potatoes on a plate and into the microwave. He got out a fork and his good steak knife—it was actually a stiletto, but he wasn't allowed to own one of those either, so he called it a steak knife—and put it on the coffee table.

On the TV, a rerun of *CSI*. Like he needed to watch that noble shit about duty and honor and esprit de corps. He changed the channel, found *The Punisher*, one of the best, most violent, stupidest movies of all time, and left it.

He flipped the steak, watched it sizzle another minute, then pulled the plate out of the microwave and lovingly laid the steak beside the steaming potatoes. Going to the couch, he sat down, put the plate on the table, and pulled the pistol from his waistband. He placed it beside the plate, within easy reach.

The movie had ended. The local news blared, the silly anchor team making much of insignificant details in the Las Vegas area while ignoring the big shit that was important. He used the remote to mute them, picking up his knife and fork, and with exquisite care, he carved the steak.

Perfect. The blood ran red onto the white plate, embracing the pile of potatoes.

Elizabeth would have turned her head away. She seldom ate steak, and when she did, it was always well done. Blood made her squeamish. Once after he'd been shot, she had rushed to the ER to see him, taken one look, and had fainted so hard and so fast she'd needed medical attention for a concussion.

So during the whole time of their marriage, Garik had eaten his steak medium. When she had told him she wanted a divorce, he'd pointed out his steakly sacrifice, but she had said, in that supremely reasonable tone which bugged the shit out of him, that if not for him and his carnivorous habits, she would be a vegetarian. And anyway, eating to please each other didn't make for a happy marriage.

Apparently not.

Now he lifted a bite of tender, rare steak to his lips, chewed and swallowed, and smiled.

Heaven.

Piercing one of the green beans with his fork, he lifted it in a salute. "To you, Elizabeth," he said, and ate it, too.

His pleasure in the moment slipped . . . Damn, but he missed that woman. He hadn't understood her. The stuff she cared about! Stuff like rocks and quakes and volcanoes. Stuff that bored him silly, and when he tried to get her interested in what was important, like crime and passion and violence, she'd pointed out that people change, come and go, but the earth was forever. She had always been so calm, so logical . . . so remote.

Except in bed. My God, he'd never met a woman like that, who hid a fiery passion beneath a cool, inquiring, scientific mind. He wished . . . well, he wished a lot of things, most of them to do with Elizabeth, and all of them impossible now.

He shrugged. Water over the dam, or under the bridge, or whatever it was. It had taken him more than a year to get himself to this point of Zen acceptance. He wasn't going to screw it up now thinking about what might have been.

Instead, he once again submerged himself in the meal, in the cheesy, salty potatoes, in the steak, in the beans and the bacon.

He'd love to enjoy a glass of wine, but he had decided he didn't want anyone to say alcohol had influenced his decision.

As a last dinner went, this one was pretty fine. Any man on death row would be glad for this, and when he had finished—he ate every bite, even the green beans—he leaned back against the couch and sipped his espresso, laced with cinnamon and whipped cream.

All he needed now was a woman. But since Elizabeth had left him, he hadn't been much good at sex. He figured that was a big part of his problem. No sex, no pressure valve, and Garik the perfect-record FBI agent gets fed up with the bullshit regulations and loses his temper. And gets in big trouble. Yeah, man.

So no, he wasn't going to go looking for sex for dessert. Going out in a blaze of impotence would be too humiliating.

Instead, he reached for the pistol.

It wasn't his service pistol. The FBI had taken that away from him, kind of like ripping the badge off an old-time Western sheriff. Garik had bought this piece at a pawn shop, though, and the Colt felt good in his hand. Solid. Cold. Uncaring. Unthinking . . .

He felt at rest with his decision.

Margaret would be angry, grieved and hurt, and he regretted that. He knew Elizabeth would mourn him, too. But Margaret wasn't related to him, for all that she'd cared for him so diligently, and Elizabeth was no longer his wife. He'd gone over the logic a hundred times, and he couldn't live with the knowledge he had started down the road in his father's footsteps. That he was a killer. Inadvertently, but a killer.

He unmuted the TV and turned up the sound. It wouldn't muffle the shot, but it might make it sound like he was watching another version of *The Punisher*.

Lifting the gun, he placed the barrel in his mouth.

He lowered it, and grimaced. For all the many times

he'd handled a gun, he'd never tasted one. Metal and gun oil had ruined the savory, lingering flavors of his meal.

Tough shit, huh.

He lifted the pistol again. That flavor wasn't the worst part of this.

The worst part was getting distracted by those phony newscasters.

The guy with the carefully applied blond streaks in his hair and dutiful concern announced, "An eight-point-one earthquake struck off the west coast of Washington State, shaking an area extending from Alaska to San Francisco and wreaking havoc in Seattle where it knocked bricks off of buildings and killed sixteen people in a bank collapse." Photos and videos took over the screen. "A massive tsunami struck the coast, tearing into the beaches." The feed switched to helicopter shots of the incoming waves battering the low-lying beaches. "The town of Forks was hard hit, and there we begin our coverage—"

Garik put down the pistol. He sat forward. "What about Virtue Falls?" he asked aloud.

The picture switched to a wide-eyed female, standing in front of a collapsed building illuminated by floodlights. "As you can see, in this small rural community made famous by the Twilight books and movies, the earthquake damage has been substantial—"

"How much truth are you telling, and how much is news hype?" Standing, Garik headed for his jacket, pulled his cell phone, and called the Virtue Falls Resort.

No connection.

He called the Virtue Falls sheriff's office.

No connection.

The news babbled on, abandoning the earthquake in Washington State and moving to the story of a local woman who had inherited a guitar once played by Bob Dylan. Because, you know, that was important.

Garik hit the Internet to get the earthquake details.

The news was right about one thing. Helicopter footage showed a huge tsunami striking the coast, rushing up rivers and swamping low-lying areas.

Elizabeth.

He'd been married to Elizabeth. He knew the theory about Virtue Falls Canyon. He knew Elizabeth was working down there on her father's project.

Had she been in the canyon when the earthquake hit?

Surely not. It had struck late in the day.

But he knew her. When she was obsessed with her rocks, time passed and she never noticed.

What about Margaret? The resort hung precariously over the Pacific. Margaret had paid for the resort's refitting, but could it withstand the assault of the ocean?

He called the airlines.

They weren't flying into Seattle right now. Not until the aftershocks stopped. They weren't flying into Portland, either. Damage at the airport.

Going into the bedroom, he pulled out his duffel bag; he had always kept it packed for unexpected trips for the FBI, and old habits died hard.

He pulled on socks and his running shoes.

He'd take his truck, a white Ford F-250, powerful as hell. After all, Nevada had a top speed limit of seventy-five miles per hour, and he still held an FBI ID.

He had claimed he lost it in the fight.

His supervisor had claimed he believed him.

So even figuring he'd get pulled over at least four times, when he flashed that ID, the cops would mostly let him go.

On a good day, he could make it back home to Virtue Falls in twenty hours.

He hoped to hell this was a good day.

Grabbing his keys and his knife, he walked out the door, leaving his pistol behind.

CHAPTER THIRTEEN

As the darkness fell, Elizabeth walked into the outskirts of Virtue Falls. And stopped. And stared.

People were firing up generators on the streets, using spotlights to illuminate collapsed buildings and crushed cars. Men and women shouted, or silently wept, or stood about with their arms crossed over their chests. Children rubbed their sleepy eyes and whined, or stared, their eyes wide in shock and terror, too scared to even cry.

Of course. Elizabeth knew the earthquake had done damage. She'd seen some of it on the way out of town, and Sheriff Foster had made clear the damage had been extensive. But she hadn't realized that the disaster would wear such a human face.

She looked down at the bandage on her hand. Compared to the devastation here, her cut was minor.

She wandered along, unsure of what to do until she got to Branyon's Bakery.

The two-story building had pancaked in on itself. Bricks were scattered across the street like a child's LEGO set. In a froth of frantic motion, a team of men and women were throwing bricks aside. She heard someone

say, "We need a dog. Mrs. Branyon's down here somewhere, but God, I can't find her."

Mrs. Branyon was one of the elderly women who wore
red lipstick that bled into the wrinkles of her upper lip,
pink blush she never blended, and enough perfume to
make Elizabeth sneeze. She was bent, stout, and refused
to wear her hearing aids, so she was very, very loud. Elizabeth knew exactly what Mrs. Branyon thought about
her, because although Mrs. Branyon's daughter had tried
to hush her, Mrs. Branyon had stated her opinion clearly
enough for Elizabeth to hear. "The acorn never falls far
from the oak, and that Elizabeth girl will either become
a whore like her mother or a killer like her father, and
maybe both."

Elizabeth had pretended not to hear. It was easier
that way.

It was always easier that way.

She watched the would-be rescuers unscientifically try
to find Mrs. Branyon, that mean old biddy . . . who didn't
deserve to die in the dark, of dehydration, in pain and
slowly suffocating.

With a deep, resigned sigh, Elizabeth climbed into the
rubble, got on her hands and knees, and started sniffing.
It didn't take long before the assault of flowery perfume
made her sneeze, and guided her to a spot where none of
the others were working. With her uninjured hand, Elizabeth plucked a few bricks off the top. "Mrs. Branyon?"
she called. "It's Elizabeth Banner. Are you there?" She
heard a faint moan. "Mrs. Branyon?" she called louder.

The other rescuers looked up.

From deep inside the piles of broken wooden studs
and broken plaster board, Mrs. Branyon croaked, "Oh,
God, it's that awful Elizabeth Banner. Are you going to
kill me while I'm helpless?"

Elizabeth sat back on her heels. Took a breath. Sneezed again.

Well. How good to know Mrs. Branyon was fine.

Raising her voice, Elizabeth called to the other searchers, "I heard her. She's under here." She moved away and let the others go to work.

After all, she didn't mind figuring out where the old harridan was located, but performing the actual salvage work stretched the bounds of her loving kindness.

Elizabeth dusted at her knees, then started toward her apartment, moving grimly through and around and over the wreckage scattered on the road.

So many buildings damaged. So many terrified faces shining in the blaring lights. Here and there, someone sat on the curb and rocked and cried, and Elizabeth felt the nervous flutter of fear she had not experienced before.

And why? Her apartment here was not a home. None of her possessions were precious to her. So many years ago, she had learned not to trust what appeared to be permanent—not her friends, not her toys, not her parents, and for sure, not Garik.

Yet she'd grown fond of Virtue Falls, probably because she'd found her life's work here, possibly because on some subconscious level, she remembered it from her childhood.

The closer she got to her apartment, the more her heart raced, until at last she stood before the two-story building, built in the nineteen thirties. Exterior walls had peeled away like soft frosting from a layer cake. Rooms gaped open wide. In the blare of floodlights, she could see into her second-story apartment. The bed she hadn't made, the refrigerator door hanging open revealing a pathetic quart of milk and a container of cheese curds, her chest of drawers that had spat her underwear across the floor. And the fake leather, lime-green, painstakingly assembled photo album of her early years in Washington.

From her aunt, she had stolen family photos and drawings. From newspaper archives, she had copied articles about her mother's acting and her father's scientific work. She had used prints of famed local artist Bradley Hoff's beautiful paintings to fill in the life she couldn't remember.

Now the album dangled over the street, half on and half off the floor.

She had thought she owned nothing that she treasured. Yet if the building collapsed, she would lose her memories. Like her father, she would be lost and alone in a world without love . . .

Oh, God. She was being so dramatic. If her cousins were here, they would mercilessly mock her. By merely glancing around, she could see how much more loss everyone else in Virtue Falls had suffered.

Yet still her bag slid off her shoulder and thumped to the ground, and she stared up at the album as if it was the holy grail.

One of the town's firefighters stopped. He was young, handsome, brawny, and covered with the dust of a man who had been in and out of collapsed buildings in search of victims. She had no idea who he was. He'd never spoken to her. But he apparently knew her, and knew where she lived. "You can't stay here tonight, Miss Banner," he told her. "You'll have to go to a shelter."

"I can't leave my book hanging there." She pointed. "It's all I've got of—" Her breath caught, quavered, steadied. "It's all I've got of my parents. Please, I need it."

He barely refrained from rolling his eyes. "Don't you have the pictures in digital?"

"Yes on the photographs. But my mother . . . my

mother took some of those photos. There are some letters she wrote to my aunt. I never copied those. There's a drawing she did of me when I was three or four. They hold a little of her essence." Which was stupid. She knew it was stupid, and highly unscientific, and . . . just stupid. But she couldn't help it. It was what she *felt*.

"Do I look like the kind of guy who's dumb enough to risk my life for a book?" The firefighter was clearly exasperated.

Yet when Elizabeth's eyes filled with tears, not manipulative tears, but tears that rose from the depths of her wretched soul, he sighed. "Right, Miss Banner. I'll go in and get it. You're going to owe me a drink."

"Any time," she said. Feeling like the wide-eyed, traumatized child who had landed on her aunt's doorstep, Elizabeth watched him climb through the rubble, up the stairs displayed with such shocking openness, and into her apartment.

Onlookers joined her, and Elizabeth heard their murmurs.

"What's he doing?" "He shouldn't be up there." "Is he rescuing a cat?" "We'll be lucky if we don't lose one of our firefighters today."

Elizabeth glanced at the lady who spoke, who stood with her hands clasped at her throat, who stared into Elizabeth's apartment with the fear and dread of a person who had seen too much pain and destruction this day.

Elizabeth looked at the building, not with her feelings, but with her usual logical good sense.

The floor was tilted, and at the edges where the outer wall had once stood, pieces had crumbled away into the street. If—no, when—another aftershock shook the town, the whole building could go down.

She shouldn't have sent him up there.

The firefighter got down on his hands and knees and crawled toward the album.

Elizabeth could see him muttering as he crept forward, inch by inch, testing the floor like a cat on a narrow branch. She held her breath; she should call him off. She couldn't stand it if he was hurt in pursuit of some old pictures. "Halt," she whispered. Then, louder, "Halt! Don't! It's not worth it!"

The firefighter stopped and looked right at her. He shook his head in disgust, as if he couldn't believe she was chickening out at the last minute. Dropping to his belly, he inched forward and with the very tips of his fingers, he nudged the album, grasped it, dragged it up over the edge and toward him. She held her breath as he tucked the album under his arm.

And the earth trembled.

CHAPTER FOURTEEN

The edges of the second floor crumbled like overdone toast.

Without the caution he'd shown before, the firefighter scooted back. He disappeared behind the door, and re-appeared almost at once on the ground floor. He bounded through the rubble, escaping from under the fragile, failing ceiling. He stepped out on the street, and the after-shock diminished.

The onlookers let out their held breaths.

The firefighter handed Elizabeth the photo album. "You owe me a drink," he said, "and maybe a kiss?"

She stared at him, working through his reasoning. "You think that because we have all faced mortality today, and you're a handsome man and I'm an attractive woman, a kiss, being a prelude to sex, will ease our tension. Also, because you risked your life for my album."

He sighed and hooked his fingers into his suspenders. "Wow, Miss Banner, you really know how to take the wind out of a man's sails."

Surprised, she asked, "Why? I'm quite willing to kiss you. It's not as if you're unfit or from the wrong age demographic."

He wrinkled up his face.

Uncertain, now, she asked, "Do you not want your kiss?"

"Hell, yes, I want it." He didn't wait for her to put down her album. He swept her into his arms, bent her backward, and kissed her with vast enthusiasm and way too much tongue.

She was overwhelmed, breathless for all the wrong reasons, and her back hurt from the backward arch.

But when he stood her on her feet again, the onlookers clapped.

"After that, you don't even have to buy me a drink," he said. "But I sure look forward to buying you one." Which apparently meant he had enjoyed the kiss. "By the way, my name is Peyton Bailey. Make sure you remember that."

"Peyton Bailey," she repeated. "Thank you."

He swaggered down the street toward the other firefighters.

She watched him. He was handsome, with wavy blond hair and bright green eyes, the sort of weary firefighter who would make the cover of *USA Today* as the face of the Washington earthquake. And from the way the women were viewing her, she supposed she was now the object of envy. But she, who had been celibate for longer than she cared to remember, wasn't attracted to him at all.

It didn't make sense. She'd had no more in common with Garik than she had had with that firefighter, yet she had been irresistibly attracted to Garik.

It was all chemistry . . . and she'd always been bad at chemistry.

For the first time, the enormity of the day's events struck her. People could die, had died, in the earthquake and tsunami that so enthralled her. This young firefighter, handsome and her age, risked his life to save the citizens and tourists in the town, and he risked his life again for her album. Because big and dumb-looking he might be, he had recognized her desperation and responded.

An older firefighter stepped around the corner and barked orders at his men, and they hustled off to the next rescue.

Rainbow grabbed Elizabeth from behind in a massive embrace. "You're alive!"

Elizabeth extricated herself.

She looked down at the album in her hand. "I am."

Rainbow rattled Elizabeth's arm. "You ran out of the diner so fast, the earthquake wasn't even over. And they said the tsunami came in on the coast."

"Yes. It was huge." An understatement. "Do you know—have they found any bodies?"

"Police say no one, that all the tourists were off the beach or they fled up the cliffs in time. Personally, I have trouble believing people would all be so sensible, but maybe the Japanese tsunami scared 'em enough."

"Yes. I hope." Elizabeth slid the album into her bag and hefted the bag over her shoulder.

"I hear you helped find Mrs. Branyon."

"Yes. I've finally discovered a logical reason to wear too much perfume."

Rainbow laughed too hard, then stopped too fast. "Kateri is missing."

"No. Oh, no!" Kateri was one of the few people Elizabeth had connected with here in Virtue Falls. "It never occurred to me . . . did the tsunami hit the harbor hard?"

"Almost wiped it out, but Kateri ordered the boats that were manned through the breakwater. They rode over the tsunami, and that saved them. She sent two of the Coast Guard cutters out, too, but the one she commanded was way understaffed and according to eye witnesses, the cutter *Ginia* was right in front of her. She backed her cutter off to the side, and before she could get turned back around, the wave came over the top of the breakwater. Right over the top. The other cutter almost foundered. Hers tipped over." Rainbow wiped at her eyes.

"The first wave capsized her?" Elizabeth had seen the waves. The second was the big one . . . "What happened to the cutter? What happened to her crew?"

"Her cutter was the *Iron Sullivan*. It rolled into the waterfront, and it's sitting on its side where Bob's Shrimp Shack used to be. The crew was on deck . . . they are all half-drowned, but they knew what they were doing better than most people. They rode the wave into shore, jumped off at the right moment, and when the wave retreated they ran like hell up the hill. It's Kateri that's missing. She stayed inside the wheelhouse, trying to steer. When the tsunami hit, the force broke out the windows and she's . . . gone." Rainbow choked up.

"I see." Like Elizabeth, Kateri was out of place, half American Indian, half . . . something else. Caucasian, Elizabeth supposed. She was a woman in the Coast

Guard, in command of the station, giving orders to a bunch of men and having to prove herself with every new Coastie who came in.

And now she was missing and presumed dead.

So much of this—the destruction in town, in the harbor, the cost in human injury, pain and life—made Elizabeth's excitement about the earthquake and tsunami seem thoughtless and reckless. "I've been selfish," she said.

"What? About the earthquake? Oh, honey. No one expects any different from you. And you're—" Rainbow paused awkwardly.

Remembering Sheriff Foster, Elizabeth suggested, "The daughter of a whore and a murderer?"

"Not that. You're kind of a variety pack, born here but not raised here, one of the scientists and a strange bird at any time." Rainbow hugged her again. "Heck, from what I heard about Mrs. Branyon, once they freed her even the old lady said nice things about you."

Elizabeth viewed Rainbow suspiciously.

"Well. Nice, if you consider the source. I was a little pissed at you myself. I thought you must have been killed, rushing off like you did to your stupid site." Rainbow sounded surprisingly bitter.

"Of course I'm alive. It would be counterproductive to put myself in danger, especially when I have been the only variety pack scientist who was lucky enough to be here today." Thinking of the spectacle she had filmed, Elizabeth patted her bag.

"I'm pretty sure the building contractors are going to decide they're lucky, too. They'll swarm like locusts all over town before the leaves fall." Abruptly, Rainbow changed the subject. "How's your father?"

"What? Why? Fine, I suppose."

"I heard the ceiling fell at the home and an old man went to the hospital."

An odd dig of emotion startled Elizabeth.

Charles . . . hurt? No. Her father could not be harmed. He was a murderer. He *did* harm.

Yet she knew that was specious reasoning. Earthquakes were far more uncaring than any one man's cruelties. She found herself saying, "I'm sure it wasn't my father. There are a lot of elderly men there, so the odds are on his side." Elizabeth reached into her bag. "I'll call."

"Cell towers are down."

"Of course they are."

"The land lines are broken," Rainbow said. "Communication is sketchy. You need to drive out there and check on him."

"Yes. You're right." Rainbow *was* right. Elizabeth could stay in town and help, but they might need help at the Honor Mountain Memory Care Facility, too, and as one patient's family, Elizabeth was a likely candidate.

She was also . . . *curious* wasn't the word.

She swallowed. She was anxious. About her father. Against her aunt's shrilly expressed opinion, she had made the move to this place to be close to her father, to talk to him, to find out while she could why he had so brutally murdered her mother.

But she had visited only once, and that one meeting had spooked her so much she had not gone back.

Now . . . perhaps he was hurt? Perhaps he could die, and her one link to the past would be severed, and she would never discover the facts about the horror that had shaped her life and character. She would never understand how a man who seemed so gentle, kind, and caring could commit such an atrocity.

Elizabeth nodded stiffly at Rainbow and started walking. "Thank you. I'll go."

"Be careful," Rainbow shouted after her. "There's no telling what's happened on the road!"

CHAPTER FIFTEEN

Elizabeth's apartment didn't offer parking, so she kept her car in a lot at the edge of town.

Good move. Out here, there were no buildings to fall apart, and her 1966 Ford Mustang was undamaged.

The paving was not so lucky. On the way to the car, she tripped on an unseen chunk of asphalt and went down on one knee—and when she put her wounded hand down, she whimpered in pain. Reluctantly, she dug her cell phone out of her bag and used it as a flashlight—reluctantly because she knew the power company would not be out here to restore electricity very soon, and the phone's battery would quickly die.

She got in the driver's seat. The car was stuffy, so she rolled down her window—the Mustang had cranks for the windows—and listened.

She could hear human activity in town; a car alarm blaring, sounds of confusion and hurry.

She started the car. The Mustang's engine was almost silent; her college energy team had won the Southern California competition for redesigning the vehicle with a combination gas and electric engine. Normally she loved the quiet motor almost as much as she loved the way guys stared when she whipped past them on the freeway. Now she wished for the noise of an internal combustion engine, anything to break the silence that rode in the car like an unwanted passenger.

As she drove through the cracks and upheavals of the parking lot to the cracks and upheavals of the road, her fingers tightened on the wheel.

For the first time in her life, she was reluctant to go off on her own. She knew what awaited her on the trip to Honor Mountain Memory Care Facility—no houses, no people, only a primal forest pressing close to a dark strip of two-lane road, while above the cold, bleak stars spun in space. The stars, the forest, the land . . . if they could care, they would probably be glad to see the human race wiped off the earth.

The earthquake must have affected Elizabeth more than she realized, to attribute emotions to the everlasting, unliving molecules of the universe.

The drive was long, treacherous, nerve-wracking, a trek across broken chunks of asphalt and around fallen trees. More than once, she heard the rumble of the oncoming earthquake, then the groan of the trees as they shifted their roots through the ever-moving ground, before all returned to a brooding silence. And more than once she wondered if she would have to turn back . . . and whether the almost constant aftershocks had already rendered her return impossible.

After two long hours—normally the drive took thirty minutes—she saw a glow; the massive generator at the care facility was working. *Thank God.* The silent forest, the restless earth, the interminable drive had spooked her. She wanted lights. She wanted people.

She turned into the parking lot and into the first empty space that wasn't crumpled and torn. Taking her bag, she hurried toward the door as if it was the gate to heaven.

Even here, the world was eerily silent, strangely empty.

She pushed the button by the metal door and when it buzzed loudly and obnoxiously, she collapsed in relief against the wall. Then she peered through the metal-reinforced window down the long, dimly lit corridor and saw one of the female nurses, a middle-aged woman dressed in a flowered smock top, scrub pants of hideous green, and sensible shoes, hurrying toward her.

The nurse pressed her face to the window. Her eyes lit up, she smiled, and she opened the door. "Miss Banner, how did you get here? Come in!"

"I drove." Had they met before? Elizabeth didn't remember. "It was not a pleasant—"

"I'm Yvonne Rudda, head nurse for the evening shift." Yvonne ushered Elizabeth inside, and shut the door after her. "I called for assistance from town, but they told me the roads were blocked."

"In places they are almost—"

"I suppose there are other priorities, but really." Yvonne herded Elizabeth down the hall with the expertise and exasperation of an overworked medical professional. "Do you know how much an earthquake like that upsets our patients? Not to mention we had to load Mr. Cook into a car and send him to the hospital for x-rays and observation. I don't even know if he got there or what his status is."

"I heard—"

"Here I am chattering away, when you drove all the way out here for one thing—to check on your father."

Elizabeth most definitely had not met this woman before. She would have remembered the frustration of trying to finish a sentence. "Yes." She nodded at another flower-smock-clad medical professional who hurried by, looking worn and worried. "Is he okay?"

"Your father is fine." They paused in the doorway of a patient's room, and Yvonne gestured toward the fragile-looking man sleeping in the dim illumination of a hospital nightlight. "As you can see."

It took Elizabeth several seconds to realize the head on the pillow was her father's. Funny—she hadn't recognized him when he was asleep. Of course, except for that one visit she'd made when she first moved here, it had been twenty-three years since she'd seen him in any way except in photos. During her visit, she had been made so uncomfortable by that creepy old guy shouting about her mother's murder, her father calling her Misty, and the general paranoia that came from visiting an entire hospital full of patients who had lost their pasts . . . maybe she had never really looked at Charles.

She advanced slowly into the room and stared down at him as he slept on his side, his hand tucked under his cheek.

Her earliest memories were of a tall man, with broad shoulders where she rested her head, kind blue eyes, and a thinning head of brown, curly hair. Now he looked . . . small. His shoulders were scrunched, but Elizabeth guessed they had never been broad. His few remaining hairs were wispy, and his eyes . . . she didn't know about his eyes, but the wrinkled skin of his eyelids showed veins under pale skin.

The monster who had haunted her childhood, who had made her a pariah wherever she went . . . was old. Ancient. "He's only sixty-five," she murmured.

"We've seen it before. Prison ages a man," Yvonne said.

"I presume that's true." Elizabeth supposed he deserved whatever misery had worn him down, but right now, he looked pitiful.

In that ever-chipper voice of hers, Yvonne said, "To-day it was weird to watch. Mr. Banner was eating at his place at the table. Mr. Cook was ranting behind him."

Mr. Cook had been the creepy old guy. "Does he always rant?"

"On some men, the dementia peels off the civilization and allows the rage to come out. Mr. Cook is an unpleas-ant man and his wife is glad to be rid of him. She doesn't visit much. Sort of tells you a lot, doesn't it?" Yvonne pushed the thinning hair off Charles's head with an af-fectionate hand.

"Yes." It took more nerve than Elizabeth could imag-ine, but she had to ask. "What about my father? Does he ever show signs of rage?"

"Never. When he first came here, we were scared of him. We were careful to make sure he wasn't alone with the other patients. We restrained him before he went to sleep. But your father's a sweetie. Never any trouble, kind to everyone, mostly keeps to himself. Except for the thing with your mother." She laughed awkwardly. "The . . . killing. No one here believes he did it."

Elizabeth turned on her. "You don't?"

Yvonne leaned back and gazed curiously at Elizabeth. "Surely you don't, do you?"

Elizabeth stared at her, and thought of all the times her cousins had taunted her that her father had murdered her mother. They had been like Mr. Cook, only younger, and meaner, and they had taught her caution in her rela-tionships.

"Oh, honey, I'm sorry." Yvonne patted her arm. "Charles Banner is a sweetheart through and through."

Elizabeth shook her head. "You're too trusting."

"Really? Do you think your mother would continue to hang around him if he had killed her?"

CHAPTER SIXTEEN

Had working here in this place of ephemeral minds and memories robbed this nurse of her sanity? "My mother's dead," Elizabeth explained carefully.

"He talks to her sometimes, and looks at this empty space beside him like she's there." Yvonne nodded her head as if that explained everything.

"Well. He does have Alzheimer's."

"I know." Yvonne looked at her, her brown eyes wide and not at all crazy. "Today, right before the quake, Mr. Banner was sitting in the dining room eating his meal with Mr. Cook carrying on behind him, and all of a sudden your father did that thing where he was talking to the air."

Elizabeth needed to clarify. "You mean, he thought he was talking to my mother?"

"I'd say so, because he nodded, like he was agreeing, got up, and moved close to the wall. Cocky as a bantam rooster, Mr. Cook sat down in Charles's seat like he was proud of chasing him away. And the earthquake hit. *Boom!*" Yvonne clapped her hands. "Everybody staggered or fell over. But the only place the ceiling came down was onto your father's chair. Ceiling tiles, steel support—*slam!*—knocked Mr. Cook out cold. We sent him to the hospital with a concussion and a broken collarbone for sure, and heaven knows what other injuries. If Charles had stayed at the table, if he would have been the one injured . . . He's a slighter man, more frail than Mr. Cook. I think the ceiling collapse would have killed your father."

"So you're saying you believe my mother warned him to move?"

"How else can you explain it?"

"Coincidence. Or luck." Yvonne's conviction made Elizabeth uncomfortable.

"Or your mother is with him. If I loved a man, and he had suffered for a crime he didn't commit, I wouldn't leave him to die alone. I'd come back for a visit, too."

It had been a very long, odd day, and in this silent nursing home filled with empty corridors and snoring patients, Elizabeth began to feel as if she'd fallen down the rabbit hole. "Perhaps he deserves to suffer. Perhaps he thinks she's here because he's guilty and he knows it."

"Perhaps." Yvonne seemed none-too-worried about Elizabeth's skepticism. "You're stuck here tonight, I think."

Elizabeth thought of the treacherous road back to town, and what was left of her apartment. She looked at her hand, still wrapped in a stiff, dried blood bandage. "I . . . yes, I think so. If you have extra blankets, I can sleep anywhere."

"We've got the staff bathroom where you can shower, and sack out in the room behind the nurses' station. We all use it when we pull a double shift and have to catch a few hours of shut-eye. The cot isn't any too comfortable, but it's better than nothing."

"But if I sleep there, you won't be able to lie down."

Yvonne sighed. "I can't lie down anyway. There's no staff to replace me. What did you do to your hand?"

"Glass. During the earthquake."

"Come on. I'll look at it." Yvonne led her to the nurses' station at the junction of three long corridors, and peeled off the bandage. While Elizabeth steadfastly stared over Yvonne's head, she examined the cut. "It's deep," Yvonne said. "You really need a doctor, but you're stuck with the medical staff we have here." She glanced at Elizabeth's stiff face. "Don't worry, we're good. Here, I'll page Sheila.

Even after all these hours on duty, she's got a steady
hand. Of course, she's younger than me."

Yvonne did have dark circles under her eyes, her
brown hair hung limply in a ponytail down her back, and
when she was not animated, her jaw sagged as if keeping it tightly closed was too much effort. But no matter
what, she looked kind, and remembering how thoroughly
she had championed Charles Banner, Elizabeth couldn't
help but feel a warmth for the woman, reluctant perhaps,
but real nonetheless.

Elizabeth gazed around at the long, dim corridors that
seemed to stretch forever, and said, "I suppose, in this
lonely atmosphere where minds silently leave the body
early, reality and fantasy are blended, and death picks off
the living one by one . . . I suppose ghosts can slip unseen along the halls." She stopped, startled to hear herself say such things.

Yvonne gazed at her almost fondly. "I did not believe
what they say in town, that you're all science and smarts
without a lick of emotion. I guess I was right."

"I suppose I, um, have the occasional lick." Although
Elizabeth didn't want to, she glanced toward her father's
room. She didn't want to have any emotion at all. Pleasant emotion—hope and love—always backfired and became pain. Always. "Do you know, is your family and
your home okay?"

"My husband's a trucker, and on the road, so he's fine.
The kids are grown and out of state. We've been meaning to take out the cedar that sits close to the house
because it leans, and it's probably landed on the roof.
But it will be what it will be." Yet Yvonne sighed and
glanced toward the windows as if to bely her untroubled
attitude. Then she looked at Elizabeth, and her eyes
sharpened. "What about you?"

"My apartment's gone. I don't know where I'll stay after tonight. A shelter, I suppose."

"Stay at the resort."

"The resort? Virtue Falls Resort?" Elizabeth blinked. "I can't do that."

"Didn't I hear you were married to old Mrs. Smith's foster son?" At the shock on Elizabeth's face, Yvonne laughed. "Your father told me."

"How did he know?"

"Prisoners do have access to the Internet, and you are his daughter. He kept up with you. Knew all about how you graduated from high school a year early, and your studies and degrees. He knew when you took this job, and he was tickled about it." Yvonne made it sound absolutely reasonable.

Elizabeth found it unnerving. She had an Internet stalker, and it was her father.

Yvonne apparently misunderstood Elizabeth's discomfort, for she hastened to reassure her. "I don't think he told anyone else who you had married, and I haven't said a word."

"We're divorced, and I . . . I have not been to see Mrs. Smith. I only met her the time she came down to visit, and it seems presumptuous of me to assume a family connection when I'm the one who severed it." Elizabeth could not have been more uncomfortable.

Yvonne waved away her objection. "I see Mrs. Smith at church, and she's an old-time Catholic. If you were once married to Garik, then in the eyes of God, you're still married to Garik. So you're family, and she'll take you in."

Elizabeth would have argued, but Sheila arrived from some far corner of some far wing, walking silently in rubber-soled work shoes, wearing yet another flowered smock and those green scrub pants.

The two women held a whispered consultation, then with a wave, Yvonne disappeared back the way Sheila had come.

Sheila thoroughly cleaned the cut on Elizabeth's hand, and didn't mock Elizabeth when the blood welled and Elizabeth found herself reclining on the linoleum, head spinning. Sheila used a butterfly bandage to close it, and gave her a shot that she sternly told Elizabeth was nothing, while showing her a bottle that identified the injection as an antibiotic.

"I understand," Elizabeth said. "As a nurse, you're not allowed to prescribe such medication without a physician's order, but you fear the infection from the cut will make me ill unless you take action now."

Sheila stared at her, shook her head, then leaned over and pressed her hand against Elizabeth's shoulder. "I never gave you a shot."

"You never gave me a shot," Elizabeth repeated obediently. "Thank you."

"Stay on the floor. I'll send Yvonne back for you." Sheila went down the hallway, as quiet as one of the ghosts Yvonne said haunted the Honor Mountain Memory Care Facility.

Spooky thought. Spooky place. Didn't matter. The hours of stress caught up with Elizabeth, and her eyes drooped and closed.

When something touched her arm, she woke with a gasp.

"It's just me," Yvonne said soothingly.

Elizabeth sat up, then stood up and swayed. "Earthquake?" she said.

"No, it's you. You're wiped out." Yvonne opened a supply closet and handed her a clean gown and robe. "Here. You can sleep in this."

Wide-eyed, Elizabeth looked at it, and wondered who had worn it last.

"It's new," Yvonne said. "We get donations."

"Okay. Thank you." Although it was irrational, Elizabeth was uncomfortable wearing a gown in which one of the patients had died.

"The staff bathroom is there. The cot is there." Yvonne pointed at the two doors behind the nurses' station.

"Do you mind if I charge my phone and camera? You've got power and I don't know when I'll get another chance to—"

"Of course. Give me the cables and equipment and I'll plug them in."

"Thank you, and thank you for, um, taking care of . . ." Elizabeth jerked her head toward Charles.

"Your father?"

"Yes. Thank you for taking care of my father."

"That's why they pay me the big bucks."

Elizabeth stared, not sure if Yvonne was joking or not.

"Oh, honey. You poor thing." Yvonne embraced her as if she couldn't stand not to. "Taking care of your father is what I'm here for."

CHAPTER SEVENTEEN

Several hours later, Elizabeth came out of a sound sleep and into a state of frozen terror.

Without even opening her eyes, she knew someone stood over the top of her.

Her father. Holding the blood-drenched scissors.

She couldn't look. She didn't dare. Didn't not dare.

She'd had this nightmare before, and it was never true.

So she forced her eyes open.

And there he was. He really was, her father, leaning over her, the night-light at the nurses' station glowing around him, leaving his face in darkness.

Elizabeth tried to scream. But as in every other nightmare she'd ever had, her throat was too tight. Although she opened her mouth and strained, no sound came out. She was mute in the face of death.

"Shh." Charles put his finger to his lips and drew back. "It's coming."

"What?" she whispered. She didn't want to startle him into action.

"The aftershock." As he spoke, the earth began to tremble, just slightly, enough to rock the cot.

"Yeah." Elizabeth glanced past him toward the nurses' station.

The shaking increased.

Yvonne was sitting in the desk chair, her arms crossed over her chest, her chin resting on her chest.

No one could sleep through this. She was dead.

No. There was no blood. And she was snoring.

An exhausted nurse can sleep through an aftershock. Yvonne *was* sleeping through an aftershock.

The earth's trembling faded.

Yvonne's head rolled as she rode the fading trembler. The trembler Charles had known about before it arrived.

Coincidence. It had to be coincidence.

"About a four-point-five, I think," he said. "Although that's difficult to judge without a seismograph."

"How did you know there would be one?"

"Misty told me."

Elizabeth eyed him. Eyed the door. Tried to figure out if she could make it past him before he caught her.

Charles collapsed onto the floor and crossed his legs. He pushed his black-rimmed glasses up on his nose, and viewed her with the bright-eyed excitement of an old gray squirrel. "That earthquake yesterday evening was the one we've been waiting for. The big one."

Elizabeth deliberately calmed herself. Hysteria wasn't going to help. Screaming would only upset the patients. And Yvonne needed her sleep.

Misty told him. Okay. Yvonne had said he was suffering from hallucinations. There was no reason to freak because he . . . he said Elizabeth's long-dead mother was talking to him.

No, the reason to freak was because Misty correctly predicted earthquakes.

Slowly, making no sudden moves, Elizabeth lifted herself on her elbow and pushed her hair out of her eyes. "Do you, um, see Mama often?"

Charles tilted his head and stared at Elizabeth as if he was trying to place her. Then his smile blossomed. "Of course. You're my daughter. You're all grown up now."

"Yes."

"I should have known. You're beautiful. You look like Misty when she was your age."

Thoughtlessly, Elizabeth said, "She didn't live to be as old as I am now."

His eyes, magnified by his glasses, grew wide. "I don't understand."

Did he not remember? Or was he lying? After all, the man who had murdered her mother would think nothing of lying about it. He had always denied his guilt.

Elizabeth had a weapon. A knife. In her backpack.

A long, sturdy pocket knife she used to cut rope, twigs, dig in the dirt if she had to. And she knew how to use it to defend herself. Garik had taught her that. Garik had insisted on teaching her that.

Charles seemed oblivious to Elizabeth's alarm. He placed his elbow on his knee, cupped his chin in his hand, and looked disarmingly like a skinny, elderly elf. "I met Misty when she was twenty," he said. "Did you know that?"

Elizabeth shook her head. When and where her parents had met and why they had married was a mystery to her. She couldn't ask her aunt Sandy. Aunt Sandy always acted stricken and upset when Elizabeth talked about her mother, as if Elizabeth didn't understand her sorrow . . . no, as if Elizabeth had no reason for sorrow. As if Misty's death had had no effect on Elizabeth's life.

Aunt Sandy guarded her memories like a hostile pit bull over a meaty bone. She did not share.

Now someone was offering Elizabeth the memories; a man who inspired such mixed feelings that she now, with the greatest of caution, opened her backpack and searched with her hand for the hilt of her knife. "How did you meet my mother?" She kept her voice polite, interested, enthusiastic.

"I was a guest professor at Berkeley for a year."

She brushed her hand over the fake leather of her photo album. If forced, she could use that as a shield if he went for her throat. "Did you like to teach?"

"Not at all! But my funding had run out on the project I had developed in Mexico, and the new project in Washington wasn't yet funded, so I took the job." Charles chuckled a little. "My poor students. I know my subject inside and out, but teaching it . . ." He shuddered. "I tend to get carried away. I'm easily distracted by the cool stuff that the earth does, and I'm not so good at hammering at the basics, which they were supposed to learn."

She found the pocket knife and grad-u-ally pulled it out of the backpack. Surreptitiously, she opened one of the blades, then slipped it under the covers with her. "So you met Mama at Berkeley?"

"I did. Remember, Misty?" He looked off to the side, seeing someone who sat beside him . . . and wasn't there. "Remember? I was thirty-seven, and you were twenty, and you took the class because you needed a science credit. Remember?"

CHAPTER EIGHTEEN

Charles stood at the classroom podium and shouted at the departing students, "Before next week, read chapters five and six in your textbook!"

None of the 237 students even waved a hand in acknowledgment.

"There'll . . . there'll be a test!" he yelled.

A few groans. Proof that he hadn't been shouting into a vacuum.

But why had he said that? Now he would have to make up a test. He sighed, went to the desk, and sat in the chair. Which was broken, and tilted off-balance. Just in time, he righted himself.

The nontenured instructors always got the crummy equipment.

"Professor?" A female voice spoke from the podium. "Professor Banner?"

"Yes?" He looked up—and saw her.

The girl who sat in the middle of the third row.

Even in California, the land of the groomed and gorgeous, she was outstanding. White-blond hair as fine as spun sugar, eyes as deep and blue as lapis, fair, translucent skin tinted by the faintest blush and with the texture of polished quartz. And she had a very nice body, not like the usual skinny California girls. More like a World War II pinup girl, all curvy and—

—and he was too old to be ogling her like this, especially when she was biting her lip and looking nervous. "May I help you?" he asked.

"I'm Misty Winston. I'm one of your students. I hope you can help me. I, um, need a science credit and this isn't what I expected when I signed up for the course."

"You'd like to drop it." Figured. Anyone that beautiful had to be skating along on her looks.

"No."

Next logical assumption. "You want me to dumb it down."

"No! I like it. I like the way you explain things, how you obviously love your work. I just, um, don't have the scientific background and I was wondering"—she stopped biting her lip and smiled at him—"would you consider some after-hours tutoring?"

He was so dazzled that for a full minute he forgot to answer.

She waited patiently, still smiling into his eyes.

Finally he woke up from his lust-inspired daze. "I could . . . I could give you a list of video tapes that explain the basics of geology. They're in the library, and they have video players if you don't have one. To check out, I mean."

"I've got a video player. I'm a theater major—"

"An actress?"

"Yes, and being an actress, it's imperative that I be able to see what I look like on camera."

"Oh." He wondered if he could get one of her video tapes to watch at night when he was alone.

No, damn it. No! She was a student. His student. And he was . . . well, he was a geologist. A boring old scientist, emphasis on old.

He said, "Those tapes I'm recommending would give you a good start. On understanding geology, I mean."

"Then I can come to you and ask questions?"

He couldn't stop staring at her pink, full lips as they shaped the words. "Yes. Of course. If they don't answer all your needs."

Why had he said it like that? He was going to get investigated for sexual harassment. Or she was going to slap his face.

He didn't dare look at her, so he talked faster. "Your questions. If the tapes don't answer all of your questions." He dug in his notebook for his list of recommended videos. "Let's go make a copy of the list."

She followed him to the door.

He stood aside to let her pass, and did not stare at her butt nicely encased in leggings and a miniskirt.

She waited for him. She asked, "Which way?," and tucked her hand into his arm.

He had never been so terrified in his life. Terrified, and thrilled, and . . . oh, God, he was horny. He was at least fifteen years older than her. That made him a dirty old man. A disgusting, dirty old man who needed to get this one simple task completed—making a copy of the list—so she would be on her way. All he had to do was walk. "I made this up in case someone like you wanted further instruction. In geology." He had been walking *since he was one. He could do it. One . . . step . . . at . . . a . . . time.*

"That was very farsighted of you." She gurgled with laughter. "Or is that nearsighted? I never can remember."

He risked a glance at her.

She was smiling at him again. Smiling with that frank and open delight, which should have made him suspicious and instead made him want to melt into Silly Putty.

He was very proud of himself. He returned her smile in what he thought was an appropriately avuncular style. He led her into the copy room. Used the Xerox machine, which jammed only once. And he firmly sent her on her way.

When she was gone, safely out the door, he sagged against the wall and tried to regain his composure, and make himself decent so he didn't get arrested for horny, disgusting dirty-old-manism while walking down the corridor.

"Professor?" Misty's soft voice spoke right behind him.

He turned so fast he slammed his knee into the copier. It hurt like a son-of-a-bitch, and thank God, because it provided him with a reason to lean down and rub the bruise, and conceal his inappropriate arousal. "Yes?"

"I heard that the San Andreas Fault ran under the Berkeley campus and there's a high probability of a big earthquake here soon."

"No. No. It's the Hayward Fault that runs under the Berkeley campus. The San Andreas Fault is to the east." He managed to straighten up. "But yes, the probability is about thirty percent within the next thirty years that the Hayward Fault will rupture in a six-point-seven or greater quake. Why?"

"I find all of this geology so fascinating. It's not like

most science, where it's protons whizzing past me that I'll never see, or DNA I can't do anything about. It could happen, right now, to all of us!"

He found himself smiling at her enthusiasm. "Yes, that's why it's always appealed to me."

She took his arm again.

Why did she keep taking his arm?

"I was wondering if you'd like to go for some coffee? There's so much I don't know . . . about geology . . . and you're so knowledgeable." She started walking toward the door.

He followed. In fact, it never occurred to him to resist.

Elizabeth wanted to laugh. Her father seemed so amazed. "She seduced you?"

Charles smiled with a kind of bewildered, nerdlike delight. "Yes! I never understood what she saw in me. I mean, I lifted a lot of rocks, so I was wiry. But I'm not tall, and I'm not handsome. Never was. And my hair was already thinning. I wasn't a virgin or anything, I don't want you to think that."

"Of course not," Elizabeth muttered. What man wanted any woman to think that?

He continued, "But females never chased me, and I was always working on some project in Death Valley or Chile or Panama, and I never thought . . . with my job and my strike-out record with women, it never occurred to me I'd get married."

Maybe Misty thought you were a nice man.

Maybe she wasn't very smart.

Elizabeth bit her lip against the sarcasm and the pain.

"Later, after we were together, Misty told me she liked me the very first time she saw me lecture. Liked my enthusiasm for my work. Liked the way I respected my students, even the beautiful ones." Charles still smiled, but he brushed away a tear that trickled down his cheek. In a lower tone, he said, "I should have known a woman as glamorous and as charming as Misty would fall in love with another man."

Elizabeth couldn't keep quiet any more. "So she killed your dreams—and you killed her?"

CHAPTER NINETEEN

Charles looked at Elizabeth in confusion. "Killed Misty? No, I can never hurt a hair on her head. Perhaps she doesn't love me anymore, but I still love her. I will love her forever."

He was talking about Misty as if she was still alive, saying stuff that made Elizabeth vacillate between wanting desperately to believe him, and wanting desperately to slap him.

He didn't notice her reaction. Or maybe he did, because he got quiet. He turned his head as if he was listening. Then he lifted one finger. "Here comes another one."

"Another one . . . what?" This aftershock hit with the suddenness of a plane crash, jolting Elizabeth half out of bed, making her press one hand against the wall and the other against the bed frame.

The aftershock threw Yvonne out of her chair.

Screams echoed down the corridors from the patients' room.

Yvonne clutched the nurses' station desk to steady herself, glanced at Charles and Elizabeth, glanced down the hall, and made her decision. She ran for the patients' rooms.

The earth was still shuddering when Charles said, "With the earlier quake of such a magnitude, multiple aftershocks of six-point-zero and more are to be expected. But it's always a surprise, isn't it? And there's that element of fear, that the shaking will grow until it's greater than the last earthquake, and we'll all be killed in the cataclysm."

"It is unlikely that we will top the big earthquake we had today, but you and I both know that"— why was Elizabeth discussing this with him? —"that earthquakes are unpredictable at best and therein lies the excitement."

He leaned forward, eyes gleaming. "Were you out there? Did you see it? The tsunami? How big was the tsunami?" He was so excited, like a kid seeing the Batman movies for the first time.

"I was out there," she said. "The tsunami was larger and more impressive than even I had imagined."

"I knew it." His knobby fists clenched on his knees. His eyes closed as if he could see it in his mind's eye. "I wish . . . well." His eyes opened again, and he sounded absolutely pragmatic and totally sane. "I wish a lot of things. Seeing this tsunami is pretty far down the list."

Still moving slowly—she didn't want to set him off— she sat all the way up. "I, um, videoed it."

"What? You . . . you filmed it?" His faded blue eyes sparkled.

"I did. I ran from the town to the canyon and got there before the first wave washed in." She glanced around. Yvonne had plugged the charger into the wall and placed the video camera on the battered table beside the bed.

The battery light now glowed green. Elizabeth reached for the camera. "Want to see it?"

A flush rose in his cheeks. He trembled with excitement. "It's all right? You'll show me?"

He looked so much like the man she remembered, the man on the seashore who had shown her the wonders of the universe, that the fear retreated to that place inside her where it resided.

Besides, she had the knife close at hand, under the covers, and she had removed the sheath. The blade was bare. She could defend herself.

"Yes, of course." She unplugged the camera and flipped open the screen.

He scooted around so his back rested against the cot.

Even from the side, she could see his eager anticipation. She started the video, saw her opening shot, heard her own voice saying, "I'm Elizabeth Banner of the Banner Geological Study . . . ," and once again the wonder of the day's events overwhelmed her. Her hand trembled as it held the camera.

Charles put his hand on her wrist to steady her.

And they both watched in rapt attention as the tsunami swept up the canyon.

Charles exclaimed several times, "I said that would happen!" and "Oh, I never imagined that." Once he had her stop the video while he showed her a small whirlpool she hadn't noticed, and once he corrected her commentary.

It was odd to talk with someone like this, someone who understood the ramifications of a tsunami, studied and filmed by a professional. Perhaps Alzheimer's disease had wiped out memories of where he had been and what he had done, but it had apparently done nothing to wipe away the knowledge and intelligence that made

Charles Banner a scientific legend, and she glowed with a sort of pride that this man was her father.

When he heard her wrap up, he sat with his knee in one hand, and nodded, and thought. Then he scooted away and asked, "What happened to the bones?"

"The bones." Her mouth felt stiff. "The bones?"

"Didn't you find the bones?"

Shock held Elizabeth rigid, and she stared at Charles Banner in disbelief and terror. "How did you know there were bones?"

"Misty told me," he said.

Elizabeth couldn't breathe. She couldn't think. She couldn't speak coherently or ask the right questions because . . . because no matter how she looked at it, this didn't make sense.

And her father sat on the floor, his head tilted, and watched her with eyes both wise and innocent.

How could she have forgotten the crime he had committed? How could she have forgotten the house drenched in blood? Yet she had forgotten all of it, or at least wiped it from the memories of her childhood.

He had forgotten what had happened.

So had she.

Were they so very different?

Yvonne's low, gentle voice spoke from the doorway. "Mr. Banner, how did you get out of bed and sneak in here?"

He spun to face her. "Misty told me Elizabeth was in here, and when I came to see her, you were asleep. I didn't want to wake you."

"Thank you. That's sweet of you." Yvonne came in and helped him to his feet. "Now Elizabeth is tired, and so will you be in the morning if you don't get back to bed."

"I'm too excited to sleep. If you had only seen the film—Elizabeth filmed the tsunami!"

"I'm sure it was wonderful." Yvonne led him toward the door. "So why don't you go to bed and think about what you learned from it?"

"I will." As he walked with her down the corridor toward his room, his enthusiastic voice faded away.

Elizabeth tucked her shaking hands around her bent knees and pondered the interlude. Those moments showing him the film had been so normal, or as normal as they could be with an Alzheimer's-stricken father confined to a care facility, in a night disturbed time and again by earthquakes.

But that last bit about the bones was too weird.

Okay, maybe he had heard the story about the prostitutes' cemetery. And maybe he had figured that it would be washed away. But with all the tons of debris that had been sucked into the sea, the chance of her finding a human bone was minuscule, and to ask about it . . . when her mother's body had never been discovered . . .

Yvonne spoke from the doorway. "He's already asleep."

Elizabeth looked at her, eyes haunted by memories . . . or lack of them.

Yvonne looked both tired and sorry. "I apologize for leaving you unguarded. I don't think you're in any danger, but I know he scares you. I won't sleep again."

"Yes. Thank you." Elizabeth slid back onto the pillows, pressed her face into the synthetic foam, and whispered to herself, "But he asked about the bones. How did he know about the bones?"

Just before she slept, she felt the naked steel of the knife blade, which she still held in her hands, and she was comforted.

CHAPTER TWENTY

Andrew Marrero finished presenting his paper, now rendered obsolete by the evening's cataclysm in Virtue Falls, to an almost empty auditorium. And not an auditorium filled with seasoned geologists, as he had rightfully expected, but a sparse number of pimply-faced students, probably visiting from the local college.

Where were his fellow geologists, the men and women who should be here paying him homage?

Down in the bar, gathered around the Internet, watching with rabid geek fascination as videos of the Washington earthquake were posted. Even his own crew pretended to pay attention, when in fact their eyes were fixed on their iPhones held low in their laps. Damn them all.

As soon as the scant polite applause died down, Andrew had them raise the house lights. "Any questions?" he asked.

Half a dozen hands shot into air.

Andrew pointed at the blond young female with the long, long legs and the short, short skirt. "Yes, Miss . . . ?"

One of the brash male geologists shouted from the back, "What changes do you expect the earthquake will have made to the area?"

"As I said earlier, I can't be sure of the changes the earthquake made to the area, but I speculate a tsunami in Virtue Falls Canyon will have proved all of the theories I've expounded tonight." He pointed again at the young woman.

The same geologist shouted, "So you're sure there was a powerful tsunami in the area?"

"Without a doubt," Andrew said crisply. "Did you not listen to any of the presentation?"

"No, I came in late." The man walked from the dim back of the auditorium toward the front. He was young, handsome, intent. "I read that you're the leading geologist for the affected stretch of the Washington coast."

Luke Baker, second in command of Andrew's team, must have finally decided it was time to do a little judicious sucking up. "That's true," he called.

The student didn't even glance at him. All his attention was fixed on Andrew. "You're this big expert, yet you didn't predict the earthquake? Of what use is the study of geology if it can't warn us of the most basic disaster so we can make preparations?"

Now Joe Cruz got into the act. "How ignorant can you be? No one predicts an earthquake."

The young man turned to the seats. "Who are you?" he asked the three guys.

"They're my team," Andrew said. "Luke Baker, Joe Cruz, and Benjamin Richardson."

The guy dismissed them with a flick of his finger, and turned back to Andrew. "I'm Noah Griffin from the local news."

A reporter. Andrew wanted to groan.

Noah pushed his fingers through his shock of blond-tipped brown hair. "The paper sent me down here today to cover the geology convention—"

The girl with the short skirt giggled and batted her eyelashes at Noah. "What did you do, piss someone off?"

He looked at her, too, and smiled, all youthful charm. "Pretty much. But there's opportunities everywhere and when the earthquake hit, that turned this convention coverage into a big opportunity." Again he scrutinized Andrew. "So your team is here with you and missed the quake?" He made it sound as if Andrew had been deliberately negligent.

"We have one member who is still in place," Andrew said.

"Who?" Noah asked.

"Elizabeth Banner, a brilliant geologist," Joe said hotly.

Luke elbowed him to shut up.

Too late.

"Elizabeth Banner?" Noah consulted his phone. "She's on the Banner Study? Any relation to Charles Banner, the guy who started the study and who killed his wife with the scissors?"

Andrew shot Joe a deadly glance. "It's his daughter."

"Whoa." Noah read his phone with intent focus.

Andrew tried to undo as much of the damage as possible. "But I assure you, she was chosen for the study based on her credentials, not on that old relationship."

"Okay." Noah slipped his phone into his pocket and faked a smile. "Thanks for the info, Dr. Marrero. If I have any more questions, I'll call you."

"Feel free." Andrew moved away from the podium, wanting to get away from this professional disaster. As he closed in on Short Skirt, the reporter swung back at him.

"One more thing—why would you hire the daughter of the guy who's an acknowledged genius in your field, a genius who has never been surpassed?"

Andrew had to unclench his jaw to answer. "As I said, of all the applicants, she had the best credentials." He waited until Noah got all the way to the back of the auditorium, and actually got the door open, before turning back to Short Skirt.

The audience was on their feet, shuffling toward the door.

"Wait," Noah shouted. "Another question—why would Elizabeth Banner willingly come back to the scene of such a hideous crime . . . which she witnessed?"

Andrew was done answering his questions.

But Joe Cruz, big mouth extraordinaire, had to reply. "Her father's been released from prison and is at a memory care facility nearby."

"Whoa," Noah said again. The door slammed behind him.

"What are you going to do about him, professor?" Luke only called him professor when he thought Andrew was angry.

In this case, he was right. Andrew was very, very angry. "Nothing," Andrew said. "It's not like his station or newspaper or whatever is going to pay him to go to Virtue Falls and report on the situation."

Benjamin Richardson, tall, smart, and quiet, got to his feet. "I wonder if he's a freelancer? Some kind of paparazzi?"

"Paparazzi at a geology conference?" Joe mocked. He stood, too.

"Lots of paparazzi in Tahoe," Benjamin said. "When the report of a major earthquake comes through, there's always a chance for a story, like how useless the study of geology is if it can't even predict an earthquake."

"A story is what he came for, and he got it," Luke said thoughtfully. "Probably not the one he had first envisioned, but that story about Elizabeth and her father is worth a rehash."

Short Skirt looked between the three young men with interest.

Andrew interposed himself between them. "It doesn't matter, there's no way to get to Virtue Falls. If there was, wouldn't I be there now?"

"Of course, professor." Luke could see Andrew's intentions, and he pushed the other two toward the door. "You would never leave poor Elizabeth Banner to deal with such a calamity. Your responsibilities weigh too heavily on your shoulders for that."

Short Skirt transferred her attention back to Andrew.

Andrew bent a darkly romantic look on her and offered her his hand.

Behind him, he heard Joe mutter, "There's always a way if you try hard enough."

Garik Jacobsen barreled across the Nevada desert at a hundred and twenty miles per hour, fleeing a past that tasted like a gun barrel, headed for a disaster composed of his foster mother and his ex-wife, and hoping to hell he got there soon enough to save them and himself.

CHAPTER TWENTY-ONE

Bradley Hoff stood in the penthouse suite in the Westin Hotel in Denver, Colorado, and wished he could remember why he had once found his wife attractive.

Vivian was tall. She wore her long, dark hair coiled into a well-tended chignon. In the last few years, she had withered into that hollow-eyed, gaunt look that very thin older women developed. But she was still handsome. She still worked endlessly to promote his career, and as his manager, he could not imagine anyone who handled publicity as well as she did.

Yet now she stood, hands on her hips, neck thrust out, saying, "I'm not going back to Virtue Falls."

He wanted to strangle her.

Too bad for him she wasn't the kind of woman any man dared to threaten.

Her eyes were big, brown, and cold as ice. She knew how to use words cruelly. She always sensed where a man's ego was frail, and went for the kill.

So Bradley kept his temper and in a level voice said, "We need to return to Virtue Falls. The town needs attention, and we can give it to them."

"There's no power. There's no water. We have no idea what shape our house is in, and I'm in no hurry to find out because there's no one there who can fix anything." Vivian tapped her foot on the floor. "Denver has at least a modicum of civilization, and I'm not going to Virtue Falls today."

"We don't have to stay in our house. The studio was built to withstand earthquakes. There are no trees close to fall on it." He ran his hand through his artfully styled, carefully dyed black hair. "We could stay there."

"I am not staying in that studio of yours. There's one single bed. The place smells like pigment and turpentine. And—" Her words hung on the air.

"And what?"

Being Vivian, she went for the slam. "I don't like it in there. It's *your* place."

He needed to win this fight. He needed to get to Virtue Falls.

So he appealed to the one constant he could depend

on with Vivian—her greed. "Aren't you worried about my paintings? That's a sizable investment to write off so cavalierly."

He could see the mere thought of his wasted work hurt her. But she was practical all the way to her chilly core. "As you said, the studio is soundly built, so all the damage would be from falling canvases and paints. Besides, I'm not writing them off, but whatever has happened, has happened. It's over. *Fini.*"

"I can save the work. For God's sake, Vivian, have some respect for my artistry."

"Your artistry. Nature's Artist." She chortled. "Don't try to play that card with me. I've lived with you on and off for how many years now? Almost twenty-four years? I know you better than you think I do. I know what you really think of your work."

"The hell you do." Nobody knew what he thought of his work, or why.

Walking to the closet, she pulled a light sweater off the hanger. "I'm going out with my friends. I'll be back in the morning. I suggest you go down to the bar and get drunk. Maybe pick someone up and have a few laughs. You can use this bed, because God knows *we* never fuck anymore."

Sometimes, when he was around Vivian, he felt as if she chipped off pieces of him until someday, he would simply disappear. "I don't like it when you talk that way."

"About fucking? Or about the fact you can't get it up?"

He grabbed her shoulder.

She rammed him with her elbow, right in the solar plexus.

With a whoosh, his breath left him. He doubled over in black and red agony.

"Don't touch me." Vivian grabbed his hair, lifted his

face to hers, and leaned over until she was at the level of his eyes. "Not unless you want a divorce."

He got enough breath to wheeze, "You wouldn't do that."

"No. You're right. You're too lucrative." She let go of him and straightened. She headed for the door, and opened it.

"I'll go back alone," he said.

She halted. Turned on her heel. Looked at him, and her eyes snapped with impatience.

"I mean it." He slowly straightened, one hand splayed on his chest.

"You will? Really? You don't know how to do one single thing for yourself. I pay the bills. I handle the publicity. I supervise the website and the social media. And I sure as hell make all the travel arrangements. *How* are you going to get yourself somewhere with no air travel and no roads?"

"I'll think of a way. I will. Vivian, my people are in Virtue Falls. My paintings." He had to say it again. *"My people."*

She drew a breath. "I'm sorry, Bradley. I lost my temper. You're right. You've got an image to protect. Tomorrow I'll start making the arrangements to return to Virtue Falls. But please, for once, think like a businessman. We've got to make this an event."

"I have to get back as quickly as I can." His chest hurt from the anxiety of not knowing what he would find in Virtue Falls.

"What's your rush?" Vivian wore that vicious halfsmile she had perfected. "Do you need to check on your girlfriend?"

"I haven't slept with another woman since I married you." He meant that.

"Then that's your problem." She meant that, too.

"Can't you figure it out?" He held out one hand in appeal. "This isn't about sex or money. It's about . . ."

"Yes, yes. I know. I've heard it all before. Your heart is there. Your muse is there." She didn't understand. She never would. "I promise, first thing in the morning, I will make the arrangements. I'll find out what they really need—"

"How? We've had no contact."

"I'll get a list from the Red Cross on what earthquake-stricken areas usually need, and we'll bring it with us. We can rescue Virtue Falls and get good publicity out of it at the same time. You'll see." She walked back to him and patted his cheek. "I'll get it done as quickly as I can. Until then, really—go get laid. That's what I plan to do."

CHAPTER TWENTY-TWO

Elizabeth got up early. So early that when she had dressed, and wandered out to look through the windows at the Honor Mountain Memory Care Facility, it was barely light, the sun still tangled in the branches of the forest that pressed and loomed so ominously close to the building.

Funny. Yesterday afternoon, she had thought the forest a green and lush paradise, a place where wild things roamed free and she could breathe air fresh and free, away from curious eyes and cruel tongues. Now the forest seemed eerie, too tall, a dark silhouette and a place where ghoulies and goblins lurked.

What happened to the bones?

She didn't even believe in ghoulies and goblins. Never had, not even as a child. She believed in facts, in science, in the eternal earth . . . all of which were changing before her eyes.

As they should. As she knew they did.

But knowing and seeing were two different things, and knowing her father was a murderer, and having him ask about the bones was creepy. Like the forest.

Didn't you find the bones?

The echo of her father's voice sent a shiver down Elizabeth's spine, and she jumped violently when behind her, Yvonne said, "You're up already! I suppose that latest aftershock woke you."

"Yes." Better to say that than admit she hadn't slept a wink after her father went back to his room.

Yvonne looked her over. "Your clothes are in pretty good shape."

"The rest are in my apartment. I don't know when I'll be able to retrieve them." Elizabeth was surprised to discover she could speak so calmly, especially considering the fact that she'd spent the last hours lying flat on her back, holding the covers to her chin, staring wide-eyed at the empty doorway, afraid that her father would return . . . or the ghost of her mother would waft into the room.

That was the part that bugged Elizabeth; waiting for her mother made her as crazy as Yvonne and her father.

"Cute shoes, though," Yvonne said. "But probably not comfortable?"

Elizabeth looked down at her battered Tory Burch sandals. "They were, until last evening when I ran all the way to Virtue Falls Canyon to film the tsunami."

"You really are an odd girl," Yvonne said impulsively, then looked sorry and embarrassed.

"I know." A movement down the corridor caught Elizabeth's eye.

A gray-haired, stooped man in a white coat shambled down the corridor toward them, looking like an aging basset hound.

"Who is he?" Elizabeth gestured. "One of the patients?"

Yvonne turned and gave a cry of joy. "Doctor! You made it!"

Elizabeth stared in awe and dismay. This doctor had a belly sagging over his belt, hair that looked as if birds had made their nest in it, and a red mustache completely at odds with the rest of his coloring. Her father looked more with it than this guy did.

"Hello, Yvonne. Yes, of course I made it. With a few detours here and there." His voice sounded like a bassoon, deep and mournful.

To Elizabeth, Yvonne said, "Dr. Frownfelter is retired, but he continues his practice at the nursing home and here at Honor Mountain. He always says that if he didn't do it, who would?"

"Because insurance doesn't pay well on these cases, you mean, and there's too much government paperwork?" Elizabeth asked.

"Exactly." Yvonne turned back to him. "Doctor, this is—"

"No need to tell me who she is." He looked Elizabeth over from top to toe. "You're either Misty's ghost or Misty's daughter. I'm guessing the daughter."

"I'm Elizabeth Banner," she said stiffly.

"Good to meet you, Elizabeth Banner." He shook her hand firmly, then didn't release it.

She was too uncomfortable to pull it back. "You knew my mother?"

"I did. When she lived here, I was her doctor. Beautiful woman, inside and out." Dr. Frownfelter squeezed Elizabeth's fingers. "Charles was a lucky man."

What could Elizabeth say to that? *Then why did he kill her?* "Some might not agree *she* was lucky," she said neutrally.

"I suppose she wasn't as intelligent as Charles, but when it came to relationships, she was shrewd. Earthy. Rock solid. She adored Charles and adored you. So you need to think about that before you accuse your father of some dastardly crime." Dr. Frownfelter's heavy eyelids sagged over his faded blue eyes. "I delivered you, you know."

"No, I didn't." The fact left her feeling vaguely uncomfortable, as if he'd peeked at her underwear.

Dr. Frownfelter didn't seem to notice. To Yvonne, he said, "How did Charles handle the earthquake?"

"He loved every minute."

"Of course he did." The doctor smiled.

"Dr. Frownfelter was the prison doctor almost the whole time your father was incarcerated," Yvonne told Elizabeth. "They spent a lot of time together, and know each other well."

Didn't you find the bones?

Dr. Frownfelter shrugged his massive shoulders. "We spoke the same language—pretty rare in that place. I wish I had been able to get him out of there sooner. An earlier application of medication might have slowed the disintegration of his brain." At last he released Elizabeth's hand. "Of course, if we had done that, he might not now be able to see Misty's ghost."

"You think the disintegration of his brain allows him

to see my mother's ghost?" After the night she had spent, Elizabeth half-expected him to say yes.

"It allows him to think he sees her. Good to meet you again, Elizabeth." Dr. Frownfelter took Yvonne's arm. "Where should I start my rounds?"

The two of them disappeared down the corridor, leaving Elizabeth feeling pleased to know Charles's doctor didn't believe in Misty's ghost, and unsure what to do next. She wanted to leave the Honor Mountain Memory Care Facility, but it seemed rude to rush out without saying thank you and good-bye. But neither was she going to hang around while Yvonne and Dr. Frownfelter toured the facility.

So Elizabeth gathered her gear, checking twice for her video camera and her notebook. She wrote a note and left it on the nurses' station, and headed out the door. She had been so glad to arrive the night before . . . and now she was so very glad to leave.

She was in her car and driving away when she glanced in her rearview mirror and saw Yvonne and Sheila rushing toward her across the parking lot.

She stopped. Of course she did.

The two nurses stood smiling and panting.

Elizabeth rolled down her window and said, "I hope someone comes soon to relieve you."

"They will," Yvonne said. "Dr. Frownfelter says he worked in town before he headed out here. Most of the injuries aren't life-threatening, and old Mrs. Smith is paying for helicopters to take the worst cases to the Portland hospitals. Virtue Falls was lucky. We were all lucky."

"Except Mr. Cook," Sheila said.

What happened to the bones?

"I do wonder how the old fart is doing," Yvonne said.

Sheila dug her elbow into Yvonne's ribs.

Yvonne smiled tiredly. "I'm getting punchy."

Elizabeth revved the engine a little. "Thank you for all the care you've taken of me."

"You bet, dear," Yvonne said.

"Take care of that hand," Sheila said.

Elizabeth flexed it, and felt the stitches pull. "I will."

"Stay away from the coast!" Yvonne spoke through the driver's window. "Go the straightest route you can to the resort, but stick with the inland roads. If there's been slough-off, it'll be on the coastal highway."

Elizabeth nodded.

"Take your time," Yvonne said. "Have you got enough gas?"

Elizabeth nodded again, waved, and eased up on the clutch.

Didn't you find the bones?

As the car began to move, Yvonne stepped back. "Let me know when you get there . . . as soon as you can. Your father will be worried!"

Elizabeth nodded again, waved again, and pressed on the gas. If she didn't get out of this parking lot soon, she was going to start screaming.

Well, she was going to scream anyway, but she didn't want to do it in front of Yvonne and Sheila. They didn't deserve that. They were both nice women, dealing with lots of crazy, frightened people every day. They didn't need to deal with her, too. She could handle crazy and frightened on her own. She'd done it before. She could do it again. It was just best if she . . . didn't speak.

As she peeled out onto the highway, she waved again, a backward wave that in no way included a glance back.

Yvonne and Sheila walked back to the building.

Yvonne swapped her employee ID through the

electronic card reader. The door unlocked, and she opened it. "I don't know what Charles Banner said to his daughter, but he scared her to death."

"Maybe," Sheila said, "she saw Misty's ghost."

CHAPTER TWENTY-THREE

"Do you need anything else, lady?" Miklós Korngold watched in concern as Margaret lowered herself, inch by inch, into the Queen Anne–style chair beside her bed.

"No, Miklós. A little time by myself should do it."

"I hang around outside your door. If you need me, you call."

"I will."

Miklós was twenty-one, with a pronounced Hungarian accent, a gold tooth, a hairy chest, and skinny shoulders. He was one of her projects, a needy immigrant she sponsored and employed. And thank God she had taken him in.

For the electric generators ran the essentials.

The elevator was not considered an essential.

But Margaret could not ascend and descend the stairs, at least not without young Josue Torres and his brawny arms, or four muscular employees. Josue was gone, whisked away by the helicopter to join his wife, and the employees were all busy. So Margaret was stuck either up in her fourth-floor suite or down on the main level. She had chosen up, with Miklós as her liaison.

Now she watched him perform a salute, two fingers to his forehead. He shut the door behind himself, and she groaned.

She needed to sleep. She needed to lay flat on her back, and close her eyes, and not talk to anyone, listen to anyone, comfort anyone, for twenty-four hours.

She glanced at the clock. It was just after three in the afternoon, but in the hours since last night's earthquake, she had hardly had a moment's rest. How could she? She was responsible for the resort and everyone in it. Even when it became clear the tsunami would do them no harm, the guests were still terrified.

She was terrified, too, yet God knows why, people expected a ninety-one-year-old woman to face death with equanimity.

She couldn't do that. Death, she supposed, she could face; it was the manner of her death that she feared. But she didn't quite have the energy to embrace life as she used to, either, so she rested and listened to the silence that had descended, and was glad.

While the staff had scurried around doing a preliminary cleaning, preparing sandwiches, and handing out drinks to the guests, Margaret had used her ham radio—she never threw anything away, not out here, not when it came to basic communication needs—to make contact with the outside world. Within two hours, she had the first helicopter landing in the parking lot, ready to ferry guests to Portland, to the hotel rooms she had managed to beg and cajole for them. Some guests left their cars parked here; she promised as soon as the roads were open, their vehicles would be delivered to them.

The evacuations had cost a fortune, digging deep into her emergency fund, but what were her choices? Broken glass was everywhere, glittering, beckoning, waiting to slice fingers and feet. Every time the earth shuddered, another picture fell off the wall, another table toppled. The resort was a lawsuit waiting to happen, and she would not allow some guest with more hair than brains—specifically Aurora Thompson—to take what was Margaret's.

At the desk, the big old ham radio squawked.

So much for Margaret's silence.

She hadn't used the walker since she had recovered from her knee replacement, but the constant aftershocks had convinced her she needed something a little steadier than a cane. So now she pulled the blasted walker close, pushed herself to her feet, and made her way to the desk. Leaning over, she flipped the switch on the microphone and with the full weight of her annoyance in her voice, she said, "I'm fine. The resort is fine."

A moment of silence, then Garik gasped out a laugh. "That's what I needed to hear."

Although Garik couldn't see her, Margaret smiled. "Ah, boyo, it's you." A relief to hear from him. He had been quiet for too long and worrisome a time, months now since he'd checked in with her, and even then she could tell he was depressed and unlike himself. "Where are you?"

"Not far away. I'm in Portland. It took me a while to remember your ham radio, but when I did, I stopped and bought one." Without taking a breath, he asked, "What about Elizabeth? Do you know about her?"

"That I don't." Margaret pulled up the desk chair and seated herself. "It's been all kinds of madness here."

"Damn. That foolish woman is exactly the type to wander into danger without a thought."

"The same could be said for you."

He grunted, and wisely changed subjects. "You're not hurt?"

During one of the aftershocks, Margaret had wrenched her back, but no point in bringing that up, not in this crisis. "No one's hurt, not really. Some of the staff and guests cut themselves on broken glass, and we've lost too many of Mrs. Smith's precious antiques, but all in all, we came out well."

"Good." With dedicated intensity, he asked, "Can you contact anyone in Virtue Falls to find out about Elizabeth?"

"That I can. Sheriff Foster sent one of his deputies around to check on the resort—"

"He didn't come himself?"

"The poor lad thinks I don't like him."

"He's right. You don't." Garik sounded amused.

"He was a pompous, self-righteous ass even when he was young, and after the Banner case, he believed his own publicity. No. I don't like him. But you—you're incredibly concerned about an ex-wife." Margaret waited to hear what Garik would say to that.

"*She* divorced *me*." He sounded defiant, incredulous—and miserable.

"And why did she do that?"

"I don't know. Something about . . . me not listening, I guess."

"You guess? You weren't listening when she told you?"

Silence.

"So you still love her?"

"Simply because I'm worried about her doesn't mean I still love her."

He was snappish now. Good. Margaret smiled at the radio again. The boy still had a thing for his wife.

"For God's sake, Margaret, this is a ham radio. Anybody could be listening." That plainly had just occurred to him. "Do you think we could discuss this when I make it to the resort?"

A strange woman's voice intruded, "Why wait? Sounds like you need a scolding, young man."

Margaret's smile vanished. She recognized that voice.

So did Garik, and the little snot sounded delighted. "Annie Di Luca! How are you? Did your resort survive the earthquake and tsunami?"

Margaret tensed as she waited for the answer.

Not that she cared. In nineteen fifty-seven, those upstart Di Lucas had come up here from California and a mere forty miles away, on the headland overlooking the long, white beach called Yearning Sands, they built a resort. Not a resort like Virtue Falls, small and intimate, woodsy and personal. No, they built a big, plush resort with exotic gardens, hiking trails, cottages, and a main hotel building that stretched out with a hundred rooms facing the Pacific Ocean. They built whale watching platforms and catered wine tastings from their own Di Luca California winery.

Virtue Falls resort served the boutique hotel crowd.

Yearning Sands played to the trendy folks, those damn Californians who wandered north wanting to spend their days pretending to rough it, and their nights cozied up on a fake bearskin rug in front of the fireplace in their suite.

Margaret wanted to say that in her heart of hearts, she hated the Di Lucas. Except Margaret wasn't subtle about hating them. Everyone was pretty clear on that, and had been for almost sixty years.

Both resorts had plenty of business. But it irked Margaret to no end that the Smiths had been here first, and now existed in the shadow of big, beautiful Yearning Sands.

"We survived the tsunami very well," Annie said. "The wave came at us from the northwest, and we were protected by a long sandbar that curved around to make a lagoon. The sandbar and the lagoon are gone now, wiped out by the wave, but it lost a lot of its punch there. The earthquake was a little hairier, at least for me."

While still in her sixties, rheumatoid arthritis had confined Annie Di Luca to a wheelchair. That had been almost twenty years ago, and Margaret admitted, only to herself, that she worried about Annie. "Were you hurt?" she asked roughly.

"I couldn't get my brake locked right away, so I rolled around pretty badly. My poor doggie was trying to help me . . . Ritter's my assistance dog, you know. Loyal and determined." Annie took a betraying breath. "But my fumbling around turned out to be a blessing, because I was in the library, and the straps that held up one of the bookcases broke. The bookcase toppled. We got out barely in time."

"The dog's all right, then?" Margaret grudgingly added, "And you?"

"We both got beat up by flying books. First time's a book has ever hurt me." Annie sounded humorous and self-deprecating.

Which made Margaret suspect she'd been injured worse than she would admit.

"How about you, Margaret?" Annie asked. "Did you fare well, you and Virtue Falls? And the resort, of course."

"The earthquake was a challenge, but we've cleared out the guests and we're relaxing a wee bit." Margaret realized her heart was beating faster than her current situation would indicate.

A panic attack. Margaret had never in her life had a panic attack, yet merely talking about the last twenty-four hours made her breathless and afraid, and to show her weakness to Annie Di Luca . . . that was unacceptable. And yet, who better to understand than her rival for the last sixty years? Her humorous tone belied her unexpected fright. "I'm ninety-one years old. I've been through my fair share of earthquakes here. Nothing like that has ever even been close."

"I'm a mere eighty-three, and from California, and I thought I knew earthquakes. Turns out I was wrong." Annie sounded as if she was breathing hard, too. "Margaret, have you contacted Patricia yet?"

Yet another reason Annie irritated Margaret; she remembered all of Margaret's children's and grandchildren's names. Margaret had never bothered to learn Annie's. "I've been busy here," she said testily.

"She'll worry." Annie had that soothing tone to her voice. Always the peacemaker.

"Then she shouldn't have sent a real estate woman in to try and talk me into selling Virtue Falls Resort," Margaret said.

Annie's response was prompt and satisfying. "You are kidding. What was that child thinking? Doesn't she know you at all?" And, "What did you do with the real estate woman? Take advantage of the earthquake and toss her off the deck?"

Garik guffawed.

With satisfaction, Margaret reported, "I sent her back to civilization in a small, private helicopter . . . and told the pilot to scare the hell out of her."

"I'll bet you did," Annie said.

Garik interrupted the women's laughter. "Margaret, this is all very well and good, but if you don't assure

Patricia that you're okay, she'll figure out a way to get there and check on you, and you know how much fun that would *not* be."

"You're thinking of yourself, because you're coming in and you can't stand my darling granddaughter," Margaret said.

"And what's wrong with that?" Garik asked.

"Not a thing, boy. But I don't actually have a way to contact her. *She* doesn't have a ham radio." Wickedly, Margaret asked, "Why don't you give her a call before you leave civilization?"

Annie interrupted his sputtering to suggest, "I've already been in touch with my Bella Terra relatives. I can have them transmit a message to her and that will probably halt any precipitous arrivals."

"Do that," Margaret said. "I appreciate it, Annie."

"I will. I'll let you know if she leaves home before they catch her."

An aftershock rippled in off the ocean.

Both women gasped and held their breaths.

The aftershock rattled, and rattled, then slowly subsided.

"That's it," Annie blurted. "I've got to go."

"You sound exhausted." Margaret couldn't help but add, "You're no spring chicken, you know." But she wasn't being ornery; Annie did sound exhausted, and she might have a mighty spirit, but unlike Margaret, she was fragile.

"I know. Talk to you later, Margaret. Good to hear your voice, Garik." Annie clicked off.

"Nice lady," Garik said laconically.

"She should take better care of herself." Having an enemy die, Margaret had discovered, left as big a hole in your life as having a friend die.

"She's got a husband. He's a good guy. He'll take care of her." Garik's tone changed to brisk. "I need to get on the road before there is no road left. Margaret, give me a list of supplies you need. I'll bring everything I can."

"Right."

"And Margaret—find out what happened to Elizabeth."

CHAPTER TWENTY-FOUR

Margaret made her way to her chair again. She sank down, easing her tired bones into the cushion . . . and a knock on the door made her groan again. "Come!" she shouted.

Miklós cautiously stuck his head in.

Perhaps Margaret had shouted a little too vigorously. "Come," she said more quietly.

"There's a lady here," he said. "A lady with eyes like a cornflower and hair like the tropical sun. She says her name is Elizabeth Banner, and she knows you. She asks if she can stay."

"Elizabeth is well? And she's here?"

"Yes, lady. She looks very well." Miklós spoke with a young man's awe of a beautiful woman.

Margaret laughed a little. "What a relief. Of course, she can stay. Send her in." Garik and Elizabeth here at the resort together. Wasn't this getting interesting? "In fact, Miklós, prepare the Pacific suite on the third floor. Both bedrooms, please. And send her up."

Miklós performed his little two-fingered salute, and disappeared.

In a moment, Margaret heard them coming up the stairs. She wanted to bustle to the door, to welcome and embrace Garik's wife, and make sure the girl was okay. But she didn't have the oomph, so when Elizabeth stepped into the doorway, Margaret smiled and held out her hands. "My dear, I'm so glad you came to me."

Elizabeth came forward awkwardly, looking remarkably like a teenage girl facing a scolding. "I know it's presumptuous, but I didn't know where else to go."

Elizabeth's hesitation made Margaret's welcome all the more emphatic. "Not presumptuous at all. We're relatives. What else are relatives for?"

"We're not exactly . . ." Elizabeth put her hands in Margaret's and lightly squeezed. "Um, thank you for having me. My apartment's pretty much down to rubble. Last night I stayed at my father's care facility." Her voice grew lower and less distinct. "But I can't do that again."

"I'm sure they have their hands full there." Margaret gestured to the matching chair close to hers. "Those poor souls must have been terrified by the quake."

Elizabeth sank into the chair. "Not my father."

"No. Charles would never be frightened by an earthquake." Margaret wouldn't have thought Elizabeth would be frightened, either, yet the girl looked pale and rabbity, with a quivering nose and mouth and hands that moved nervously over her dress, her face, her hair. "We'll get you something to eat. Would you like that?"

"I think so, yes. I didn't have breakfast." Elizabeth sounded surprised.

"Go to the door and tell Miklós to bring up a tray with a little of everything for us both."

"A little of everything." Hope sparked in Elizabeth's face. "That sounds wonderful."

Margaret watched her walk toward the door.

She liked Elizabeth. Her figure reminded Margaret of the movie stars of the forties. Her intensity reminded Margaret of Charles Banner, back before the murder. Her smile reminded Margaret of Misty . . . Margaret remembered the newly married couple's arrival in Virtue Falls, and never had she foreseen the tragedy that had occurred between them.

Yet sometimes from a tragedy, a triumph was born. A triumph like the marriage between Garik and Elizabeth. Margaret had orchestrated that meeting; she had believed the two would be perfect for each other. Yet now they were apart. Children these days gave up too easily on love.

Margaret waited while Elizabeth spoke to Miklós, then asked, "What did you do to your hand?"

Elizabeth lifted her bandaged hand and looked at it. "The earthquake. But this is all. I was lucky."

Margaret sighed. "We're here, so we're lucky . . . Have you heard from my boy lately?"

Elizabeth looked startled. "From Garik? No, he doesn't call me."

"He has barely called me, either"—no use telling Elizabeth that he was on his way to the resort, the surprise would be good for them both—"since the incident that got him put on leave from the FBI."

"He's on leave?" Elizabeth sank back down in her chair. "That must be killing him. Why?"

"He wouldn't tell me the details." Margaret only knew that somehow, his spirit had been broken.

"That doesn't surprise me. When I first met him, I

thought he was so open. He would talk about things that happened on his cases—the car chases, the gun shots, the tackles. He was such a good storyteller it took me a long time to realize that he never told me about himself, and what he felt and thought. He never told me about the hours spent watching for a suspect, or the paperwork, or the times when a case went bad." Elizabeth laughed without humor. "It was like living with a bad action movie, all excitement and motion, and no character development."

Margaret had to refrain from rubbing her hands together. This was good. Garik asked about Elizabeth. Elizabeth went into an unprovoked diatribe about Garik. Feelings. They still had feelings for each other.

A knock on the door.

"There's our tray," Margaret said, and called, "Come in!"

Miklós shouldered his way into the room, flashed his gold tooth at the ladies, and put the tray on the table between them. He lifted the covers and showed them fruit and cheese, bread and olives, fragrant blood orange jam and a pot of clotted cream. In one corner was a plate with tiny squares of lemon tea cakes and small ginger cookies. And . . . "Mimosas," he said, and poured champagne into wide, flat-bottomed glasses unlikely to tip in the next aftershock, and added a splash of orange juice.

"Perfect." Margaret nodded at him. "This will feed two hungry women. Please tell the kitchen staff thank you."

"Call when you want me to take away the tray." Miklós saluted, and left.

"We still have fresh food, lots of it, enough to feed the resort guests, so enjoy." Margaret figured it would be at least two months before she could reopen the resort, and that was probably optimistic.

There was never good timing for these things, but at her age, with her family wanting her to retire, this was bad. Very bad.

Elizabeth stood and went to the tray. "What would you like?"

Ah, the child had good manners. Margaret asked for bread, clotted cream, and fruit.

Elizabeth filled a plate, handed it to Margaret, and said, "You have staff here still. Don't they want to be home?"

"I have eight who live here full time—students on summer break and immigrants I've hired. I was an immigrant once myself, so I've got a soft spot for them. The rest of my staff are local, and when three of my people went home, they discovered those homes aren't livable." Margaret spread a napkin in her lap. "Now they are back, living here, working their hours. Thank God I've got them."

"And thank God they've got you." Elizabeth filled her own plate. "It's good of you to accept us refugees."

"The good people who work for me, and you, are a blessing on my house."

"I don't know how much of a blessing I will be. I don't have any clothes." Elizabeth settled in the chair, spread a slice of crusty bread with marmalade, and placed a slice of Brie atop.

"Guests leave things all the time, and sometimes they don't want them back," Margaret said comfortingly. "We always have a stack of clothes to go to Goodwill. We'll find you something."

Elizabeth chewed, swallowed, and said, "Thank you," although whether for the food or the clothes, Margaret did not know. Then, as if she couldn't drop the subject of Garik, Elizabeth said, "I mean, really. Did he have to always be the hero? Couldn't he simply sometimes be a man?"

CHAPTER TWENTY-FIVE

Margaret sipped her mimosa and meditated on Elizabeth's obsession with Garik. Promising. Very promising.

Elizabeth continued, "All I wanted was a man who I could love and who loved me, who I could share my secrets with and know his."

"He is private," Margaret acknowledged. "He doesn't like to talk about things that hurt him."

"But I'm not psychic. If he wouldn't talk, how was I supposed to figure out what *did* hurt him?"

"He doesn't like cruelty to those who are helpless." None of that fancy French cheese for Margaret—she piled clotted cream onto her bread.

"Children. Yes." Elizabeth leaned forward. "When he dealt with cases where a child was hurt, he got very quiet."

"His own childhood was difficult." An understatement. Margaret ate her bread and watched Elizabeth think.

"I gathered from the few tidbits he dropped that his father was an alcoholic?"

"Did you never ask Garik about his childhood?" Margaret countered.

"Every time I did, he led me to talk about mine."

Elizabeth leaned back with a sigh, and drank her mimosa with thirsty pleasure. "It took me a while to realize what he was doing, never allowing me to know him."

"No matter how unreasonable it is, the boy blamed himself for what happened to him." Margaret was sprinkling conversational bread crumbs, hoping Elizabeth would follow them back to Garik, and a heart-to-heart that would bring them back together.

"What *did* happen?"

"You should ask him."

Like a stubborn mule, Elizabeth set her jaw. "He's gone. We're divorced. It was better that way."

"Better for who? Not for him. He's lost his wife and his job, and I think the two are connected."

"Better for me. I may be selfish, but in the end, living with him was like being in a five-star restaurant"—Elizabeth waved at the tray—"watching the food go by, smelling the scents wafting under my nose, knowing I was so close to heaven . . . and starving to death." For the first time, Margaret saw misery settle onto Elizabeth's shoulders. "He wouldn't talk, so I wouldn't talk. So he stopped listening, so I . . . left."

Margaret hurt for them both. "I had hoped you children would love and help each other."

"We did love each other. So much. That made it all the more painful, to live together, yet be apart, only touching in our bodies, never in our minds."

"In your souls?" Margaret leaned her head back and allowed herself the old-woman pleasure of reminiscing. "When I first married my Johnnie, he didn't know what to do with me. He was older. I was very young. He was bone lazy. I worked like a dog. He wanted a playmate. I wanted a man. It took about ten years of me doing what I thought best and him thinking he could go on being the dilettante, but eventually we worked things out." She smiled. "When I came to the United States with my dear Mrs. Smith, I saw Johnnie as a means to an end, a way to achieve wealth and security. And he was. That we became soul mates was an unforeseen bonus."

Elizabeth took the bowl of blueberries and raspberries and ate as greedily as a child. "These are fabulous."

"They're local to Washington, best in the world." Margaret waved a hand. "I don't want them. Please finish them."

Elizabeth obeyed in record time, and put the bowl down. She blotted her mouth, and said, "I don't have your patience, waiting on a relationship that may never mature."

"You're not Catholic. Johnnie and I were married, and I was stuck with the man. We were like two angry cats in a burlap bag. We had to work it out."

"Garik and I had very different careers pulling us in different directions." A wisp of a smile crossed Elizabeth's face. "We're not stuck in the same bag."

Yet. Margaret chuckled. Because Garik was on his way.

"What's so funny?" Elizabeth asked.

Margaret lied easily; at her age, she had plenty of experience with it. "I was merely remembering my own refugee experience. Very different from yours, and linked to the Smith family heirloom." She gestured to the case in the corner. "It's called the Singing Bird, bought by Mr. Smith for the first Mrs. Smith to express his joy at the birth of his first child, a son. He commissioned it from Tiffany's when the Smiths were at the height of their wealth and power."

Elizabeth set her plate aside, and walked over to the case where the exquisite piece of jewelry rested against a black velvet background. Clasping her hands behind her back, she leaned forward slowly, her eyes fixed on the piece. "A mythical bird. A phoenix."

"Exactly. The plumage is emeralds and rubies, the eyes are aquamarines, and the bird stands on the justly famous seventeen-carat Smith emerald." Margaret had been familiar with the piece for seventy-six years.

"Whoa."

"That is exactly what I thought when I first saw it. I was a chambermaid in Dublin at the time. I had no idea then I would be traveling back to the United States with her." Actually, the Singing Bird had been Margaret's ticket out of Dublin and poverty, but she had no intention of ever telling the truth of that story. "I keep it on display here. You'll note the earthquake didn't shatter the glass in that case. Nor will any earthquake. The glass is bulletproof, and that brooch is protected by the most up-to-date security in the world."

"Why not place it in a museum?"

What a ripe old disaster that would be. "I'm a selfish old woman. I like to look at it in the morning, when I rise, and at night, before I go to bed. Johnnie and I had four children, and they all went on to do God's will and populate the earth, and some of my descendants say that with the brooch up here, it's safe enough and I shouldn't bother paying the security firm to protect it. Those are the same members of the family who, when they visit, I lock up the silver."

Elizabeth looked startled, then horrified, then, when Margaret laughed, she laughed, too.

Droll and amused, Margaret said, "We like to say they must be in-laws, but in fact, every large family births a few of the light-fingered folk. It's inevitable."

"Yes, I suppose so." With a last glance at the brooch, Elizabeth returned to her seat. She took another sip of mimosa and nibbled on a cookie. "Some people envy whatever others have, be it belongings or intelligence or happiness."

Margaret put her plate aside. "You sound as if you have some experience with that envy."

"Yes." Like a tired child, Elizabeth fretfully rubbed her forehead. "I don't understand how it happened. One moment I was that poor, awkward kid who saw her father kill her mother. All the adults felt sorry for me and all the kids made fun of me, and my cousins beat up on me. The next moment I was fast-tracked for college, guys were hitting on me, and I got a gig in modeling."

"Sounds like quite a successful puberty happened."

"Yes." Elizabeth's mouth quirked. "But my cousins still made fun of me."

"That seems cruel." More than cruel, considering the circumstances. "Didn't your aunt stop them?"

"My aunt was frustrated with me. I never did what she wanted."

"What did she want?"

"She wanted me to remember the murder." Elizabeth put down her mimosa, stood and stretched. "Thank you, that meal was good and I was hungry."

"I like to see a girl with appetite. Now—help me make my weary way to the powder room." Margaret gathered herself to stand. "Then you can have Miklós take the tray away."

Elizabeth moved immediately at her side.

"Give me a little push."

Elizabeth pushed.

Margaret strained. Between the two of them, they managed to get Margaret on her feet and into her bathroom.

God, she was tired. After this, she had to send Elizabeth away and stretch out for a nap.

But when she came out, the tray was gone and Elizabeth was on Margaret's private balcony, leaning over the rail, head tilted, wearing a frown. "There's debris down there from the tsunami, a whole pod of it sloshing on the swells in that inlet. I can't figure out what that one object is. It looks vaguely . . ." She tilted her head the other way. "Vaguely . . . maybe human."

Margaret made her way to Elizabeth's side, and followed Elizabeth's pointing finger. "Yes. You're right. Get the binoculars, dear—they're in the drawer—and take a look."

Elizabeth fetched the binoculars and trained them on the mass of floating debris. "I can't tell for sure. It looks like someone in an orange life vest, bobbing in the water. Dark hair, head drooping." Abruptly she pulled the binoculars away from her face, blinked, then brought them back. "I think . . . I think that's Kateri." Her voice rose in excitement. "That's . . . Kateri!"

CHAPTER TWENTY-SIX

The wind blew, waves crashed at the base of the cliffs, a smear of pink clouds glowed against a pale blue sunset sky. The vapor trail of an airplane passed from east to west, leaving the continent and heading for the lush tropical islands or the structured orient, or beyond. The universe was indifferent to the small group of people who lined the cliffs beside Elizabeth, who prayed or cried, and watched as if Kateri's life depended on it.

It didn't. Elizabeth knew Kateri couldn't be alive. Not after being rolled by the tsunami, snatched out of the cutter, and sucked out into the ocean. Not after so many hours in the frigid Pacific. But if they could at least recover her body, what a relief for her family and friends. Friends like Elizabeth.

Elizabeth used the binoculars to watch three of Margaret's bravest employees motor through the tsunami debris field in a tiny launch. Massive logs, floating coolers, overturned boats were in constant motion, the ocean swells lifting them up . . . and dropping them down. A dislodged forest of kelp bound everything together. And in the middle, a bobbing piece of jetsam that looked so much like a human floating in a life vest . . .

Kateri. Could it really be her?

Elizabeth glanced up at Margaret, standing on her fourth-floor balcony watching intently. The old woman nodded encouragingly at her.

Elizabeth put the binoculars back to her eyes.

The crew signaled to Margaret—it was indeed human, a body. Then as they used the grappling hook to catch the life vest, the head rolled back.

It *was* Kateri.

Thank God. They had found her, and she wouldn't be a name lost forever in the vastness of the Pacific Ocean.

Elizabeth scrubbed her tears away—it was not yet time for that—and focused again on the recovery.

All of a sudden, the launch was a flurry of activity.

Elizabeth stared harder, trying to figure out what had happened. Then someone shouted, "She moved. She moved!"

The crew now spared no attention for the onlookers, but grabbed Kateri's arms and tried to pull her on board.

Even from this distance, Elizabeth heard her scream. The horrific cry made the horizon waver, and brought Elizabeth to her knees.

The crew had no choice. They had to bring her to shore. So they dragged her up and over the side into the launch.

Another of those screams reached across restless space.

Elizabeth experienced an anguish and a pity that almost broke her. Almost.

Instead, she found herself shouting, "We need a stretcher. Blankets. First aid. Down at the dock." She glanced back at Margaret's balcony.

Margaret had disappeared.

Elizabeth knew why—at the first sign of life from Kateri, Margaret reached for the ham radio to call in the helicopter and medics. "We've got to keep her alive until help arrives," Elizabeth said to the circle of people around her.

They broke then, running toward the hotel, all of them showing the innovative attributes Margaret required of her staff.

When at last the launch escaped from the debris field and headed toward shore, Elizabeth hurried toward the crooked wooden stairway that led down the cliff to the dock. At the top landing, she met Harold Ridley, directing traffic. He handed her a blanket and the first aid kit and waved her on.

She ran down, two steps at a time, and got there as the launch was pulling up. Even as the crew was securing the boat to the dock, Elizabeth crawled aboard and tucked the blanket around Kateri's shoulders.

Slowly, Kateri turned her head.

She looked as if she'd been beaten, slashed, and mangled. Her swollen, bloody lips were twice their normal size. Her bronze complexion had taken on a bluish cast. She must be suffering from hypothermia, and that perhaps was a good thing, sparing Kateri the worst of her pain.

But she saw Elizabeth, and recognized her, for her eyes blazed with unexpected, intense need. Her lips moved, and she whispered . . . something.

Elizabeth knelt beside Kateri and opened the first aid kit.

Kateri's hand latched on to Elizabeth's wrist. "Not yet. I'm not going to die. Not again."

Elizabeth paused.

That voice. It was so changed. Kateri sounded like a longtime smoker, like someone whose voice had been taken by torment and returned in some different, ruined form.

The crew slowly climbed out of the launch and up the steps.

"Can I give you water?" Elizabeth asked.

"They gave me . . . now I want to tell you . . . I want to tell you what happened."

But you're hurt, maybe dying . . . "Yes. Tell me," Elizabeth said. For these might be Kateri's last words.

"I . . . saw the wave cresting. Tried to turn the clipper. Too late." A shudder shook Kateri. "Then I saw him."

Elizabeth leaned closer. "Who? One of your crewmen?"

"The god of below. The giant frog monster who made the earth break apart."

"Oh." *Okay.*

"The god broke the clipper's windows, reached in . . .

dragged me out." Kateri paused to rest. "And flung me into hell."

Elizabeth nodded. In a way, that made sense, that as a Native American, Kateri would see the Pacific Ocean as a god pulling her from the safety of the clipper and into the maw of death. "You were in the water."

"I rolled in the wave, over and over, while the god beat me, broke me, stole the breath from my lungs and drank the blood from my body." Kateri's breath rasped in her lungs. "Now. Water. Please."

Elizabeth feared to touch her.

But Kateri turned her head to the side and took short sips from the bottle. She swallowed painfully, then closed her eyes as if exhausted.

Elizabeth's heart hurt for her friend. "You don't have to tell me now."

"Now. It has to be now." Kateri opened her swollen, bloodshot eyes. "I woke underwater, in the cave of the god. He was green, with hands and feet that wavered in the currents, and a mouth huge and black. I knew . . . what had happened. I was drowned. My body was worthless, my soul trapped within. The god reached for me and squeezed me, chewed me and swallowed me." She whimpered, the low, animal sound of pain and anguish. "And I died."

"You're here," Elizabeth said in a voice meant to comfort. "You didn't die."

Kateri was not comforted. "I did. I did. I saw things . . . a person should never see. Heaven and hell. Eternity and beyond. The pain disappeared . . . and I saw the light. You know . . . the light I was supposed to go toward?"

"The light that calls you after death." Elizabeth didn't believe, but Kateri did. "Yes. Of course."

"I tried to go toward it—and the god snatched me back. He made me return."

Elizabeth didn't know what to say in the face of such delusion. "We're glad he did."

"Not me. I'm not glad. Like a candle, the light blew out. Without warning, bubbles, blue seawater, green kelp surrounded me. I was in agony . . . again. I was rising to the surface. I saw a shark. I knew I was bleeding and I knew he could smell it, and I thought . . . I thought he would rip me to shreds." Kateri coughed, and flinched as if that cough caused her a spasm of pain. "The big shark. Came at me, mouth open, pointed teeth . . . at the last moment, he veered away." Tears sprang to her eyes and trickled down her cheeks. "Then I knew what I was."

"What are you?"

"One who has returned." Beneath the tears, Kateri's eyes blazed with that terrible anguish. "The shark did not dare touch me. The god would have punished him."

Elizabeth nodded as if she understood. She did not.

"I bobbed to the surface." Kateri's voice came easier now. She was talking faster, as if she knew she was out of time. "I took a long, sweet breath. The ocean slid a piece of debris beneath me, and I floated through the night and into the morning. When I woke, the pain was too much, and I pushed myself into the cold water and hoped to die. Elizabeth? Do I still have my legs?"

Elizabeth lifted the blankets and looked. "From what I can see, you have all your parts. But you are . . . battered." Beyond belief. She didn't know how anyone could live with so many injuries.

"The god gave me back to the earth, but I am changed. I have been reborn . . . and transformed. I will never be the same Kateri again." She closed her eyes, as if the effort of speaking had exhausted her . . . or as if saying good-bye to her former self. "Listen. The god said to tell my people that the might of the earth would free them from the past."

Elizabeth carefully tucked the blankets back around her. "When you're healed, you can go to your tribe. You can tell them."

"Not my tribe. You. The god spoke to you. You are my people. You are like me. We are alike." Kateri's eyes opened. "Listen to me. Listen to the earth. No more surprises. You know it all already." Her lips stretched into a broken parody of a smile. "You don't have to *remember*. You simply have to *listen* . . . Listen . . ."

From far away, Elizabeth heard a sound that shimmered in the air. Louder and louder, until she could identify the chop-chop of a helicopter blade, the roar of an engine. Like a mighty bird of prey, it swooped off the edge of the cliff and lowered over the dock, over the launch.

Coast Guard.

They had come for one of their own.

Two men descended on cables.

The resort staff scrambled backward.

Elizabeth found herself shoved aside, then impersonally hoisted out of the launch, out of the way.

Coast Guard medical corpsmen stabilized Kateri, then signaled for a flat stretcher/basket to be lowered. The corpsmen slid her onto the basket and signaled again. The helicopter lifted her into the air. Above them, more Coasties caught the stretcher and pulled her inside. Within minutes the corpsmen had been winched back aboard, and the helicopter whisked away toward Seattle, toward the hospitals and surgeries that could save Kateri's life.

Elizabeth stared into the empty air, in awe of a crisis that had ended so abruptly. Feeling apart, surreal, she climbed the steps.

At the top, Harold took her arm. "What did she tell you?"

Elizabeth stared at his inquisitive face, and made a decision to save Kateri's career and reputation. "She told me how she saved herself. She's an amazing woman, and I'm proud to know her."

CHAPTER TWENTY-SEVEN

"Shit." At the sight of the dozenth roadblock, where three police officers stood beside a fallen log, Garik rolled his truck to a halt and wondered when his luck had turned from *just about wonderful* to *every minute sucked*.

Oh, wait. That had been about the time Elizabeth left him.

Now, as he looked through the bug-speckled windshield at Sheriff Dennis Foster, the snottiest, most self-important asshole of a law enforcement officer in the continental United States, Garik knew he'd about hit rock bottom.

But by God, this time he was going to bounce.

Foster's fair, freckled skin was burned. His nose was peeling. His green eyes drooped like a drunk's after a three-day binge. His uniform hung on him. But with one hand on his firearm, he headed toward Garik's truck.

Garik got out and slammed the door.

The two men gave that *size you up, you're an asshole* nod.

Foster spoke first. "Jacobsen, how did you get here?"

"I drove." It had been more off-roading than driving, and it had taken Garik as long to get this far as it had to get from Vegas to Portland. "In Portland, I did some recon, plus I grew up here and know the side roads. That helped. Of course, you know I grew up here."

"I remember. I remember those years when you should have been in juvenile detention, and Mrs. Smith bailed you out." Foster never passed up the chance to snark at Garik. "She's a sentimental old woman."

"Don't tell her that. She's got power in this community, and you've never had quite as much support, have you?" *Take that, asshole.*

The asshole said, "Go back. This area is restricted, we've got troubles and don't need another mouth to feed."

"I figured. That's why I brought supplies." Garik waved a hand at the truck bed, packed full of food, bottled water, and filled gas cans.

Foster's eyes narrowed. "I still can't let you pass."

Knee-jerk reaction, Garik diagnosed. Foster was the kind of guy who took a stand and couldn't back down, no matter what the circumstances.

Garik didn't care—one way or the other, he was going to win this. "Sure. The law is the law, and you have to enforce it." He moved toward his truck.

Foster stepped forward. "Don't you want to know if Mrs. Smith is okay?"

Garik climbed into the cab. "I know Margaret's okay. In Portland, I got the supplies and had a ham radio installed." Hearing Margaret's voice on that ham radio was the best moment of his life.

"A ham radio." Foster pushed his hat back on his head and scratched his forehead. "I wondered how she got those helicopters here so quickly."

"Not bad for a sentimental old woman." Garik shut the door and rolled down the window.

"How about Elizabeth? Don't you want to know about your ex-wife?" Foster smirked. The smug bastard had investigated her. Or Garik. Or both.

"Sure." Garik braced himself. "Tell me about Elizabeth."

"She managed to get herself almost killed within two hours of the earthquake." Foster wasn't smirking now.

Which was good, because Garik was not amused. "How?"

"She was filming the tsunami—"

"Of course." In the throes of a scientific orgasm, no doubt.

"—And afterward, she crawled into the canyon because she saw a bone."

Garik was going to kill her himself. "A bone? Like a dinosaur bone?"

"No, human, but *she* thought it was a prehistoric find." Garik recognized the expression on Foster's face. Law enforcement officers wore that look when citizens did stupid stuff. "I had the coroner look at it. Nineteenth century. Female. Probably from the whores' cemetery."

"I always heard about that cemetery." Garik started the truck. "Never stumbled on it. There really was one?"

"Apparently. If the tsunami raked it over, we'll find more bones—the quake has unearthed all kinds of weird stuff. I just wish your wife didn't feel as if she had to kill herself over it." Foster's pocket squawked. He looked surprised, pulled out his cell phone, and in a vicious tone said, "Goddamn son-of-a-bitch."

"You got cell service?" Garik looked at his own cell phone. "I don't."

"I've got cell service." Foster turned off the sound and stuck the phone back in his pocket. "Because God hates me."

"It's a text, right? Aren't you going to read it?" Garik asked.

"It's Mother. She wants me home." Foster pulled off his hat and crushed it in his hands. It looked like he'd been doing that a lot. "I'm busy here!"

"Right. Okay." Garik kept his hands on the wheel. "I'd better get going."

"You ought to get those two women under control."

"What two women? You mean . . . Margaret and Elizabeth?" Garik laughed out loud. "*Those* two women? Right. I'll do that." He put the truck in reverse.

Before he could move, Foster slapped his hand on the door. "You're going to the resort anyway, aren't you?"

Garik looked down at him, right into his mean little eyes. "I might not be able to get control of those two women, but I sure as hell can protect them."

Foster shouted to the guys manning the roadblock, "Let him through!"

Garik pressed on the gas. With any luck, he would be home before lunch.

Garik pulled into Virtue Falls Resort, stopped the truck, and stared. The windows had been blasted out. The wraparound porch had lost a post and the roof hung drunkenly to one side. Shingles paved the parking lot. But compared to some of the damage he'd seen while skirting Virtue Falls, the resort looked good.

He drove around to the service entrance, grabbed one of the coolers out of the truck bed, and headed for the kitchen. He walked in on a dozen dirty, tired-looking people eating lunch. He lifted the cooler high, then set it beside the restaurant-sized refrigerator. "I brought milk!"

The members of the resort workforce laughed, gave him a general thumbs-up, then returned to their meal.

"You made it," Harold said. "Good thing. The old dear's been fussing—she thought you'd be here when she got up this morning."

Garik put his hand on Harold's shoulder and kept him in his seat. "Her and me both. Where is she?"

"In her room. But Elizabeth's not with her right now."

"Elizabeth has been here? She's staying here?" Garik kept his voice cool, but his skin prickled in anticipation.

"Yes, and she went for a walk this morning. She didn't return. I don't know where she is. Ask the old dear. Miss Banner would have told her."

"She better have." Garik tossed his car keys to Harold. "When you finish eating, there are supplies to be unloaded."

"Good," Harold said. "I've got most of the staff working in Virtue Falls doing rescue and cleanup, and Chef and his cooks have committed themselves to fixing lunch everyday at the shelter, so we've got a lot of mouths to feed."

"We'll get the town put back together," Garik said, and headed into the great room and up the stairs. Margaret's door was open, so he knocked on the sill.

She came in from her private deck with her arms outstretched. "My darling boy!"

He hugged her tenderly, marveling at how tiny she was. When he had first met her, he had been eight, and she had seemed tall. Actually, she'd only been five-three, and as she aged, she lost five inches in height. Now she was stooped, and skinny, all bird bones and thin skin . . . yet her heart was as big as ever.

She looked him over. "You're a little thin. We'll feed you."

"I have no doubt about that." He led Margaret to the chair beside her bed. He sat her down, then pulled the other chair around so it faced her. Seating himself, he stared into her face. "How are you?"

For him, she let down the mask, and wilted. Even her gray hair drooped as if it was weary. "When I was younger, I might have been better prepared to face a calamity of this magnitude." She sighed, and straightened her shoulders. "But I'm surviving. Did you know your wife came to me for shelter?"

"Harold told me."

"Damn the man! He never allows me the fun of breaking the news."

Garik couldn't help it. He laughed.

Three days ago he had been alone as no man had ever been before, and seconds away from killing himself. Now, within a few moments of arriving in Virtue Falls, he was alive again. He had a function. He was needed by one old, independent, hardheaded woman and one determined, oblivious, far-too-intelligent young woman.

Both of them could function on their own. Neither of them would ever admit to needing him. And yet they did.

"Where did Elizabeth go?" he asked.

Margaret winced.

"God. Damn. It." He pushed back the chair, stood, and paced away. "She went to her fucking dig, didn't she?"

"Language!"

"You taught me that language."

"That's no excuse," Margaret said. "But yes, she did. She called."

"She *called*?" He spun to face her.

"She called, and it rang through." Margaret relaxed and smiled. "It would seem cell service has been restored."

Garik took his phone out. He shook his head. "Restored . . . sporadically." He could hardly contain his annoyance. "Has it occurred to Elizabeth that there's been a major earthquake and tsunami, and another one could arrive at any time and sweep her away?"

"She knows that, none better, but she also noted that since we recovered Kateri, the number of aftershocks have markedly deceased." Margaret seemed bemused.

"When I was in Portland, I heard Kateri Kwinault was lost." Garik knew her. Not well, but he knew her. "She's found?"

"Here in the bay." Margaret brushed a tear away. "Cracked spine. Both hips broken. Ribs, arms, legs, feet, hands . . . bones broken and crushed everywhere. She'll require reconstructive surgery. She'll never be the same."

Garik scrubbed his face with his hands. "God in heaven. What's the prognosis?"

"She may live, but if she does, she'll never walk again."

"The Coast Guard's taking care of things?"

"For her care? Yes. She's getting the best care Seattle can offer, and the newspapers are painting her as a hero. But the government . . ." With an Irishwoman's contempt for authority, Margaret said, "What a bunch of morons."

"What's the government doing?"

"In town, there's talk that the government is going to charge her with incompetence in the loss of the cutter."

"Not surprised. I know the stupidity of the bureaucrats better than most." Hated it more than most, too. "But I don't understand—what would Kateri have to do with aftershocks?"

"Her Native American relatives are talking about their legends, especially the one about the frog god. They think she saw him and he gave her powers."

"I'm so glad you told me. I feel one hundred percent better." When Margaret didn't answer, he said, "That was sarcasm!"

"Yes, dear. I'm not deaf or stupid. Push that ottoman up, will you?"

He did as he was told, and helped her lift her feet onto it. "I wish you would remember how old you are and make allowances."

"I wish I could forget how old I am, but my body won't let me," she snapped. "Now—would you like a map of the canyon where Elizabeth is working?"

"Yes." He looked down at himself and sighed. "But no matter what, I've got to shit, shower, and shave before I go see her."

"You do have a manly aura." Margaret waved a dismissive hand at him.

He grinned, and stood. "Eighteens hours of moving timber out of the road, sweating, and driving to get here from Portland, so don't give me any trouble, Margaret."

"Of course not, boyo. I put you in the Pacific Suite downstairs. I'm sure that when you're presentable, Elizabeth will still be in the canyon." Margaret sighed. "Give me a hand onto my bed. Now that you're here, I can sleep. You damned kids keep me worried all the time."

CHAPTER TWENTY-EIGHT

Elizabeth knelt in the drying mud at the place where twenty-five years of excavation had once been, and took photos and measurements, and treasured every moment of being alone, in charge, without the team . . . when a shiny pair of size eleven black shoes stepped into her field of vision.

She stared at those shoes, musing at her own immediate, visceral reaction: amusement that anyone had tromped down a steep, nonexistent wilderness trail wearing such inappropriate footwear, a probably futile hope she wouldn't have to defend her activity here, and most of all, the hard, rapid heartbeat caused by breathing the same air as Garik Jacobsen.

Because she knew it was him.

His presence always made her heart beat faster, in anticipation of a fight, or of good sex, or in this case, of simply seeing him after more than a year of wrenching separation. She had known separation was the right thing to do, and she had known, too, that the anguish would gradually fade. But it hadn't yet, and here he was, all shiny-shoed and spiffy.

Gradually, dragging out the anticipation, she lifted her eyes to examine the starched black khakis, the black golf shirt, the broad, stiff neck, and the handsome, disapproving face.

She couldn't remember the last time Garik Jacobsen had looked at her with anything but disapproval.

Reason number one she had hiked out of their marriage.

He'd grown his hair out; the blond ends curled around his earlobes and down his neck, and that was weird. He'd kept his head shaved before, he said to avoid giving the bad guys something to hold on to. This look softened him a little, made him less action hero and more . . . whatever. He looked good.

His eyes were still the most striking gold-speckled green she'd ever seen, accented by lashes dark and so long they tangled when he blinked. He'd had the guts to gripe about his lashes once while she'd been applying mascara; he'd ended up with a black blob on his white shirt, one that never came out.

He had quite an aristocratic nose, pronounced, thin, and crooked. At some point before she'd met him, he'd had it broken. He looked down that nose now, without smiling.

"What's wrong *now*?" It seemed as if she was picking up the conversation where they left off.

"Why would you say something was wrong?" His voice was the same; deep, dangerous, derisive. "Three days ago, there was an earthquake."

"Almost four!"

"There are still a hundred aftershocks a day, some of them sizable. And you're down in the canyon where the tsunami struck, looking at rocks."

She considered the best way to answer him. "You have a point—"

"Really?"

"But I didn't mean to come down here. I went for a walk and found myself at the canyon rim, and wandered down . . ."

"You have tools," he said icily.

Busted. "Well, yes."

"The tools at the previous site have to have been swept away, ergo, you brought them with you."

She admitted, "I did think I might need them if I spotted anything that required investigation."

"You stole them from Virtue Falls Resort's gardening crew."

"I didn't *steal* them! I *borrowed* them." She put down her trowel, then defiantly picked it up again.

"You're wearing gloves. You brought gardening gloves to protect your hands."

"During the earthquake, I hurt my hand." She looked at the glove on her left hand. "I cut it. I have stitches."

"You have stitches and you came out here to work?" His voice rose.

"There hasn't been an aftershock of more than five-point-zero for the last twenty-four hours. In fact, since yesterday afternoon, the seismic activity has markedly diminished." Although she, as a logical scientist, did not believe the change was the result of Kateri's rescue.

In a tone of exquisite sarcasm, Garik said, "A noted geologist of my acquaintance once told me an earthquake can occur anytime, especially along the Pacific Rim."

"The descent to this site was easy and if climbing became necessary, the return could be swift." Damn. She sounded defensive.

"That same geologist said that frequently one large earthquake triggers another, and landslides are a frequent consequence, which would make the ascent hazardous if not impossible."

She tapped her saw-toothed trowel on the side of a displaced boulder. "Should another earthquake occur in the same location, I would have time to seek a way out before the tsunami arrived."

"That noted geologist once told me—"

"Would you stop quoting me to myself?" She took a breath and pushed a dangling strand of hair off her forehead. No one ever made her lose her temper . . . except Garik. "I had to come down. There's so much to see, to check on. Look at the exposed bare rock! The patches of mud!"

He lifted one shoe. The mud he stood in appeared not to impress him.

"Look at the displaced sea creatures that swept in from the tidal pools! No wonder we find their fossils in the rocks. My team is still MIA, and there's no one else except me to . . ." She could see by his expression she hadn't convinced him, would never convince him. "I brought all kinds of ropes and climbing supplies, and I'm healthy and will start up as soon as there's the slightest sign of . . . Oh, to hell with it." Sweeping her arm in an arc, she slammed it and the flat side of her trowel behind his knees.

CHAPTER TWENTY-NINE

Garik had considered a grounding in self-defense necessary for the wife of an FBI agent. He had taught Elizabeth how to hit, how to fall, and most important, how to surprise her opponent.

But she'd never before gained the advantage of him.

This time, he stood on a downhill slope on the edge of a pool of mud. When she hit him, his knee buckled.

He windmilled his arms. His leather-soled shoes slipped out from underneath him.

He slammed flat on his back in the soft muck. He splatted.

"Oh, dear," she said.

He shook his head to clear it.

Mud flew from his goo-covered hair.

"Oh, dear." She covered her mouth with her hand.

Lifting his head, he focused on her and glared.

She sputtered. Tried to contain herself. Snorted, and sputtered again.

Outrage blossomed on his face.

And she laughed until she couldn't breathe. She laughed so hard she bent over from the waist, holding her aching ribs. She laughed so hard she had to contain tears with a dig towel pressed over her eyes. She laughed so hard, she was hiccuping.

Every time she started to slow, she looked up to see him leaning on his elbows, glaring, with black, sticky mud caking the back of his head, splattered on his shoulders, his arms, between his legs, all over those pristine, shiny black shoes . . . and she started cackling again.

He waited until she contained herself enough to search for a clean towel and silently offer it to him.

Grabbing her wrist—the wrist on her good hand—he pulled her on top of him and rolled.

Now she was on her back in the mud, staring up at him. And still laughing.

He was *not* laughing. He gripped her shoulders and shook her. "Do you know how scared I was that you and Margaret were hurt, were trapped in debris or swept away by a wave, were dying . . . and I wasn't here to help you? Do you *know* the horrors I imagined?"

He was ranting—and the Garik she remembered did not rant. "Yes, it would have been very bad if I'd been in my apartment."

He continued, "I drove for goddamn ever, had to throw my weight around as an FBI agent and a former Washington resident with an elderly relative to even get past the roadblocks law enforcement set up around the whole coast—"

"But I thought you weren't FBI any—"

"—talk my way past that stupid fool of a sheriff who still thinks I'm a juvenile delinquent. Then I got to the inn, and Margaret's all right, and she says you're staying there, and I think my troubles are over." His voice started rising. "Then you know what she told me?"

"She said—"

"She said you'd left to check on your rocks."

"Not just rocks, but the results of—"

"The results of a million years of earthquakes and tsunamis that shake the ground and sweep up this river and destroy everything. Everything! For a million years!" He pointed his finger in her face. "Millions . . . of . . . years. And you have to come down here *now* to look at your rocks?"

She wasn't laughing anymore. "I'm not careless, you know. I did call."

"You were lucky to get through!"

"You always make me feel like the village idiot. But I'm not stupid!"

"Worse than that," he said bitterly. "You're dedicated."

The injustice stung her. "You're one to talk."

"But when I walk into danger, it's because—"

"I know. Because your job is important." She could do bitter, too. "Mine is not. It can wait another million years or so."

"I didn't say that."

"You don't have to. You're not exactly a subtle thinker."

He didn't answer.

So she'd finally stumped him, finally won the fight. She didn't feel triumphant, just let down and gray. Although perhaps she hadn't won. For he was staring at her face, her body . . .

A lot of things occurred to her then, silly things: that the towel she'd used on her face had been dirty, that she had been shoveling rocks and was covered in sweat, that she'd tied a bandana around her head to try and keep her hair out of her way, that she hadn't been sleeping well because every time she shut her eyes, she heard her father's voice saying, *What about the bones?*

"I must look like hell," she said.

He shook his head. In a voice deep and rich and lavish with desire, he said, "You look absolutely . . . beautiful."

"Ohh." It was more of a sound than a word, a quick sip of breath as she recognized the look on his face, remembered the weight of his body, gloried in the scent of his desire.

No matter how they fought they had always been like this: balanced between anger and passion, between hurt and glory.

When they first got together, she didn't understand how two people who had so little in common could be so madly, passionately in love.

When they split, she had realized madness and passion could never keep a couple together.

But the hunger . . . it still seethed between them.

The earthquake had given him reason to fear for her life.

And she had been lonely, an outcast among the townspeople and the scientific team.

Now the gold in his eyes intensified to a heated amber, the air grew thick and warm and so still it almost shimmered . . . and his lips descended to hers.

He kissed her.

He tasted like toothpaste and desperation. He smelled like cinnamon and teak wood and explosive need. He felt . . . oh, God, he felt right, his weight a memory of good times and bad, of long afternoons of leisurely sex and quick morning gropes in the shower. And the way he kissed her . . . familiar, with all the same moves, yet so intense it felt like the first time, a flashfire that could not be contained.

She wrapped her arms around his shoulders, slid her hands up his neck.

He was muddy, and she wanted to laugh.

He was skinny, and she wanted to scold.

He was so desperately unhappy, that she wanted to cry.

Grabbing his hair, she pulled his face away from hers. "Garik. Why . . . ?"

He answered by grabbing her hair, too, and tugging her head back, and tasting her neck. He pressed his lips over the artery, sampling the excitement that spread through her veins. "Damn you for leaving me." His lips moved against her skin, his breath touched her lightly as a scent, the words were barely audible.

She didn't need to hear. She knew how deeply she had wounded him.

Yet she had left to save herself. All the days of their marriage, she had ached with fear and loneliness. Fear that he would be killed in the line of duty. Loneliness because if he was, she would have nothing, not even the memory of their closeness to warm her through the rest of her desolate years.

So now she yielded, allowing him to kiss her throat, the hollow at the base of her neck, then her lips again. It was no sacrifice; he kissed as he did everything, expertly, thoroughly, with the passion that gave her a hint of the soul he hid so well. Those kisses, those hints, had first seduced her, then kept her·in their marriage long after she should have given up.

Now he stole her breath, and her heart.

Not again. Not again.

She gave him a push. "Garik. That's enough. Off!"

He rolled with her, bringing her on top of him, freeing her from his weight, and with his head cradled by mud and his hands barely touching her waist, he looked up and said, "Then *you* kiss *me*."

"No." Even as she pressed her mouth to his, she said, "That would be stupid."

Oh, my God. Even with her eyes closed, he was beautiful. He let her have her way with him, let her kiss him, suckle his tongue, savor his tenderness spiced by desire.

He'd been the first man she'd ever slept with—and she'd slept with him on the first date.

She'd been a twenty-one-year-old virgin, not for any dedication to purity or for religious reasons, but because the men who'd pleaded and arm-twisted never moved her to anything but annoyance. She had figured she was frigid, that passion was one of those things that her warped upbringing had stolen from her.

One kiss, and Garik convinced her otherwise. She had jumped on him, so eager for a taste of genuine lust that he'd had to slow her down, warn her away . . . and all the while he'd been taking off her clothes, and ripping off his, and thank God the man showed power and stamina in the back stretch . . .

She lifted her head, and looked into his face. She pushed his hair off his forehead, and whispered, "Garik." She wanted to say more: *Take me, love me, need me.* And she knew he would do all those things.

But *talk to me*? Not so much.

"In my truck," he murmured, "there's a blanket. We could put it on the seat, and I could take off your clothes and kiss you here"—he touched her mouth—"and here"—he touched her breast—"and . . ."

She put her knees down on either side of his hips and sat up.

He was hard. His body was making her a promise . . .

"And here." He slid his index finger between her legs and put slow, hot pressure on her clit.

She tilted her head back, seduced, tempted, on the verge of coming, shuddering with . . . No. Wait. She opened her eyes, saw the green pines trembling against the blue sky—and realized that wasn't the earth moving for her.

It was *moving*.

"Earthquake," he said hoarsely. "Earthquake!"

She jumped up, scrambled away from him, gave him room to stand.

He vaulted to his feet, too, his mouth tight with tension, his hands held at the ready for battle. But what would he battle here and now? If the walls of the canyon came down, he could do nothing about it.

The walls did fail: plumes of dirt rose up and down the river as landslides large and small bore witness to the instability of the region.

The shaking increased. Her feet slipped in the mud. Roughly he pulled her close, watching, prepared to move on a moment's notice.

Two great boulders ripped off the canyon rim and

plummeted down the slope. One boulder missed them by twenty feet. The other, smaller boulder bounced into a nearby massive pile of brush.

Dust rose. Twigs and branches clattered and broke. The boulder hung there like a bird's egg in the middle of a nest, then slowly subsided, sliding out of sight and all the way to the ground.

The shaking became trembling, then ceased altogether.

She clung to him anyway, and she remembered the other thing she had so loved about him—when he held her in his arms, she felt safe and cherished.

She could have stayed here forever.

Then he pushed her back, and looked down at her accusingly, no doubt remembering her assurances about the aftershocks and how she was safe here.

She glanced around, prepared to defend herself . . . when she saw it. Sprawled on the pile of brush, revealed by the broken branches.

She freed herself, and walked closer, hypnotized by the sight of . . . bones.

Bones . . . shattered secrets revealed by this day's disaster.

But these bones had not yet spent over a century in the earth. Flesh still clung to these bones, and clothing . . . a flowered dress, marked by mud and an older, darker, more ominous stain. Patches of short, blond hair cluing to the skull.

Elizabeth knelt by the outstretched, skeletal hand.

The ring was gone from the finger, but she recognized the material of the dress. She recognized the body. And the stain on the material—that was blood.

In a calm voice that seemed to come from a great distance, she said, "This is my mother."

CHAPTER THIRTY

Their trip into town went swiftly, for Garik drove like a maniac along roads cracked from the earthquake. He drove like a man about to report a recent crime.

Their visit to the sheriff's office had not gone smoothly, for Foster had been incredulous and insulting, both about their find and about the mud that coated them.

The drive back to the canyon involved a convoy of police cars that followed close on Garik's bumper, and a monologue from Elizabeth that sent chills down Garik's spine.

"I'm not even that surprised," she said. "My father warned me I would find her. Which is weird, I know, but the nurses at the care facility say he talks to my mother, so I suppose if one believes that is true, one could hypothesize that my mother knew her bones would be discovered. There's a weird sort of logic there." Elizabeth's eyes were bright, her color was good. She appeared to be fine.

But she was chatting. Elizabeth never chatted.

Always, Elizabeth weighed her words. She spoke carefully, as if the speechlessness of her childhood had taught her the heft and power of language. During their marriage, as time went on, she had been more and more reticent.

So one good thing had come from the shock and horror of finding Misty's body—Elizabeth was talking to him now.

And he, by God, was listening.

Garik nodded and kept driving.

"Garik, do you believe in the afterlife?" Elizabeth asked.

"You know I do. When I was eight, Margaret adopted me. Margaret is Catholic. Therefore, so am I. It's a requirement for living in her house." He drove slowly, his attention torn between the rutted dirt road and his ex-wife.

She was in shock, whether she knew it or not, and if chatting was what she needed to do, then he would listen. And learn. Because she was saying things he had never heard before.

"I never have believed in an afterlife," she declared. "I've seen no proof of ghosts. I've seen no sign of a just God. So why would I believe?"

"God works—"

"I know. In mysterious ways."

"Actually, I was going to say, at His own speed and with His own timetable. Sometimes justice takes longer than we would like." Bitterly, Garik reflected on the truth of that in his own life. "Sometimes justice doesn't come in a lifetime . . . and that's what the afterlife is for." He hoped. He knew a few candidates he would nominate to burn in hell.

"I suppose that makes some sense. I mean, if you believe that the universe must remain balanced and justice must be fulfilled." Elizabeth looked like a dirty urchin.

No matter; she was still beautiful, and right now, she needed somebody.

She needed him.

She continued, "Personally, I find it fascinating that the nurses who work at the Honor Mountain Memory Care Facility, men and women who deal with death every day, do believe in ghosts and the afterlife."

"Maybe they know something you don't."

"Maybe." Elizabeth looked out the window at the pines, green and lush, bent and twisted by the eternal winds that blew off the Pacific Ocean. Finally she said, "Beautiful here, isn't it? For millennia, it's been an important ritual to humans to inter the bodies of the beloved of their family in a place of honor. If one was to think in such a manner—because it's not like it matters to the person who has died—then this place is appropriate for my mother."

He wanted to pull Elizabeth close and hug her, tell her Misty would be buried with honor and Elizabeth would have a place to visit where she could place flowers in tribute to the woman who had given her life.

But he couldn't. Not now. They were on a mission to retrieve her mother's bones, and until they had completed that mission, Elizabeth would have to be strong all on her own. Instead he infused his voice with support. "This peaceful, ancient forest has been a good resting place for your mother."

Elizabeth sat now with her hands in her lap, palms up, and she nodded. "Yes. Peaceful and ancient."

"And you work nearby. She knows that."

"She's dead," Elizabeth said with impeccable logic. "She can't know that."

"Some people might say you didn't find her, Elizabeth. Some people might say she found you." Which he was pretty sure was going to bug him later.

Elizabeth frowned. "That doesn't make any sense."

He thought she understood him perfectly well.

She ran her fingers through her hair, shedding leaves, twigs, and chunks of mud onto the back of the seat.

He started to protest, then shut his mouth.

They were dealing with bigger issues here than the

cleanliness of his truck. And after that drive across four states, through a billion bugs and a dozen McDonald's drive-throughs, he had no business whining about a little mud.

She looked behind them. "Sheriff Foster is tailgating."

"Yes. He doesn't want us to think we can get away."

"Why does he have his police lights flashing? Why did he bring his deputies with him? Does he think *we* committed the crime?"

Garik glanced in the rearview mirror, at Sheriff Foster's clenched jaw and furious eyes. "He has issues."

"What kind of issues?"

"For one thing, he doesn't like me. I was nobody, a vagrant's kid. Then Margaret adopted me and made me somebody. Then I became a juvenile delinquent, and he got to say, *I told you so.*"

"To Margaret Smith?"

Her openmouthed horror made him laugh briefly. "I know. What he lacks in intelligence he makes up for in balls. She's been gunning for him ever since."

"I would not make Margaret Smith my enemy," she said fervently.

"No. No, it's not a good idea. What really pisses off Foster is that I straightened out, went to college, went into the FBI, and was by definition cooler than him." Garik still loved that that was true.

"Even suspended, you are cooler than him," Elizabeth said.

"No arguments here."

"That is not so large an accomplishment," Elizabeth pointed out. "I don't think Sheriff Foster actually qualifies as cool."

"My darling." Garik patted her knee and chuckled. "Honest to the last."

She looked at his hand, then at him. "You are, however, younger, more intelligent, and more pleasing to the eye."

"That, too." He was glad she had noticed.

"And taller. I have noted that men who are less than five-ten seem to have issues with men of your height."

"True. And he lives with his mother."

She sent Garik a startled glance. "Oh, dear."

"She's in bad health, always has been."

"But has he never had a relationship with a woman?"

"Not that I know."

"Or a man?"

"Not that I know."

She seemed confused. "After living with you, I find it hard to believe a man could abstain from sex, but I have read some men are not at all interested."

"It is hard to believe, isn't it?" Today, it had taken a jolt from the earth itself to throw Garik off Elizabeth, and even then, as soon as the aftershock had ceased, he would have tugged her up to the canyon rim, tossed her in his truck, and had his way with her.

She would have gone, too.

Today, only one thing could have called a halt to the sex. And had.

Her mother. For a woman who had been dead for twenty-three years, she did a good job of protecting her daughter.

"I don't understand it," he said, "and I don't like things I don't understand. Foster's not happy with us, and you'd think finding your mother's body would be the culmination of his lifetime's law enforcement work."

Elizabeth mulled that over. "You're right. When we were at the courthouse, he went out of his way to insult us. It's one thing to insinuate that we're muddy because we've been having intercourse on the ground, but when we told him about . . . about my mother, he refused to believe us. He said it must be one of the . . . the whores from the cemetery. Then I told him about her . . . her dress. You told him she had blond hair. White . . . blond hair."

Garik listened to the hitch in Elizabeth's voice, and wished he could help her through this.

But Elizabeth shouldered past her pain. "Misty Banner's body was never recovered. How would he know whether it was my mother or not?"

"Exactly."

"I think Sheriff Foster should be happy. The forensics experts will examine her body and at the least, they'll say yes, she was killed with the scissors that my father held." Elizabeth placed her hand on her throat, as if she could feel the fatal blow. "If Sheriff Foster is very, very lucky, DNA will link my father to the crime."

"And with this discovery, Sheriff Foster will be thrust into the spotlight again, which would make his next run for reelection easier." Garik realized how good he and Elizabeth were together—not just in the sack, but also tracking the sheriff's illogical reaction. "So why is he angry?"

Elizabeth answered promptly. "It would follow that he fears some new evidence that will reveal incompetence and strips him of the glory of the case."

Garik glanced again in the rearview mirror. "A fair assumption."

"Garik . . . do you believe there's a possibility my father is innocent?"

He hesitated. He could see it—she was hopeful. He hated to crush that hope, but he couldn't lie to her. "I read the file on the Banner case, and if there had been reason to believe him innocent, I would have investigated further."

"Oh." Elizabeth picked at the mud on her arm. "The nurses say my father was innocent. But if that's true, who is guilty?"

"Since it's never happened again, someone who is long gone from this place." That was always the theory to which all communities subscribed. *It couldn't be one of us, we're nice people. It must be a vagrant.*

In Garik's experience, it was almost always someone local, almost always a spouse or family member . . . or lover.

"I wish . . . I wish I could find out for myself he was innocent." Elizabeth's big blue eyes were pleading. "It would change nothing and yet it would change . . ."

"Everything. I know. Having a father guilty of heinous behavior casts a long shadow." Garik *knew.* "There's always the belief that a parent should love and protect his child, and the knowledge that your parent, your own flesh and blood, failed in that basic requirement . . . hurts."

"Yes." She pushed at her hair again, and more dust drifted across her face. "In the news reports, people who knew my father said he was so kind, so decent. No one expected he would fly into a jealous rage and murder my mother. So I always fear I'll do that. Change personality, turn into a monster, be like him."

He wanted to tell her it was impossible, it couldn't happen, that no one had two disparate sides to their personalities. But he knew better. "That is the fear." That fear could drive a man to attempt suicide. "You watch for that moment when you turn into a monster exactly like the man who gave you life."

"Statistically speaking, either through environmental

observation or genetic propensity, there is a high likelihood of that occurring."

"You mean, as the twig is bent, so grows the tree? And the sins of the father are delivered on the son?"

She touched his hand on the steering wheel. "You express these matters better than I do."

"Not better. Differently. We complement each other."

"What a nice thought." Her voice grew wistful. "It doesn't seem fair, though, that every person who walks this earth is doomed by . . . by things over which we have no control."

A year ago, he would have said he had control. Now he knew it wasn't true. But other men and women, better people than him, had risen above their pasts, and he felt able to assure her, "We don't have to turn into our parents."

"No, but people constantly expect that we will."

"Yes." That was the sad truth. People did constantly expect the worst—and were thrilled when their expectations were fulfilled.

He applied the brake. "We're here." Back at the rim of the canyon where her mother's ruined body had been torn from some hidden grave by the tsunami.

Now Elizabeth's flush faded to a cold white marble. "Do you think he buried her in the prostitutes' cemetery? Do you think she's been there all these years, without one person to mourn her or a flower for remembrance?"

He put the truck into park, turned off the motor, and faced her. He took her bandaged hand and kissed it. "No matter where your mother came to rest, she was mourned. Wasn't she?" It was more a statement than a question.

Elizabeth's gaze dropped away from his.

Lightly he touched her shoulder. "Flowers are to comfort the living."

Elizabeth bit her lip, and nodded.

And jumped when Sheriff Foster rapped his knuckles sharply against her window.

"Come on," he said roughly. "Get out and show me this body you found."

Elizabeth's complexion turned almost green, and she put her head on her knees and moaned.

Garik was abruptly, coldly furious. *The mean fucker.* He unfolded himself from the driver's seat, jumped down on the ground, leaned across the hood of the truck, and said, "I'll show you the body."

Sheriff Foster stared back at him, his eyes narrow and spiteful and scared.

Yeah. The guy was guilty of something. At the very least, being an asshole. Maybe of incompetence. And with that thought came another.

What better way to cover up a murder than to investigate it yourself? "Where were you," Garik asked, "when Misty Banner was killed?"

CHAPTER THIRTY-ONE

Foster gaped as if he couldn't believe Garik had the nerve.

He stalked around the front of the truck. "You want to accuse me of something?"

"No. I want to know where you were when Misty Banner was killed."

Elizabeth opened her door and slid down out of the truck.

Garik flicked her a glance that warned her away.

She nodded. But she obviously wanted to hear the answer.

"You little bastard. You get rescued and all raised up by Margaret Smith, and ever since then"—Foster pointed to his throat—"you've had this attitude that sticks in my craw."

"Because I didn't have a mother who kept me home my whole life?"

Foster's face turned red, his green eyes blazed, and he vibrated with rage. "Don't you talk to me that way. Always visiting Virtue Falls, always so much more important than local law enforcement. I know what happened to your FBI career. I know what you did. I looked it up."

Elizabeth looked back and forth between the two men.

"Yeah. And I still want to know where you were when Misty Banner was killed." Garik stepped closer, lowered his voice, and ruthlessly used his height advantage to piss Foster off. "I could make everyone here speculate where you were that day. All I have to do is raise my voice and ask the questions, and your deputies would start wondering why you won't explain. Want me to do that, Foster? Because this little bastard might have been thrown out of the FBI, but I still know the tricks. I could make your life awkward, and you don't want that."

Foster immediately went into his belligerent stance; shoulders back, elbows out, one hand on his weapon. He stepped close, very close, to Garik, and glared, eyes unblinking. He glared and glared, and when Garik didn't budge, he finally muttered, "I was out on patrol."

Elizabeth sidled around to stand in front of the chrome grill.

"Got any alibis?" Garik asked.

"No, I don't have any alibis. I didn't need them."

Foster flung out a hand. "Do you know how big this county is? Do you know how long it takes an officer to make his rounds?"

"I know the guy who's first on the scene is frequently the perp."

"I wasn't first on the scene. First on the scene was the Banners' postal worker. He took that photograph of Charles Banner holding Elizabeth, and the scissors, and both of them covered in blood."

Elizabeth turned her face away.

Garik wished she'd get back in the truck. Because he had Foster on the ropes, and he wasn't going to quit now. "You were the first *officer* on the scene."

"Because I was in the area."

"Exactly."

Foster's face worked violently. "I could arrest you right now and throw you in jail, and who among your fancy law enforcement friends would know or care?"

"I don't have any fancy law enforcement friends, but you'd have to have some reason to arrest me, and I'm pretty sure that even in this county, an arrest would go through due process. It's not the Wild West, no matter how much you or I would like it to be." Garik stood solidly in place for another three counts, long enough for Foster to know he didn't give a crap about his threats. Then he eased back. "I'll study the case."

"You mean you didn't do that when you first met Elizabeth?" Foster mocked. "I thought that must be what attracted you to her, the chance for a damaged control freak to mess with a real live head case."

"Shut up," Garik snapped. "She just found her mother's body."

Elizabeth stood with her chin up, no expression on her

face, but the red eyes and blotchy cheeks told their
own tale.

Foster might be a gold-plated asshole, but he didn't
like the world to see him in action, and his deputies were
definitely getting an eyeful right now.

"Goddamn it." He whipped around to face his men,
and shouted, "Let's get this crime scene cordoned off."

The deputies moved, but none too fast. The three guys
were young, under twenty-five. They had heard stories
about Misty Banner's murder, but they didn't remember it. And the scene unfolding before them held them
enthralled.

Foster snarled, and they pretended to move a little
faster. Then he turned back to Garik, and in a furious
undertone said, "I did good work on the Banner case.
Charles Banner was guilty of killing his wife in a jealous rage. It was logical."

"Logical?" Garik couldn't believe Foster had to guts
to say that. "Crime is logical?"

"All evidence pointed to it."

"Nice dodge."

"I challenge you to find out anything different."

"You sure you found all the evidence? Because I did
read through the Banner case, and I don't remember anything about Misty Banner's hair being cut off."

Foster froze in surprise . . . and denial. "Off? Her
hair—Misty Banner's hair—is cut off?"

"Oh, yeah."

Foster looked like a man right after he's been hit between the eyes with a tire iron and right before he falls
over dead.

Garik went on alert.

Foster started talking, fast and defensively. "We didn't

know for sure. There were some loose strands in the carpet. But the body was gone. Criminology wasn't as good then as it is now. How were we supposed to know?"

Garik picked right up on the pertinent information. "You found loose strands—strands that had been cut from her head—and you didn't mention them in the report?"

"We didn't see that they were pertinent."

Garik laughed. One snort, really, but it completely expressed his opinion of Foster and his investigation.

What mattered, of course, was that Foster knew Garik was right.

Garik walked to Elizabeth and put his hand under her arm. "Let me help you back into the truck while I show Foster and his men the right location."

"If you don't mind," she said. "I'd like to stay out here and . . . pace."

"Sure." Garik couldn't resist; he smoothed a lock of muddy hair off her forehead. "Don't go far, though, huh?"

"I'm not going to go back to work, if that's what you mean." She sounded a little snappish. And that was good.

"Yeah, that's what I mean." But it wasn't. The discovery of Misty's body, combined with the realization that Foster's reputation as an investigator had been exaggerated, provided Garik with a fear he'd never experienced before.

If Charles Banner hadn't murdered his wife, someone else had. And who was that someone else? Where was that someone else? And would this discovery flush him out of hiding?

"Come on, Foster," Garik said. "I'll show you the body, and then I'm taking Elizabeth home."

CHAPTER THIRTY-TWO

Taking Elizabeth home was a journey taut with fears, unspoken questions, and too many missteps from the past.

But finally Elizabeth lifted her head off the headrest, looked at Garik, and asked, "Is Sheriff Foster right? Did you study the Banner case out of curiosity, so you could see what it had done to me?"

Man, was Garik glad to be able to answer this one truthfully. "No. I told you, I read through the case. I did that before our first blind date." He kept glancing at her. "Look. I didn't have to *study* it. I knew who you were. The case was well known at the time, is still famous in law enforcement—and I'm from Virtue Falls. Here, it's notorious."

Her color washed away; she looked like she was going to throw up.

He did not want her to toss her cookies in his truck. So he talked faster. "But I didn't go on that blind date because I considered you a test case. I went on the blind date because Margaret was matchmaking and strongly suggested we meet and"—he ran his hand through his hair—"and because I checked out your photos and you were hot."

Silence from beside him.

He glanced at her again. "I'm shallow. So sue me."

She looked at him sideways. "Shallow works for me. Shallow—*she's hot*—is better than nosy—*she's a lab rat*."

He breathed a sigh of relief. Her complexion was no longer Wicked Witch of the West green.

His truck was safe.

With utmost sincerity, he said, "Honey, looking at you, I have never once thought of any kind of rat. I promise, I didn't do my best Bond imitation for any other reason than to impress you. Because I'm a disgusting, horny guy."

She nodded and smiled. "Okay. I like you disgusting and horny."

Elizabeth was always so successful at presenting a calm façade, he found it easy to think she had dealt well with the murder and its consequences. But today had conclusively proved that wasn't true. Her emotions were fragile, raw, anguished. She was a lonely, wounded soul, who even now was easily injured . . . and she needed reassurance. She needed reassurance from him.

"If you will recall, I spent our first date using every excuse to show my muscles, I talked all the time about my testosterone-laden job, and I pretended to be interested in geology. I think that qualifies for disgusting and horny, right?"

"All that stuff you said about geology was just pretending?"

"Yes. But since then . . . do you know how many Discovery Channel episodes I've watched so I didn't feel like an idiot every time you mentioned your work?"

"No." For the first time in the last two hours, she sounded warm and amused. "How many?"

"Lots."

She slid down in the seat and looked out the window at the passing scenery. "Good."

Garik concentrated on his driving; on this stretch of road, the asphalt was crumpled like a starched shirt after a tough day of work. When they reached a smooth stretch, he said, "I will say, I thought the Banner case was predicated on the assumption that your father was guilty."

Which, speaking as an FBI agent, Garik totally comprehended, not that he would ever admit that to the public, and most certainly not to Elizabeth.

"You're saying Foster did do sloppy police work? That the case was not well investigated?" She sounded hopeful again.

"I wouldn't say that. At the time of the crime, law enforcement didn't have the technology we have now, especially not a small, remote town like Virtue Falls." Especially not if Foster was out to make his name. "Before and after the trial, the evidence, the testimonies, the verdict was typed up, then copied and sent around to the various agencies. A dozen years ago, somebody, probably some gofer with a thousand pages and fifteen minutes, scanned and uploaded it to the Internet. Lots of room for neglect and error, not to mention lots of smeared print. So I'd have to get up close and personal with the evidence before I could say anything for sure." And as soon as he could, he intended to.

He pulled out his cell phone, glanced at it, and silently cursed. No reception. If it was working, he could set it up as a router to access the Internet . . . but Elizabeth's phone had worked. "Do you still have reception?" he asked.

She pulled it out of her toolbox. "No. It's dead. But it worked this morning. I didn't think when I called Margaret, but the call went through."

Okay. Elizabeth was doing better. Not so tense. Not so pale. She was going to be okay.

Then she asked the question Garik dreaded. "What *did* happen to get you thrown out of the FBI?"

CHAPTER THIRTY-THREE

Garik pulled into the resort parking lot. He parked next to the front door, and put his truck in gear.

Elizabeth started to snap at him, to ask whether it was the same old, same old, where she talked and he didn't.

Then she glanced at him.

He looked bad. His complexion was pale. His jaw was locked so tight it looked as if it might shatter. He turned off the motor and looked straight out the windshield. And he answered her. Sort of. "I haven't been thrown out. When I can pass the psychological test, I can rejoin the force."

"What precipitated the, um . . . what incident . . . ?" For the first time, Elizabeth appreciated how carefully Garik had had to tread with her when discussing her mother's murder. Because she was trying to be sensitive here, and she didn't quite know what words to use.

Garik understood. "I lost my temper."

She had never in the two years that they had been married seen him lose control . . . except in bed. "Because?" she asked faintly.

"Exactly what we were discussing earlier. I turned into my father." He smiled the kind of smile that looked as if he was chewing razor blades. "I deserve to be on probation. And I can never go back to the work, because I now realize that my father's always there, inside me, waiting to spring out, and there's nothing I can do about it."

"What did you do?"

He looked at her, and those green-and-gold eyes revealed ice and anguish.

Never had she expected to pity Garik. She pitied him

now, and reached for him, to kiss him, to comfort him. "Everybody loses their temper. I do, and I mean, look at Margaret! She's as Irish as they come. It doesn't mean you're going to kill somebody, or hurt somebody."

"I already did."

"You hurt somebody?" He hadn't killed anybody. She would have heard about that.

"He deserved it." Garik clenched his fists. "And I'd do it again if it would change"—he shook his head—"anything."

"You're one of the good guys, Garik. If you hurt someone, I know you did it to right a wrong." She took his hand, smoothed out his fingers, and petted them until he relaxed. "You're one of the good guys," she said again, "and I trust you to never hurt me. Does that mean anything?"

He closed his eyes as if pain stabbed at him.

Then he opened them, and looked toward the porch. "There's Margaret," he said.

Elizabeth dropped his hand.

As if he couldn't get away from her fast enough, he swung out of the truck. "Margaret! How did you get downstairs?"

Elizabeth opened her door and slowly got out.

Margaret pushed her walker toward the edge of the porch. "With enough staff and a great deal of determination." She offered Elizabeth a shaking hand. "My dear, I heard . . . what happened. How are you?"

Elizabeth walked up the stairs, and took her hand. "I'm fine."

"Are you?" Margaret searched Elizabeth's face. "You look dreadful."

"Yes. After a day of work, I'm always dirty. But even for me, this is extreme." Elizabeth touched her hair. She looked at the grubby gauze that wrapped her wounded hand. "I should go wash."

"Do that, then come down to the dining room. The staff is preparing a wonderful meal for us." Margaret watched Elizabeth go inside, then turned to Garik. "How is she really?"

"In shock. But holding it together. She always does."

"Early life training never goes away." Margaret had dressed for a special occasion, in a gray dress, diamond earrings, and her jade bead necklace. She snapped her fingers at him. "Knock that dirt off before you step inside my inn."

He started kicking his shoes against the steps, whacking the back of his pants with his hands. Most of the mud disintegrated into dust. But some of it clung, thick and black, on his back and in his hair.

Margaret shook her head. "Come on, then. I won't even ask what the two of you were doing to get plastered in mud."

"Better if you don't."

Margaret led the way into the resort. "Has Elizabeth remembered . . . anything?"

"Not about the murder. She's certainly remembered what it's like to be the center of attention." He followed. "How did you hear?"

"Harold was in Virtue Falls, distributing the supplies you brought, and someone saw you and Elizabeth go in the sheriff's office, and come out with the escort." Margaret had that sneer she wore when people made her angry. "Within minutes the news was all over town that Misty's body had been found."

He remembered the middle-aged, gray-haired dumpling of a grandmother who worked at the sheriff's office. She always wore a kindly smile while she spread the news of who was in trouble and why. "That secretary of Foster's, right? What's her name?"

"Mona. Mona Coleman of Coleman Wood Products." Margaret's tone made it quite clear what she thought of Mona and her products. "And yes, she is the Virtue Falls broadcasting system."

"I remember her from before." From when he was a teen delinquent, he meant. "I hated her then, too."

"Not that everybody in town wouldn't have gossiped anyway, but I'm sure the news made a welcome change of topic from the earthquake." Margaret walked toward the kitchen. "I hope for Elizabeth's sake there's closure in finding her mother's body."

"And a rough couple of weeks while everyone re-hashes the time Charles Banner killed his wife with the scissors." A big chunk of mud fell out of his hair and landed on Margaret's antique Persian rug.

She sighed. "You'd better go shower."

"Long shower? Short shower? How's the water situation?"

"The well is fine, the pump is working, the cistern's full, but I'm worried about propane, so don't linger."

He started up the stairs.

"And, um, Garik?"

He recognized that tone of voice. Warily he turned back.

"Wait a little before you go into the bathroom that you're sharing."

It took him a moment to realize what Margaret had done. "You put both Elizabeth and me in the Pacific Suite?"

"Why not?" Margaret leaned hard on the walker and looked up at him. "There are two bedrooms, one on ei-ther side of the living room."

"Heaven knows there are no other suites free in the resort."

Margaret laughed.

"You are a wicked old matchmaker," he said.

"A man and his wife should be together."

No use reminding Margaret they were divorced. She did not believe in divorce. "Until this is over, I'm going to stick close to Elizabeth," he told her.

"For a start, that will do very well," she said.

CHAPTER THIRTY-FOUR

Garik stepped into his room.

One door led into the connecting sitting room. Another led into the connecting bathroom. In there, he could hear water running, and he spared a moment to remember better times, when he would have stripped down and strolled in, and joined Elizabeth in the shower, and helped her wash . . . and made love to her . . . and helped her wash again.

She had said she equated him with an active sex life.

He was glad to hear that, because today, despite being furious that she'd returned to the canyon while aftershocks still rattled the area, he'd leaped on her.

He hadn't seen her in over a year, and within five minutes, he'd rolled her body underneath his and considered—no, not considered—had been *driven* to kiss her, to take her, there in the mud. No matter that the earth was unsteady beneath them and a tsunami could at any moment sweep in off the ocean.

Those geological forces were primitive, powerful, inexorable.

So was his need for her.

The shower turned off. He considered the fact that if he imagined her getting out, drying herself, gathering her clothes, and heading into her bedroom, it would be another long night alone with a spectacular erection. Then he imagined the whole scene anyway, because imagining Elizabeth nude was one of his favorite pastimes, exceeded only by getting Elizabeth nude and having great sex with Elizabeth . . . anytime, anywhere.

The jeans and T-shirt he'd worn to travel had been washed and laid out on his bed. He said a silent thank-you to the resort staff, waited until he heard the bathroom door open and close, and headed in.

The Pacific was one of Margaret's luxury suites. He would have never been placed in here if the resort was full . . . but Margaret must have seen the earthquake as a gift from God, for she'd certainly acted quickly and decisively to throw him together with his ex-wife. It had worked out well, though, because after their discovery today, Elizabeth shouldn't be alone.

The bathroom sported an enormous tub and shower done in waves of blue tile, the work of a local artist who had made her name working on the remodel of the inn. The resort's signature bergamot and cinnamon soap scented the lingering steam, and he saw Elizabeth had tried to clean up her trail of dried mud with her used towels.

He stripped off his clothes, adding a fair amount of mud to the floor. He showered quickly, dressed in his jeans and T-shirt, and headed downstairs. Sticking his head in the kitchen, he saw Harold speaking to the chef. "Thought you'd want to know—Elizabeth and I dropped mud like breadcrumbs all the way up to the Pacific Suite, and we made a mess of that bathroom."

Harold gave him a thumbs-up and went back to discussing how to transport the huge baked hams and pans of baked macaroni and cheese to the homeless shelter in town.

Garik stopped outside the library door and looked; Margaret sat in the high-backed, comfortable chair, Elizabeth on the broad, low couch. Both were sipping Irish whiskey on ice and chatting.

Elizabeth looked better, less pale and shocky, but still remote.

Margaret had a square-jawed, determined expression that boded ill for anyone who dared make Elizabeth miserable.

Seeing them together made him feel good, in a way he hadn't felt since Elizabeth had first told him she wanted a divorce. No, even before that—when he realized he'd managed to screw up his marriage, and didn't know how to fix it.

When he was a kid, Margaret had saved his life, probably literally.

As an adult, Elizabeth had lavished him with love.

They were the pillars of his life.

Not his job. Not the FBI.

Margaret and Elizabeth.

Somewhere along the line, he'd forgotten that, and he'd damned near killed himself over shit that didn't matter. Yes, he was a good agent, but he could move into a less stressful form of law enforcement, live a slower pace, be closer to Margaret and Elizabeth . . .

He was in control of his life. As they faced the events of the next days, that was something to remember.

Elizabeth turned her head, her white-blond hair like a halo around her head. She caught sight of him; her blue eyes widened, and she smiled as if the sight of him gave her pleasure.

And that gave *him* pleasure.

"Boyo! Come in here." Margaret rattled her ice. "It's been a hell of a week, and I need a refill."

He strolled in. "Trust you to sacrifice some of your ice for the cause."

"It's a good cause." Margaret's Irish accent came on strong.

He refreshed her drink.

Elizabeth shook her head and covered her glass.

He poured himself a red wine.

"One of the few bottles in the wine cellar that didn't break," Margaret told him darkly. "Thank you for using a stemless wine glass. If the earth's going to move again, we don't need red wine spilled on my antique rug."

Garik seated himself on the couch beside Elizabeth. He sipped the wine. "It's good. Of course it should be— it's a zinfandel from the Di Luca winery." He grinned wickedly at Margaret.

"I wouldn't know," she said haughtily. "I don't drink their wines."

Elizabeth swirled her glass and stared as if fascinated by the mix of icy water and whiskey.

Margaret looked to him in appeal.

So Garik addressed the elephant in the room. "Margaret, I always respect your opinions, especially about people. What do you remember about the Banner case, and Charles and Misty Banner?"

Margaret's jaw dropped.

Elizabeth straightened, and her eyes kindled with

interest. "Yes, Margaret, what do you remember? I've always wondered how the murder looked to the people who knew my parents. Were you surprised?"

Margaret snapped her mouth shut.

Garik raised his glass to her. He knew Elizabeth; he knew she would feel better trying to untangle the mystery of her father's rage and her mother's murder.

Margaret realized it now, too. "Everything about your parents surprised me. He was so much older and not sophisticated. Your mother was a Disney princess Barbie, shedding glamour like stardust wherever she went. She didn't even try to charm, she simply did. I mean, I liked her, and I don't normally like younger, taller, beautiful women." She gave her toothy, patented Margaret-smile.

"Did you think my father . . . ?" Elizabeth's voice trailed off as if she couldn't quite finish the thought.

"Did you think Charles Banner was the jealous type?" Garik asked for her.

"Not at all. I would swear it never occurred to him to think anything but the best of Misty. I admit, that summer when rumors started to swirl, I wondered what he would do. But I never thought what did occur . . . would occur."

"Back up." Garik wanted the chain of events laid out in order. "You met Charles and Misty when?"

"The year they moved here. In the spring, before the tourist season really hit, I had the scientific team to dinner. Misty was pregnant. Charles was proud. They seemed happy. Really happy." Margaret sipped her whiskey. "It's always a surprise and a pleasure to see that kind of affection between man and wife. It felt like . . . like they'd rescued each other."

"Rescued each other?" Elizabeth put down her drink. "From what?"

"I don't know," Margaret said. "It was just an impression, anyway. Then the tourist season hit, and I didn't see them again until after Elizabeth was born. I sent a gift, of course, a silver christening cup engraved with her name and date of birth."

"Did you?" Elizabeth looked delighted. "Thank you! My aunt kept it for me, one of the few things I have from . . . when I lived here."

"You're welcome. Every precious girl should have a gift to commemorate her birth." Margaret looked toward the door where Miklós stood dressed in a waiter's clothing. "Ah. Dinner is served. Shall we?"

Elizabeth got to Margaret before Garik could put down his glass.

Margaret smirked at him as Elizabeth helped her to her feet. "Some young people have manners," she told him. "I wish you had brought your wife to visit earlier, when I was younger and more spry."

He got to his feet. "When you were only ninety?"

Appalled, Elizabeth said, "Garik!"

Margaret leaned heavily on Elizabeth's arm and in a pitiful voice said, "He has always been cruel to this old woman."

Elizabeth thought about it for a minute, looked between Garik and Margaret. "You are joking. You don't care if he makes fun of your age."

"Well." Margaret put her hands on her walker. "The difference between ninety and ninety-one is about the same as the difference between passing gas and farting. It's semantics, and it all stinks."

Garik laughed at the expression on Elizabeth's face. Putting his arm around her, he said, "Margaret is known for her plain speaking." He smiled at Margaret. "And the older she gets, the plainer it is."

"Who's going to tell me no?" Margaret asked.

"Not me." Garik walked ahead of them into the dining room, held Margaret's chair.

As always, the dining room was immaculate, but rather than the usual white linen tablecloth, lit candles, and expensive place settings, the table was plainly set. For beneath Margaret's carefully acquired polish, she was an Irish chambermaid, practical to the bone, and Garik guessed that whatever remained of her crystal had been packed away until all the aftershocks had ceased and the resort could reopen.

Margaret groaned as she seated herself. "Earthquakes and old bones don't go together."

Garik pushed her chair in, then knelt beside her until she looked at him. "You'll tell me if there's something wrong with you, right?"

Margaret brushed his damp hair off his forehead. "You can't cure what's wrong with me, boy. Only the Grim Reaper can do that."

"And on that cheerful note," Harold said from the doorway, "Miklós will serve dinner."

CHAPTER THIRTY-FIVE

While Miklós served gazpacho and Garik poured wine, Margaret instructed Harold to pull up a chair and give her a report.

He seated himself. He stretched out his bad leg, rubbed his thigh, and informed her of the town's progress.

She told him to make sure none of her people took unnecessary risks or did too much, and when she said it, she sternly looked at *him*.

"I'm fine," Harold said with irritation. "If I didn't kill myself all those years ago with the drugs, I'm not going to die from a little hard work."

"I'll take it amiss if you do." For all that Margaret was a despot who expected perfection of her staff, she treated them as family, and fiercely protected them from harm.

Garik was proud to be part of her family.

"Have you received word of Kateri via the ham radio?" Harold asked.

"The doctors put her into an induced coma to keep her from moving, and to try and stop the internal bleeding," Margaret informed him.

Elizabeth's mouth trembled with anguish.

"We're praying for her." Harold put a bell beside Margaret's elbow, said, "Ring when you're ready for the entrée," herded Miklós out, and shut the door.

"I don't know what I'd do without that man." Margaret picked up her soup spoon. "He always handles everything, but he shines brightest during a disaster."

"Disaster seems life-changing. For me, it seems as if the earthquake broke me apart, and perhaps . . . when I put myself back together, this time all the pieces will be there." Elizabeth's gaze skated over Garik, dutifully eating the gazpacho, then returned to Margaret. "Please tell me more about your memories of my parents. I want to know how it all looked from the outside looking in."

Garik was glad she asked; when Foster said he hadn't reported all the evidence, that had reopened the investigation, and Garik needed as much insight as he could gain.

Margaret was warmly pleased. "Of course, dear girl. Glad to. Back then, Betsy, you were the apple of everyone's eye—smiling, outgoing, a chatterbox. The dinner with the scientific team became an annual event, and Charles and Misty were always there and seemed happy. I don't mean that everything was perfect. They were married. They argued. They completed each other's sentences and interrupted each other's stories. It was very *real*, if you know what I mean."

"Aunt Sandy said before my mother met my father, she was an actress." Elizabeth stroked the napkin in her lap, and stroked it again as if it couldn't be flat enough. "Maybe she was acting."

"Have you ever seen someone *act* happy? Eventually they slip. They *overact.*" Margaret rang the bell. "No, I flatter myself I can tell the difference."

Harold and Miklós whisked in, removed the bowls, and replaced them with the main course. Harold told them, "Miso-glazed salmon, rice pilaf, and roasted kale. Simple and delicious, so please enjoy, because with Chef dividing his time between the shelter and resort, he is fussing about the preparation."

"Tell him it looks wonderful," Elizabeth said warmly.

Garik tried to choke out some praise, but the words stuck in his throat.

"I know, Mr. Garik. You hate kale." Harold accepted a bowl of salad from Miklós and placed it beside Garik. "Here you go."

"Thank you!" Garik piled his kale onto Margaret's plate.

Margaret viewed the operation with a critical eye. "They spoil you, boy."

"Yes," Garik said. "I had forgotten how good it is to be Margaret's son."

"I never knew when I adopted him how much trouble he would be," Margaret said to Elizabeth.

"Then you weren't paying attention," Elizabeth answered.

Margaret looked startled, then laughed long and loud. "We'll get along fine, Elizabeth Banner Jacobsen."

Elizabeth opened her mouth to correct her on the last name, then shut her mouth again. She wasn't going to win this fight.

Harold shooed Miklós out and once again shut the door behind him.

Margaret, Garik, and Elizabeth ate in a companionable silence, and when they were done, Garik returned to the conversation. "Margaret, what happened to the marriage?"

Margaret pointedly looked over her eyeglasses at first him, then at Elizabeth. "That's what I've been wondering."

"The *Banner* marriage," Garik said in a deadpan voice.

Margaret faked surprise. "Oh, Charles and Misty's marriage . . . I don't know. That summer, rumors started to whirl that she had taken a lover." She spoke more softly, "Then she was dead."

With her fork, Elizabeth pushed what remained of her food around her plate. "My father was always assumed to be the killer. Did no one suspect the lover?"

Margaret shook her head. "No one knew who the lover was."

"Elizabeth's got a point, and a good one," Garik said. "Was there no attempt to discover his identity?"

"Before the murder? Everyone watched and wondered. After the murder . . . whoever it was slipped away." With a clink, Margaret put her fork down. "You have to realize what the photo did to the case. It was so visually damning. In those days, not everybody had a camera on them all the time. But the Banners' postman was an amateur photographer. While he made his rounds, he kept an expensive camera with him. He took arty coast-line photos and sold them to tourists, and made a good amount on the side. As Charles walked out of the house, the postman drove up. Charles was holding Betsy and the scissors, and both he and the child were covered in blood. The postman took the picture."

Elizabeth looked as if she was holding her breath, hoping for a different resolution.

"Bad luck for Charles," Garik said.

"That picture was so visceral it made the front page of every national paper and the cover of every news magazine. When the country saw it, it made its decision. Without a good lawyer, which Charles did not have, he never stood a chance with a jury. Personally, Charles was the last man I would have ever thought could murder any-one, much less his wife." Margaret looked back and forth between Garik and Elizabeth. "But I know Garik would tell us the neighbors say that about every serial killer and child pornographer."

"Not all of them. Some serial killers are damned weird." Something niggled at Garik. "What did the postal worker do after he snapped the photo?"

"He drove to the nearest neighbor's and called nine-one-one," Margaret said.

Garik's mouth curled with disdain. "He thought Charles had murdered his wife and was going to kill his daughter, and he ran away."

"I didn't say he was an admirable man, only that he took the photo." Margaret rang her bell.

Dessert and coffee arrived via Harold, and to a grim silence.

Garik stood and took the tray. "We'll manage. You go and eat, and rest."

"The staff is back, so we've had our dinner." Harold gave his report to Margaret. "They tell me that in Virtue Falls, the chaos is coming under control."

"Thank you, Harold." Margaret took her tea from Garik. "And thank the staff for me."

"Right now, they're grateful to have a place to stay," Harold said.

"Then we're helping each other." Margaret nodded at him.

He nodded back, and left.

Garik poured himself and Elizabeth coffee, put the pastries in the center of the table—

"Frozen," Margaret sniffed.

—and rummaged in the drawer in the antique buffet until he found a small, battered spiral notebook. "Are we sure there was a lover?" he asked.

"I was sure at the time. For those summer months, Misty had that shiny *I'm in love* look about her." Margaret's hand had a tremor as she poured her tea. "Top on my list for the candidates? Andrew Marrero."

Elizabeth's intake of breath was shocked and audible.

Margaret's eyebrows rose. "Surely you realized he fancies himself a ladies' man?"

"No, but I don't hang with him," Elizabeth said. "I see him on site."

Garik found a battered pen advertising the resort, seated himself, and started his list. "Andrew Marrero . . . Elizabeth, he's never put the moves on you?"

"Please understand, I'm good at what I do. But he always seems annoyed with me." Elizabeth spread her hands in puzzlement.

Good. He can live. But Garik said nothing, merely sat with pen poised.

"Write down Dr. Frownfelter," Margaret said.

"He . . . really?" Elizabeth seemed astonished. "I met him yesterday morning at the Memory Care Facility. He seemed really old." Elizabeth wrinkled her nose. "Older than my father, so definitely too old for Misty."

Margaret added cream and sugar to her tea and stirred gently. "Not long after Misty's murder, his wife of twenty-five years divorced him, citing infidelity. Dr. Frownfelter let her have whatever she wanted, and he moved away. Then I heard he was working at the penitentiary where Charles Banner was imprisoned."

"Now, *that's* interesting." Garik filed the information away as something that warranted investigation.

Elizabeth cleared her throat. "He said he was my mother's doctor, and he delivered me. That was weird. Sort of TMI, although I don't know why."

"The doctor made you uneasy." Garik made a note. "Margaret, anyone else on the list of potential lovers?"

Margaret said testily, "Misty Banner was a woman that every man wanted. It's not a question of who wanted her. It would be easier to ask who didn't."

"Okay." Garik could go at it in that direction, too. "Who didn't want her?"

"Dennis Foster."

Garik turned to Elizabeth. "I told you. No sex drive at all."

"I believed you!" Elizabeth said.

"Foster hadn't been elected sheriff yet, and he was trying to impress the constituency as an upright law officer, a man who cared for his ailing mother, never drank, and didn't cavort with the wild women. Or even the tame ones." Margaret lowered her eyelids to hide her scornful gleam. "A man should have a few vices. If he doesn't, either he's a saint, or he's hiding something."

"What's he hiding?" Elizabeth asked.

Garik noted she didn't for a moment consider that Foster could be a saint.

"I never have figured it out," Margaret said, "but I know if you turned over the rock that hides his soul, you'd find it crawling with worms."

To Garik, Elizabeth said matter-of-factly, "You might add Rainbow . . . who likes me a little too much. It's interesting. She protects me like I'm a chick to her hen." She saw that Margaret and Garik gaped at her. "I'm not saying she killed my mother, only that she should be on the list for possible lovers."

Garik made a note, and took a pastry that oozed cheesecake filling. "She's a tall woman with broad shoulders, capable of overwhelming another woman."

"The Native American, Stag Denali. He's rich, he's powerful, he's ruthless. But . . . he likes women. He likes me, and while I know it's hard to believe, some men don't value an outspoken woman." Margaret's eyes gleamed with humor.

"Some men need quiet, submissive women to make them feel important." Elizabeth took a bite of her lemon tartlet.

"I like quiet, submissive women—or I would if I knew any." Garik poured himself another cup of coffee. Later, when he was awake all night, he would be sorry. But right now, sugar slid through his veins, caffeine percolated in his brain, and he felt as if he had found the Garik Jacobsen who solved crimes like crossword puzzles . . .

He had found himself again.

"Misty's lover had to have a flexible schedule." Margaret drummed the table. "No eight-to-five job would do it, because Charles worked during the daytime hours, and the rest of the time, he was a homebody. So . . . Bradley Hoff."

"The artist. Yes." Elizabeth nodded. "I've met him. He told me he knew my mother. She and my father took his art class."

Garik went on alert. "Why would Bradley Hoff give an art class? He's rich."

"Not in those days. In those days, his paintings were intense, deep, unnerving. Powerful stuff. Compelling work. I urged him to continue, to delve into men's souls, to take the more difficult road to fame. But he opted for instant money." Margaret smiled. "I'm not judging him. I did whatever it took to get ahead, too, and if you look into his background, you'll discover he was an only child of wealthy parents. Art commanded no respect from his family. He bucked a lot of pressure, got cut out of the will for being an artist."

"Poor baby," Garik said sarcastically.

"It takes strength of will to progress, knowing you're going to lose your family." Margaret clearly admired Hoff. "He was very handsome, which made his art class more popular than one might expect."

Elizabeth broke into a smile. "In my scrapbook, I have some of my parents' drawings. They both were very good."

"Okay, fine," Garik said. "Why would *Charles* take an art class?"

"To make his wife happy," Margaret said promptly.

Elizabeth gave a different answer. "In the past, before cameras and cell phones, when field researchers came across a plant or a rock formation that warranted documentation, sketching was the only way to capture the evidence. Sketching is still much valued in the scientific community. It has cachet."

"But nonetheless I think Charles did it to indulge Misty. Her mother died that winter." Margaret's mouth drooped. "Misty came back from the funeral restless and wounded. For a long time afterward, Charles was assiduous, but Misty worked hard to present him with the appearance of being fine—"

"Why?" Garik asked. "Why lie?"

"She wasn't lying. Sometimes not saying what you feel is easier than trying to explain." When Elizabeth realized what she'd revealed, and to who, her eyes opened wide, and her mouth snapped shut.

But Margaret drove the point home. "Women are like that. Sometimes it's hard to explain emotions. And sometimes *men*"—she said the word like an insult—"who really don't have a clue, will scoff, and that hurts."

Garik knew Margaret was talking about him, and that pissed him off, because maybe he wasn't at fault for every damned thing that ever went wrong between a man and a woman in every marriage that ever existed. "Got it. Charles drifted back to his dig. It was summer, he worked long hours. Misty was alone and in emotional turmoil. Even I, Mr. Insensitive, can see the setup for tragedy."

The conversation went dead. Margaret and Elizabeth looked away.

Garik supposed he should apologize. But he *wasn't* a jerk. He *would* have been understanding if Elizabeth had told him what she felt. He would have. If she'd told him. And he was pretty sure all she'd said was that she wanted Garik to talk about his tortured past.

Yeah. Like that was going to happen.

This past year, he had suffered, too. Maybe these women who valued emotions and shit should realize he had put a fucking gun in his mouth, and the only thing that had stopped him from shooting his brains out was the earthquake and the compulsion to care for Margaret and Elizabeth, the same two women who were now making him miserable.

Nervously Elizabeth tapped her spoon against the table. She watched it intently, finally cleared her throat and said, "My aunt said their mother went crazy after Misty married my father, and killed herself with drugs and alcohol."

Okay. They were going to talk about the case again. Good.

"Sometimes a woman experiences more grief over a bad mother than a good one." When both Garik and Elizabeth would have objected, Margaret held up one hand. "Mothers, good and bad, wield a mighty influence. With the death of a bad mother, a woman swallows a potent cocktail of guilt and unhappiness that is straight poison."

"So you think Misty had an affair because her mother's death screwed her up?" Garik knew a parent could totally ruin a kid's life. Look at him—exhibit A. "Then it follows that someone realized she was vulnerable—"

Margaret interrupted, "And that Charles was oblivious."

"—and her lover moved in to claim what he wanted." Elizabeth rubbed her forehead with her fingertips. Rubbed her forehead as if the brief confrontation with Garik had given her a headache.

"We have a personality type—the predator." Garik stood and made his way to the liquors. "Could be Bradley Hoff."

"But if Hoff killed my mother," Elizabeth said, "it seems odd to tell me that he knew her."

Garik unwrapped the brandy from the towel that protected it from aftershocks. "Not if there are people who know he knew her."

"There's one other person who can shed insight into

the case." Margaret turned to Elizabeth. "What does your father remember? Has he talked about the past at all?"

"He told me about meeting my mother. His memories seemed realistic."

"Any information he could give us would be helpful." Garik brought snifters to the table, placed one in front of Margaret and one in front of Elizabeth, and seated himself again. "Does he remember in bits and pieces, or in chunks?"

"I've only visited him twice, so I really haven't . . ." Elizabeth's voice trailed off, and with careful precision she folded her napkin and placed it on the table.

"I thought that was why you moved up here. To get to know him and figure out what happened and why." Garik had thought it was a dumb idea, but when she made her decision, the divorce had been very, very final and she hadn't asked his opinion.

"Not . . . exactly. Well, yes. But he . . ." Elizabeth swallowed. "It's difficult."

"Difficult?" Margaret exploded with vibrant, Irish indignation. "When are relatives not difficult? He's your father. This is your only chance to get to know him. He has Alzheimer's, and you haven't got much time to do it!"

"He thinks I'm my mother. When he doesn't think that, he talks to the *ghost* of my mother." Elizabeth spoke too fast, too defensively. "And he scares me . . . I remember him with those scissors."

"You remember? I thought you didn't remember at all," Garik said.

"It might be the photo. The one in the paper. Maybe I've seen it so often that's what I remember. I don't know. Sometimes I wish I knew the truth, but most of the time I wish I had never started this. What difference does it make why Charles Banner killed my mother? She's still dead. Nothing can change any of that." Elizabeth was magnificently defiant . . .

. . . For all the good it did her in Margaret's eyes. "Suck it up, girl!" Margaret said. "When you came to Virtue Falls, you as good as told everyone that you intended to find out the truth behind Misty Banner's murder."

"I did not!" Elizabeth sniffed. "I know it's a surprise to a lot of people in Virtue Falls, but my father's study is important, and it's an honor to work on it."

"An honor you were willing to forego until Charles Banner was diagnosed with Alzheimer's and sent here to live out the rest of his life! But you're too afraid to visit him." Margaret didn't *look* over the top of her glasses at Elizabeth—she *glared*. "I expected better of you, Elizabeth."

Elizabeth squared her jaw. "I do the best I can, Margaret, but sometimes I feel I'm lacking certain social skills." She stood. "Now I am exhausted. If you'll excuse me, I'm going to bed."

CHAPTER THIRTY-SIX

Garik stood, too, and remained on his feet as Elizabeth left the room.

Margaret pursed her lips. "I may have been a little rough on her. After the day she had, I mean."

"I think so. Yeah." Garik sat down again. "But you made a good point. If Charles Banner is not Misty Banner's murderer, and the guilty party is still around, then the one reason Elizabeth has remained safe is that she hasn't visited her father and asked questions."

Margaret absorbed the information. "We're fooked no matter what we do."

"Succinctly put," Garik said.

"But she needs to go before it's too late. Charles hasn't got a lot of time before his mind is gone. I've seen it before, lost friends this way. Lost them . . . when they were sitting right in front of me." Sorrow echoed in Margaret's voice. Then she sounded brisker. "As long as you're here, Elizabeth's safe."

"If I stay with her every second."

"Yes," Margaret said with satisfaction. "Do that. Do we have any real reason to believe that Charles *wasn't* the murderer?"

"No. Foster ran a flawed investigation, but that doesn't mean the conclusions were wrong." Garik waved a hand that encompassed the day, the dining room, and their discussion.

"What's your gut tell you?"

"Absolutely nothing." He put his hand on his belly to quiet any rumblings. "Last time I listened to my gut, I got thrown out of the FBI."

Margaret's smile faded. "But your gut wasn't wrong then."

She believed he had done the right thing, God bless her. "If only I had thought it through . . . But I was so angry . . ." His eyes burned with anguish.

Margaret touched his cheek. "Don't let the guilt eat you up."

"Why not? I deserve every drop of guilt." He knew what she was going to say next. She would urge him to go to confession, to seek an absolution he didn't deserve. So he stood again. "I'll take you up to your room."

She watched him with troubled eyes as he helped her to her feet, swung her into his arms, and headed toward the stairs, up, and into her bedroom.

She pointed at the chair. "There. Vicky will help me get ready for bed."

"In a minute." He placed her, then seated himself on the ottoman. "Did Bradley ever paint Misty?"

"Not that I know of. In those days, he was deeply involved with Vivian. She had money, and an art gallery—he needed both—but she didn't want to leave New Orleans, and he had to be here to paint."

"Whether or not he was involved with Vivian, he still could have had an affair with Misty."

"Yes, but Bradley was brooding. Intense. He didn't seem a fit for Misty. She always smiled. She always made you feel better. She was like . . . sunshine." Margaret looked uncomfortable. "I really did like her. And it's possible that Charles did kill her. I didn't want to say so in front of Elizabeth, but I was there when that bitch Louisa Foster told him about the affair."

"Louisa Foster . . . Dennis Foster's mother?"

"She was—is—one of those holier-than-thou women, pillar of her church, mean little eyes that watch and judge. She didn't get married until she was well into her thirties, and her husband died when Foster was a little boy. I figured the husband dropped dead to get away from her."

"I remember her." And not fondly.

"That scene . . . I'll never forget it." Margaret bunched her bony fists in her lap. "It was lunchtime. She walked into the Oceanview Café where Charles was talking to his team. She stood on the other end of the table, and announced he was the laughingstock of Virtue Falls. He looked bewildered, which made her madder, so she got louder. She told him his wife was running around on him, and when he couldn't seem to comprehend, she got into his face and said that Misty had taken a lover, someone younger and handsomer than Charles, and Misty was spending all the time Charles was at work having disgusting sex."

"It sounds as if she knew who Misty's lover was." And if she knew, Garik could find out.

But Margaret quashed that hope. "If she had, she would have outed them both. When she saw sin, she took it upon herself to repair the situation."

"So was Louisa after Charles in particular?"

"Not Charles. Misty. Misty treated Louisa kindly. As if Louisa was someone to feel sorry for. Which Louisa liked because the woman is a world-class hypochondriac. Until!" Margaret raised a finger. "One time, Louisa was railing against this young tourist couple who got caught doing the wild thing in a car—railing at them to their poor, mortified faces—and Misty defended them. *Then* Louisa's minister agreed with Misty and chided Louisa in public. I think the man despised her and welcomed the chance to knock her down a few notches. It rebounded on him, of course—within a year, Louisa got him ousted from the job and he and his family had to leave Virtue Falls. And Misty's actions rebounded on Charles, because after that, Louisa was gunning for them both. Louisa told Charles his wife was a whore who corrupted their young child and daily betrayed him, and if he was a real man he would go home and kill her, and then kill himself for being so weak and gullible. Nasty old harridan."

"What did you do during this whole scene?" Garik asked.

"I sat there with my mouth hanging open, just like

everyone else. Finally, when it was too late, I intervened, but Louisa had dragged herself off her perpetual death-bed to make Charles miserable and nothing short of a bazooka could have stopped her." Margaret had one helluva temper, and her faded blue eyes now gleamed with fury.

"Charles believed her?"

"Not at first. Not until he looked around the café and nobody could meet his eyes. It wasn't Louisa who convinced him. It was the rest of us, and our guilty faces." As she remembered, Margaret's face *was* guilty.

"What did he do?"

"He got furious. He . . . turned colors. Have you ever seen someone who is normally pretty calm get mad? Really mad? A tide of red rose up over his cheeks and flooded his forehead. His eyes got bright and hot. I swear his jaws popped, he had them clenched so tightly. He put his fists on the table and hoisted himself to his feet like he *was* going to kill someone. We were all voting for Louisa, and she thought so, too, because she backed up, first slowly, then faster and faster. But he strode around her like she was unworthy of his attention, and left." Margaret lifted a hand and helplessly let it drop. "And for over three hours while Misty was killed and her body hidden, he went somewhere where he had no alibi."

"Shit."

"Exactly."

"Where did he say he'd gone?" Garik vaguely remembered, but vaguely was as good as it got.

"One of the digs."

"None of the team were there, because they were all in town." Garik rubbed his forehead. "Do you remember anything else about the case? Anything of interest? Anything at all?"

"I was there for that one moment. Everything else I know was hearsay."

"At least I trust you as a source. After so long, most people don't remember what really happened, only what was reported." He stood. "With a mother like that, no wonder Foster is such a self-righteous prick."

"He didn't have to take Louisa's teachings as his own. He could have moved out, married, had kids, been normal." Margaret leaned forward and locked eyes with him. "I might not know what happened between Charles and Misty, but I know Dennis Foster is odd, especially in these last few years. I've seen him in his patrol car, parked on a highway turnout, sitting and staring."

"Sitting and staring?"

"Out the windshield. Every Sunday I drive myself to church—"

"Very slowly?"

"More slowly than I used to," she allowed. "Which is why I've noticed him. Once I stopped and asked if I could help him, and he told me he had been making a call. I didn't believe him. To get his attention, I had to tap on his window."

"A cop, and he didn't realize you were there?"

Margaret nodded.

"All right," Garik said wryly. "You win. My gut is talking to me, and it's telling me there's more to this case than any of us have ever realized."

CHAPTER THIRTY-SEVEN

It was one in the morning when at last Dennis Foster pulled up in front of the darkened single-story rambler he shared with his mother. He stopped the car. Shut off the engine. Took a long breath.

Three days since the earthquake, and this was his first time home.

He got out, slammed the car door—and he knew his mother had heard. She had the hearing of a hawk, and used words like talons. He knew she now waited in her big chair with her arms crossed, her mouth pinched, and her eyes narrowed.

God, how he hated the flutter deep in his belly as he walked up to the front door and stood, afraid to go in. All his life, his mother had made a coward of everyone. But more than anyone in the world, she had made a coward of him.

That's why he had gone into law enforcement. That's why he was a master marksman with every kind of firearm. That's why he learned self-defense and how to fight with his fists. He had to prove to everyone that he was the bravest man in the county.

Unfortunately, he had never succeeded in convincing himself.

No matter how often he told himself she couldn't harm him, no matter how often he swore he would face her with indifference, he always cringed at the sight of that skinny, rigid figure, at the sound of that high, cruel voice.

But there was nothing for it. He had to go in.

For three whole days, he'd left her alone. He hadn't gone to check on her. He hadn't sent any of his deputies in his place. Of course, every one of his deputies would defy him and refuse to come to the house. One encounter with Mother was enough for anyone.

But Dennis was her son.

He ought to be ashamed of himself; Mother would soon tell him he should be ashamed of himself. He supposed if everyone in town ever found out he had left his mother alone for so long after that earthquake, they would also say he should be ashamed of himself.

He wasn't.

He had his excuses. His duties as sheriff had kept him busy. The disaster took precedence. And he knew if he went home, he would spend his time helping Mother pick up the thousands of religious knickknacks she collected to hang on walls and place on shelves.

He had better things to do. And she wasn't as sick as she pretended. Once she realized he wasn't coming home, she would pick up a broom and sweep away the debris. If there was one thing he could depend on, it was that she'd clean the house. Cleanliness was next to godliness.

How many times in his lifetime had he heard that?

Once or twice in the last seventy-two hours he might have wondered if she had been hurt in the quake—the neighbors detested her, so there was no one to check— but about the time he figured he had to send somebody to investigate, she texted him. And she called. And texted. And called.

He refused to answer the calls, which made her texts terse and threatening.

Come.

Come home.

You'll be sorry.

He was already sorry.

At last he put his key in the lock and opened the door.

Usually as soon as he opened the door, she was yapping at him about something. Tonight, he heard nothing.

So Mother was refusing to talk to him.

In so many ways, that was even worse than her nagging.

He walked into the darkened house.

The breeze whispered in his face; the windows were broken. Yet when he shined his flashlight around the living room, the place looked pretty good. All the walls were standing, all the furniture was upright. Except for the crosses and pictures of Jesus scattered across the floor, the house had sustained very little damage.

Not even God dared mess with his mother.

Ceramic and glass crunched under his feet as he walked through the living room. So she hadn't cleaned up. Maybe he'd misread her, or maybe . . . The silence was so ominous that he surrendered, and spoke first. "Mother, I'm home."

No answer.

He headed for her bedroom.

He groped for the light switch, couldn't find it for the junk that still clung to the wall, then remembered it didn't matter since Virtue Falls had no power.

Damn, that was a hard thing to get used to. He hoped to hell the power company arrived pretty soon; citizens were starting to complain to *him* about their lack of electricity, and when he explained the sheriff had no jurisdiction in this matter, they told him to do something anyway.

The moon was out, shining brightly through the windows, but he shone his flashlight around the room, hoping to blind her with the beam. Childish and petty, he knew, but her eternal whining and constant reproaches had been his main meal for almost fifty years. Nothing he did made her happy.

Mother wasn't seated in her big chair or propped up on the pillows on the bed.

Hunger must have driven her to get up and rummage around in the kitchen for "a few crackers and a dry prune," which according to her were all she survived on when he wasn't home, never mind the cans of soup and tuna he found tucked in the bottom of the garbage can.

He walked into the kitchen, stepped in a puddle of something wet, and grabbed for the counter. "What the hell . . . ?" He shone the light around.

The damage was here. The kitchen was trashed. The upper cabinets on one wall had shaken loose and smashed onto the counter, each spilling its contents. At the end of the kitchen, the refrigerator had tipped over, slamming into the countertops opposite. Canned goods, food, silverware, dishes were everywhere.

And where was his mother? In the utility? The other bedroom? Had she left the house?

He started to turn away, and heard a scrabbling noise, like a rodent.

He shoved his way through the stuff on the linoleum, shining his light back and forth—and found her.

Mother. Sprawled on the floor, the open refrigerator door resting on her back, cutting her in half, blood congealed underneath her. She scratched blindly with her fingernails at her cell phone. When he shined the light directly on her, she feebly turned her head from one side to the other, but she didn't open her eyes.

She wasn't really conscious anymore.

He stood over the top of her, feeling nothing. Feeling numb.

At last he dropped to his knees beside her. He felt for her pulse; her heart still beat.

But she felt cool to the touch.

In a somber voice, he said, "Oh, Mother. So this is the end at last."

CHAPTER THIRTY-EIGHT

Garik moved like a wraith into Elizabeth's bedroom.

Elizabeth's bedroom matched Garik's own—a richly textured gray carpet on the floor, blue satin drapes, a king-sized bed with tall bedposts, draped with silver gauze. Outside, the waves played music as they caressed the cliffs, tossed the pebbles on the beach, filled the tidal pools and drained them again. Inside, the half-moon slipped through the open windows like the pale scent of jasmine, perfuming the furnishings, the curtains, and especially Elizabeth's sleeping figure, clad in a white T-shirt, sprawled under the white sheet.

The scene was pure romance . . . for all the good it did Garik.

He was here for one thing—Elizabeth's phone.

It rested facedown on the bedside table, and when he picked it up and checked, it showed full bars.

Yes, the area was recovering in fits and starts.

Good thing. He needed information. He needed to burrow into the Banner case and find out the truth.

He didn't want to look down at her, but he couldn't resist, and his heart twanged as if it caught on a string of emotion. When it came to Elizabeth, his soul sang a country-western song. One of the morose tunes, about a lost love, a cold, lonely house, and way too much guilt because it was all his fault.

He couldn't resist dropping to his knees, either, nor brushing a lock of her white-blond hair off her cheek. She moaned slightly, and turned her head into his hand. He closed his eyes as his fingers absorbed the warmth of her, as her smooth skin tempted him to continue touching . . .

Elizabeth was beautiful, ethereal.

Elizabeth was earthy, practical.

So was his need for her.

From the night he'd first seen her—her pale complexion, her platinum blond hair, her wide blue eyes, the dimple in her chin, that sinful mouth—she had been desirable. From the first moment he'd heard her voice, listened to her expound so logically, realized she was hiding a wounded soul so similar to his—she had been his mate.

Nothing could change that. Not even a divorce.

How had they gone so wrong? The first year had been dusted with gold. Then they settled down to real life, discovered their differences were greater than their similarities, and the marriage had chilled, become disapproval on his part, unhappiness and worry on hers. And no talk.

His fault, he thought, because for all that his earliest years had sucked rocks, when he was eight, Margaret had taken him in, showed him how to have a loving relationship, filled him in on the emotional stuff he didn't understand. Even now, he couldn't remember if the chasm between Elizabeth and him had opened all at once, or slowly over the months, only that it was suddenly irrevocable, impossible to cross, and painful. So painful.

His fault the marriage didn't work. Because yeah, he could open up with an FBI-approved psychiatrist and share all the ugly, nitty-gritty horrors of his early life, but with Elizabeth, it hadn't been simple. It mattered. He feared that if he showed her his old scars, she would tell him to get over it, to grow up, to stop whining.

Then his soul would have bled to death.

How did it make sense that with the one person he wanted to be close to, he didn't even try?

It didn't.

Yet there it was.

She breathed heavily as she always did for those first few hours when nothing could wake her except possibly . . . an earthquake.

He bent down to her and pressed his nose to her hair.

The resort's bergamot and cinnamon fragrance scented her, of course, but richer and warmer was the scent of Elizabeth, complex, clever, kind, and his.

He wanted her. He wanted to kiss her, wake her slowly to his touch, hold her under him and stake his claim.

Because, damn it, the one thing that had always worked for them was the sex. Standing, sitting, lying down, upside down. Fucking and making love. Being wild and being sweet. The best sex ever.

He lifted his head, and his hand.

The best sex, and the worst relationship.

Yet although their relationship had sucked, she still cared for him. Why else would she tell him, *You're one of the good guys?* Why would she bother? For the husband she'd chosen to leave?

Without even knowing the whole story, she had tried to make him feel better. She had tried to make him stop blaming himself.

Funny thing was . . . he almost felt as if he could breathe easier. Almost.

With a sigh, he touched her cheek one more time,

and stood. He retrieved her phone, and returned to the suite, leaving the bedroom door half-closed to shield her from the light, and half-open so he could hear her if she cried.

He downloaded the app to set up the router, opened his computer, and got online. As soon as the Internet lit up, he gave a sigh of relief. It had been claustrophobic, being confined on all accounts to Virtue Falls, especially when he needed information, especially when—

A million e-mails, give or take a hundred thousand, popped up.

Crap. Never mind what he'd thought about being claustrophobic. He didn't need his penis enlarged, or to be thinner. He didn't need more hair on his head or anywhere else, and he sure as hell didn't need to hear from Tom Perez, his supervisor at the FBI, demanding to know where he was. Garik scanned the increasingly urgent subject lines, picked one at random, and opened it.

"Ah." It was actually kind of sweet.

In between the stern demands that Garik report in, the sharp questions about why he'd missed his last psychiatrist's appointment, the temper tantrum about him taking advantage of Perez's sweet disposition, ran a real concern.

Come on, man, I need to hear from you. I went to your house to see where you were. Neighbors wanted to know if you were one of the Ten Most Wanted and I was hunting you, which doesn't say much for your social skills. They said you were a loner and went tearing out of here four days ago and they haven't seen you since. You left a pistol on the coffee table, for shit's sake. You're not supposed to own a pistol. Check in, damn you. Check in.

Garik wiggled his two index fingers, his typing fingers, and went to work. *You were in my house. Breaking and entering is a crime, too.*

Thirty seconds later. *You son-of-a-bitch. Am I glad to hear from you. Where the fuck are you?*

Virtue Falls, Washington, home of the biggest, baddest earthquake ever.

I hoped that was it. Your old granny okay?

She's not my granny, and she's fine. So's my ex, thank you for asking.

Hunky wonderful.

Nobody could do sarcasm as well as Tom.

His e-mail continued: *Your phone is going right to voice mail. Scared the shit out of me. Virtue Falls is preferable to you offing yourself, and the way that psychiatrist was talking, I thought you really had turned into your father and done the deed.*

Garik winced. Perez never minced words . . . and he was way too close to the truth.

Now get your ass back here.

Can't. Roads are impassable.

You got there. You can get back.

Sure. Right after I clear up a few things. Any chance we could move to the secure network for this?

I dunno—can you tell me my wife's name?

Your ex? Lorena Bobbit. Good thing I saved you that night before she—

Let me see what I can do.

Garik didn't know how, but a minute later, the software appeared on his monitor.

He clicked on it. It asked for his password. He asked for a hint. His question was, *What's the name of Tom's best friend?* He didn't even have to think. *Dick Mole.*

The password said no. Then it disappeared, and a message popped up.

My dick may be my best friend, but do we have to talk about my mole? You wouldn't even have seen it if you hadn't come to untie me that time when Lorena tried to cut it off.

Trust me. I have tried to forget. Now . . . ever hear of the Banner murder case?

You're in fucking Washington State investigating a thirty-year-old murder case?

Twenty-three years old. My ex and I found Misty Banner's body today.

Okay.

It's my ex's mother.

The answer was a lot slower coming this time. *That is interesting. But Garik, you're confined to Nevada unless you receive FBI permission to leave.*

So give me permission. Because there was something about the body that didn't get reported. Misty Banner's hair was cut off.

Wasn't reported? Are you sure?

The local sheriff who handled the case admitted he didn't think reporting the hairs he found on site was important.

You're trying to distract me.

No, I'm trying to see if the guy who got convicted of the murder really was the killer. The sheriff is a loser . . . C'mon, Tom. It's Elizabeth's father.

She's your ex. I'd be thrilled if I could make my ex miserable.

Ever seen my ex?

The blond in the photo on your desk? Yeah. Never mind.

Charles Banner has Alzheimer's. Memory is going fast. Give me access to the FBI files.

Give you access? I can't fucking give you access. Pause. *But I'll send you everything the FBI has.*

You old softie.

Shut up, asshole, and keep the fuck in touch. It's the only way I'll keep the boys in DC from using your guts for garters.

Garik grinned and waited.

In five minutes, the file arrived in his e-mail in-box with a pithy *You're welcome.*

Aloud, Garik said, "Thank you, Tom."

The pages were pretty much as he had told Elizabeth. Typed on a typewriter, filed for years in a manila folder, scanned when the techs got around to it, haphazardly, most times not even square on the page. Even more than Garik remembered, the case was Foster's one-man show. Garik would bet that Foster made sure no surprises occurred, that Charles Banner was convicted and Foster was a hero.

To figure out anything different would require access to the evidence . . . or a chance to examine Misty Banner's body. And the latter, perhaps, could be arranged. After all, Garik had pretty much grown up in this town.

He looked up the name of the coroner.

Heh, heh. He'd gone to high school with Mike Sun. He'd done favors for Mike, like at prom, after Mike got dumped, Garik had taken him drinking. When Mike went on a crying jag, Garik had held him over a bridge and shaken him until he barfed. Then he had delivered him to Mrs. Sun, who thanked him, led her son into the house, shut the door—and yelled so loud the windows rattled.

Yeah. Garik had connections with Mike Sun.

He started to type up an e-mail request to Mike, realized he had Internet access and probably no one else did, and there was a good chance phone service at the county morgue was still out, too. He'd have to go down there and—

From Elizabeth's bedroom, he heard a muffled sound, like someone straining to run away.

In a flash, he was on his feet. He pushed open the door and in the light, saw her thrashing at the covers in grip of an agonizing nightmare. He ran to her bedside. Kneeling, he pulled her close.

She was sweating.

He petted her head and murmured, "It's okay. I've got you. You're safe. Elizabeth, I won't let anyone hurt you."

She woke up with a start and looked into his face in stark terror.

He thought she was going to scream.

Then recognition lit her face, and she burrowed into his chest as if he was her only refuge in a terrifying world.

CHAPTER THIRTY-NINE

Elizabeth always woke early, and this time when she did, she was on her back, staring at the ceiling, wrapped in a man's arms. Garik's arms.

He was snoring in her ear.

He had a nice, even rhythm, not too loud, very relaxing for a woman who had spent too many silent nights assuring herself the divorce had been the right thing to do.

Cautiously she turned her head and looked.

He always said he was a light sleeper, but she'd never seen evidence of that. Usually she saw him as he was right now, deeply unconscious, uncaring about anything but getting his Zs. His dark lashes pressed against the hollows beneath his eyes . . . he really was too thin and tired looking. Still attractive, of course . . . Actually, he was gorgeous with his longer blond hair. But she knew she was prejudiced, especially when she was looking at his lips. He had those vampiric I'm-going-to-suck-on-you lips, and the sucking she imagined had nothing to do with her neck and everything to do with prowling, primitive sex. Also prize and primal and a few other *p* words she couldn't remember right now.

None of which had happened last night, because he was still fully clothed, and she still wore her panties.

Too bad. Last night, if she'd been asked to vote, she would have been in favor of him taking advantage of her.

She had always liked watching him sleep. When he was awake, he protected himself with smiles, with frowns, with jokes, with dinner invitations and kisses and good sex. But when he was asleep, all barriers went down, and she could pretend he was hers, and that she knew him inside and out. That had been the fantasy, and far too fragile for the light of day.

Sometimes when she had a nightmare, he held her close, as he was doing now. Which was good, because she definitely remembered last night's nightmares. She also remembered the other door in the suite, the one that led to another bedroom.

Had Margaret put him in there? Had he moved himself in?

It didn't matter. He was here, and last night, she had needed him.

She looked back up at the ceiling, and sighed. Nightmares were to be expected, she supposed. Finding a decomposing body would always be an unsettling experience. Finding her mother's body . . . In a sudden, childish reflex, she whimpered and rubbed her fists at her eyes.

Garik woke immediately, proving he actually *was* a light sleeper. "Hey." He took her hand and kissed it. "You okay?"

It took her a moment to organize a sensible answer. "I am. In this case, distress is to be expected, and will fade with time."

"It'll never fade all the way," he said with assurance, as if he knew what he was talking about.

"I wish it would."

"No, you don't. It's your mother. You don't want to forget her as if she had never existed."

"But I have forgotten her. To me, she's nothing but a picture in my scrapbook." No matter how painful, that was irrefutable logic.

"Somewhere deep in the recesses of your mind, she's there. She made you who you are." His warm green eyes closed as he kissed her forehead. "So I thank her for that."

A lovely sentiment. Elizabeth remembered why she had liked him.

"What did you dream?" he asked.

Her pleasant feelings faded. "Stupid dream."

"They usually are, like the one where my elephant crosses the street, steps on my foot, buys a Coke at the vending fireplace, takes a drink, snorts it through her nose, and turns into Tim Conway." He looked totally serious.

"You've had that dream?"

"Sure."

"Me, too."

He grinned at her. "So last night, what did you dream?"

One of the things she hated about Garik was the way he latched onto something and never let go. He would bug her about this dream until she told him, and the trouble was, she didn't want to tell him. It was dumb, full of symbolism . . . and it betrayed far too much of her inner turmoil.

She thumped her head onto his chest hard enough to make him wheeze, and when he had caught his breath, she said, "I'm on the street in Virtue Falls, and I see Andrew Marrero and the boys, and they patronize me because I can never be as good as my father. I want to yell at them, but I'm afraid I'll cry. Besides that, I can't breathe. Then I realize I'm dressed in a shirt and a heavy, tight sweater and I'm hot. I have to get the sweater off. I wrestle my way out of the arms. I look up. The street is empty. Weirdly empty. The sweater is thick. I'm hotter and hotter. I pull it over my head, but the neck is too tight and I can't take it off." Her heartbeat picked up. Even in the light of day, she couldn't breathe. "I'm stuck inside the sweater, fighting to get out. It's dark in there. I can't see the street. I'm vulnerable. I'm hot. I'm hot. I panic . . . And you woke me up." She took a long breath. "Dumb, huh?"

He did not laugh. In fact, he looked sober and thoughtful. "Had that dream for long?"

"It's a new variation of the same old dream. Dark. Hot. No air. And I know someone's coming for me, but I can't see him." She huddled closer.

He wrapped her tighter. "Had it since you were a kid?"

"Yes . . . but more since I moved to Virtue Falls." She took a shaky breath. "Yesterday may have triggered it again."

"Yesterday was a good day to make nightmares."

"Yes." She didn't move away. She didn't relax. Finally, she sighed, short and sharp. "I need to get up." She pushed her way out of his arms and onto her feet. "Thank you for sleeping with me."

"My pleasure." He watched her, eyes alight with interest, as she tugged at the hem of her shirt.

She started for the bathroom, then stopped and turned back to him. "What's going to happen to her . . . body? My mother's body?"

He sobered. "It's a murder case. The coroner will perform an autopsy, and Foster had better damned well hope nothing contradicts the evidence presented at the trial. I've got files from the FBI and I— Oh, shit!" Garik leaped off the bed and ran into the other room.

She sat up and listened to him shuffling around and muttering. She went to the door.

He stood holding her phone and looking disgusted. "Honey, I'm sorry, I used your phone last night to establish an Internet connection, set it to never allow sleep, and then forgot about it. It's drained."

"It's okay. Plug it in."

"Will do, but it's going to be pretty dry." He looked so dismayed he was comical.

"I can do without a cell phone if I have to, especially since"—she rubbed her sweaty palms on her shirt—"today I'll spend some time with my father."

Garik looked quizzical. "Yeah?"

"Before I went to sleep, I was thinking—you and Margaret are right. I have no natural affection for my father. I don't remember my very early life, or the time before or after the killing, and I in no way connected with Charles Banner. But it is a good idea for me to go see him and discover what he remembers of me and my mother."

"Agreed." Garik took off his shirt and tossed it on the floor, and headed into the bathroom ahead of her. "Let me get done in here, and I'll go with you."

CHAPTER FORTY

Elizabeth was pleased to note that this morning sunlight had vanquished the isolated, spooky atmosphere of the Honor Mountain Memory Care Facility. The building buzzed with motion, with sound. At one door stood a flatbed truck where two burly men wrestled an ancient steamer trunk up a ramp.

One of the elderly patients had wandered out that door; Yvonne had him by the sleeve, and Elizabeth could hear her clearly say, "Now, Mr. Mohr, come back in. You wouldn't like living in town with Mrs. Perry. You two don't even get along!"

"We don't?" Mr. Mohr frowned and walked in a circle to head back into the facility.

Catching sight of Elizabeth and Garik, Yvonne added, "And if you leave now, you won't get to meet Charles Banner's children."

"I would like to meet them." Mr. Mohr waved at them.

Garik waved back, and headed over to shake his hand. "Good to meet you, Mr. Mohr. Beautiful day, isn't it?" He took over from Yvonne, chatting cheerily as he led the patient inside.

Yvonne fell back to walk with Elizabeth. "Is that Garik? My God, I haven't seen him in a month of Sundays. You have a very handsome husband."

"Ex-husband." Elizabeth corrected her automatically. But she was right. Garik was handsome, although his jeans were baggy in the rear, and his arms were without a single ounce of fat to soften the impact of his heavy muscles.

"A tragedy, that divorce. You two look good together."

Elizabeth glanced down at herself.

Unlike Garik, she wasn't wearing her own clothes. She had on a flowered summer dress that was a little too tight across her breasts, and a pair of metallic gold sandals with big colored rhinestones. Not her style at all, although she supposed she should be glad to have them. "Thank you. But looking good together is hardly a criterion for a successful marriage. But we did look very good in our wedding picture." And this morning, on the way to the care facility, every time Elizabeth shifted her bare legs, Garik had noticed.

Elizabeth would not say that she frequently moved on purpose. But she felt triumph in knowing she could still keep him enthralled with an incremental adjustment of her hem.

Yvonne gestured toward the moving van. "Mrs. Perry's relatives are taking her home until the facility has been inspected and the damage fixed. We found more damage than was immediately visible, and recommended families come for their relatives. So far four have left. Unfortunately, a lot of them don't have families, or nobody who can or will take them." She sighed wearily.

Elizabeth thought Yvonne looked exhausted. "Have you been home at all?"

"Yes, once, to change and pack a bag. It's thirty minutes north of here . . . a lot of trees are down on the acreage, but they missed the house, thank God. Last night, my husband managed to get through to me on the phone, and he told me he'd take care of everything when he gets home. But he's a trucker, and it's going to be a while before he can get his semi over the roads."

Elizabeth noted that Yvonne seemed sincerely fond of her husband, even though he hadn't been here to help her through the crisis. "You're working too much. You need more sleep."

"We got two more orderlies back to work today, so I'm going home tonight." Yvonne clasped her hands at her chest. "I can't wait to sleep in my own bed. How's your hand?"

Elizabeth showed her the bandage. "Okay. It hurts and the stitches pull, but it's okay."

"When Dr. Frownfelter gets here, I'll send him in to look at it."

"Okay." It wasn't logical, but as they stepped across the threshold of the care facility, Elizabeth's nerves tightened and her breath got short.

"I hear you've had a bit of a shock, too," Yvonne said.

"What shock?" Elizabeth found herself looking around for a ghost.

"You found your mother's body yesterday."

"Yes. That. That's why we're here." Elizabeth inhaled deeply. That didn't help; the hospital smell reminded her of that moment when she'd come awake to see Charles Banner standing over her bed. "We want to talk to my father about Misty, to see if the news that she'd been found would have an effect on him."

Yvonne started to say something, then shook her head as if she changed her mind, and said, "He's been quiet since you left. He mentions you, calls you Misty, then he corrects himself."

Garik shook Mr. Mohr's hand, introduced him to an orderly, gave him a wave, and walked back to join Elizabeth.

Sweat had sprung up at the back of her neck and now trickled down between her shoulder blades. Since the earthquake, she had become a bundle of neuroses; she was afraid to walk into the Honor Mountain Memory Care Facility.

As if Garik knew it, he took her hand and held it

between both of his. Smiling, he said, "Hello, Yvonne, you're prettier than ever."

Elizabeth couldn't believe it when Yvonne blushed and preened. "You're as delusional as some of my patients. Have you come to meet your father-in-law?"

"We're not married," Elizabeth said. What was it with these people? Did they not understand the meaning of the word *divorce*?

Garik winked, and smiled. "We'd like to visit with Charles, if it's okay."

Elizabeth wanted to slap him. He was feeding this myth that they had an ongoing relationship. Didn't he want to move on?

She did. Whether or not he was nice to sleep with, whether or not he sympathized about her nightmares . . . she really, really did want to move on. It was the only sensible thing to do.

"Okay." Yvonne spoke to Garik. "Down this hall, room three-two-three, he's usually working this time of day."

"On what?" Garik asked.

Yvonne walked with them. "Right now, he's working on the earthquake and what he expects the scientific community to find. For all that he's an Alzheimer's patient, he still has quite a following online among the geologists." She sounded proud, as if his admirers gave her prestige.

"You have Internet?" Elizabeth was astonished—and excited. She had a video to upload.

"It's blinked on a couple of times. But no. Not yet. If we had Internet, the patients' families wouldn't be so worried. My husband wouldn't be so worried." Yvonne looked to Garik as if he could fix the situation.

A typical guy, he responded as if he could actually

cure the problem. "The power will come first. The Internet will be back soon. Then they've got to fix the roads." He rolled his eyes.

"Rumors say the DOT is working Highway one-oh-one as hard and as fast as they can," Yvonne said. "I hope it's true."

"I'm sure the state officials will not want to leave us without power and water for long," Elizabeth said.

Yvonne snorted. "State officials only care about Seattle. They'll get to us folks in the country after they get the important city folks fixed up."

"Cynical." But Garik sounded as if he agreed.

Room 323 had the door closed.

Yvonne put her hand out to stop them. "Listen, Elizabeth, I tried to call you yesterday and couldn't get through. This is not good news. Your father had a seizure."

Elizabeth swung to face her. "What?"

"Late in the afternoon, in the rec room, he stiffened, fell out of his chair, started shuddering, was unconscious, and when he revived, he was unable to speak or move for about thirty minutes." Yvonne gave her report in a cool tone that belied the anxiety in her eyes. "The nursing staff took care of him, and when Dr. Frownfelter came in last night to make rounds, he examined him. Your father seemed rather distracted and as if he was looking for something. But he's fine."

Elizabeth swayed.

Garik caught her arm. "Is this the first time this has happened?"

"That we know of." Yvonne spoke to him, but kept an eye on Elizabeth.

"Is he in danger?" Elizabeth asked.

Yvonne opened her mouth, sighed, and nodded. "For a man his age, he's not in the best of health. Prison, the stress of losing his family, the beatings he's taken . . . Dr. Frownfelter doesn't think there's any immediate danger. We put a monitor on him, so if he seizes again, we'll know immediately. But there's a good chance this is his first seizure. There's a good chance he'll never have another. Try not to worry. He's doing fine today. It seems sometimes the mind chooses what it can bear. Your father usually doesn't remember his years in prison."

"Twenty-three years are gone?" Elizabeth asked.

"For the most part. When he does remember, he's agitated, unhappy. So we like it better when he remembers you and your mother. It's a gentler, happier memory for him, and he likes to tell us about those times."

"He's told you about meeting my mother?"

"Yes, that she was his student and made all the moves on him." Yvonne chuckled. "Which doesn't surprise me; it fits his personality, I think." She looked down at her pager, turned, and hurried away. She called over her shoulder, "I've got to go. We're still short-handed. Don't worry!"

"Don't worry?" Elizabeth repeated to Garik. "I almost didn't come back to see him."

He put his arm around her. "We're here now. And we'll keep coming back for as long as he needs us."

For no reason, without ever meeting her father, Garik was taking responsibility. So Charles wasn't merely her charge, but also Garik's, and sharing the burden made her relax a little, feel as if life could be within her control.

Garik opened the door.

She walked into room 323.

Charles sat at his desk, typing on his aging laptop. "Hello, Father."

Charles looked hard at her, adjusted his glasses, and said, "Hello, dear, how good to see you."

Elizabeth braced herself. "I'm Elizabeth, your daughter."

"I know." He sounded slightly irritated, as if she was stating the obvious.

Elizabeth leaned in to kiss his cheek.

"Before she left," he said, "Misty explained all to me."

Elizabeth pulled back. He'd had a seizure. She knew he was delusional. But those delusions made her feel sort of itchy, as if someone—Misty—was stroking ghostly fingers across her skin. "Mother left?"

"Yes, but don't worry, she said she would be back," Charles assured her.

Elizabeth did not feel measurably reassured.

From the doorway, Garik watched her. "Won't you introduce me, Elizabeth?"

Charles looked at him, broke into a smile, pushed his chair back, and stood. "I recognize you. Elizabeth's husband, Garik Jacobsen. Margaret Smith forwarded me a photo when you two got married."

Which explained a lot.

"Good to meet you!" Charles offered his hand.

Garik took it. "You're looking well, sir."

Charles adjusted his glasses. "I'm feeling well, too. I wish Misty was here to meet you, though."

"I wish that, too." Garik scrutinized Charles, then said softly, "Elizabeth and I found Misty's body yesterday. Did you know?"

"No, but I'm not surprised." Charles turned to his daughter. "I did ask if you'd found the bones, you know."

"I know." Her lips felt numb, and she was sweating

again. "That's why I wanted you to tell me more about how you and Misty met and got married."

Charles chuckled softly and collapsed into his desk chair. "Marrying Misty was the best thing I ever did."

CHAPTER FORTY-ONE

Charles waited in the lobby of the hotel, nervously tugging at his suit and wishing Misty would hurry up.

If she had a fault, it was that she was always late. Although in her defense, she was always late because people stopped her and talked to her.

Men told her she was pretty, and she smiled and thanked them. Women asked her about the color of her lipstick or how she made her eyes appear so big, and she smiled at them, too, and talked to them as if her makeup tips would help create full lips or large eyes. She charmed everybody, and that took time, so she was always late.

He hated the late part, but he always waited without reproach. He couldn't urge her to ignore the people who spoke to her. If she did that, she wouldn't be the Misty he adored.

Right now, though, they needed to get to the chapel on time or they'd have to wait another day to get married. This hotel was full, and he didn't have enough money to stay another day in Las Vegas. Not with a baby on the way.

A baby on the way.

He felt almost faint with terror and pride. He was going to be a father.

He stood facing the outer doors, worrying that he wouldn't be able to get a cab in time, when he heard that particular hush fall across the lobby, the hush that meant Misty had finally made her appearance. He turned . . . and there she was, the most beautiful woman in the world.

She wore white; she had somehow managed to come up with a dress that looked like a fifties-era prom gown, with a wide, crisp gathered skirt, a fitted bodice, and cap sleeves. Her satin heels were low, and her little hat had an attached veil. She held a bouquet of white roses, and she smiled at him as if he was the only man on earth.

He swallowed.

She walked toward him across the lobby, floating, incandescent with joy. At marrying him? It seemed impossible. But he had to believe the truth in her blue eyes.

She loved him.

"Darling." Her low, warm voice sent chills up his spine. She slipped her hand into his arm. "Are you ready? Because I can't wait any longer to marry you."

He nodded, mesmerized, like everybody else, by her glow. "I'll get a cab."

Of course, he didn't have to do anything.

Misty smiled at the doorman, and prettily explained that because she had taken so long getting into her gown, they were late for their own wedding, and could they cut the taxi line?

The next cab was theirs.

The doorman helped her in, and when she waved, the people in the line waved back and called out congratulations. She enchanted them as much as she enchanted Charles.

Charles heard one guy say, "He must have money."

And he wished everyone would stop looking at him as

if they knew what he'd done to a girl who was almost young enough to be his daughter.

He leaned forward and told the cabbie they wanted to go to the White Shoulders Wedding Chapel, and quickly.

The cabbie nodded, hit the gas as hard as he could, and Charles slammed back against the seat. "Crazy driver," he muttered.

"Never mind him." Misty took his hand. "Do you like it?"

"What?" He stared at her, half-crazed with amazement, embarrassment, and mad, possessive, giddy happiness.

"My dress." She smoothed a hand down the skirt. "It's vintage. Old-fashioned clothing fits me well, because in those days women had curves. And so do I."

"You look beautiful." If he could, he would kneel at her feet.

Instead, he hoped they didn't hit any more speed bumps, because he was tired of being airborne.

"Thank you." She fluttered her lashes. "I didn't know if you'd noticed."

In deep, heartfelt sincerity, he said, "There is not one moment of the day when I forget how beautiful you are, and how lucky I am."

Tears sprang to her eyes, and he was suddenly digging for his handkerchief.

She took it and dabbed at the corners of her eyes. "Really? Because I feel guilty. I knew you didn't think you ought to sleep with me, and then when I got pregnant, I thought, Oh God, he's going to insist on marrying me and I'll let him because my father left before I was born and that's no way to raise a child. But I don't want you to be unhappy, or feel awkward. I'll *do whatever you want, live wherever you need . . . as long as we can be together. I love you, you know."*

She'd said it before.

This time he believed her. "I love you, too."

Elizabeth couldn't quite get up the nerve to glance at Garik.

She remembered a time when Garik had looked at her the way Charles described looking at Misty. And their wedding . . . their wedding had been very much like her parents', not a grand and glorious religious ceremony, but a civil union in a courthouse in Santa Barbara. It was a beautiful spot, but the location didn't quite make up for their bleak lack of relatives.

Margaret had come down to meet her and witness the ceremony, but the trip had proved too much for her and at the last minute, she had had to admit defeat and rest in her hotel room.

Aunt Sandy, Uncle Bill, and the cousins "just couldn't make it."

Elizabeth had been prosaic about the quiet ceremony; she told Garik that having each other was all that was important.

Remembering now, she blinked away tears.

That stupid sentiment had proved quite untrue.

Yet as if Garik was remembering that same thing, his hand stroked her shoulder.

The quick, gentle contact made the tears harder to subdue. She had to take a long breath before she could speak, and when she did, her voice wobbled a little. "I have a photo of your wedding." She opened her scrapbook and found the photo taken in front of a glittering sign proclaiming them JUST MARRIED, and underneath, in smaller letters, THE WHITE SHOULDERS CHAPEL.

"Mama was beautiful, but you looked handsome, too, Daddy."

Charles stared at Elizabeth with detachment, then studied the photo and nodded. "I did look very presentable. I had such doubts about our union, but she believed in us. She believed we could make it, and she convinced me of it, too." He gave a single, dry chuckle. "Then I met her family."

CHAPTER FORTY-TWO

As a cliffhanger, Garik thought that couldn't be surpassed . . . pretty impressive for a man with Alzheimer's. "After Elizabeth and I got married," Garik said, "we drove up to Santa Clara so I could meet Aunt Sandy and her crew. I thought they put the diss in dysfunctional. Is that who you met?"

"Did you meet my grandparents?" Elizabeth asked, her eyes wide with curiosity.

"No, not Misty's father. He decamped before she was born, fled like a coward into the night, and when I met Misty's mother, I knew why. That woman . . ." For a mild-mannered scholar, Charles projected scorn very well. "Frankie Winston was the reason Misty took theater arts as her college major. From the moment Misty was born, Frankie decided that Misty would be her ticket to Hollywood. She put that little girl in tap, ballet, gymnastics, voice, deportment, all by the time Misty was five."

"What about Aunt Sandy?" Elizabeth asked.

Charles looked at Elizabeth in that way he had, his head half-tilted as if he could almost remember who she was . . . but not quite. "Sandy was pretty enough, and she had a pleasant singing voice, but when she stood next to Misty, there was no comparison. Misty was . . . luminescent. Sandy never stood a chance. Not in a contest where she was pitted against Misty. And Frankie always made sure she compared the girls. Misty loved me, I know, but I also know she wanted to get away from her mother, and she saw marriage to me as a way out."

As they drove to Sandy's house in Santa Clara, Misty presented a calm front, but Charles could tell she was nervous. "Hey," he said, "I'm meeting your family. I'm the one who's supposed to be scared."

"If you knew what you were getting into, you would be."

That explosive, irritated gasp of words startled him. Misty was always so composed, almost placid, even when in the grips of passion. And he . . . hated that. Worked hard to make her crazy with desire. Sometimes he thought he succeeded, but when he caught his breath, she was always placid again.

"I'm sorry." She was trying for placid now, and not quite succeeding. "I didn't mean to take out my fear on you. I've never told you about my mother. My sister, too. But mostly my mother."

"What's wrong with her?"

"Stage mother in the complete sense of the word. I mean, I feel bad for my mother. When she was young, she had a lot of talent and worked to get into movies, but she never got beyond the bit parts. She got pregnant with Sandy, got married, got divorced, and tried to get into movies again . . ." Misty sighed, a brief, breathy gasp. "I

think my sister was neglected when she was young. Sandy's married now and expecting her third child."

"That is great news. Our baby will have cousins!"

"Yes." Misty smiled.

But Charles had learned she always smiled most when she was stressed. How did he know when she meant it? "Is there something wrong with your sister's children?"

"No! Not at all. They're just kids. The house is small, though, and Sandy works, too, so another child . . . I don't think Bill and Sandy meant to have another child. It's sort of stretching their resources."

He nodded, trying to comprehend the morass of family Misty was describing.

"My sister tenses up when my mother is around. Everybody does, but after thirty minutes, you can tell Sandy wants to shriek at Mother, and if she gives in then Mother wins." Misty touched his hand as it rested on the steering wheel. "You'll see. Mother always wins."

He smiled at her. "Your mother sounds like a challenge."

"She's a monster." Misty pointed to the small bungalow tucked into a fifties pocket Santa Clara neighborhood. "There it is."

"Do you want me to park on the street so if we have to make a quick getaway, we can?"

"Yes!" For a moment, Misty's eyes lit up. Then the anticipation faded. "No. I can't abandon Sandy. It wouldn't be fair." She nodded at the low-slung sports car in the driveway. "Mother's here." The two words dropped like distilled poison from Misty's lips, and after Charles turned off the car, she sat with her hands clenched in her lap. Abruptly, she turned to him. "Promise me you'll still love me when this is over."

*He smoothed her hair off her forehead. "I've got it. I
understand. We're stepping into an ugly, mean swamp
of emotions. But listen to me, Misty. You're beautiful. But
more than that, you're kind, you're caring, you're generous, and for some reason that I don't understand, you
love me. And I love you more than . . ." At the crucial
moment, he realized what he was saying, how important
this was. "More than . . ." His eloquence dried up, and
he began to panic.*

The dimple blinked in her cheek. "More than rocks?"

"Definitely more than rocks."

"More than volcanoes?"

"Definitely more than volcanoes."

"More than . . . earthquakes?"

He hesitated.

*With a wail, she flung herself on his chest. "Not more
than earthquakes?"*

She was crying.

Was she crying?

Yes, she was crying.

He tilted her chin up.

No, she was laughing.

*"Wretched wench," he said, and pinched her ear. "I
love you as much as any earthquake under seven-point-
five on the Richter scale."*

*"Oh!" She punched him in the chest. "At least an
eight."*

"Seven-point-five, and I'll throw in the aftershocks."

*She laughed again, a little too long and a little too
hysterically, but when she dug out a tissue from her purse
to dab at her eyes, she said, "Thank you. I feel better.
Not quite so afraid."*

"She can't hurt you."

Misty touched his cheek sadly, as if he was a pleasant fool. "Let's go in."

Sandy and her husband, Bill Frisk, were middle-class American normal.

Bill was six-two and looked like an aging football player, which in fact he was. He patted his stomach and joked that he used to have a six-pack, but now it was more like a keg.

Their kids, Hope and Mary, were five and almost two.

Hope was in kindergarten; she'd already received three pink slips but she promised her mommy not to bully anyone ever again.

Mary had an ear infection and was going in next week to get tubes in her ears. In the meantime, if she wasn't crying, she was whining.

Sandy was hugely pregnant; they were having a boy, Bill Junior.

Charles discovered all that in the first two minutes of Sandy's overly bright chatter; she never drew a breath through all the nodding and hand-shaking and hanging of jackets.

Charles noted the rather desperate hug Misty and Sandy gave each other, and the much more gingerly hug Misty gave her mother. In fact, Misty looked like a detonation expert taking stock of a particularly deadly ticking bomb.

Frankie Winston, aka Mother, was a California beauty. Too thin, too blond, too worked-out, smiling tightly, dressed exquisitely. Her face had been lifted, and yet for all the stretched immobility of her expression, she managed to convey scorn in her glittering blue eyes. With a nod, she acknowledged Charles and dismissed him at the same time.

Turning to Sandy, she said, "Bill Junior? Wasn't it bad enough that you named your daughters names like Hope and Mary? Do you have to saddle a boy with Bill? Do you have a thing for four-letter names?"

"I don't have any aspirations for my children to go into show business, Mother, and plain names are more acceptable in the real world." Sandy's eyes glittered as hard and blue as her mother's.

"True," Frankie agreed. "These kids would never make it in Hollywood."

Bill Senior thrust a glass of red wine into Charles's hand. "Here. You'll need this," he muttered.

Sandy asked, "Why don't we sit down for dinner?"

CHAPTER FORTY-THREE

They sat shoulder to shoulder at a round table in the tiny dining area.

In an undertone, Misty told him, "Sandy bought a round table for the same reasons King Arthur seated his knights at a round table—to give everyone the same importance in seating."

"Your mother likes the head of the table?" he murmured.

"Um-hm."

Bill pulled a pan of lasagna out of the oven.

Sandy stood at the counter and tossed the salad with dressing and croutons, and handed it around, followed by a basket of sourdough garlic bread.

Frankie poured herself a big glass of wine. "Darling,

you do know these overflowing pans of lasagna went out a good ten years ago?"

Sandy paused, her spatula ready to cut into the steaming, cheesy casserole.

Misty shook out her napkin. *"Sandy makes the best lasagna I've ever tasted. Why would she change?"*

Sandy plunged the spatula through the noodles with a clean, stabbing motion.

"Yes." Frankie ran her fingers through her blond, short-cropped hair. *"Of course. It is very good. But so many calories!"*

Charles watched the scene unfolding before him with a sense of helplessness. Outside of a play by Tennessee Williams, he had never seen anything like Frankie. The unexpected attacks, the words chosen to cut and maim, the constant undermining . . . it was terrifying. It was fascinating.

But this wasn't a Broadway play, and this woman was hurting his wife. Had hurt Misty her whole life.

He was beginning to comprehend what Misty's life had been, why she smiled, how much of her grief and uncertainty she managed to hide—

"So!" Frankie turned on him like a striking cobra. *"Misty tells me the two of you are married."*

He had never in his life made a suave, romantic gesture.

He made one now.

Prying Misty's hand free of her death grip on the tablecloth, he carried it to his lips and kissed it. *"We are. I was privileged enough to win her heart."*

"She says you're one of her professors." Frankie looked him over disparagingly. *"Old enough to be her father. I suppose you regularly seduce your students."*

It was so absurd, he laughed, a brief burst of bright

amusement. "Do I look like a man who regularly seduces women?"

Frankie's expression went from speculative to vicious.

Misty's hand tightened on his.

"Do you think I'm a fool, Mr. Banner? I've met men like you, lecherous old bastards who prey on young women like Misty and rob them of their youth and careers—"

"Mother!" Misty said.

"—and then toss them aside—"

"Mother!" Misty said again. "I don't want to act!"

At the same time, Charles said, "Misty says she's not a good actress."

Frankie slapped her hand on the table.

Plates rattled.

"Yes, you do want to act," she said to Misty. And to him, she said, "Misty's a wonderful actress. If not for you, she could be in contention for an Academy Award. Did you know she turned down the lead for Cape Fear?"

"What's Cape Fear?" he asked.

Frankie's expression made it clear he had committed the ultimate faux pas. "It's only the movie cited as most likely to win the Academy Award, with the meatiest female lead ever!"

"The lead was never actually offered to me, Mother," Misty said.

"If you had offered that producer the slightest encouragement—"

"He wouldn't have liked sleeping with me." Misty's dramatic pause proved she did know how to hold center stage. "I'm pregnant."

Misty's announcement slammed into the conversation, silencing Frankie at last. Silencing everyone, until

Sandy laughed, a short burst of nasty amusement, then said hastily, "Congratulations, darling!"

Only the whiny two-year-old was oblivious to the up-coming grandmotherly explosion.

But Frankie did not explode—and that was worse. "A child? With your figure, dear? Your hips would expand, you'd lose your waist, and you'd be fit for nothing more than parts as the fat friend."

"Misty won't lose her figure," Sandy said. "She'll be beautiful."

"Like you," Bill said.

"Yes, Sandy, she'll look like you—a huge bloated whale with swollen ankles. Three children, and you have to work." Frankie took a long swig of wine. "Bill, with your lousy salary, you'd think you could keep it in your pants."

"Mother, Sandy is happy!" Misty said.

"She didn't even get around to putting on mascara." That, apparently, was Frankie's ultimate condemnation.

Sandy's hand flew to her lashes.

Frankie leaned toward Misty, stared into her eyes, said, "I know a good doctor. Safe. Sanitary. We'll take care of the problem. No one ever needs to know."

For the longest time, Charles didn't understand. Then he did.

An abortion. She wanted Misty to have an abortion.

That bitch. *How dare she? In a level voice, he said, "Misty and I are married. We're having a baby. I hope you'll take this moment to congratulate us, but if you don't, nothing will have changed. We* are *still married. And we* are *still having a baby."*

Beside him, he heard Misty take her first unrestricted breath.

Frankie shoved her chair back. In the tight confines of the dining room, it bounced against the wall, denting the Sheetrock, then slammed back under her, knocking her back onto her butt.

Bill grinned.

Frankie was unfazed. Tapping her index finger on the table, she leaned toward Charles. "Who are you, really? Who do you think you are to try to come between me and my daughter? I raised her. I sacrificed everything for her. She has what it takes to be a star, and if I have anything to say about it, she's going to be a star. There's nothing a skinny, old, balding scientist can do about it. You're nobody. No one even cares who you are."

Her eyes glittered with malice. She expected him to shrivel. She expected to him to stammer in his own defense. She thought she could make him run away. She didn't understand him—or Misty—at all.

Charles had never in his life thought he could use his scientific knowledge to take out a competitor. But he had never before in his life had Misty to defend. "I understand what you're trying to say, Frankie, and I completely agree. Misty is your daughter, the light of your life, and I came along and without acknowledging your role in her life, swept her off her feet and into a wedding chapel. I should have applied for your permission to marry her, but since I did not, let me assure you of my capability to love and support your daughter. You mentioned my age—yes, I am substantially older than Misty, but I've never been married before so you can clear your mind of any fears that I am a serial sexual predator. Misty is my first love, my first wife, and my only wife. Ever."

Frankie tried to interrupt.

Charles spoke right over the top of her. "I'm mature

enough to handle this relationship, and I also am a well-respected scientist in the field of geology. In fact, I might immodestly call myself the foremost scientist in the field of geology concerning the Pacific Ring of Fire and specifically the West Coast."

"Geology." Frankie made the word sound like an obscenity. "What does that even mean?"

"I'm so glad you asked." Utilizing that same on-camera smile he'd seen Misty use to deal with unfortunate situations, he segued into a description of his work. Twenty years of his work. Hours and days and weeks and years of field work. Degrees in chemistry, biology, and geology. Evenings in a chemistry lab, nights in the library. He delved into college lectures. About geologic theories.

Misty propped her chin in her hand and stared adoringly.

Whenever he drew a breath, Sandy brightly asked a question.

Whenever Frankie tried to speak, Bill harrumphed and said, "How fascinating!" in a tone that clearly conveyed his absolute and total ignorance.

Charles took the stage as the villain, and came away the hero, and by the time he finished talking, Frankie stood outside, smoking a cigarette like Bette Davis on speed.

The silence that fell on the kitchen was pure unadulterated relief.

Bill picked up the drooping five-year-old. "I've got to put this little girl to bed, but good to meet you, Charles. You did something I thought no man could—you took out Frankie Winston."

Sandy hugged her sister and laughed softly. "That'll teach Mother to complain about my lasagna."

Misty hugged her back, then put her head on Charles's

shoulder. "Charles has a grant to excavate a canyon in Washington State. As soon as the school year is over, we're moving. I'm sorry to leave her with you, but I have to get out."

"Don't worry about it." Sandy glanced out the window at the glowing tip of Frankie's cigarette. "Without you, she won't come around much. As far as she's concerned, I'm a lost cause. Always have been." She stroked her hand across her belly. "I really don't care, but when she visits, I have to remind myself of that."

"Why would what she thinks matter to you?" Charles asked. It was an honest question. "What is her influence on you?"

Neither woman spoke for a long moment.

Then Misty took a deep breath. "She's our mother. But more than that, she's . . . I know you couldn't tell tonight, but when we were younger, she could be charming. Exciting! Fun! She played games with us and our friends. She took us places. She wrote plays and gave us parts and we acted them out. She put us in ballet, then did parodies of The Nutcracker. She was pretty and she talked to us like we were adults. All of our friends envied us our mother. We—Sandy and I—always knew that pleasant charm was a façade, and it would shatter at the slightest provocation, for no reason, sometimes in public, which was so embarrassing, and sometimes in private, and she . . ." Misty turned her face away.

Now he wanted to go out and choke Frankie. No one should make Misty writhe as if she was in pain. No one. But he kept his voice gentle. "Did she hurt you?"

"No. Not usually. Not physically. But if we weren't smarter than everyone else in school, if we didn't dance better and sing better and make her proud . . ." Misty's *voice grew hoarse with pain. "Then she told us we were nothing without her. I guess I've always been afraid . . . it was true."*

Charles scrubbed his hand across his face. "Misty and I never saw Frankie again," he told Elizabeth and Garik. "The day that I was done teaching, we went to visit my parents in Ohio. They were older—I was an afterthought—and dismayed when they saw how young Misty was. But she won them over. Of course. When they found out they were going to be grandparents, there wasn't anything they wouldn't do for her. The next year, my mother was diagnosed with Alzheimer's. The year after, my father died of a heart attack. At the time I thought all that was tragedy, but now . . . thank God, Dad never saw me go to prison, and Mom never knew what happened to me."

Elizabeth hadn't realized the emotional traumas of her mother's life, nor Aunt Sandy's, when it came to that. She had a picture of her paternal grandparents in her album, sitting together on a flowered couch, dressed up and smiling, but she hadn't known that Charles's mother had also succumbed to the disease that now preyed on his mind, or thought about the fact she had barely missed meeting her father's father. She could almost hear the wailing of the Fates as they wove the destiny of these lives . . .

She turned the page of her album and pointed to the photo of Misty, with a baby bump, standing in front of a small, neat, white painted house. The wind was blowing her blond hair, and she beamed at the camera as if she'd won the lottery. Elizabeth couldn't help smiling at that Misty. "Then you moved to Virtue Falls."

"Yes," Charles said softly. "That's Misty. That's our place."

Garik leaned closer. "Nice!"

"This is one of my favorite pictures." Elizabeth stroked the edges of the photo. "Look how happy she is."

"Did you take the photo, sir?" Garik asked. "Charles? Mr. Banner?"

Charles didn't answer. He didn't answer, didn't move, didn't even seem to breathe.

Elizabeth put her hand on his shoulder. "Father?"

He started as if she woke him. He looked at her, at Garik, and in wondering voice, he asked, "Who are you?"

CHAPTER FORTY-FOUR

Rainbow stood in front of the Oceanview Café and smoked a cigarette.

As a general rule, she didn't smoke tobacco, but the last week had made her think of the Lloyd Bridges character in *Airplane*—"I picked a bad day to quit sniffing glue."

She was tense. She was tired. Waitressing at the Oceanview now took Herculean effort. She wanted the aftershocks to go away, wanted everyone to stop looking scared, wanted the news helicopters to stop flying over the top of them on their way to cover the destruction in Forks, wanted her pretty little town back. Most of all, she wanted electricity flowing through the lights and stoves and water heaters. According to the rumors floating around, that wasn't happening soon. So she smoked, and watched Old Man Namkung's battered, rusty, out-ofalignment Ford F-350 farm truck weave down the street toward her.

Old Man Namkung was the best organic gardener west of the Olympic Mountains, and she hoped to hell he was headed her way because the town vegans were getting surly at being told all they had to eat was corn tortillas and stale peanuts out of a broken courthouse vending machine. If someone didn't fling some kale at them pretty soon, they were going to lift their feeble little arms and pound their puny fists on the big, mean omnivores, and Rainbow would hate to see the slaughter that would ensue.

The truck slowed down and stopped against the curb.

She crushed the cigarette out against the building and got ready to rush forward and grab a crate of cantaloupes.

Andrew Marrero got out of the passenger side and slammed the door.

Hot damn. He looked mad.

His apostles, Matthew, Mark, Luke, and Joe, climbed out of the back.

No, wait. It was Benjamin, Luke, and Joe. But they were still nothing but sycophants hoping to make their ways up the geology chain of command by sucking up to Andrew Marrero.

From the looks on their faces, lately they hadn't done too well.

Goodie. That made it a fine time to stroll over and have a chat.

She strolled, and when she got close she called, "Hey, Marrero, that's not your usual mode of transportation. Something happen to your car?"

Marrero finished paying Old Man Namkung, put his

wallet in his pocket, and smiled coldly. He was not happy to see her.

In the kind of precise English a guy would use when he was making sure he didn't drop into colloquial Spanish, he said, "My car is a wreck."

"Where? How?"

"It's off the road halfway between here and Portland up by Willoughby Goddamn Creek with a crumpled fender, a punctured oil pan, and God knows what other damage"—Andrew's voice swelled—"because these guys thought we could get back to Virtue Falls in my Jaguar!"

"What were you doing up by Willoughby Goddamn Creek?" she asked.

A pause.

Joe said, "We got lost."

"Wow. Marrero's beautiful Jaguar is in a ditch?" She liked repeating that.

"It is," Andrew said.

"You tried to drive your Jaguar home after that earthquake?" She guffawed, and actually saw the blood vessels burst like fireworks in Andrew's eyes. "That's bad. No use blaming your sycophants, though. You're a big boy, Andrew, and you're in charge. It had to be your decision to leave Portland."

Andrew stalked toward her like a guy who expected this feeble little woman to back up in the face of his displeasure.

She didn't back up.

He stopped short.

Jesus. You'd think he would remember sleeping with her. But no. He was the kind of guy who forgot who he'd fucked as fast as he could, especially when it was someone like the town waitress. Now, if she'd been the state governor, she'd bet he would remember . . .

He flicked his hand at her as if to ward off an annoying mosquito. "There's no use talking to you."

"Nope. No use talking to me . . . except I know what happened to your house during the earthquake."

He froze.

"You know . . . since we live so close?" She made it sound salacious enough that Luke's eyes widened, Joe grinned, and Matthew looked conspicuously impassive.

Actually, she and Andrew both lived in the old downtown housing development. In the forties, the now-defunct town sawmill had built one square block full of tiny one-story houses and rented them to their mill workers. When the mill went out, Rainbow had bought the house on the corner closest to the Oceanview Café. When Andrew moved into town, he had bought the house on the complete opposite corner.

She could see the back of his house over the fence.

"What happened to my home?" Andrew asked.

"Same thing that happened to mine," she said. "We all lost our windows. That fragile old glass shattered. Mrs. Rutledge kept her husband's ashes on the shelf over the stove. The urn fell off and broke, and it was Mr. Rutledge all over."

Luke laughed, brief and sharp, then shut up.

"The automatic turnoff for the gas main worked like it was supposed to. It turned off the gas. The gas company can't turn it back on until the pipes are checked, and the gas company's officially decided they'll get to us when they get to us. We're all taking cold showers and eating cold cereal. Except the electricity is off—downed power lines, you know—and all the food in the refrigerators is spoiled, so it's cold cereal with curdled milk." She turned on the sycophants. "Where do you guys live?"

"In the apartments on First," Matthew said.

"Not anymore you don't," she said. "The officials shut that place down. You're in the gym at the high school."

The apostles looked dismayed.

"What? Did you boys not understand the power of an earthquake? Or maybe you thought, because you study earthquakes, you would be exempt from damage?" Rainbow chuckled.

The three glared. But they didn't talk back.

"You should go check." Andrew waved them away.

The apostles turned and headed toward the downed apartment building.

Andrew waited until they were out of earshot. "So you were merely trying to humiliate me? My house is intact?"

"If that's all it takes to humiliate you, you've got a fragile ego. Not surprising. As far as I know, your house is fine." She lit another cigarette. "Why did you come back to Virtue Falls? You would have been a lot better off staying close to civilization."

"I had to come back to supervise the digs." His eyes lit up the way they always did when he talked about his job.

God, these scientists were predictable.

"Some important changes have no doubt been made to the terrain," he said, "and I can't trust that girl to document them."

That girl? "Elizabeth?" Andrew really was a nasty little bully.

"Yes! Have you seen her?"

"Not since right after the tsunami, but I'm sure you're

pleased to hear she lived through it and the earthquake and was only a little hurt." A tactful reproach, she thought.

Too tactful. He brushed it away. "Sure. Do you know? Did she observe the tsunami?"

"She filmed it." Rainbow didn't know why he trembled. Jealousy? Or anticipation? Probably a dollop of both. "If I see her, do you want me to tell her you're around?"

"If you see her, tell her to report in at once!" He started to stride off toward his home.

"Please," she said.

His head whipped around. "What?"

"I'm not one of your sycophants," she said. "Tell Elizabeth I want to see her . . . please."

He didn't want to say it. She could see he hovered on the verge of a simple, rude gesture.

She straightened, squared her shoulders, took a step forward, and looked him right in the eyes.

"For shit's sake." He backed away. "*Please*, Rainbow, tell Elizabeth I want to see her right away."

"Of course, Andrew. I'm delighted to do that favor for you." She watched him steam away down the street like the little tugboat that could.

He was an annoying bastard who needed to be taught some manners, and she was just the woman to do it.

CHAPTER FORTY-FIVE

Dr. Frownfelter's windowless office in the Honor Mountain Memory Care Facility held a small desk and three chairs, was lined with medical texts, and smelled of antiseptic. With one fluorescent fixture shattered by the earthquake, twilight lingered in the room.

Around his head, Dr. Frownfelter wore an elastic band with an attached light. With it he illuminated the stitches on Elizabeth's palm, and as he cut them loose, Garik held her free hand between both of his and rubbed her cold fingers.

She kept her eyes closed as if not looking would help get her through the ordeal, and, in a joking tone, Garik said, "For such a logical woman, you're not very logical about a little cut."

Her eyes flashed open. She shot him a dirty glance. Then shut her eyes again.

Aware that Dr. Frownfelter regarded them curiously, Garik made sure it appeared as if all his concern was for Elizabeth. Which was true, in its way. But right now, he expressed that concern by observing the good doctor, sizing him up, judging what kind of man lived beneath his shabby white coat and stethoscope. Because Margaret had named him as a possible suspect for Misty's lover.

"There you go." Dr. Frownfelter pulled the last stitch free and pressed his thumb lightly on the thin red scar.

Elizabeth pulled her hand back and opened her eyes.

"Sheila did a good job, but because your hand is a delicate, complex instrument and you use it constantly, for the next couple of weeks, I want you to keep it bandaged and clean." Dr. Frownfelter viewed Elizabeth sternly.

"When you work, especially if you work in the canyon, make sure you wear a latex glove."

She nodded her head.

Since her father's most recent lapse of memory, since the moment he had blinked at them and asked, "Who are you?," Elizabeth had said very little. Garik could see her mind working on the problem of Charles and his broken intellect, and not paying attention to Dr. Frownfelter's warning. "Do you have a latex glove, Elizabeth?" Garik asked.

"What? Oh. No."

Dr. Frownfelter reached into the cabinet behind his desk, brought out a box of gloves, and handed it over. "I know you'll want to work before you should, but take it easy. No heavy lifting. Get a stress ball and an ergonomic hand exerciser, and use them several times a day." He huffed. "I mean, get them as soon as you can. We're not yet ordering items off the Internet and getting them the next day." He stripped off his own gloves. "Now, about your father."

Elizabeth straightened her shoulders as if bracing for a blow. "You said he had another seizure."

"A petit mal seizure, now called an absence seizure. For a few seconds, he simply wasn't there." Dr. Frownfelter pulled the light off his forehead and clicked it off. "All seizures are present as symptoms of Alzheimer's, and of course of other diseases and syndromes. You have to understand, in prison, he was beaten up, received a lot of head injuries, multiple concussions . . . I think it's a miracle we haven't seen seizures before."

"So my father's brain is not functioning as it should, probably for the reasons you've suggested." Elizabeth's face was expressionless, her voice quiet.

Other men might have viewed her composure as indifference, but Garik saw her pain.

She asked, "Is there a chance we're dealing with a brain tumor, also?"

Dr. Frownfelter inclined his head. "Anything is possible. We'd like to do tests, but the state holds guardianship of Charles, and getting permission will take time, especially with so much of the state government impacted by the earthquake and the hospitals full of the injured."

Garik jumped at that. "Can Elizabeth have guardianship of her father?"

Elizabeth looked startled. "Me? Have guardianship of my father? I . . . you want me to have that responsibility?" Then she caught herself. "Yes, I suppose I am the logical choice. I would make the right decisions for him."

"I agree, that would be a good idea. But that would also take time." Dr. Frownfelter's mouth turned down. "Trust me. Between the government and the insurance companies, when it comes to medicine, good patient care is a miracle."

"I can't see anything except for my father's bewildered face." Elizabeth rubbed her forehead. "He asked, 'Who are you?' Immediately after, he had said, 'Oh! It's Garik and Elizabeth. How good of you to come for a visit!' We had been with him for two hours. He'd told us stories about their wedding, and meeting my mother's family. I showed him the pictures I had." She sighed deeply, then continued, "And he didn't remember us being there at all."

"He told you about being with Misty?" Dr. Frownfelter's eyes flicked between Elizabeth and Garik.

"Yes. And during my previous visit, he told me about how he met my mother. It was like a gift. I've never heard any of it before." Elizabeth stood, paced the short distance to the door, and grasped the door frame as if to steady herself. Turning back to the two men, she said,

"But now I wonder . . . is it even possible for him to remember?"

"Certainly it's possible for him to remember," Dr. Frownfelter assured them both. "With Alzheimer's patients, memory loss is progressive, but seldom linear. Sometimes a patient clearly remembers what happened fifty years ago, but not what he ate for breakfast."

"I'm like that now," Garik said.

"We all are. The familiar and everyday don't impress us. The big events of our pasts cling relentlessly, no matter how much we wished they wouldn't. Which is why diagnosing Alzheimer's takes time and is a difficult science. Charles Banner diagnosed his condition first." Dr. Frownfelter cleared his throat. "I fought him, not wanting to believe it."

"Why not?" Elizabeth asked.

"I was the prison physician. Most of the inmates have below-average IQs, their education seldom goes beyond high school, if it goes that far." Dr. Frownfelter shrugged his massive shoulders. "He and I had a lot in common—advanced education and a scientific background. We could talk, and did . . . I didn't want to lose his companionship."

"Now he's here, and you're here. You certainly seem to follow where he leads." Garik smiled benignly, but the answer greatly interested him.

"I was born in Virtue Falls. It's not surprising I would choose to retire here." Dr. Frownfelter folded his hands over his stomach, for all intents a benevolent, kindly physician.

"You have a very busy retirement." Garik waved a hand around at the facility.

"If I don't visit the memory care center and the nursing homes, who will? Small town doctors are hard to find."

Garik believed that. It appeared that Dr. Frownfelter worked hard and discharged an important duty. But to think it was a coincidence that Charles Banner and Dr. Walter Frownfelter had been in three different locations at the same time?

No. Not even.

Since Charles had not voluntarily made the move to prison or back to Virtue Falls, that made Frownfelter the man responsible.

Yet was Frownfelter guilty of something other than curiosity? Perhaps he had a crush on Charles Banner. Perhaps he was one of those groupies to whom a specific crime held total fascination. Or perhaps he was writing an insightful tell-all book about the perpetrator of the crime. Although why would Dr. Frownfelter wait so long to publish?

Which took Garik back to his original question—was Dr. Frownfelter Misty's killer?

If Dr. Frownfelter had any inkling of Garik's thoughts, he didn't show it. He was far too focused on Elizabeth—and given Garik's train of thought, that was worrisome, too. "You know everything about the Banner family." Garik watched the doctor's face.

"Medically speaking, I do. I was practicing here in Virtue Falls during the . . . tragedy. I cared for Charles in prison and Misty was my patient." Dr. Frownfelter returned Garik's scrutiny. "I thought I knew all the kids in Virtue Falls, but I don't remember you as a boy."

"I moved here when I was eight. You were already gone."

"Yes." Dr. Frownfelter stroked his chin. "Of course. The Jacobsen case. One of my colleagues at the time told me about it."

Garik wanted to smack him for bringing it up, for now Elizabeth looked between the two men, her eyes bright with curiosity.

Dr. Frownfelter stood and patted Elizabeth's shoulder. "Try not to worry about your father. We'll do some tests. We'll find out what's going on. No use imagining the worst when answers are merely weeks away." He shambled out and down the hall.

Elizabeth watched him go, then swiveled around to face Garik. "Why did one of his colleagues tell him about you?"

Garik should tell her. If she hung around Virtue Falls long enough, she was going to hear about it, anyway, and she might as well hear it from him.

But not here. Not now. Not until absolutely necessary. "It wasn't easy for Margaret to gain custody of me. It took a lot of string pulling, talks to doctors and lawyers, and I think some bribery."

"Why did she want custody of you?" Elizabeth was zeroing in on the story.

Not here. Not now. Not until absolutely necessary. "Because even at the age of eight, I was the charming sort." He smiled toothily and put his arm around her shoulders. "Come on. Let's go into town and see how the locals are faring. When you write the companion volume to the PBS mini-series on the quake, perhaps you can add a chapter about the recovery in the area and how the people reacted. Readers love that stuff."

Elizabeth looked down, and seemed to gather herself. Then she looked up and said, "I'll be bigger than Ken Burns!" But her eyes watched him wisely.

And Garik knew his attempt at distraction had failed, and he had disappointed her . . . again.

CHAPTER FORTY-SIX

Elizabeth watched the pitted, broken road that led from Honor Mountain Memory Care Facility to town, and remembered her aunt Sandy's rant.

You're moving where? Have you lost your mind? It's cold and it's wet. There're no restaurants or nightlife. The people are all hippies and organic freaks. Not to mention your mother was slaughtered there. And you're going back to work on your murderous bastard of a father's geological study and to visit your murderous bastard of a father in a nursing home? I swear, Elizabeth, sometimes I think living with us didn't give you any sense at all.

Elizabeth pushed her hair off her forehead.

"What's wrong?" Garik asked softly.

She rolled down her window and let the air wash over her face. The August day was warm, but that wasn't why she felt sick. Aunt Sandy was right. Elizabeth didn't have any sense at all, and now she was paying for it.

"Elizabeth?" Garik drove slowly, carefully, and glanced at her frequently. He wore a concerned frown and defiant green eyes. "Are you mad at me?"

She wanted to tell him he didn't need to worry. She wasn't mad that he'd evaded her question about his past. Right now, she was far too scared about her father to do more than sigh about Garik.

They hit a pothole deep enough to make her teeth snap together, and she burst out, "This road reminds me of my life. It's going somewhere familiar, but every time I look up, there's a new obstacle to jump, another hole to fall in."

"Luckily, you don't have to wait for the DOT to come in and repave you."

She was not amused, and showed it with a quick glare and a hard sigh.

"Okay, okay!" Garik patted her bare knee. His touch lingered . . .

And she liked it.

His hand flexed, then as if he suddenly recalled the divorce, he took his hand away and put it back on the steering wheel. "You know what Dr. Frownfelter said. The second seizure wiped your father's short-term memory. Forgetting is to be expected after a seizure. Your father has Alzheimer's, which makes it doubly to be expected."

"I know. But I was *listening* to my father. I was hearing him, believing him, and I felt as if he was telling my own history, as if what he said put me into context. Now, I don't know if any of what he said was true." Even to herself, she sounded whiny.

Garik pulled into the driveway that led into one of the state parks. The picnic area was empty, the restrooms demolished by three tall Douglas firs that had been uprooted and tossed like pick-up sticks. He turned off the motor, and the silence of the forest enveloped them. He faced her, his expression serious and intent. "You tell me. The pictures sure match the stories."

"You're right. They do."

"You know your cousins. You know your aunt and uncle. Did what your father was saying sound real?"

"My uncle and that line about how he used to have a six-pack and now he has a keg—I've heard him say that a thousand times. My cousin Hope *is* a bully. She made me miserable. Aunt Sandy is always angry because Uncle Bill won't push and get ahead in his job, and they live in the same tiny house Dad described. The table is round. There's a ding in the Sheetrock that's never been fixed." Like the ding Frankie Winston had put in the wall when she shoved her chair back.

Garik nodded. "Nothing about the stories your father told seemed like fantasy, and everything was backed up by a photograph."

"I don't have a lot of photographs."

"How many do you need for proof?" When she would have replied, Garik leaned across to console and put his fingers on her lips. "Let's acquit your father of being devious enough to know which pictures you have and making up stories to go with them. To me, he is guileless, so there's no criminal intent in his stories. Which makes the stories credible. Even now, he recognizes that he and your mother's ages were very disparate. He's not painting a pretty picture of himself. He is, though, painting a pretty picture of their lives . . . and their love."

She pushed his hand away from her mouth.

It settled around the back of her neck.

That was okay, a chance to lean into the comfort offered by the man she had loved . . . did love. "Yes. It's a relief to hear that they loved each other. Aunt Sandy made me doubt . . ."

"Honey, your aunt Sandy came out sounding good in your father's story."

"Aunt Sandy was angry about my mother's death. Really angry."

Garik's eyes heated until amber coals glowed in the depths. "So she took it out on you . . . what a sweetheart."

"Not deliberately, I don't think. But she worked and she was always tired and they already had three kids . . . and I think she missed my mother."

"If she missed Misty, she should have treated Misty's daughter better." Garik's jaw looked like granite.

No use talking to Garik about it. He was a lawman, seeing life in black and white, and Elizabeth's existence with her aunt and uncle was, in Garik's eyes, definitely black.

Elizabeth liked his attitude. It helped make up for her cousins' opinion that Elizabeth had taken family resources they rightly deserved, and so she should pay in blood, pain, and lunch money.

"Look," Garik whispered.

They watched a doe lead a wary fawn across the park's campground, the long-legged creatures picking their ways through the debris left by downed trees.

"What do they think of the earthquake and the aftershocks?" Garik said.

"They think it's all part of nature," Elizabeth answered. "And they're right."

Garik massaged her neck. "Honey, you have to stop worrying about your father. You're afraid you're going to lose him too soon."

What a great explanation. She should agree and let Garik think the best of her. Yet he always seemed to be the guy with the least expectation of exemplary behavior. That freed her to speak the truth. "No, I'm selfish. It's that my father is so smart. Or was. If there's one thing I've taken comfort in, it's that he is a highly intelligent individual, like me. But look how fragile his mind is! I don't want to know a mind can be so easily broken, or slip away silently in the night."

Garik's gaze grew sober.

"I know," she said. "I'm selfish and illogical."

Wrapping his hand around her neck, he pulled her

close and put his forehead against hers. "I swear to God, if I hear you try to understand this stuff logically one more time, I'm going to—"

"Going to what?"

"Spank you." He sounded half-humorous . . . and half not.

"That's not logical," she said.

He laughed and gave her a quick kiss.

She let him. When he drew back, she remained in place, her eyes closed, her lips parted, breathing him in, tasting him, knowing if he would, he could make her forget . . .

He leaned in again and gave her a slower kiss, deeper, warmer.

All of her apprehension melted away . . . for the moment. And to have it melt away for this moment was enough.

She slid her arms around his neck and her hands into his hair. She breathed his name against her lips. "Garik . . ." And tugged at him.

He gave a muffled curse, and suddenly he tasted of urgent need and total desperation. "Too soon," he muttered.

"Hurry up," she answered.

He did. He lowered the back of the seat. Pushed her away from the dash. Climbed over the console and knelt over her, his knees on either side of her hips. He held her head in his hands and kissed her . . . and kissed her.

He kissed her behind her ear, nuzzled the base of her skull and inhaled, and chuckled softly, as if she was a flower and her fragrance filled him with delight. Drawing back, he looked at her face, really looked at her, his gaze touching her forehead, her nose, her cheeks, her lips. He pressed his lips to her eyes and closed them.

Elizabeth placed her hand over his heart, and it beat for her, hard and fast, the rhythm of desire. "Garik . . ." Her soft voice stroked him from the inside out, slipping into his bloodstream, reminding him of the times they had fought, made up, made love, and fought again . . . until one day she wasn't there to fight with, and his soul resided in silence and isolation.

She was here now, sighing in his ear, lightly sliding her hands down to his waist and over his thighs, touching him until his skin warmed and at the same time, goose bumps chilled his spine. She lifted her hips in a slow, voluptuous roll.

He slid his hand up the inside of her thigh, under her panties, into the warm, damp beckoning center of her body.

He had been there before. He knew her scent and how to touch her. He recognized her whimpers and her moans. Yet with him every time was new, real, glorious. Elizabeth always seemed unconquerable, and making her yield and grow wet against his fingers made him feel like the man who owned the world.

She moaned now, softly, then as he pressed firmly, and then deeply, her moan grew . . . and quavered.

He watched her face, at the way she tilted her head back against the rest and stretched into his touch. Inside, her body flexed against his fingers, inciting him with promises of a sensuality beyond recollection, beyond any previous encounter.

Then she convulsed, quick and hard, coming while he pressed the heel of his hand against her clit. Her fingers dug into his ribs. Her groans were deep, heartfelt, and glorious.

Now. Now he would strip off his jeans and rip off her panties and—

Out of the corners of his eyes, he caught sight of something—someone—moving outside the truck.

A fist slammed against the driver's-side back window.

Elizabeth startled out of her sexual daze, pushed at Garik, and shoved her skirt down.

At the same time, Garik rose onto his knees, fists clenched, ready to fight for her.

Sheriff Foster—Sheriff Son-of-a-Bitch Foster—stepped up to the open front window. His green gaze swept them scornfully, observing their dishevelment, the way Garik protectively crouched over Elizabeth. "This is a public park," he announced. "Zip up. Get dressed. No lewd behavior allowed."

Garik could barely control himself. He wanted to leap across the console, over the steering wheel, and through the window to grab Foster by the throat and choke him. Instead he stared at Foster while the red tide of fury rose from his gut to wash over his face, and the fires of hell kindled in his eyes.

He'd been told he was a fearsome sight while in a rage.

Foster proved it when he stepped back, broke eye contact, and said, "Just doing my job. Thought you might be stranded here. Shouldn't be, um . . . teenagers might see and get the wrong idea."

"Get. Out." Garik's voice was soft and lethal.

Foster got. Out.

Garik watched through the rearview mirror as the sheriff climbed in his cruiser, put it in reverse, and drove in the opposite direction from town. The opposite direction from where they were going. "Damned good thing," Garik muttered. Then he glanced down at Elizabeth.

She sat with her eyes closed, her head bowed, a disgusted moue on her lips.

Garik sank back down on top of her. He slid one arm around her waist and one under her shoulders.

Her head fell back; she opened her eyes and looked at him. "In my whole life I have never been caught making out in a car. I am twenty-seven years old and now, with you, in the middle of a forest in the middle of an earthquake zone . . . I'm busted." She wasn't livid. She wasn't swearing at him for humiliating her.

Which for some reason made it okay for Garik to explode. "That worthless piece-of-shit sheriff bastard cocksucker."

"Who am I to argue?" she said.

"How dare he . . . teenagers, my ass. Nobody's out here except us people who have places to go and the gas to get there. Teenagers . . . like we're the damn corrupters of America's damn youth who already know more from the Internet than I knew when I was twenty-damned-five." Garik was raging. He knew he was raging. But damn it! If they'd had another fifteen minutes, just fifteen minutes—less!—he would have been cured of his perpetual hard-on.

Elizabeth petted his cheek. "We couldn't have done it in here anyway. The space is very constricted."

"Are you challenging me? Because I assure you, I have done it in a lot smaller vehicles than this. I'll have you know the first time I got laid was in a girl's Volkswagen Bug, not one of the later models, either. It was her father's classic Volkswagen Bug, and it didn't even have sealed headlights."

Elizabeth laughed. "I'll bet you didn't have sealed headlights, either."

Okay. She thought he was being stupid. He *was* being stupid. He didn't care. "I did, too. Carried the headlight cover around in my wallet for two years before I got to use it. Between my body heat and my fierce desire to put it on, it's a miracle it didn't disintegrate when I pulled it out of the foil packet."

Elizabeth started really laughing now, laughing hard enough to weep, so he gave her his handkerchief and let her wipe her eyes.

He liked the sound, liked the way her breasts bounced, liked the rosy color returning to her cheeks. "I was really hoping to put that handkerchief to a different use," he said wistfully.

Which made her laugh more. "Come on." She lightly punched his shoulder. "We've got to go."

"You're right. God damn it."

The moment had vanished. He had stuff he wanted—needed—to do, and it wasn't sex with Elizabeth. So he climbed back into the driver's side, helped her adjust her seat into the upright position, watched her buckle her seatbelt, buckled his and winced at the pressure on his lingering erection, and headed to town.

He hit the potholes a little too hard, and pretended Foster's balls were under the tires.

CHAPTER FORTY-SEVEN

Elizabeth looked around Virtue Falls' streets in wonder. "It is amazing to me that in three and a half days, the town has managed to gain some semblance of normalcy."

"The place never changes." Garik barely glanced around, and he did not sound complimentary.

"No, really, Garik. It's even more amazing when you consider that aftershocks still shake the region, communications with the outside world are mostly limited to emergency and law enforcement agencies, and road travel is almost nil." A group of four people, locals, stood talking on the sidewalk. She didn't know their names, but she recognized them, so she smiled and waved.

They stared at her and Garik in the cab of the truck, feebly waved back, then leaned their heads together.

Pleased that she had elicited a courteous response, Elizabeth sat up straighter. "How often in the height of the tourist season do we see the streets so empty?"

"All we need is one good storm, rain coming through the roofs, everybody jam-packed into the emergency shelters, and the whole town will go into meltdown." He glared at the gossips. "They're quivering with frustration already."

"But they brag about their fierce independence and survivalist instincts."

"They're fiercely independent as long as they have clean running water. Cut that off and they're nothing but a bunch of stinky, pissed-off citizens demanding their rights."

She didn't understand why he was so cynical. But she didn't care. His lovemaking, however cut short, had released some of her anxiety.

Garik, on the other hand, seemed more tense.

"Do you not like the town?" she asked.

"I like the town fine."

"You don't *sound* as if you like it."

"I sure as hell don't like the sheriff." If possible, Garik sounded even more savage than he had when they were interrupted.

"He was certainly in the wrong place at the wrong time." She arranged her skirt hem primly on her knees.

He watched out of the corners of his eyes.

"So it's not the town that makes you grumpy, it's—"

"I'm *horny*." He was very loud, and the windows were down. "Okay? I'm *horny*. And likely to stay that way, which makes me grumpy, as you put it."

She half-smiled. "We could drive out to the other side of town and—"

"And have the perverted bastard Foster follow us? I don't think so." Garik took an exasperated breath. "I've got stuff to do in town. It looks like the Oceanview Café is open."

It was. As she watched, one of the regulars opened the door and walked in.

Of course, the door was nothing but a metal frame with a handle. The window that had made up the primary door panel had been swept into a dust pan and tossed into the restaurant's overflowing trash can.

"Drop me there. I'll grab lunch, then I'll walk out to Virtue Falls Canyon and check on some of the markers I placed." She thought she was talking sweet reason. "I suspect the aftershocks will have moved them."

Garik's head whipped around. His face turned an odd puce.

"I want . . . to . . . document . . . the, er . . ." She faltered to a halt.

"Like hell you will," he snapped.

Being horny really unbalanced the guy. "Why not?" she asked gently.

"You found your mother's body yesterday. We discussed the fact Foster did a lousy job investigating her death, and we speculated that your father was innocent— which makes someone else guilty and possibly vengeful. Foster just proved himself to be the major asshole in the state. Dr. Frownfelter is one weird guy. Rainbow is here somewhere. I don't know where the other possible suspects are, but I do know your phone battery barely got charged this morning."

She pulled the phone out of her bag, and made a face. "It's dead," she said.

"And you want to go out alone and work in the field?" Garik double-parked next to a battered white pickup, and turned to her. "Not even, sweetheart."

His tone put her back up. "I hardly think you're in charge of how I spend my time."

"Elizabeth, I don't know jackshit about rocks, but when it comes to killing people"—he tapped his chest— "I'm the expert. And I'm right. You know I am."

She wanted to disagree—except he was the expert. He had the creds; he was an FBI agent. She would be stupid to argue. She wasn't stupid. She might be resentful. But she wasn't stupid. "Since you put it that way . . . okay."

He watched her cautiously. "Really? You'll stay in town?"

"We both agree that I am an eminently logical person, and doing as you wish in this case is logical." But she was curious, too. "What are *you* going to do?"

"I've got a friend I need to visit. School friend. Name of Mike Sun. I'll introduce you someday." Leaning across her, Garik opened her door. "Can you plant yourself at the Oceanview and catch up on paperwork until I finish?"

"Sure." She gathered her bag. "How long will you be?"

"A couple of hours. I'll be back for you." He turned his face to hers and kissed her hard. "Wait for me."

She kissed him back, and for one swift and glorious moment, she forgot about Virtue Falls and the earthquake and her father and the onlookers, and fell deeply and beautifully in lust with Garik. When she was breathless, he let her go, and they stared at each other. "I will wait for you," she said. "But I wish . . ."

"I do, too, but there's not a damned thing we can do about it now." He slid his hand under her hip. "Hurry up and get out while I remember that."

She slipped out of the truck and slammed the door.

He yelled out the window, "Stay out of trouble," and drove off toward the courthouse.

She turned toward the Oceanview, and muttered, "What possible trouble can I get into here?"

CHAPTER FORTY-EIGHT

For the first time since the earthquake, Elizabeth stepped inside the Oceanview Café.

Customers were eating at the tables, chatting as if they didn't notice that the windows beside them were blown out, the floors were catawampus, the tables were tilted, and the food consisted of coffee brewing on a camping cook stove and sandwiches served on paper towels.

"Hey, hon, grab a seat and I'll be with you in a minute." Rainbow sounded cheerful as she bustled past. "But be careful! We've cleaned and swept three times, and we're still finding glass in the damnedest places." She shook her fanny suggestively.

Elizabeth stared, then put that resolutely out of her mind, and went to the table in the far back corner where she'd be out of the way and have plenty of sun. She pulled out her chair and checked the seat, then sat down, placed her bag on the chair beside her, and heaved a sigh of relief. This was the most normal she'd felt since she'd seen the dog sit down in the middle of the street and brace himself.

She heard someone at the counter say, not quietly enough, "That's the girl who saw her father kill her mother with the scissors."

That was normal, too.

What wasn't normal was a guy calling, "Miss Banner, can I buy you a drink?"

She stared at the young blond firefighter who sat at a table full of firefighters, holding up his coffee cup. He was smiling, but tentatively, as if he wasn't quite sure she would smile back.

Everyone in the café got quiet.

So she did smile. "Peyton Bailey, thank you for saving my album. I've been showing it to my father, and it means so much to both of us."

His smile became a grin.

The customers went back to their conversations.

She felt as if she'd passed some test and was suddenly part of the group.

Peyton called to Rainbow, "I'll buy this young woman a drink!"

"Yes, Peyton. I got it. You're the BMOC." But when Rainbow stepped up to the table, she winked at Elizabeth and recited, "I can offer you coffee or a soft drink, and a sandwich on white or wheat, with baloney or cheese. You can have mustard, no problem. If I were you, I wouldn't touch the mayo. If you take the coffee, it'll be hot. That's all that'll be hot. The soft drink will be tepid, because everybody's using their ice to keep their meat cold and we can't get any more."

"Half a cheese sandwich on wheat, and do you have a bottle of water?"

Rainbow looked around. "For you, I do."

"Any word on when the electricity will be back on?" Elizabeth asked.

"The highway's a mess. The DOT is working on it, but it'll be a couple more days before trucks can get through. The mayor decided to ration water and gas. That caused a tizzy. We can't get anything into the harbor because it's so torn up and there are boats scattered everywhere on dry land, including the Coast Guard cutter, which no one is allowed near because it's government property." Rainbow put her hand on one hip. "Thank God lots of folks here have generators—with the winter storms we get, it makes good sense, but most of them run on propane and sooner or later, everybody's going to run out. Then there'll be trouble. No one will give us any update on Kateri's condition, which has me scared to death. So short answer—we don't know anything."

Elizabeth nodded. "I'm staying at the resort."

"I heard." Rainbow cleared her throat. "I heard you found your mother's body yesterday."

Of course. The sheriff and his deputies ate in here. "Who else knows?"

"Everybody." Rainbow put her hand on Elizabeth's shoulder. "I knew Misty. I knew her really well. She was my . . . friend. I am sorry."

"Thank you." It felt weird to be offered condolences. When she was a kid, no one said *I'm sorry* at all. They merely gossiped and speculated. Rainbow's words took Elizabeth into a different place, one where she could handle the situation maturely.

Of course, if Rainbow was the one who had killed her mother, that put a whole different light on the situation.

"Are you okay? I mean, finding any body is going to be tough, but this . . ." Rainbow shook her head as if at a loss for words.

"I am okay. Thank you. It helped to know where she is."

"Good." Rainbow patted Elizabeth's shoulder again, then spoke to the next table. "Yeah, yeah, keep your shirt on, I'll get your coffee." She walked off.

Elizabeth pulled out her notebook and her laptop, and looked through her notes, trying to appear well-balanced and pleasant when she now knew the whole town was gossiping about her and the murder . . . again.

Rainbow deposited the dry cheese sandwich and bottle of water on Elizabeth's table, which started a ker-fuffle from customers demanding their bottle of water, and Rainbow announcing that if they wanted special treatment, they should have tipped better before the earthquake.

Elizabeth listened, smiled, and ate, her eyes on her work. In only a few minutes, she was involved enough in creating a spreadsheet for slippage caused by after-shocks, she didn't notice when the firefighters pushed back their chairs, nor did she notice that as Peyton left, he sighed morosely.

Then a shadow fell across her table.

Absorbed in her work, she paid no attention.

Someone cleared his throat.

She paid no attention.

"For God's sake, Elizabeth," a man's voice snapped, "do you ever notice anything?"

She looked up in surprise. "Andrew. You're back!" One look at his scowling face, and her heart sank. He was irritated with her already.

"I've been back for over three hours." He said that as

if she should have sensed his return by a lightening in the atmosphere. "The earthquake made a mess of my house. The sites are completely overwhelmed by the tsunami. All our work has been swept away."

"Yes." She beamed. "Exactly as we predicted."

With the exaggerated patience he so often showed with her, he pulled out the chair opposite and seated himself. "Yes. Unfortunately, only you were here to experience the earthquake."

"I'm so glad you left me on site!" She thought he should be, too. After all, after so many years of constant monitoring, if no geologist had been here, that would have been a great tragedy.

He seemed unimpressed. "Rainbow says you witnessed the tsunami."

As if on cue, Rainbow showed up with a cup and a pot of coffee, and poured it for Andrew.

He didn't even acknowledge her presence, or her kindness.

Elizabeth tried to subdue her enthusiasm, and spoke in a quieter tone, but her fervor bubbled over with her choice of words. "The tsunami was magnificent."

"I'm sure it was." Leaning forward, he stared at her, and sniffed. His brown eyes narrowed. "You've had a bath. And your clothes are clean. How have you had a bath?"

She leaned back, away from him and his weird question. "I'm staying at Virtue Falls Resort. About the tsunami—"

He straightened up so fast his spine cracked. "They're letting people stay at Virtue Falls Resort?"

She shouldn't have said anything. She could see where this was going. But if she lied, Andrew would find out, so what were her options? "No, not exactly." She tore little bits off her paper towel. "I'm sort of . . . related."

He took a sip of his coffee. "I can afford to pay."

That surprised her, considering how, when the dinner check arrived, he was always in the men's room. "I don't think Mrs. Smith is interested in payment. The earthquake shattered the windows and created a lot of hazards inside and out, so she's only offering hospitality to people who are—"

"Sort of related? It's that marriage of yours, isn't it?" Andrew hitched his chair forward. "Listen, you can swear for me. I won't sue her, but I need someplace where I can get a hot shower and wash my clothes."

Elizabeth squirmed with discomfort. "I don't have any influence in this case. Mrs. Smith has been quite firm that she won't take guests."

"I wouldn't be a guest. I'd be like a ghost, hardly there except to bathe. And eat." His brown eyes lit up. "She has food, doesn't she?"

Elizabeth looked down at the half sandwich on her paper towel, and slowly pushed it toward him. "Do you want this?"

"No, I don't want *that*." He pushed it back. "I want a real meal!"

"Was your house destroyed? If it was, I might be able to plead—"

"There's no water or sewer or gas. There's stuff knocked out of the cupboards and off the shelves, and half of the furniture is overturned." He nursed his coffee. "My project helps support this town twenty-four/seven, winter months, too. Margaret Smith knows that. Use your influence. Persuade her."

"I really don't think I can." Nor did Elizabeth want to. When she thought of last night's dinner, and how Garik, Margaret, and she had talked about the past, explored the possibility that her father might not be guilty . . . putting

Andrew into the mix would ruin everything. They couldn't discuss anything personal, because he talked about himself all the time.

"Do it," Andrew said. "It would be good if you could get the whole team in there, but if you can't—make sure it's me."

Under the table, Elizabeth clenched her fists.

When she didn't reply Andrew's color rose in his cheeks. "Just do it, Elizabeth." It was clearly a threat. He wanted to be at the resort, and he would make her miserable if she failed.

Rainbow appeared again with the coffee pot. "Warm that up for you, Andrew?"

"Yes." He didn't look at her.

She poured coffee to the brim.

He took a sip. "Now, Elizabeth—you documented the tsunami?"

"I got it on video."

His color subsided, leaving him almost gray. "You got it on video. Where were you when it hit?"

"Here."

"And you—"

"I ran to the canyon and got there before the first wave came in." She opened her case and pulled out her laptop. "I uploaded it to my computer as soon as I could. So I have a backup. Do you want to see?"

She had thought he would be pleased. But he stared at her as if she aggravated him beyond belief. He barely moved his lips when he said, "Show me."

She flipped up the screen. Bringing up the video player, she pushed PLAY.

And she showed him.

Watching it again renewed her excitement, made her

want to point and explain, and once, she did pause the video and clarify a detail her father had identified.

When the video finished, Andrew tapped his fingertips together. "So you showed this to Charles Banner."

"I knew he would enjoy it, and as it happened, he had those new insights."

"Have you showed it to anyone else?"

"No. No one else is interested," she said truthfully.

"You haven't been able to upload it online?"

"It's been impossible, but the Internet is coming back. I plan to send it first to the Geological Society of America."

"Yes. Of course. They would be interested, I suppose." The finger tapping stopped. Andrew reached across the table and grabbed her wrist. "I hear you found your mother's corpse."

Elizabeth jerked back in shock at his touch and his words. "Yes."

He didn't release her. "Was there anything new there? Any detail we hadn't heard about before?"

"I . . . I don't want to discuss it."

Andrew's eyes narrowed, and he studied her like a bug under a microscope. "All right. But finding the corpse must have greatly upset you."

She didn't know quite how to respond. It was like he was digging at a recent wound. "The sight of the body was traumatic, yes, but I . . . already knew she was dead."

"But to actually see your mother's corpse." Andrew stared into her eyes. "I'm sure it was in a horrible state of decomposition."

"Of course." She swallowed.

He released her. "In light of the circumstances it might be better to hold back on releasing the video."

"Hold back?" Incredulous, now Elizabeth leaned

forward and spoke rapidly, persuasively. "This is an opportunity the scientific community has never enjoyed. Not even the footage of the Japanese earthquake and tsunami can compare to this cataclysm at this site, which has been studied for years. This video proves our theories about the geology of the area are correct. Not to mention that the drama of the footage will enthuse the public and help fund our research!"

"That is all true, but I'm thinking of you. With the recent developments in your mother's case, I'm afraid you'll face an on-camera collapse." When she would have objected, he held up one hand. "I have long thought of you as a protégé, much as your father thought of me. Elizabeth, trust me in this matter. You're a practical young woman, but logic cannot protect you from the trauma you suffered as a child and the renewed distress of dealing with your father, who has lost his memories of his terrible deed, and on top of all that—to find your mother's rotting corpse."

Andrew's voice, deep and dramatic, made a shiver run up Elizabeth's spine. But she kept her own voice quiet and level. "It's a fine point, Dr. Marrero, but would you please not call my mother a corpse? That is a horror film word."

"See?" He nodded as if he was wise. "You're more upset than you realize."

"I don't really know how that proves I'm upset." Although she was getting there, with a sick feeling in the pit of her stomach.

Nothing she said seemed to slow Andrew down; he kept rolling along. "Furthermore, you know that socially, you're not the most competent of women. I fear that when you were the center of attention, if you failed at a critical juncture, you would do our cause more harm than good."

He stood. "Keep this video quiet for the moment. The scientific value will remain when the fuss is over, and that's really why you took the video, isn't it? For the good of the scientific community?"

She surrendered at last. "Yes. Of course."

Uncharacteristically, he thumped her on the back, then turned and marched out the door.

Slowly, she put her laptop away.

Rainbow appeared and cleared away Andrew's coffee cup. "I heard."

"You did?"

"Of course. I was eavesdropping. How do you think I find out everything that goes on in this town?" Rainbow pulled a new bottle of water out of her apron pocket, unscrewed the cap, and put it in front of Elizabeth.

"If I didn't know better," Elizabeth said, "I would think Andrew Marrero was intentionally trying to upset me."

"You would, would you?" Rainbow wore an unpleasant expression as she watched him march past the windows toward his home.

"But why would he do such a thing?"

As if Elizabeth wasn't the brightest thing, Rainbow patted her shoulder. "Why, indeed."

CHAPTER FORTY-NINE

Noah Griffin looked in his backpack and knew he should have packed more clean underwear. A lot more underwear. With electricity and water scarce and the Virtue Falls Laundromat a wreck, he was reduced to turning his boxer briefs inside out and wearing them again. And he wasn't the kind of reporter who went out and pounded his clothes on a rock in the stream, although that might come if he didn't get out of this disaster of a town.

But he didn't want to leave. Maybe he wasn't a tough reporter who faced impediments without complaint, but he was a smart one, and he recognized opportunity when he saw it.

There were stories in Virtue Falls. Interesting stories. Stories about the hardships the earthquake had brought. Stories about the brave survivors. Stories that tugged at the heartstrings. Stories that blamed the geologists for not predicting the earthquake and stories about the incompetent government that responded too slowly to the emergency.

But best of all, there was the Elizabeth Banner story.

In that, he had the ingredients for a bestselling book: a vicious domestic crime committed by a husband on his wife, an innocent child who witnessed it and who, twenty-some years later, returned to the scene of the murder to discover her mother's missing body.

Oh, and the child had grown up to become a woman as beautiful as her mother with the intelligence of her father.

Oh, again. In the meantime, the father had gone crazy.

Did it *get* any better than that?

The guy Noah rented a room from, Old Man Landau, said he'd heard Elizabeth had returned to Virtue Falls to clear her father's name. And Rainbow at the café had told him Elizabeth's ex-husband had rushed to her side, and Garik Jacobsen was an FBI agent. So maybe the FBI agent also thought the father hadn't done it.

In that case, who had? *Heh, heh.* Finding the real

killer wasn't likely, but even the mere chance made Noah's mouth water.

In the meantime, Rainbow had also confided that Elizabeth had taken eye-popping video of the tsunami that she hadn't been able to release yet because of the size of the file and the crappy Internet connections.

Noah wouldn't mind being the one who helped her with that. After all, that would thoroughly piss off that total jerk, Andrew Marrero. Plus Elizabeth might be grateful, and the FBI agent was also the *ex*-husband.

Noah liked the way Elizabeth looked, and as long as he was in Virtue Falls collecting stories, he might as well create one of his own.

Grabbing his computer tablet, he headed for the Oceanview Café.

Yes, there was money to be made and fame to be found, because stories abounded in Virtue Falls, and Noah intended to find them all.

CHAPTER FIFTY

Garik walked into the courthouse intent on using his status as an FBI agent, or his background as a local, or whatever means possible to get to the morgue and view Misty's remains.

Subterfuge wasn't necessary.

The courthouse was quiet, staffed by a bare minimum of workers.

He asked to visit the coroner.

The officer manning the desk waved him in and went back to filling out paperwork with an ancient typewriter dragged out of some deep dark storage.

The morgue was in the basement, a dim, tiny, cold, stainless-steel-lined room with drawers where the dead rested in peace. Or not.

Mike Sun sat scowling at his old typewriter, typing with one finger at a time and cursing at every other letter. When he saw Garik, he scowled and asked, "Did you bring Wite-Out?"

"Wite-Out?" Garik laughed. "I would have, if I'd realized I was visiting the nineteen eighties."

"This week has been one surprise after another." Mike stood and offered his hand. "Somehow I knew you were going to find your way down here. How have you been?"

"Good." Garik shook the outstretched hand, then the two former school friends did an affectionate fist bump. "How's your mom?"

"Good. She doesn't yell at me anymore." Mike swiped his shoulder-length straight black hair off his forehead. "I've got a wife for that now."

Garik worked incredulity into his voice. "Who was dumb enough to marry you?"

"You remember Courtney Clenney?"

"The babe with the . . ." Garik thought better of saying that. "The babe who went off and became the Victoria's Secret model?"

Mike smiled. Smugly.

Garik looked the five-foot-five, half-Chinese and half-Aleut Mike up and down. "I mean, you're good-looking enough, but she's twice as tall as you are."

"Yes. When we dance, I've got a great view. My dad says he can't see my face, but he thinks I'm smiling."

Garik cackled. "Good work, man."

Another fist bump.

"Now," Garik said, "why did you know I could find my way down here?"

"I knew you'd want to examine Misty Banner's body. You didn't get a good look when you found her, and everybody in the building heard you yelled at Foster for sloppy police work." Mike grabbed a flashlight off his desk. "Sorry about the gloom. Half the fluorescent tubes broke, replacements, too, and anyway, no one's going to give me more power than they have to. Autopsies are not priority after an emergency like this. Everybody figures if someone died, it was the fault of the earthquake. Usually it is." He walked over to one of the drawers and pulled it open. "By the way, Foster told me not to let you down here."

"So you're going to break the rules?" Garik had forgotten how much he liked Mike.

"I don't work for Foster." Mike flipped back the sterile sheet. With a wave, he indicated the decomposing body of Misty Banner. "No matter how beautiful a person is in life, everyone ends like this."

"Every coroner I've ever met is a philosopher." Garik walked around the body, trying to reconstruct Misty as she had been the day she died.

"Coroners spend a lot of time alone, except for—" Mike indicated the drawers. "Anyway, that's the full extent of my philosophy."

"Come to think of it, that's the same thing I always hear." The body bore the thin markings of a well-wielded scalpel. "You already did the autopsy?"

"A coroner doesn't get a famous corpse like this on the table often. Besides, it had to be done quickly. Out of the ground, she's going to decompose rapidly."

"Tell me what you found out."

Mike clicked on the flashlight and used it to illuminate the pale, intact stretches of skin on her face, belly, and legs. "First—no way is she as decomposed as she would be if she'd been buried in the dirt, so she's been in a container of some kind."

"A coffin." Garik thought out loud. "The killer took her to the prostitutes' cemetery, dug up and dumped one of the other bodies, placed Misty inside, and buried her. Then the tsunami struck, lifting coffins, opening them, and spreading the contents up and down the canyon. First Elizabeth found a bone from one of the nineteenth-century prostitutes . . . then she found the corpse of her own mother."

"Good theory. A coffin would have protected Misty Banner. The killer didn't kill her with the first blow." With the flashlight, Mike showed Garik the flesh peeling back from her ribs. "The bones here show skid marks where he slashed at her. The ribs at the back show the same slashing, but more powerfully—he was above her, while she was on her hands and knees, trying to crawl away. There's a chip off her jawbone, right here on her left side."

Garik examined every site Mike indicated, and leaned closer to see the knick on her jawbone. "Was all the violence done with scissors?"

"I think so."

Garik looked up at Mike in surprise. "You think so?"

"Don't give me any shit, Garik." Mike pointed to a pile of twisted metal and broken glass swept into the corner. "During the earthquake, my one puny piece of cool autopsy equipment jumped off the table and onto the floor. But your intrepid coroner got out his good ol' magnifying glass and examined the evidence on Misty Banner's body, and noted that there are double scrapes on the bones."

"The tips of scissors."

"Yep. Banner was in a rage. Which I suppose makes sense when you think that his wife was cheating on him." Mike viewed the body with mingled disfavor and pity.

"Hm." It was so logical. Charles seemed very pleasant, but the blow to his pride and his manhood must have hurt. Garik liked his theory that her lover was the killer, but why would her lover turn on her so violently? . . . Unless she had threatened something . . .

To end the relationship? To reveal it?

He asked, "Which was the death blow?"

Mike shone his flashlight at her throat. "Here. Look at the larynx. The bones are shattered, broken, completely ripped open. He slashed, and slashed again, long after she was dead."

"She said something he didn't like."

"I think we can assume that—probably that she didn't love him anymore and she was running away with her lover."

"So he came at her in a rage, grabbed the scissors, and stabbed her in the ribs." Garik enacted the scene. "She went down, tried to crawl away. He stuck her in the back. She fell. He turned her over and ripped out her throat, nicking her jawbone at some point."

"He dug deep enough, he even notched the number-four vertebra from the front." Mike handed Garik the flashlight and let him get a good look. "Scissors don't slice neatly like a knife or a garrote. Look at where he cut off her hair. He got a pretty good chunk of flesh, too. He killed her, then he killed her again. This was a crime of passion and rage. No wonder Elizabeth Banner was traumatized."

"That she was." Garik indicated the area with the hair.

"Foster said there was hair at the crime scene he didn't report."

"What a dumbshit." Mike put his hands in his pockets, and shrugged. "But do you really think that would have made any difference to the verdict?"

"Maybe not, but I'm sure happier when I know the work was done competently."

"I heard that was one of the things you yelled at Foster about." Mike rocked back and forth on his heels. "That, and you pretty much accused him of killing Misty himself."

"I didn't accuse him, exactly," Garik corrected. "I asked where he was when she was murdered and how he got there so fast after the call came in."

Mike couldn't contain his sarcasm. "No, that's not an accusation. Not at all. Garik, Foster's really not a good guy. He's always been weird and he's getting weirder, and he . . . Well. You know he never liked you. You stick around here, and at the best, you're going to have more traffic tickets than you can pay."

"Probably." Garik shrugged back at Mike, but the memory of this afternoon's scene on the highway made his temper simmer.

"You're not going to back down," Mike said.

"No."

"Look, I've studied the case. Everyone in law enforcement has studied the case." Mike counted off the salient points on his fingers. "Charles Banner was on the scene. He had motivation. He was covered with blood. He was holding the scissors. Hell, his fingerprints were all over the scissors."

"But were they the only fingerprints? I read the reports. I can't find that Foster bothered to check." Garik waited a heartbeat. "If only I could see the original evidence . . ."

Mike pointedly ignored that. "Who do you think did this?" He took the flashlight back and pointed it at Misty's torn throat.

"Probably Charles Banner." Probably. "But as I said, I prefer competent work on behalf of law enforcement. Where is the evidence, do you know?"

Reluctantly, Mike said, "Local evidence stays here in the courthouse, in the evidence room."

"Really?" Garik couldn't believe his luck. "It's right here?"

"You going to break in?" Mike sounded hopeful.

"Not me." Garik lifted his eyebrows, tilted his head, and smiled at Mike.

Mike retreated. "No. No way. Not me. I've got a wife with an expensive underwear habit to support, and I like it that way."

Garik advanced. "What if Misty's lover killed her, and he's still hanging around? That's someone with a lot of fury simmering. What if he hates blondes? Isn't your wife blond?"

"Sometimes. Depends on what her and her hairdresser are up to this week." Mike dismissed that with a wave of his hand. "But Garik, that's the only murder there's been in this town, so even if it's not Charles Banner, whoever it is is never going to kill again, or he's moved on, or he went nuts, or he drove into the ocean. He's not around anymore."

"Or the discovery of Misty Banner's body is going to scare him and bring him out of hiding."

"No, I'm not stealing evidence for you. No, no, no!" Mike's voice got louder with each repetition.

Which meant he was tempted. So Garik backed off. "Okay! You don't have to sound like a reluctant virgin. I'll do it myself."

"Don't get caught."

"I won't if you give me your keys."

"Yeah, that'll get me off the hook. Anyway, I don't have the keys for the evidence room. And honest, Garik, I don't think you ought to break in. I'm telling you . . ." Mike stopped talking. He put his hands in his pockets again. He shifted from foot to foot, avoided Garik's gaze.

"Men's room's up the stairs," Garik said.

"It's not that." As if he'd made a decision, Mike set his chin. "You've been in on a few autopsies in your time?"

"A few. I do everything in my power to avoid them. Afterwards I have nightmares, and the dead are always, like, talking to me." Garik shuddered.

"The dead talk to me, too, if I examine them correctly." Mike shut the drawer, hiding Misty from sight. He pulled a couple of latex gloves out of a box on his desk and said, "Come and look at this." He opened another drawer.

Garik stared at the body of a shriveled old woman. "Who's that?"

"Foster's mother."

"His mother?" Garik searched his memory, and remembered an ancient sighting of her driving herself to church. "God, it is her, isn't it? She looks like hell."

"Dehydrated. After the earthquake, Foster didn't go home. Finally when he did, and this was last night, he found her crushed under the refrigerator. Took three men to lift it off so I could drag her out."

"She was dead?"

"Yes, and a long, painful, unpleasant death it was. Internal bleeding, bruising from being battered with cans, cuts from the broken dishes."

"The day I came into town, she texted him while we were talking." Garik remembered the way Foster had acted when the call came through. "He never went to check on her?"

"It gets better." Mike flicked on his flashlight and carefully rolled Mrs. Foster to one side. "I couldn't quite figure out what caused bleeding on her skull, lower right, so I shaved her hair and took a look."

Garik looked at the dent. "What caused that?"

"Not a can."

"The shape looks like the butt of a revolver."

"That's what I thought."

Garik put the clues together. "The old battle-ax wasn't quite dead when he found her, and he wasn't taking any chances she might survive."

"Pretty much what I thought, too."

The two men looked at each other.

"I never really imagined Foster did kill Misty, because I was thinking if it wasn't Charles, it was definitely the lover. And I don't believe Foster ever slept with a woman in his whole life." An ugly thought wormed its way into Garik's brain. "But I never considered the fact he was raised by a religious fanatic. Like you said, he's weird. Maybe he's more than weird. Maybe he's a sociopath. Say his mean old mother knew about the affair, and she carried on about sin and adultery. Maybe Foster figured God wanted him to kill the adulteress."

Mike watched him, jaw dropped. "No wonder you're in the FBI! You've got the most suspicious mind of any person I ever met."

"Yes, I do have a suspicious mind, but I'm not with

the FBI anymore," Garik said absently. "Or rather, I'm on leave."

"But you love the FBI! Why would you go on leave?"

"I didn't *go* on leave. I was *put* on leave. Because I lost my temper." And not even Elizabeth's assurances had eased his guilt.

"Does Foster know you're on leave?" Mike asked.

Garik snorted. "Of course. He makes it his business to know all the crapass stuff he can use for leverage."

"Against you."

"Against everyone. Foster is one of those guys who likes to have the upper hand."

Mike groped his own throat, as if he could feel a noose tightening. "I don't disagree. That's why I don't think you ought to be pissing off Dennis Foster. Not when we're trapped in this town. Not when he holds all the power. The guy is most likely off his rocker."

Garik stared at the skinny, naked, bruised body of Foster's mother, and contemplated the surprising multitude of options he had to consider about the murder of Misty Banner. "Rage or cold-blooded murder. Which is worse? And did the same man do them both?"

CHAPTER FIFTY-ONE

Another shadow fell across Elizabeth's table.

This time she looked up immediately and in alarm.

A pleasant-looking young man, about her age, stood with his hand on the chair Andrew Marrero had so recently vacated.

"Do you mind if I join you?" He didn't wait for an answer, but sat down.

"Do I know you?" She was pretty sure she had never met him.

"I'm Noah Griffin." He used his fingers to push his shock of brown hair, tipped with blond, across his forehead and over to one side. "I'm a reporter and I'm doing a news story on the earthquake and tsunami. I understand you're the expert."

Elizabeth didn't have any warm memories of reporters—on the tenth anniversary of her mother's death, one had popped up and caught her as she left school, and badgered her all the way home, asking what she remembered of the day, recounting the events as they were believed to have unfolded in an effort to make her talk.

Her aunt had been furious, then ended up giving an interview, rehashing her niece's mental problems, and creating even more trouble at school and at home for ugly duckling Elizabeth.

But this guy looked nice, not obnoxious, and more important, he was asking about the tsunami. So, cautiously, she said, "I'm not *the* expert. I'm *an* expert."

"That's not the way I understand it. I heard you were the only one of that research team who was in town when the earthquake hit. I heard you took some great footage of the tsunami."

He knew too much, and that made her feel squiggly. "How did you hear that?"

"Rainbow is a big cheerleader of yours." He saluted Rainbow with two fingers to his forehead.

Rainbow nodded genially.

Elizabeth relaxed and admitted, "I did get some great footage."

"Could I see it?"

She debated whether she should show him.

Andrew wanted her to keep the footage secret.

But what harm could it do to show it to this reporter? Especially when her father's reaction to the footage and Elizabeth's commentary had been so positive. And regardless of what Andrew said, she knew showing the video to the world was the best thing she could do for the Banner research site.

Her excitement, so recently snuffed by Andrew, revived.

After all, she hadn't really agreed to keep it secret. She had merely sort of agreed to not post it online or send it to the Geological Society of America.

Reaching into her bag, she pulled out her laptop. She placed it so they could both see the screen. "Watch this!" She kept the volume down and watched the tsunami unfold again, transfixed by the majesty and excitement. She didn't notice that Noah watched her as much as he watched the film, or that the other customers craned their necks. She didn't notice that Rainbow came to stand at the end of the table to watch and listen, too, her mouth curved in a half-smile.

After ten minutes, Noah pushed OFF and turned to face Elizabeth. "Look, I have some contacts in the news and on the Discovery Channel. They'd kill to have this, and you're a natural. Why don't I get ahold of them?"

"I had planned to turn the film over to the Geological Society of America, then send it to . . . I don't know, some science channel. But the head of our project arrived this morning." She realized her lips were stiff and the words came with formal reluctance. "After reviewing my work, he suggested I not post the film."

"The head of your project." Noah got a nasty smile on his face. "That would be Andrew Marrero?"

The reporter had done his research. "Yes. That's him."

"Andrew Marrero suggested you not release this? May I ask why?" Noah lightly touched her hand.

He had a way of making her feel as if she knew him, as if she could confide in him. "Many years ago, my mother was killed and her body disappeared. I just found her body, and Mr. Marrero said bringing myself to the public's attention now would stir up all the old news stories and make it difficult for me to work."

Rainbow gave an explosive snort and walked away.

"I'm forced to agree with *her*." Noah tilted his head toward Rainbow. "That's bullshit. This is brilliant stuff. You're succinct, well spoken, you know how to explain stuff in layman's terms. You've got a great on-air voice. You deserve recognition for your work."

"I'll get that recognition. Just . . . not right now." She was trying to convince herself as much as him.

Rainbow came back with a baloney sandwich on wheat, a pickle, and a canned Coke. She placed them in front of Noah. "Can I get you something else?"

"No, thanks. One sandwich is my limit." He waited until she had gone before saying, "Are you very upset about finding your mother's body?"

"At the time, I was. Now I'm mostly glad to know that after law enforcement studies her, I'll be able to lay her to rest." Talking to Noah was like talking to a long-lost brother. "Death rituals facilitate the grieving process, and I believe performing those rituals would be healthy for both me and my father."

"Your father killed her, right?"

A week ago, she would have said yes, and with assurance. Now she said, "He was convicted of the crime."

"I read the reports. You saw the crime." Noah popped the top on his Coke. "Did he do it?"

"I don't remember."

"He denied doing it. But then he would, wouldn't he?" Noah shot the questions at her as if he had the right to know.

That made her withdraw into the cool, logical façade she wore so well. "Yes. Sadly, he's suffering from Alzheimer's and doesn't remember that my mother is dead at all, although he does remember their relationship. When I spoke to him this morning, he told me about their early time together. I hope he can continue to recall what their marriage was like; it will shed some light on what happened to her."

Noah's eyes grew wide and intent. "It sounds as if you don't believe he killed your mother."

"Anyone who knows my father well doesn't believe he did it. So perhaps there is room for doubt." She was proud of her levelheaded response.

Noah picked up the sandwich and took a big bite. "Who do you think is guilty?"

"I don't have any idea."

He chewed, swallowed. "Her lover?"

"I don't know who that is or even if there really was a lover. That was rumor, wasn't it? And the issue was never addressed during the trial." Which, come to think of it, was illogical. Had her father's attorney been so incompetent?

Noah took another bite of the sandwich, a big bite, as if he feared he would never have another. He seemed to mull things over. He got to his feet as abruptly as he had seated himself. "Thank you, Miss Banner. You put a face on the tragedy of the earthquake, and I appreciate that." Taking his Coke, he walked away.

His abrupt departure left her confused. "Wait," she called. "Do you intend to write about me?"

He walked back. "In my article, I'd like to include information about you and your video. The video really is spectacular."

She was torn between wanting to get her beautiful video out to the public, and not wanting to deal with an angry Andrew Marrero.

Maybe she should trust to fate. The Internet in the area was seriously compromised. There was a good chance Noah wouldn't be able get his story released, anyway. "I suppose, but—"

"Good. I'll let you know when the article goes live."

He didn't have to let her know when the article went live. About an hour and a half later, she found out when she looked up and discovered Andrew Marrero storming toward her.

CHAPTER FIFTY-TWO

Garik headed into the Oceanview Café, wondering what the hell he was going to say to Elizabeth about her mother's autopsy, wondering what he should do about Sheriff Foster and his crime, and thinking he felt altogether like a better person than he had been an hour ago. At least he hadn't killed any of his relatives . . .

Garik froze in midstep.

The memory of his father's face rose in his mind. The vivid green-and-gold eyes, aflame with rage, the red-mottled cheeks, the blond hair strands soaked with sweat, the mouth open and screaming with rage.

Garik took a breath.

His father was dead. The past . . . was dead. Garik might be guilty of unforgivable crimes, but nothing he did could bring the dead to life. Nothing.

He opened the door the rest of the way, and walked in. He searched for Elizabeth, then caught sight of something rushing at him from the side. He turned swiftly—and faced Rainbow, her face hard and angry.

She grabbed him by the arm and in a hurried, hushed voice, said, "Andrew Marrero has Elizabeth cornered and he's throwing a shit fit."

Garik searched the restaurant with his narrowed gaze. "What? Why?"

"Some reporter put an article in the online papers rehashing the whole Banner murder case—identifying Charles as the world's foremost geologist, telling how he founded the study, how he killed his wife, what Elizabeth saw, how she says her father didn't do it."

That brought Garik's attention squarely onto Rainbow. "She said her father didn't do it?" Talk about creating complications.

Then he caught sight of Elizabeth at the back corner by the window, backed against the wall, her eyes wide, horrified, and fixed on her boss.

Marrero stood, his palms pressed flat to the table, every line of his body hostile and aggressive.

Garik had never seen Elizabeth look like that. Not when they were fighting—she had never been afraid of him. He wanted to rush to her side, to shove Marrero's face through the wall.

But that would be the act of a man who was out of control.

Elizabeth could handle herself for another few minutes, and Garik needed to know the facts before he stepped in. "So what has Charles's guilt or innocence got to do with Marrero? Why is he picking on her?"

"Because this reporter said she recorded a mind-boggling video of the tsunami and Andrew won't let her release it because he's jealous. The article claimed she is so much more talented that Marrero is afraid he'd be left in her dust." As Rainbow watched Marrero and Elizabeth, she clutched the sleeve of Garik's shirt in her fist.

"I don't believe it. She didn't say that." True, Elizabeth was distressingly honest, and she knew very well how intelligent she was. But he'd never heard her slam other geologists.

"No, of course she didn't. But that's the way the reporter wrote the article. Andrew came charging in here, carrying on about how she sabotaged him." Rainbow watched Marrero as he leaned farther and gestured with hostile motions.

Garik shook Rainbow away. "Okay, thanks, I'll take it from here."

She caught him by the back of the shirt. "Earlier, he put the pressure on Elizabeth to make Margaret let him stay at the resort."

Garik laughed once, shortly. "You are shitting me."

Rainbow looked at him.

He looked at Rainbow.

They nodded.

Then he headed to the table in the back corner by the window where Elizabeth sat, staring at Andrew Marrero.

Garik heard the phrases Marrero flung at Elizabeth: "You want to be a star, even at the cost of the study," "Recklessly putting yourself forward without thought to the results," "Ignoring my recommendations made with nothing but your best interests at heart," "Proving your inadequacies . . ."

Garik slapped his hand on Andrew Marrero's shoulder hard enough to make him jump. "You're upset, Marrero."

Marrero turned on him with ferocious intent . . . then saw who it was and backed away.

Garik had recognized him as a specific kind of coward: the man who picked on women, children, the elderly, and never someone who could beat him.

Never Garik.

Garik spoke pleasantly. "A man so upset deserves to take a few moments to formulate his thoughts. Perhaps you should go away and consider how best to handle this situation with the press, maybe approach the reporter and explain your reasons for not wanting Elizabeth to present her video to the waiting world. I'm sure you have good ones. In the meantime, considering how you feel about Elizabeth, I understand how you would be reluctant to stay at Virtue Falls Resort. I'll express your regrets to Margaret."

Marrero needed a few minutes to comprehend and respond. Then, like the selfish bastard he was, he latched onto the tidbit that impacted him most. "Margaret was going to let me stay?"

"Of course!" Garik used all his FBI-honed acting ability to drive a stake into Marrero's heart. "Elizabeth requested that you be allowed to move in. You and your team."

Elizabeth started to speak.

He shook his head back, an infinitesimal shake to warn her off.

Before, when they were married, she was oblivious to all but the most blatant of hints. Now she caught on, and subsided.

Garik continued, "Margaret adores Elizabeth, so she said she would welcome you into her resort. But after this disappointment, you don't want to be around Elizabeth."

Taking Elizabeth's hand, he pulled her up off her chair. "I respect your feelings." He picked up her bag and slung it over his shoulder. "I'll tell Margaret *not* to prepare your room. Good evening, Andrew."

"But I can . . . That is, this is nothing but a misunderstanding." Marrero backtracked fast, and too late. "The reporter probably misrepresented everything Elizabeth said. I've met him before. He draws rash conclusions. Elizabeth is probably innocent of maligning me."

"Probably." Garik smiled tightly. Turning to Elizabeth, he said, "Come on, sweetheart."

Her face looked pale and shell-shocked, like someone who had been slapped when she least expected it.

His wife was in anguish.

Garik lost his temper. He turned ferociously on Andrew Marrero, and with withering sarcasm said, "Thanks so much for supporting Elizabeth. Next time, make sure of your facts before you start bullying your staff."

"No." Marrero still thought he could repair the situation. "Listen!"

Putting his arm around Elizabeth, Garik walked with her to the door.

CHAPTER FIFTY-THREE

The truck was parked at the curb.

Garik put Elizabeth in the passenger's seat, walked around, and got in the driver's side. One look at her, at her pale, still face, and he smacked the steering wheel with his palm. "That son-of-a-bitch!"

She took a quavering breath. "He thought I had slandered him."

"No, he didn't," Garik said. "He's not stupid. He knows you would never do anything to harm the study."

"Apparently, the article accused him of being afraid I would be the future voice of science."

Garik glanced into the diner.

Marrero was headed their way. Going to make a last ditch appeal for resort housing, no doubt.

Garik waited until Marrero's hand touched the café's door, then he put the truck into gear and peeled out. Squealing his tires appeased his wrath, and his voice gentled. "Of course he's afraid you're going to supplant him. Is there any other reason why he didn't want you to release that video?"

"He said it was because I had just found my mother's body and I was upset." She fumbled in her bag, put on her sunglasses. Hiding.

"Elizabeth, you *are* upset about your mother. That's natural." Garik headed out of town and toward the resort, driving quickly and efficiently. "But what has that to do with the video? The video is your work, and showing it to the public would bring attention and funds to the study. He knows that. So the only thing left is that he doesn't want to be overshadowed by an attractive woman who took amazing video, who clearly knows her subject, who can explain things in layman's terms. He doesn't want to be over shadowed by you!"

She looked out the window at the passing forest. "He said I'm socially inept and . . . and that would lead to my collapse and . . . and my emotional state would reflect badly on the study." Her voice wobbled more and more.

"He said a lot of shit, didn't he?" Garik slammed on his brakes right in the middle of the road, and turned to her in a rush of mingled compassion and impatience. "I've been around assholes like this before. The ones who pretend to care and undermine you all the while." Gently, he pulled off her sunglasses, looked her in the eyes, and pointed at himself. "Do you know who I am? Do you know?"

"You're Garik Jacobsen." But she watched as if she was unsure of him.

He'd surprised her, with his actions, and with his words. Good, because he was about to crucify himself. For her. "Garik Jacobsen, the boy whose father tried to kill him. Yeah. I'm the kid whose father got drunk and punched him, broke his ribs, his jaw, his nose, and tried to rip off his arm."

"Oh, Garik." Her blue eyes grew wide and horrified— and surprised.

How about that? She hadn't suspected. "My father was always like that. He was a gardener, for shit's sake. I never met a man who knew more about plants than him. I remember the way he would cradle a seedling in his palm. He would tell me the Latin name, how he had prepared the soil to nurture this plant, how much water it needed, and sunshine." Memories swept up from Garik's past, from his soul. Emotions, too. The pure, sweet admiration of a little boy awed by his father's wisdom, his father's skill, his father's tenderness. "I watched him plant seedlings, watched them bloom under his loving care." Garik willed her to understand. "And I remember him coming home drunk, crushing those flowers in his fists, throwing them and cursing, and then, as if that wasn't enough, flattening them under his heels." Nightmare emotions, now. Panic. Terror. And guilt. Bleak, overwhelming, useless, stupid, irrational guilt.

"Your father did that . . . to the plants." Elizabeth put

her hands to her cheeks and watched him, eyes wide and somber.

"When he was sober, he was the greatest dad in the world. He treated me like one of his seedlings, said the right stuff, fed me, clothed me." Garik recalled the pleasure of those times. Recalled, too, the little boy's futile hope that if he did everything right, said everything that needed to be said, his daddy would love him forever.

She knew the punch line of this story. He told her that, first. Yet still she led him with a softly spoken, "But . . . ?"

"But Dad could only do sober for so long. We'd move somewhere, he'd get a job on some posh estate or at a big garden center. He'd impress the hell out of his employers. Women always thought he was sweet. Then he'd start drinking. Again." Garik talked too fast, remembered too much. "A little at first. A couple of beers. A shot of tequila. All of a sudden, he was out of control. When he was like that, I'd try to keep him out of the way." Stupid, desperate kid that he had been. "Some rich lady would knock on the door and want cut flowers for her garden party, or to tell him weeds had invaded the roses. I'd try to cover for him. Tell them I was sick and he couldn't leave me, and she'd get all sympathetic. Trouble was, he had the hearing of a lynx. He'd rouse from his stupor and come roaring to the door, screaming obscenities to the woman he'd spent so much time impressing. 'I'm independent, I don't have to take orders from a cunt.'"

Elizabeth flinched.

"Yes. His favorite drunken insult to any female. It always worked. He'd always get fired, and . . ." Garik dangled, bleeding, on the hook of old horrors.

"He would hurt you," Elizabeth said.

"He would hurt me." Garik felt jumpy, like a cat walk-

ing across an iron furnace vent. He was telling his story
to Elizabeth, and unlike his father, he was in control.

He didn't expect her to stick with him after this. Although he hadn't admitted it even to himself, he had been
nursing some hopes of a reunion. But now she knew how
pathetic he really was.

Still, if he made her feel better about that dumbshit
Andrew Marrero, it was okay. Garik did not ever want
to see that misery on Elizabeth's face again. "My father
would hurt me. He'd tell me everything was my fault. My
fault he started drinking again. My fault his employers
got mad at him. My fault my mother ran away. All crap,
of course. He was a raging, abusive alcoholic."

"What happened to him?" Her voice was soft, slow,
kind.

Great. She did feel sorry for him. Which was exactly
why he hadn't told her earlier. "Oh. That. He beat me,
broke my face, broke my arm pretty good. Twisted it, shattered both bones between the wrist and the elbow, then
passed out. For that matter, so did I, for a while. Then I got
myself to the hospital—I'd had practice. I told the emergency room personnel some craptastic story about how I
fell down the stairs. They didn't believe me. I knew I was
in for another stretch in a foster home."

"You'd been in foster homes before?" She took her
sunglasses back from him and looked down at them.

"That's one of the reasons we kept moving. Dad didn't
want me raised in a foster home. And I didn't want that,
either. The kids in foster homes were always . . . damaged." With finely tuned irony, he said, "I didn't want to
be damaged."

Elizabeth shifted toward him. She stroked his arm as
if taking the old, bad pain away with a brush of her hand.

Deliberately, Garik slowed down his rush of words. The worst was over. He'd told Elizabeth the truth. She felt bad for him. She realized she wasn't the only one who had had a tough life and been maligned by jackasses like Marrero. Garik's story had done its job. He was glad. He was proud. Of himself. Really. "Margaret was also in the emergency room—she actually *had* fallen down some stairs, and Harold insisted she come and get checked out. She heard the medical personnel talking about me, and it pissed her off good. That little Irishwoman doesn't like bullies. She has a thing about taking down bullies."

"I'm sure she does." Elizabeth seemed to think for a moment. "With her background, I understand."

"Next thing I knew," Garik said, "my father had disappeared and I went to live with Margaret."

Elizabeth petted him with more strength, more conviction. "Thank God. He might have killed you."

"But I . . . he was my father." Garik remembered the way he had cowered at the resort for days and weeks, the tears that soaked his pillow as he waited to be beaten and then discarded. "I was scared, reluctant, amazed to be living at the resort, thrilled to have three meals a day that I didn't have to scrounge out of a garbage can." Then more tears soaked his pillow . . . as he missed his father.

Elizabeth scrubbed away her own tears with one hand. "Don't cry. C'mon, this is the good part."

"I know." She sniffled. "I'm happy for you."

"I went to school, worked hard to catch up. Margaret was strict about that, I can tell you, and she told me the only way a kid like me would get ahead was to be smarter than everyone else."

Elizabeth smiled, a wobbly smile of fellowship. "Aren't we lucky that we *are* smarter than everyone else?"

Garik repeated, "But . . . he was my father, my only parent, and he was gone." Good, Garik. Tell her the pitiful stuff, then moan about your good fortune. She had to be impressed.

"You missed him."

"I loved him. It doesn't make sense, I know."

"He was your father, your kin, your blood. And you missed him."

She understood. Garik couldn't believe it, but she did understand.

When someone leaned on the horn behind him, she jumped, and Garik was almost relieved to see a cop car in his rearview mirror. Not Sheriff Foster this time, though. Garik waved the boy deputy around, rolled down his window, and called, "Sorry, I dropped a Coke in my lap. We've got it cleaned up now."

"You don't need assistance?" The cop was obviously disappointed. "Then move along—it's dangerous to block the road."

Garik watched him drive off. "Right. We're the only two on the road, but it's dangerous to block it." Putting the pickup in gear, he drove slowly, sensibly. No more tire skidding.

"What happened to your father?" Elizabeth hadn't taken her hand off his arm.

Garik should have known she'd want to know the whole story. And he was going to tell her, because . . . why not? Once he'd come this far, he might as well spill all the beans. No more secrets. No more lies. Give her the straight stuff and let her run as far and as fast as she could to the other side of the world. "When I was a teenager, he came back. He jumped me after school and said he wanted his share of the good life. He wanted me to get money out of Margaret."

"Oh." Elizabeth took a breath. "That's why you got into trouble. With Foster, I mean."

"Yes. I robbed a few stores. Gave my father the money. Got caught and Margaret bailed me out." He didn't want Elizabeth feeling sorry for him. Too late for that, of course. "I wanted to handle it myself, and having Margaret bail me out made me . . . it humiliated me. I swaggered. I shouted. I was a little asshole."

"But your father wasn't gone."

Of course she figured that right out. "No."

"What did he do?"

"He . . . my father told me I was a failure. He listed all the reasons. I never stood with him. I was my mother's son. I ran when the going got tough. He made it sound like it was my fault he abused me. He undermined me. Sound familiar?"

Elizabeth pulled her hand away. "You're saying Andrew Marrero has abused me."

"Marrero knows too much about you. He knows the buttons to push. Yes, he has abused you, and the reporter is right. Marrero doesn't want to stand in your shadow, he doesn't want you to be the spokesman for the scientific community. He saw the video you took of the tsunami, heard your commentary, realized that with your looks, scientific credentials, and pure good luck at being the only knowledgeable person on site during the earthquake and tsunami, you'll supplant him and be the new star of every PBS and History Channel geological special for the next twenty-five years. So Marrero's going to keep that video hidden until the earthquake is old news. This is no time to be naïve." Garik pulled into the resort parking lot. "The guy's an egotistical, self-centered bastard."

"He's one of the men who could possibly have been

my mother's lover." She squinted through the sunny windshield, then, as if she had just now remembered she held them, she slid her sunglasses on her nose.

"That, too." Garik parked right next to the front porch steps. "If she told him it was over, he had every reason to kill her. Hell, he had every reason to kill her even if he wasn't her lover. He could have killed her to set up your father as the killer so he could direct the dig." Another motive, and one all too obvious.

"That's absurd, to kill someone over something like a job title."

"Nothing's absurd when it comes to power. Men will do anything for power." If Garik had ever doubted the truth of that, the recollection of another father's smile made him writhe with anger and pain.

"Power regardless of the price. I don't understand that, but I've read about it, and I believe you."

"I know this stuff, Elizabeth. It's part of my training." And his memories.

"Tell me the end of the story," Elizabeth said. "What finally happened between you and your father?"

Garik looked up at the resort, all four stories of it. "He broke in, but this time he didn't come after me. I was now taller, stronger, more reckless than him. He came after Margaret, because she was old and frail."

"Oh, God." Elizabeth sighed. "Of course. What happened?"

"The next day, when the sun came up, my father was dead on the rocks at the bottom of the cliff below Margaret's balcony—and she faced manslaughter charges."

Elizabeth thought it over. "Who killed your father?"

"I did. I shot him, and when he didn't die, I threw him off the balcony."

CHAPTER FIFTY-FOUR

Somewhere in the depths of her mind, Kateri lived.

She couldn't move. She didn't eat or drink. She didn't think. She floated in time, in space, like a galaxy formed from a billion stars, like a fetus awaiting rebirth.

As she floated, she was growing, changing. Molecules realigned themselves. Bones knit. Bruising healed.

But cells mutated. Her body was not what it had been before.

Occasionally she caught a wisp of humanity hovering close. Occasionally she smelled antiseptic and flesh. Occasionally she heard voices, muffled by distance or time . . . or pain.

The pain was always there, her newest companion. A constant companion. She almost felt it. If she could grasp the tendrils of that pain, it would guide her up, out of this darkness.

But every time she tried, every time her fingers brushed the writhing tendrils, she didn't feel pain. She felt agony . . . blistering, tearing, ripping her soul and her sanity.

Then she sank back into the depths, and floated. Floated . . .

A tendril of crimson pain flicked at her consciousness. Taunted her. Enticed her.

Come back. Be a person again.

She caught. She pulled.

Anguish. Torture. Legs, arms, back, belly. So . . . much . . . pain.

But she pulled again, nerves burning, muscles trembling, brain afire.

She heard things: beeping, voices, cloth rustling, a tuneless humming. The sounds got nearer. Nearer.

No. Go back, Kateri. Don't come up.

She opened her eyes.

Movement. Above her. Around her. Humans working, saying things, urgent sounds she didn't understand.

To the side, gauges popping with colors.

On the wall, a television set to . . . to the Weather Channel.

A window. Sunshine slanting in.

She tried to speak. Something in her mouth.

She tried to move. Something holding her down.

And pain. Pain exploding in all the far reaches of her universe.

Her heart beat loud in her ears.

Her breath rasped in her lungs.

She fought, and trembled with the effort to be free.

Then . . . the effort broke her will. She let go of the writhing pain tendril.

At once she sank back down into space and time . . . and isolation.

But she would be back.

Soon.

CHAPTER FIFTY-FIVE

The ground started trembling.

The truck started trembling.

The inn started trembling.

"There it goes again." But there were things that

needed to be said. "The only other person in the world who knows that I killed my father is Margaret."

"I understand." Elizabeth wasn't paying attention to Garik. She looked toward the ocean, blue and glittering in the sun. At the parking lot, wrinkled from previous aftershocks. At the resort, which swayed like a tall ship in a storm.

He had to raise his voice to be heard over the creaking of the truck and the cracking of the asphalt. "If the FBI ever finds out, my career will be toast. It already pretty much is, but I could do time, so don't tell anybody."

"No, of course not." She spared him a glance. "But that explains a lot."

He wanted to ask what exactly she thought it explained, but abruptly the shaking got worse. He grasped the door frame to hold himself in place, reached a hand across to Elizabeth, and wrapped his fingers around her wrist. Like that would protect her. But even after his confession, he needed to hold her.

People staggered out of the resort and onto the porch, grasped the rails and uprights, looked around in panic.

"The truck is hopping around." Leaning and rolling with the ground waves. Garik spared a thought to his shocks and struts.

"This is a major aftershock, well over six-point, I think." Even Elizabeth's voice shook.

Then the shaking died away, moving on inland to wreak more destruction on the already broken landscape.

"It's a great thing for me to have experienced such a cataclysmic event," Elizabeth said. "Professionally. But it can stop now!" She yelled the last two words out the window, then looked surprised at herself.

To Garik's amazement, he wanted to laugh. He'd just

torn out his guts for her, told her all his long-held secrets, and he wanted to laugh? Really?

He needed to face facts; he was never going to be more important to Elizabeth than an earthquake. That's why she wasn't reacting to his confession. He didn't need to imagine she was okay with the fact that he had been a sniveling kid who had grown up to be a murderer. Because she did mind, or would later when she'd had time to think about it.

Yet another glance at her aggravated face again made him want to laugh.

He must be hysterical.

He cleared his throat. He let go of her wrist. He looked at the people lining the porch. "What is Mike Sun doing out here?"

"I don't know. Who's Mike Sun? Oh, wait, I remember—he's your friend."

"Yes." Garik might as well tell her. "He's also the coroner."

"You went to see him today." She remembered that, too, of course.

"Yes." No need for more explanation, unless she demanded it. Garik looked around the parking lot. "Where's his car?"

"Did he perhaps ride a bicycle?" Elizabeth pointed to two road bikes chained to the resort's racks.

Garik slid out of the truck, came around to the passenger side, and opened Elizabeth's door. As she descended from her seat, he took care not to touch her.

But she put her hand on his shoulder to steady herself, and moved close to him as Mike and a woman—wow, that must be his wife, Courtney—came off the porch and across the parking lot toward them. Both looked windblown and healthy, and had helmet hair.

So Elizabeth was right. They had come by bike.

"Hey, good to see you, and so soon!" Garik raised his eyebrows at Mike.

Mike said, "Courtney wanted to take a ride—you remember Courtney, don't you, Garik?"

Garik offered his hand.

Courtney took it, pulled herself into him, and did the double cheek kiss.

She was almost his height, built like a Barbie doll, top-heavy with no hips and long legs. She had a tan so natural and smooth it looked fake, hair so black it was obviously dyed, and she was as gorgeous as Garik remembered. He didn't know quite what to do with her, so he gave her a hug and stepped back as fast as he could.

"Of course I remember Garik. When we were in high school, I thought he was the only man I could ever love." Courtney tucked her hand into Mike's arm. "Until I saw Mike."

"I was there all the time. You overlooked me." Mike grinned at Elizabeth and offered his hand. "I've seen you around. It's good to meet you at last."

"It's good to meet you, too," she said.

Mike's grin got bigger. "You don't have the foggiest memory of me, do you?"

"No." Elizabeth scrutinized him now, though. "But if I don't look up, I don't have to see which people are gossiping about my parents."

"Whoa. There's a burden I never imagined." Courtney embraced Elizabeth and did the cheek touch with her. "I like you. You're real. Shall we go in and see how Mrs. Smith is doing? When the earthquake started, she grabbed an unbroken vase and refused to leave."

Elizabeth laughed. "I'm sure she's okay. She's too stubborn for anything else."

The two women wandered toward the resort, chatting. Mike and Garik watched them go.

"Ya done good, Mike," Garik said.

"You, too. What the hell does she see in you?"

"Nothing. She divorced me." Even now, that tasted bitter. "Remember?"

"She seems awfully fond. When Courtney hugged you, Elizabeth didn't like it at all."

"Really?" *Cool.* "What are you doing here?"

"I've got that stuff you asked for, so we made the trip." Mike headed toward the bike racks.

Garik followed. "What stuff?"

Mike dug around in his duffel bags and came up with a huge, shiny, pink, padded envelope. He handed it over with a flourish.

Garik still wasn't getting it. "Nice packaging, man. Is this how you send out your reports?"

"Courtney got the envelope from a cosmetics company. They want her to endorse their products. I took some papers to work in it, and it seemed like a good camouflage for . . . this stuff."

Garik opened it and looked inside. The smell of musty old papers whooshed out, and he saw a glint of metal. He started to reach in.

Mike caught his hand. "I brought you gloves. Handle everything with gloves. We don't want your fingerprints on the evidence."

"The evidence." Garik stuck his head almost inside and stared in disbelief. "You brought me . . . the evidence? Of Misty Banner's murder?"

"What did you think it was?" Mike sounded disgusted. "A random bunch of old papers with a random pair of scissors? Yes, it's the evidence!"

"All the evidence? Holy shit, Mike. Holy . . . shit."

Garik looked up at his friend in awe. "How did you get it?"

"I stole Foster's keys, snuck into the evidence room, and cleaned out the box." As if the heat of the day was getting to him, Mike lifted his black hair off his neck. "The box is still in there, empty."

"Holy shit." Garik couldn't seem to think of another thing to say. "What made you do it?"

Mike got an ugly look to his face. "I went to lunch, came back to my office, and that bastard Foster was in there looking at his mother's body."

"And?"

"He had her half-turned over, looking at the back of her head where I cut the hair so I could examine the wound."

Garik's gut tightened. "He knows you know he killed her."

"I'd have to examine his service pistol for blood first. But yes, assuming he did it . . . he does. So I figured if he was going to kill me, too, I might as well get you the evidence first." Mike talked fast. And he grinned as if he was joking.

Garik wasn't laughing.

Mike sobered. "You don't think this is melodrama."

"Do you?"

"No. I wish it was, but no."

Garik looked down at the evidence again. If Foster found out . . . An unstable sheriff with a couple of murders on his plate could do a lot of damage, and right now, Garik couldn't be responsible for Mike's safety, and Courtney's, and Elizabeth's, and Margaret's. "Have you thought of leaving town?"

Mike glared. "Yeah. Because that's so easy right now."

"It's tough, but not impossible. I got here. You got a four-wheel drive?"

"Yes." Mike paced away, then came back. "You're serious."

"As death." Garik wished he wasn't. "Everyone agrees Foster is strange and getting stranger, and for the first time in his life, he's free of his mother's restrictive influence."

"She may have been holding him together, you mean?"

"That's exactly what I mean. An extreme life change frequently triggers aberrant behavior."

"Now you're talking like an FBI agent." Mike couldn't quite work up one of his cocky grins.

"Occupational hazard." Garik was thinking it through. "He knows you know he killed his mother. Plus you stole evidence for me, evidence of a murder I accused him of committing. Even if he didn't kill Misty Banner, he has a lot riding on the accuracy of his investigation. But he didn't see you get the evidence. Did he?"

Mike hesitated a moment too long.

"You are kidding." Garik couldn't believe it.

"He didn't see me get it. But I had it when I walked back into the morgue and caught him looking at his mother."

Helpless with despair, Garik lifted his hand, and let it drop.

Mike pointed. "It was in that stupid pink envelope!"

Garik shook his head and started for the resort.

"Crap." Mike followed, moving fast, heading for the porch, passing Garik.

"It's you," Garik called. "You're a superhero concerned with justice for all."

"Bite me." Mike turned and walked backward. "Promise me you won't tell anyone you've got it."

"I promise."

"No one. Not even Elizabeth."

"Not a problem, man. She's the last one I'll tell." In all his life, Garik had never meant anything so much. "Elizabeth has this unnerving habit of blurting out the truth at the most unfortunate moments."

"Right. Good." Mike walked forward again, then backward. "What am I going to tell Courtney about our unexpected trip?"

"That you want to take her to the city to ride out the earthquakes?"

Mike stopped, and said in disgust, "She's got big tits. That doesn't mean she's stupid."

"That's too bad." Garik meant it, too. "Then . . . you'll tell her the truth?"

"I guess."

Garik flung his arm around Mike. "Let's get this over with. We'll get a map. I can show you some of the trouble spots, and then, let's get you on your way. I'll feel a lot better when you're gone."

"Yeah, me too." Mike sighed. "When I saw you, I knew you were going to be trouble."

"You sound like every girl I ever dated."

"If that's what you think"—Mike shoved at him—"take your arm off me."

It wasn't funny, but they laughed like it was, and walked into the resort.

CHAPTER FIFTY-SIX

That night, after dinner and some quiet, civilized conversation with Margaret, Garik and Elizabeth went to their respective bedrooms. They faced each other across the suite, wished each other good night, then Garik firmly, carefully, shut the door between them.

He didn't want Elizabeth to surprise him now.

Picking up the shiny pink padded envelope, he spilled the contents on his desk. Papers, brown-edged papers, lots of them, slid across the brown wood surface, and on top of them—the scissors, enclosed in a Ziploc bag.

The scissors.

This relic had the same impact for an FBI agent as the golden mask of King Tut had for an archeologist.

Using the disposable gloves Mike had given him, Garik picked up the bag by the corner and held it aloft, close to the desk lamp.

A little rusty, still bloodstained, with long blades and sharp tips. Good scissors. Sewing scissors. Scissors Misty had used to make the curtains for her home, dresses for her little girl, maybe that flowered dress she had worn when she was murdered . . .

Taking the bag, he headed downstairs to the resort's mail room. He enclosed the scissors in bubble wrap, slid them into a medium-sized Priority Mail Flat Rate box, sealed, addressed, and put postage on it. He didn't know when he would have the chance to mail it, but he knew the local postal carriers. He'd gone to school with a couple of them. And that kind of connection had turned out pretty well with Mike Sun . . .

As he headed back to his room, package in hand, he spared a thought to the Suns.

Courtney was not pleased with Mike.

Mike was not pleased with Garik.

But Garik had helped them pack their four-wheel-drive Wrangler, close up their house, and waved them off as they set out across lousy, broken roads toward Portland, because better safe than sorry.

Now he had the paperwork from the Banner case to examine, and all night to do it in. Good thing he wasn't going to sleep anyway, not after almost scoring with Elizabeth today in the truck. He'd march right into her room and give it another hot shot, except if she didn't yield, he'd wonder if she couldn't stand to sleep with a pathetic loser whose father beat him up, and if she did yield, he'd wonder if she did it because she felt sorry for the pathetic loser . . .

No use telling himself he wasn't a pathetic loser, that that was the memory of his father yelling abuse in his mind. As Elizabeth would say, he knew that logically. But what the hell did logically have to do with emotions that snapped at his courage and ripped at his heartstrings?

Better concentrate on the work at hand. When it came to this kind of research, he knew himself to be the best on the force, and thus in the world.

He shuffled through the reports. Found the one he wanted, the one that identified the fingerprints on the scissors.

Misty. Charles. And three others, unidentified.

Not surprising. In any given household, scissors got used by a lot of different people: residents and visitors. Lots of people had never been fingerprinted, so again, not surprising to have unidentified prints. Yet the failure of this report was that it didn't mention the position of the prints.

People handled scissors by the handles, of course, unless they were handing them to someone else, and then they grasped the blades.

But someone, the killer, had held the handles of the scissors backward, and slashed and stabbed and killed. The fact that those fingerprints hadn't been specifically located and proven to be Charles Banner's showed gross negligence on the part of the investigator. And that investigator knew it, too, because this paper hadn't been scanned and included in the report pertaining to the case.

Garik was glad Mike and Courtney had left town, because Dennis Foster had a lot to answer for.

Garik looked at his computer, and sighed. He'd stalled long enough. He had to check in with Perez and tell him what was going on, and for that, he needed Elizabeth's phone.

So he made his way through the sitting room to the open door of Elizabeth's bedroom. Not that he wanted to; after his confession this afternoon, he didn't want to see her again tonight.

But he sucked it up and knocked on her door.

"Come in," she called.

He swung the door open. "Can I use your . . ."

She sat on the floor, clad in a man's oversized white shirt, her right hand pressed on the floor, her fingers spread wide, frowning as she put polish on her nails.

". . . phone?" he croaked.

She didn't look up. "Sure." When he didn't move, she added, "It's on the night stand."

He crossed the room, picked it up, noted the signal was strong, and headed for the door. He shouldn't say another thing, but he couldn't stop himself. He had to ask. "What are you doing?"

"Painting my nails."

"Painting your nails."

"Yes."

He rubbed his head and wondered if he'd fallen into another dimension. "Where'd you get the stuff?"

"From the resort's spa."

"Oh." He supposed that made a weird sort of sense. Except . . . "I didn't know you knew how."

"Just because you never saw me do it, doesn't mean I don't know how. I learned in college, when I was a shoe model."

Women. Did they ever make sense? "You painted your nails so you could model shoes?"

"The photographers loved to take photos of me doing this." She stood, struck a pose, and cupped her boobs with her own hands.

He halted in midstep.

The polish was red. Her shirt was white, and unbuttoned to the middle of her chest. She was barefoot. She was not wearing a bra. And her cleavage swelled, rich and sinful as whipped cream. "It sold shoes. Shiny, high-heeled, fuck-me shoes." She let herself go, sat back down, and returned to painting her nails.

"Yes. I can see it would." Somehow he got out of her room, across the sitting room, and into his bedroom without falling to his knees and begging that she sit on his face. Because he was in control of himself.

Either that or he was a rank coward who was afraid of being rejected.

Plugging Elizabeth's phone into his computer, Garik brought up the FBI's secure instant messaging, logged in, and and typed a message to Tom Perez. *Got the contents of the evidence box for the Banner case. I'm sending you the scissors via Priority Mail, or however else I can wrangle it. Still no mail service, but as soon as I get it sent, I'll give you the heads-up so you can be on the lookout.*

Five seconds later. *Did you get the evidence by legal means?*

Best not to ask questions you don't want to know the answer to.

You know the shit I'm getting because you're missing in action? Why should I do this for you?

Garik rubbed his hands together, and typed, *Hey, you're right. I'll send the scissors from the* infamous *Banner murder case to someone else to get the prints. Maybe . . . let me think . . . that detective with the Las Vegas police. What's her name? Alexis Long. Didn't you sleep with her for a while? She would do me a favor to have a shot at this celebrated piece of crime history. And she'd be gettin' all that publicity when it turns out Charles Banner didn't commit the murder . . .*

Mail me the scissors.

I don't want to get you in trouble.

Mail me the scissors.

If you insist. If you really want them.

Mail me the fucking scissors.

Of course, boss.

A pause. Then, *You have any reason yet for thinking Charles Banner didn't do it?*

Not all the reports got uploaded to the online case file.

This reply returned immediately. *Juicy.*

The sheriff is one scary dude.

Suspect?

Right now, my number-one. But there are others. Garik thought about Marrero. He liked Marrero for the crime. That slimy little bastard.

Then he thought about Rainbow, about that grip she'd had on his arm earlier today. She was a big woman, strong, with man hands, and Elizabeth had named her as a possible for Misty's lover.

Dr. Frownfelter with his weird psycho obsession with Charles. Who else had Margaret named?

Are you just entertaining yourself, or is there real cause for suspicion?

"You suspicious bastard," Garik muttered, and typed, *I'm just entertaining myself.*

Don't get yourself killed entertaining yourself. Keep in touch.

Will do.

A knock on the door connecting to the suite made Garik jump, turn, and look.

Elizabeth leaned against the doorsill, white men's shirt brushing her thighs, red bottle of polish in one hand, girly paraphernalia in the other. "Can we talk?"

CHAPTER FIFTY-SEVEN

Elizabeth didn't wait for an answer. She walked past him toward the bed, and she smelled good, like citrus and cinnamon. She sat on the floor, and spread out her nail supplies. She put her foot on a little white drop cloth, stuck some foam thing between her toes, unscrewed the lid on the polish, and started painting her toenails.

He tilted his head, trying to see . . . to see . . .

"What are you doing?" she asked.

"Um . . ." *Trying to see your panties?*

She clarified, "What's with the papers?"

Garik tore his gaze away from her upraised knee and glanced at his desk. Shit. The evidence was all over the place. The evidence Mike stole for him. The evidence Garik had promised to keep secret. Evidence clearly marked with a red stamp that said EVIDENCE REPORT and in the upper left-hand corner, BANNER MURDER in black magic marker.

He started gathering the papers, squaring them up with each other, keeping the writing turned away from her. "Mike brought me a bunch of old papers from high school. Teenage boy stuff, you know." Lame.

But Elizabeth bought it. "Okay, I won't look." She wasn't watching him, anyway. She was observing her own hands as they carefully dabbed red polish on her little toe. "I was thinking about the stuff you told me this afternoon."

Oh, God. She wanted to talk about his big, whimpery confession.

And to think he had been grateful she wasn't interested in the evidence.

A quick glance proved she had finished with one foot, and she had both legs stuck straight out in front of her. Which was better than the other pose, except that she wiggled the red-painted toes and smiled at them . . . Damn, that was endearing.

Picking up the pink envelope, he started sliding the papers inside. "Do we have to talk about this afternoon?"

"No . . ." She pulled her other foot in close and put it on the drop cloth. She shook the bottle of polish—

With this leg up, the light on his desk shone in at the right angle, and—

She wasn't wearing any panties.

Like a Disney character whose animator dropped the

brush, he froze, eyes bugged, jaw dropped, fingers clenched around a pile of papers.

He could see . . . everything.

Through the buzzing in his ears, he heard her say something . . .

Something like, "But I feel closer to you than I did this morning."

And he came back to life.

Think, Garik. She's wearing a see-through shirt unbuttoned to her navel, she's doing girly stuff with her fingers and toes, her hair is tousled, she smells like flowers, and she's not wearing panties. She has something on her mind besides talk.

Well. She could just think twice about that.

He stuffed the rest of the evidence into the envelope, placed it up on the top shelf of his closet, walked over, and stood over the top of her. He clenched his fists on his hips. He scowled. He said flatly, "I do not want to be your pity fuck."

She looked up, all the way up, taking a flatteringly long time to make the journey. "Really?"

Wait.

She had a point.

Did he really care about his pride if he was going to get—

No, damn it. He didn't want her to have sex with him because she felt sorry for him. "Yes. Really."

Her gaze wandered back down his body, lingering on the bulge in his jeans, which didn't mean anything except that he hadn't been laid for over a year and that circus in his pants had a mind of its own, and she said, "Why would I pity you? If I pitied you, I would have to pity myself."

Her lips were moving, but he had absolutely no idea what she was talking about.

She went back to work on her toes. "I always wondered why we connected when we had nothing in common. Turns out we have everything in common."

Garik frowned. Elizabeth was such a strange girl. He knew that. He'd always known that.

But her feet, especially her painted toes, were looking good. Sexy. Flirty. Seductive . . .

She continued, "We were both kids who survived the worst kind of trauma—our fathers hurt us, destroyed our lives, made us the objects of scorn for our peers. Yet look at us! We're successful adults with good careers and you know what? We're pretty well adjusted." As she worked on the little nails at the outside of her foot, she concentrated hard, her tongue massaging her lower lip as if that would help her get this right.

And it might. As he recalled, she had a very talented tongue.

When she finished dabbing the last of the polish on her tiniest toe, she grinned in triumph, capped the polish, and looked up again. "We're made for each other."

She was starting to make sense. That meant his brain was compromised by lack of blood flow. So he retreated to his desk and sat down in his chair. "You're saying because we both had trauma in our childhoods we're a match?"

She laughed. Gently, but she laughed. "Honey, we didn't just have trauma. We had the kind of stuff that makes most people alcoholics or drug addicts, or makes them go to bed and pull the covers over their heads and never get up."

She had a point.

But so did he. He was straining, straining, to remember he did not want to be her pity fuck.

So he said the thing guaranteed to make her run away and never look back. "I'm in therapy."

She didn't leap to her feet. She rose in a leisurely fashion. She looked at him. She straightened her shirt, tugging it down like it mattered whether she was covered or not when in fact he'd just seen the most toothsome display of female goodness he ever remembered in his whole life. Or maybe only since their divorce. But the fact was, he couldn't remember ever having spotted it displayed so temptingly, so innocently, so . . . naughtily.

She strolled over to the desk—strolled, her long legs moving deliberately—and stopped with her knees against his knees. She leaned forward and put her hands on his shoulders. Her full lips moved, purposefully articulating each word. "I've been there, too. I'd go back if I felt like I needed to. How about you?"

How about him? Well. Her shirt was unbuttoned down to mid-boob and when he looked left, he could see inside, all the way to the pale swell of one breast. He couldn't quite see her nipple; it was hidden by a fold of cloth. When he looked right, he could see the pale swell of the other breast, and about half of her buff pink nipple.

He looked right.

"So?" She shrugged.

Shirt and boobs shifted and moved.

She said again, "Therapy helped me. How about you?"

He cleared his throat. "I didn't think so. But yeah. Maybe. Since I got here, I've thought a few of the things the therapist said might be valid."

"Because if the study of psychology helps you track a serial killer, then it has validity?"

"Possibly. But also, there's a difference between a psychotic human mind, and a normal human mind."

She cupped her hand under his chin and lifted his face so his eyes met hers. "If there is such a thing as a normal human mind."

"Gotta be."

"Says who?" She was mocking him, her big eyes wide and amused.

"I do."

"So you have a normal human mind?"

"Sure. Normal."

"Then explain why we shouldn't do this." She slid one knee onto the chair with him. Slid the other knee onto the chair with him. And sat, with her legs spread, on his erection.

He thought his heart was going to explode.

No. Wait. The explosion was going to take place a lot lower.

But he thought he sounded almost normal. "Because my jeans are in the way."

She chuckled, warm and throaty and charmed. "You're right. That's a shame." She kissed him on the lips, slid her tongue inside his mouth, tasted him and sighed with pleasure. Pulling back, she said, "I wonder if I can remember how to work a zipper." She slid her fingers into his hair and massaged the back of his neck and head, pressing the heel of her hand against the tense muscles, easing away stress and anxiety and replacing them with something much, much more potent.

He was being seduced. He knew he was being seduced. He knew he didn't have a choice—he was going to yield, and yield fervently and thankfully. But he couldn't help it. One question gnawed at his mind. "What did you mean, it explains a lot?"

She shook her head slightly. "What?"

"This afternoon, after I told you about my father, you said, 'That explains a lot.'"

"Oh." She gathered her thoughts. "Your father. Knowing about him explains why you don't like to talk about yourself, your past, your feelings. You loved him, and he abused that love in every way possible. So you're afraid if you love too much or show it too freely, the person you love will rip you apart. Then you're afraid you'll become your father, and hurt that person in return." She relaxed against Garik again, wrapped her arms around his shoulders, and leaned her forehead against his. "You keep closed up to protect yourself, and to protect me. But I have never been afraid of you, Garik Jacobsen."

"Perhaps you should be, because now you know the truth." Or . . . most of it.

"Yet here I am, a logical woman with acute and trained observation skills, and I'm open to you in every way." She snuggled closer, rested her breasts against his chest, and smiled into his face. "Trust me, Garik. I see you as you really are."

He stared at her, trying to breathe, trying to think, trying to figure out the hole in her reasoning. He couldn't. He just couldn't, because there wasn't one, or because he suffered from testosterone poisoning.

Either way, he had no choice. If there was one thing their time apart had taught him, it was that he needed Elizabeth. He needed her body, her mind, her heart, and he would do whatever it took to win her. Really win her. And keep her this time.

He unfastened another button on her shirt. And another. "You have an advanced intellect." Her breasts now almost escaped from the material. Almost. "So if I can do this, certainly you can—"

She pressed her hips closer, spread her legs wider.

The heat of her vanquished thought, and speech.

"If I remember correctly, sliding down your zipper is like opening a really great Christmas present." She leaned back, her hands against his knees, her chest thrust out. "Guaranteed to bring joy all the—"

He slid his arm inside her shirt and around her back, baring her left shoulder and left breast. He lifted her to his mouth and tasted her nipple.

Now *she* forgot how to speak.

During the years of their marriage, he had dedicated himself to the study of what gave her pleasure. He knew how to ease her into desire, to take his time, to build her enjoyment . . . and his. He licked her softly, swirled his tongue around, then suckled with increasing pressure.

She writhed in his lap, her fingers digging into his thighs, and when at last she gave a low, deep moan, he lifted his head.

She opened her eyes. At the sight of his smile, they narrowed. Sitting up straight, she yanked at the hem of his T-shirt until he raised his arms and let her pull it off. She pressed her palms to his chest until she felt his heart jump, then slowly she trailed them down toward his waistband. With firm, deliberate movements she popped the button on his jeans and eased the zipper down. "Look at that," she said. "I did remember how. Let's see what else I remember." Now *she* smiled, her lips open, as she slipped backward off his lap.

She tugged at his jeans.

He lifted his rear, let her slide them down and off.

She eased her hand under the elastic of his boxers. "What do you want?"

He wanted to tell her to hurry.

He needed to warn her what would happen if she—

She grasped his dick, slid her fingers up and down. "Do you know what I'm doing?" she murmured.

He could barely form the words. "Killing me slowly."

She tsked like a displeased schoolteacher. But she did not look like any kind of schoolteacher he'd ever had.

Well, except for the middle school fantasy . . .

She said, "No. I'm relearning the contours of your body."

"Learn faster."

She chuckled. "I find I learn better if I avail myself of all the methods at my disposal. Touch. And—" Putting her head in his lap, she sucked him into her mouth.

He tensed, lifted himself about an inch off the chair, remained there, blind and deaf, while she sipped and suckled, circled the head with her tongue, and drove him nearly to the brink. He hovered there, in torment, until she released him and sat back on her heels.

He looked at her, and he would have sworn even his eyes were swollen.

Standing up, she parted her legs a little, enough to tease. With one red-tipped fingernail, she circled a button on her shirt, over and over, a slow, sensuous circle. And in a spuriously innocent tone, she asked, "Did you like that?"

He surged to his feet, picked her up, sat her on the desk, stepped back, and dropped his shorts.

Abruptly, her smile vanished. She was serious, intense . . . needy.

"You shouldn't trust me and my patience so much," he said. "I'm going to make you scream."

Her blue eyes grew wide. Her tongue massaged her lower lip. "You, first."

CHAPTER FIFTY-EIGHT

Yvonne stepped out of the Honor Mountain Memory Care Facility and paused, waiting to hear the door shut with a solid thunk behind her.

The night was cool, like every night on the Washington coast. Midnight was quiet, the parking lot almost empty, the light over the entrance an island in the forest dark.

She walked toward her Ford Bronco, parked in its usual place, six spaces out and two lanes to the right.

She was exhausted. Her feet hurt. Her back hurt. Even her emotions hurt. And she was so very, very glad to be going home at last.

She was about halfway to her vehicle when her cell phone rang. She pulled it out of her purse, stared at the number, answered it with a glad cry. "Sweetheart. You got through to me!"

John laughed, deep and low in his chest. "I've been trying every hour. How are you?"

"So good. Now." She stopped walking, and smiled into the darkness. "I'm going home for a whole twelve hours for the first time since the earthquake hit. How are you?"

"No problemo. I delivered my load in Salt Lake, got the money wired to our account, and we're in the black, baby." He sounded so proud.

"I'm glad. So glad. Because"—she hated to tell him—"there's some damage to the house."

"I figured there had to be." She could almost see his face as he sobered. "Bad?"

"Nothing you can't handle yourself." He knew his way

around construction, thank God. "All you'll need is electricity to charge your cordless drill and some two-by-fours . . . which I hope you bring with you, because at this rate it's going to be a long time before Virtue Falls gets any supplies."

"I'll bring whatever you tell me to bring." He didn't sound happy. "I just can't get there right away. Every trucker who wants to drive Highway One-oh-one is lined up at the truck stops, waiting for the DOT to clean it up so we can go home. Baby, it's a mess."

"I know. You can't do anything about it." But her voice betrayed her loneliness, and quivered and broke.

"I could leave the truck and get home."

That offer snapped her out of her self-pity. "Have you lost your mind? If you abandoned the truck and someone took it, or vandalized it, what would we do? We need that truck!"

"I know." Now he sounded wretched. "But what about you?"

"I'm fine. Don't I sound fine?" She made a concerted effort to sound fine. "I'm going home now, I'm going to sleep for twelve hours straight, then I'm coming back to work—"

"What about the crazy people you've got at that place?"

"They're not crazy. Not that kind of crazy."

"Oh, yeah? How did they take that earthquake?"

She thought about the general hysteria every time they had another aftershock, about Mr. Banner and his enthusiasm, about Mr. Cook who had been smashed by the ceiling and who was still unconscious. "Really, babe, hearing your voice is the best thing that could have happened to me." She almost cried with sincerity. "Promise me you'll take care of yourself."

"You know I will. We're having a card game at the rest stop tonight."

"Don't lose the farm." She wasn't really worried. He was cautious, and he had a poker face that revealed nothing.

"Are you kidding? I could win us all of eastern Washington."

She laughed. "But who wants eastern Washington?" She didn't say it often, but she hadn't talked to him in so long, and he was her guy. "I love you."

He never could say it, and it always made him uncomfortable when she did. But she understood, and she didn't mind.

"I know," he said. "Gotta go. Game's gonna start in ten minutes." Then he yanked his attention back to her. "Listen. You be careful. Promise me."

"I promise. I'll see you when you get home." She said it again. She had to. "I love you."

He grunted.

She hung up. She smiled at her phone. She slipped it into her purse and started toward her Bronco again. She got within five steps when she heard a whisper of sound from the edge of the trees. She turned fast, but a blow knocked her to her hands and knees. The torn asphalt ripped her palms; she screamed.

Her attacker landed on her, slamming her flat on her face, knocking the wind out of her. The man grunted, then flipped her over. He knelt on her chest, on her boob, leaning so hard the agony almost made her black out.

But he pressed his knife to her throat, and terror kept her conscious.

The point pricked her skin right over her carotid artery.

No one knew better than her; one firm slash, and her life was over.

Her heart beat hard. Desperate with fear and pain, she gasped for breath, but his knee, his weight, made it impossible to draw a full breath.

A knit ski mask covered his face. His mouth was a round hole in the weave. His eyes blazed from the two holes above. "Where are your keys?" His voice was hoarse, a whispered threat.

"What keys?" Stupid question. "Oh. To the care facility."

Drugs. He wanted drugs.

She couldn't give him access to the hospital filled with vulnerable patients and weary medical staff, not even to save her life. "My keys are in my purse."

He groped on the ground, found her purse, dumped it out. She heard the phone hit the pavement. Wallet. Lipstick. *Keys.*

He reached for them. But he never took his gaze away from hers. He watched her as if he wanted to kill her, and all the time, the point of the knife pressed against her skin.

Please, God, no. No, please, God, I don't want to die.

The keys jingled by her ear. "Which one?" he asked.

"The brass one with the red plastic cap."

He bent his head close to her ear. "If you are lying to me, I will get you."

Did this mean he wasn't going to kill her . . . now? "I'm not lying." She wasn't. That had been the key to the facility . . . a year ago, before they went digital.

Her breath wheezed in her throat. He pulled his knee out of her chest. The point of the knife disappeared from her throat.

She took her first, full, unobstructed-by-fear-and-pain breath.

And the blade settled onto her upper cheekbone.

Beneath the ski mask, his eyes glittered with sick excitement. He pressed the point on the skin.

She pushed her head against the pavement. Useless. She couldn't back away. The tip pierced her flesh, slid toward her eye—and at last she gave into terror. She didn't know where she got the air; she must have brought it from the depths of her being, and screamed, loud and shrill.

He looked up, across the parking lot. He looked down at her again, and his eyes were now cold, pitiless, bleak. "Bitch!" He gave the knife a spiteful twist, then he was gone, racing across the parking lot toward the forest.

She sat up. Scrambled to her feet. Couldn't stop screaming. She held her face, pressing hard, trying to fit her skin back in place, to mold it to the bone. Blood filled her palm and ran down her arm to her elbow.

A man ran up.

She flinched back, throwing out her free hand to fend him off.

But it wasn't ski mask guy. It was Mr. Villalobos; his father was a patient, and he must have left the facility soon after she did.

Thank God. Thank God. His arrival had chased away ski mask guy.

She could see Mr. Villalobos's lips moving. He was talking to her, although she couldn't hear him over her own shrieks. He showed her his phone, dialed, spoke into it.

Tears welled in her eyes. *John. She wanted John.*

Across the parking lot, the door to the nursing home slammed open. Orderlies and nurses ran out.

Sirens sounded in the distance.

Yvonne's screams became sobs. She sank to her knees.

Voices. A lot of voices now. Safety in numbers.

He couldn't get her now.

CHAPTER FIFTY-NINE

This morning Garik couldn't stop smiling.

He had had a very good night. Not much sleep, but a very good night. There had been screaming. And as promised, some of it had been by him.

Now he walked into the dining room, pressed a kiss on Margaret's forehead, pressed a kiss on Elizabeth's forehead, and seated himself. "How are my favorite ladies this morning?"

"I would sleep better if fewer earthquakes rattled the hotel," Margaret said.

We're almost sure the aftershock last night wasn't our fault! But he didn't say that. Instead, he helped himself to two pitted prunes from the bowl in the middle of the table. And smirked.

"Prunes," Margaret muttered. "In August. When it should be fresh peaches. We have indeed fallen far."

Elizabeth sprinkled brown sugar over her oatmeal. "It could be months, years, before the earth settles down again."

Margaret's eyes narrowed. "I'm ninety-one years old. I would hope that the earth stops this infernal shaking before I go to meet my maker. I want to rest easy and not have my bones rattle out of my—" She stopped, and looked guilty.

Because Elizabeth's mother had not rested easy in her grave; in fact the earthquake and tsunami brought her out of the ground.

An awkward silence settled over the breakfast table.

Margaret patted Elizabeth's arm. "I'm sorry, that was thoughtless of me."

"It's fine. You didn't mean . . . and I think my mother will rest easier now, don't you?" Elizabeth looked hopefully from Garik to Margaret and back to Garik.

"Indeed I do," Margaret said warmly, "when she's had a proper burial with proper rites said over the grave. Prayers, I mean. That will set everyone's mind and heart to rest."

Elizabeth's phone sat by her elbow, and when it rang, she looked surprised and then complacent. "Some of us obviously deserve phone service. Like me. Like Margaret."

The two women nodded at each other.

"Garik, have you got phone service yet?" Elizabeth sounded prosaic, but she looked at him with (he thought) affection.

He glanced at his phone. "No. Are you going to answer, or are you going to gloat?"

Elizabeth picked it up—and paled. She read the screen, THE HONOR MOUNTAIN MEMORY CARE FACILITY, and answered. She listened. Her mouth turned down. She blinked and frowned. She exclaimed in horror.

Garik and Margaret exchanged concerned glances.

Elizabeth said, "Okay, I understand. I'll come by later to see my father. Thank you for letting me know." She hung up, and stared at the phone as if it had bit her.

Garik's gut stirred.

Margaret placed her cup of tea precisely on her saucer. "What?"

"Last night, Yvonne Rudda—"

"The nurse at the care facility?" Margaret asked.

"Yes. Yvonne. She was attacked in the parking lot by some guy with a knife. He knocked her down, put the point to her throat, and got her keys to the facility. Then he cut her face." Elizabeth touched her cheek.

"How badly was she hurt?" Margaret asked.

"I don't know, but she's in the hospital. Someone chased him off . . . she was finally going home, and someone attacked her?" Elizabeth's eyes kindled. "That's bullshit."

"Life's bullshit." But Garik took her hand and laced their fingers together. "What happened with the keys?"

"While the police and EMTs were helping Yvonne, the guy went around to the far door and tried to break into the facility. That's why they called me. They're calling all the relatives of the patients to assure them everyone's fine." Elizabeth wet her lips. "My father's fine. The burglar didn't get in."

"Hm." The stirring in Garik's gut became a roiling. Elizabeth had discussed the Banner case with a reporter, told him they had been talking about the past with her father, and the news story had made it online. And Charles Banner, after all, was housed in the Honor Mountain Memory Care Facility.

"They didn't catch the burglar?" Margaret asked.

"I don't know," Elizabeth said.

"Is there video?" Garik asked.

"I don't know," Elizabeth said.

"We'd better go this morning." So he could view the

video, if there was one, Garik meant, and examine any evidence.

"Do you think Charles is in danger?" Margaret was too sharp not to know what Garik intended.

"No. The facility is secure. It keeps the patients in, keeps the bad guys out. When we visit, somebody who works there has to buzz us in through the main door, then check us in. The people who work there have to slide an electronic ID so they're logged in when they're there." Garik's mind clicked through possible criminal types. "Whoever this guy is, breaking and entering isn't his main occupation, or he'd know that."

"The authorities think he was a stray addict who got stranded in the area by the earthquake, and got desperate for drugs." Elizabeth pushed her oatmeal away.

Almost at once, Harold appeared in the dining room and picked up her bowl.

Elizabeth continued, "Although that really doesn't make me feel any better. He didn't get any drugs, so he'll be more desperate. Next time he'll break a window."

Garik watched Harold as he removed more dishes off the table.

Why was he clearing off? Why not Vicky? Why not Miklós? Had Harold been listening at the door?

For Elizabeth's sake, and Harold's, too, Garik asked, "The facility's windows are reinforced glass. It has to be, or a resident could bash his way out and escape. No one will come through the window."

Harold left carrying a tray full of dirty dishes.

"Do you think my father will have more stories to tell about my mother?" Elizabeth asked.

"Have you decided you believe him?" Garik asked.

Harold was back again with a fresh cup and pot of tea.

"Yes . . . it was very weird, but last night I dreamed

about my mother. She was talking to my father. I couldn't see him, but I could see her, and she looked the same as she does in the pictures. I woke up feeling happy. And oddly enough, reassured that he does remember what really happened." Elizabeth looked alarmed. "Which isn't logical at all."

"No, not at all," Garik said firmly.

"I wonder if that was a memory of her?" Margaret mused. "Or simply your mind building on a photograph?"

"Probably the photograph." Garik didn't need Harold to speculate that Elizabeth's memory was coming back. Too much publicity had already occurred about her, the Banner case, and her search for the truth. Now violence had occurred, and Harold lingered in the dining room.

Probably Harold had been working for Margaret long enough that he considered himself one of the family. Or maybe he was carrying gossip back down to the kitchen. But Garik no longer trusted anyone, not even Harold, an elderly veteran with one leg, a man who, even if he had left the resort to attack Yvonne last night, could never have run away fast enough to escape pursuit.

Because Harold was the right age to have been in love with Misty Banner, and he had been to war. He could have murdered her. He knew how to kill.

"Harold, could I get a thermos of coffee?" Garik asked.

Harold nodded and left.

Elizabeth stood, looked down at the table, and traced the wood grain with her fingertips. "Actually, I do need to drop by the facility every morning for a few minutes to help rebuild my relationship with . . . well. Margaret, you're right. If I want to know my father, and hear what he has to say, I need to do it now."

"I am very glad you've made this decision," Margaret said.

"If you'll excuse me," Elizabeth said, "I'll go get ready."

Garik and Margaret watched her leave.

Margaret sighed and pushed her oatmeal away, too. "Do you think it's a stray drug addict in search of a fix?"

"I don't know." Garik stood, wrapped his arm around her skinny shoulders, and gave her a gentle hug. "I hope so. It beats all other scenarios."

"Boyo, what did you get on your jeans?" Margaret craned her neck and looked down at the leg of his jeans. "Paint? Red paint?"

He straightened, and saw the smear of red nail polish on the side of his right thigh. And on the side of his left thigh. Color flooded his face. A smile tugged at his lips. "Damn. And it's not like I'm overwhelmed with clothes here."

"How did you do that?"

He knew *exactly* how he'd done that. When he thought about last night, it was amazing he didn't have red fingernail polish on his chest and shoulders and . . . places less obvious. But no way would he discuss this with Margaret. "You know," he said vaguely. "Helping around the resort."

"I thought maybe you'd got into some paint mucking around at Elizabeth's dig," Margaret said.

"Good one." He wished he had thought of that excuse. "I'll go change, and ask the staff if they can clean this off. Or maybe they can make it fade. I'll have to wear my slacks today. Elizabeth will mock me." He looked toward the door where Elizabeth had vanished. "We'll see you tonight, Margaret, and catch you up on anything we've discovered."

Margaret watched him hurry off. She poured herself a fresh cup of tea. She added lemon, cream and sugar, and stirred it slowly and thoroughly.

How could a man get paint on both sides of his jeans? She was old, and she had forgotten a lot, but even so, she could only think of one way . . . and come to think of it, this morning, Elizabeth had red polish on her nails.

Margaret chuckled. "At least one good thing has been brought about by this earthquake. A very good thing, indeed."

CHAPTER SIXTY

Today, the medical staff at the Honor Mountain Memory Care Facility looked grim, sad, and confused. Garik had seen situations like these before: people dazed by the sudden onset of violence. Time, and a return to normalcy, would bring them solace.

But these days normalcy was difficult to achieve. How much longer until Virtue Falls had heat, light; until homes were repaired; until the staff worked routine hours again? Days or weeks to rebuild the infrastructure—water, gas, electricity, roads—but years for home life and business procedure.

The attack on one of their own had added another dimension of stress—and more important, fear—to already difficult lives.

Garik stopped Sheila in the corridor and asked, "How is Yvonne?"

"Okay. Non-life-threatening injury. She'll be scarred,

and she's terrified." As if she felt the knife, Sheila pressed her hand to her throat. "She never did anything to hurt anybody, and she doesn't understand how she became a target."

"She wasn't the target," Elizabeth said. "She was in the wrong place at the wrong time."

Sheila smiled tightly, and without any apparent appreciation of Elizabeth's attempt to be supportive. "She's tired, and not taking comfort from such sensible comments." The words *sensible comments* held a bit of a snap.

"We'll visit her today, and see if we can't cheer her up." Because Garik liked Yvonne, but more important, he wanted to question her about her attacker. He wanted to know what she had seen, heard, smelled, and whether *she* believed the man had been after drugs—or attempting to gain entrance to the facility for other reasons. "In the meantime, how is Charles Banner?"

Sheila smiled with sincere pleasure. "He's fine. A dear man who, when he heard the news this morning, did everything in his power to bolster our spirits. And I don't think he remembers who Yvonne is. Yet the poor man learned about violence the hard way."

"You mean when he killed my mother?" Elizabeth asked.

Sheila viewed Elizabeth thoughtfully. "No. I meant when he was repeatedly beaten in prison."

"So you don't believe he killed my mother?" Elizabeth insisted.

"No. I don't," Sheila said.

Elizabeth tucked her hair behind her ear. "I respect your opinion. Thank you for giving it to me."

Sheila nodded, glanced down at her pager, and hurried away.

Elizabeth turned to Garik. "The preponderance of belief here is that my father is innocent. At first I thought their surroundings and the patients they cared for must have affected the medical staff and their thinking, but as I've grown to know them, I find myself hoping that they're right, and we can discover a different truth about my parents than the one the jury decided upon."

Taking her hand, he drew her into the open restroom, shut the door, and locked it behind them. "I'm hoping that, too. But we don't want to talk about your father at all, to anyone. If your father is innocent, then we have an abundance of suspects and a violent attack last night that may be connected to the case—but probably is not. So let's act casual. We'll visit your father, I'll search for evidence, we'll behave as if the one thing that really consumes our attention is the earthquake and getting back to normal."

Elizabeth listened, and thought. "Of course. You're right. If the DOT doesn't fix the roads soon, the whole town will have trouble getting potable water, so getting back to normal could really be the issue that consumes our attention."

"Exactly." He kissed her hand, then opened the door and stepped out into the corridor.

A male orderly stopped and stared, then hurried on toward the dining room.

"We just gave the medical staff something else to discuss besides potable water and the attack on Yvonne," Garik said.

"What?"

Garik mocked her with his gaze.

"You mean he thinks that we—" Elizabeth looked behind her. "We were in the restroom."

"Together." He led her toward Charles's room.

Elizabeth was clearly appalled. "Who would do it in the restroom?"

"Restrooms are private."

"They're a germ factory!"

"Sex is a germ factory. But I'll take my chances . . . with you." He stopped outside her father's room and kissed her lips. "Are you ready?" he asked.

Elizabeth adjusted her bag on her shoulder. "I've got the laptop in case he wants to see the tsunami again. I've got my album. And I want to know what he knows. So yes, I'm ready."

Misty didn't even wait for Charles to sit down and take off his muddy boots. She was almost dancing with joy as she announced, "I found our house."

Charles blinked at her.

They'd lived in an apartment in Virtue Falls for two months, and he had thought Misty had looked at every property up and down the coast trying to find the perfect place for them to buy. "Our house? Really? Did it just come on the market?"

"No! That's the weird thing. The realtor didn't want to show it to me because she thought I wouldn't like it." Misty tossed her blond hair in disdain. "Realtors are like beauticians. They think they know best and they try to handle you to get their own way. I found our house when I was walking toward the dig and got lost."

"You found a house? When you got lost on the way to the dig? Where is it?"

"On the flat above the canyon, about a half mile from the ocean."

"On the plateau? There's nothing out there."

"Yes, there is. Our house." She laughed excitedly. "Come on. Let me show you."

She took him to the flats above the ocean cliffs where the wind blew with ceaseless force off the Pacific and the trees grew like misshapen beasts, claws pointed inland.

As if the location wasn't bad enough, the house itself had been an old woman's abode, neglected for years, until she died two years before. Then the salt breeze battered the last of the paint off the exterior. Humidity leaked through the old single-hung windows to make the plaster swell and fall off the walls in chunks.

Charles thought it strange that Misty, who had been raised in Southern California among the bustle and decadence of the movie business, would desire to live out in the middle of nothing. "We'll have no close neighbors," he said.

"I know. Isn't it wonderful? No one to see us coming and going. No one to gossip about us. No one to interfere with the way we raise our child."

"I don't understand. Why would anyone gossip about us?"

She laughed. "Darling, it's a small town. Gossip is the main entertainment."

Bewildered, he said, "But we don't do anything worth gossiping about."

"Gossips don't let facts like that stop them. I can't tell you the number of times I've been asked about you and me, and how we met, and whether we're happy together." She put her hand on his chest. "I tell them we are."

"Of course . . . you are happy, aren't you?" His work engrossed him, but even more, he was engrossed in Misty, in the changes pregnancy was creating in her body, in her constant enthusiasm for her new surroundings.

"I am so happy." She gestured around at the rundown home. "I feel free here!"

He looked around again, at the mildewed carpets and the doors swollen with moisture; they stuck at the top or the bottom, or both.

Misty said, "Rainbow down at the diner wants to pry every last detail of our sex life out of me."

"What do you say?" Such rampant curiosity made him cringe.

"I tell her I married you for one reason, and it wasn't because of your lofty intellect." She gurgled with laughter. "Haven't you noticed the way all the women in town watch you now? They think you're the biggest stud on the West Coast. And of course, you are." She slid her arm through his and kissed him.

He kissed her back, but her kisses, no matter how delicious, couldn't distract him from the reality that surrounded him. "The house is going to need remodeling. I don't know how to remodel."

"I already bought books at the hardware store. I can do a lot of it."

He looked at her doubtfully. She was four and a half months pregnant, had been showing for a month, and he secretly worried she was carrying twins.

She continued blithely, "During the off-season, I can hire the workers from the resort."

"But can we afford to remodel?"

"For the price I've negotiated on this house, we could tear it down and start over. Except that I like the house. It has character. And don't you see? I love this land." She drew him out onto the big, ocean-facing porch. "Watch the grasses ripple. It's like seeing music. Listen. The ocean's out there, eternally pounding the shore, and beyond that is the horizon, and infinity. And freedom. So much freedom. This place makes me feel as if I can fly. It is the perfect place to raise our baby. She'll be happy here."

"She? Do we know it's a she?"

"I know." Misty stroked her hand across his forehead. *"And she'll be as smart as you."*

"But she could never be as pretty as her mother."

Misty laughed, a merry chime that blended with the Pacific's breeze. "You say that now. Wait until she's born, and you hold her in your arms. Then you'll say she's the most beautiful thing you've ever laid eyes on, and you'll do anything for her, to keep her happy." Misty's smile slipped. *"Promise me you'll do anything to keep her safe and happy."*

Remembering her mother, he understood, and he made the promise.

Charles stood in profile by the window of his room, looking out into the parking lot . . . and yet looking into the past.

Garik and Elizabeth sat together on the visitors' uncomfortable chairs. Garik had his arm around Elizabeth's shoulders. She had her head on his chest.

Charles's stories irrevocably drew them together, made them realize how brief and precious life could be, and how quickly its joys could end, leaving nothing but memories, and even those were soon lost.

Charles smiled faintly. "The remodeling went perfectly well. People liked to do things for Misty. She could always find someone who was willing to rewire the switches or replace the sinks or install the Sheetrock. She worked alongside the men, and at night she would laugh and tell me how hard they labored because they didn't want to be shown up by a fat lady."

"Was Misty fat?" Garik asked.

Elizabeth poked him in the ribs. "Garik means, did she gain a lot of weight when she was pregnant?"

"*He's* the one who said fat," Garik argued.

"I don't care," Elizabeth said. "That's rude."

"She gained so much weight. You should have seen her. By eight months, she was a blimp." Charles's voice crackled with delight. "Every night I would massage her back, and then rub her belly with lotion because the skin itched. She didn't get stretch marks, but she had every other symptom of pregnancy. Morning sickness for the first five months. Swollen ankles. Her breasts were—" He stopped. "Never mind that."

"Right. Never mind that," Garik said.

"But she reveled in impending motherhood. She glowed with happiness. When she went into labor, it wasn't as painful as she expected, so she didn't tell me right away, and we didn't make it to the hospital. Elizabeth was born in Dr. Frownfelter's office in town on his examining table. That baby came out, and Misty held her." Charles's voice caught, and he whispered reverently, "She thought Elizabeth was beautiful."

Elizabeth blinked to push back the tears. "Misty must have been a wonderful woman."

"The most wonderful woman in the world," Charles said.

Garik found himself aching for Charles, for the loneliness of so many years, and the knowledge he would die bewildered and alone, unable even to remember the people who surrounded him. "I don't understand. *Wasn't* Elizabeth beautiful?"

Elizabeth elbowed him again.

Charles made a disgusted sound. "She looked like she'd been stewed in a hot bath for too long. She was all wrinkled and covered with white wax, and she screamed. My God! That child had lungs on her. But Misty didn't care. She bonded . . . they bonded right away."

"Did you not bond with me?" Elizabeth asked.

Charles looked at her uncertainly.

He had forgotten who she was again.

Elizabeth rephrased it. "Did you not bond with the baby?"

"It took me a few more minutes." Charles smiled. "I'll never forget how I felt when I looked at the two of them, sweaty and bloody and both of them crying. I felt as if I'd been created for that moment, for those women. I knew I would keep my promise, and I would do anything for my daughter." With the suddenness of a winter storm, he dropped his head into his hands and wept, terrible, painful tears. "But I failed her. I failed them both, and I will never forgive myself."

CHAPTER SIXTY-ONE

"Here's my professional opinion." Garik stared straight ahead, intently watching the road to the hospital. "I agree with the medical staff. I don't think your father killed your mother."

Elizabeth swallowed a lump of hope that gathered in her throat. "Why not?"

"I thought maybe he had. I mean, in my job, I've seen everything. And he's always talking about how beautiful she was—"

"Is," she said.

"What?" Garik glanced at her.

"How beautiful she *is*. He thinks she's still alive."

"He doesn't think she's still alive. He knows she's

dead. But he sees her. It sounds as if she comes around quite often." A tall, slender Douglas fir was down across the road, and Garik slowed the truck.

"Do you believe my mother is a ghost, too?" Elizabeth asked in exasperation.

"I don't believe she's a ghost. But she certainly gave him good advice when she told him to move out from underneath the ceiling that was going to fall." Garik braked to a halt. "Hold on." Getting out, he dragged the tree into the ditch.

Elizabeth didn't understand it at all. How did her father manage to convince sensible, practical people like Yvonne and Garik that Misty was visiting the Honor Mountain Memory Care Facility?

Garik got back into the truck, seemingly unaware that he'd wandered into the land of delusion. In that factual, no-nonsense tone Elizabeth thought of as his FBI voice, he continued, "Before today, Charles was always talking about how beautiful your mother was, and I thought the way she looked was the big deal to him. Which makes sense. This none-too-attractive guy manages to snag a gorgeous babe, knowing all the time she was using him to escape a bad family situation. When she bops off and has an affair, proving she doesn't value him as anything but a way to get away from her mother, the reality of the situation sends him into an uncharacteristic rage and he murders her. So all the time he's been talking, I'm thinking he sounds like a great guy and he's telling the story in a way that tugs at your heart, but my money is still on him as the killer."

Elizabeth turned in the seat to face Garik, fascinated to hear his thoughts so coolly stated.

Garik continued, "Then today he said your mother gained weight with her pregnancy. And you showed us the photos. She really did. A lot of weight." Briefly, he lifted both hands from the steering wheel to indicate a broad beam. "He was laughing about it, talking about how she glowed and he was so proud when he massaged her back and rubbed her belly. That's not a man who owns a possession, who has a trophy wife. That's a man in love."

"So you're saying men in love don't kill their wives?" Elizabeth had once known the answer; now she was not so sure.

Garik also hesitated. "What I'm saying is, if a man in love can kill his wife—that's not my definition of love."

"Okay." Elizabeth contemplated everything Garik had said, everything she had heard from her father, and her own thoughts, and put them together as coherently as she knew how. "I keep thinking that Charles might believe what he's saying. But memory is a tricky thing. Is he remembering it the way he wants to? To lose his memories after a savage murder like this is so convenient."

Garik got that shit-eating half-smile on his face. "I know of a child who after viewing a horrific tragedy lost her power of speech, and was unable to tell anyone what she witnessed until that moment when she managed to forget it all."

Indignant, Elizabeth said, "But I really did lose my power of speech!"

"Then maybe it was convenient. But it was real."

She chewed her lip, seeking a way out of this well-planned maze.

"Wanting to forget a tragedy is not a shame. It's a blessing. His mind rejects it. Your mind discarded it." Garik took her hand and squeezed it. "It's normal. If you hadn't forgotten, you would be forever in pain. Your young mind chose life. Your father's older mind couldn't discard the memories so easily. I find it fascinating that he still recalls the important parts of his life."

"You've really thought about this."

Garik glanced at her in surprise. "I was in the FBI. We're taught to think about it. Our mission is to catch the bad guys, and to do that, we have to understand them, walk in their shoes, then outsmart them. Did you really think it was all gun battles and testosterone?"

"If I were to try and understand you when we were married, I would say the distance that I felt from you was the wall you set up to prevent me from experiencing the ugliness of the rapists and the killers."

"And the child abusers."

"Why would you shut me out like that?"

He pulled over to the side of the road. "You had suffered the kind of trauma no child should ever have to face. On some level, you remembered it. I mean, yes, people faint at the sight of blood. But look at you. The color's draining from your face at the mere mention. And after that time in the hospital, when I was shot and you fell so hard you got a concussion—do you remember your nightmares? You woke up screaming night after night, terrified of some man who stalked you with bloody scissors."

He was right. Even now, she felt suffocated, unable to catch a breath.

He continued, "There's something there in your mind, and you're afraid to see it."

"I'm not . . ." But she couldn't deny she was afraid. She was. So afraid of the darkness that hid, shivering, in her subconscious. "I think sometimes I would rather face the truth than be such a coward. Then I push toward the memories, and I unravel like an old sweater in the dryer. I think I can't be whole until I know, and then I think I'm fine with a piece taken out of me."

"You are fine, and not a coward at all. You're one of the bravest women I know. Why do you think I didn't ask your father to go on and recall the scene of the murder? I can't do that while you're in the room." He caressed her shoulder. "You don't need another concussion."

"We should go back and I'll remain outside the room."

"How about if I drive you back to the resort and let you lie down, and I'll do a little research?"

She wished she didn't feel sick . . . but she did. Sick with terror and anticipation, and all from talking about the blood. Her mother's blood, all over the carpet, and her father reaching for her, crooning her name, a pair of bloody scissors in his hand . . .

"Or we can go on and talk to Yvonne about the attack on her?" Garik suggested.

Elizabeth nodded, and closed her eyes and leaned back against the headrest.

From the power panel on his side of the truck, Garik rolled down her window, put the car into gear, and drove.

She breathed deeply. The wind came through the window, cool enough to dry the sick sweat off her forehead and upper lip.

When she sighed, opened her eyes, and pushed her hair out of her eyes, he said, "I do want you to remember something. Your father hasn't told one single story that you haven't had the photo to verify. He might be making it all up—but he's making it up to fit the photos you have. The photos he didn't know that you had, and that he hasn't seen in twenty-three years."

"So now we're back to it again . . . if my father didn't kill my mother, who did?"

"Someone had better find out, huh?" He shot her a smile. "Good thing your former husband is a former FBI agent. He's got contacts on the force."

CHAPTER SIXTY-TWO

Garik and Elizabeth stepped quietly through the door of Yvonne's hospital room; they had been warned, and warned sternly, that they were not to disturb her if she was sleeping.

But she wasn't. Or rather, one moment she rested on the stack of pillows with her eyes closed, and the next she sat straight up, staring at them in a wild panic.

Elizabeth halted in her tracks. "Yvonne? Are you okay?"

A white bandage covered half of Yvonne's head: one eye, one cheekbone, most of her scalp and forehead. Bruising extended below the bandage into her lips and down to her chin. She looked wild, fierce—and terrified.

Garik stepped back and put up his hands to show he had nothing in them.

"Oh. It's you two." Yvonne withered back onto the pillows. "I'm sorry. I'm so sorry. I know you're not killers. But they've got me on painkillers and the meds make me loopy. Whenever I drop off and someone comes into the room, I think it's . . . him again, come to finish the job."

"Yvonne, don't worry. We completely understand."

Garik's voice was almost operatic in its warm, slow sincerity.

"I know you do. Better than anyone, you understand." She wasn't looking at Elizabeth, but at Garik, and she nodded in timid, nervous little dips, the kind that made Elizabeth's heart bleed for her.

Elizabeth went to the bed and took her hand. "The medical staff weren't going to let us in because we're not family, so Garik told them he was your cousin. I don't think they believed him, but they must have decided we were harmless."

Yvonne tried to smile. "Probably. They know I need somebody. I haven't had many visitors. I don't have family here. John is still gone. My friends at Honor Mountain Memory Care Facility are all working. I was just wishing I had someone to sit with me." She squeezed Elizabeth's fingers.

Garik moved at the foot of the bed. "How many stitches did it take to close the wound?"

"Quite a few." Yvonne touched the bandage self-consciously. "Because he . . . when he twisted the knife, he did a lot of damage. Shredded the skin."

"Oh, God," Elizabeth whispered.

Garik pushed a chair under Elizabeth's bottom.

Thankfully, Elizabeth sank down.

Yvonne continued, "Since the cut's on my face, putting it back together was delicate work. I really should have had a plastic surgeon, but the one who visits this hospital is stuck in Denver and can't get home."

Garik walked to the other side of the bed. "Can you tell me anything about your assailant?"

"No." Yvonne closed her eye. "I didn't see him. His face was covered by a ski mask."

"I know you don't want to remember." Garik leaned

over Yvonne, his voice warm, slow, kind. "But it's important. What did you see? What color was his skin? Was he thin? Fat? Broad-shouldered? You smelled his breath—did he smoke cigarettes or weed? Did he smell like frying grease, or a hospital, or wet paint? What did his voice sound like?"

Yvonne's hand trembled in Elizabeth's. She turned her head and looked at Garik. "Last night, I answered all these questions for Sheriff Foster. Can't you get the information from him?"

"Sheriff Foster and I are not the best of friends." Garik smiled with such charm Yvonne visibly relaxed onto her pillows. "Add to that I think he's a crappy law enforcement officer and I told him so—"

"You didn't." Yvonne laughed a little.

"I did." Garik waggled his hands back and forth. "Imagine my surprise when he didn't take it too well. Anyway, I want to hear it all from you." Garik got very serious again, and very quickly. "I want to catch this guy, for you and for whoever else he might attack."

Yvonne's one eye filled with tears.

Elizabeth leaped to the side table and pulled a tissue out of the box, and handed it to her.

Yvonne dabbed at her tears, and her voice wobbled. "I don't want to remember it again. But I can't . . . I can't forget it anyway. I wish I could. God. I wish I could."

"I know. I don't blame you. If there was any other way I could find all this out, I would. But it's got to come from you. I have to hear it from you. I promise, if you tell me, you'll be helping immensely."

Elizabeth stared at Garik. She had never before seen him use his voice, his stance, his words to cajole a witness. This was a side of his job she had never imagined, one that took every gentle skill and dexterity. He understood what it was to be a victim, and he used that understanding to get what he needed.

It seemed every time she turned around, she was learning more and more about Garik . . . and falling more and more in love with the man who commanded her body, and her heart.

"We'll start with just one thing," Garik said. "You can do that, can't you, Yvonne? Just one. Tell me about his voice."

Yvonne answered obediently, "His voice was hoarse, but I think he was doing that deliberately to disguise it."

"Any accent? Foreign? Southern? New York or Boston?"

"No. He sounded like he grew up here."

Garik nodded encouragingly. "That's important."

"He smelled clean, like soap. Maybe a little smoky . . ." Yvonne frowned as she tried to remember. "Smoky, and like some kind of fuel."

"Fuel." Garik seemed in doubt.

"My husband's a trucker," Yvonne insisted. "He almost smelled like diesel. But not quite. Something else."

"Okay. That's good. Very helpful." Garik hovered protectively over the bed. He used that soft, slow, hypnotic voice, and he kept eye contact with Yvonne. "Is it possible it was a woman?"

Yvonne frowned. "Not unless it was a very husky woman." She strained to recall the attack. "No. What kind of woman could overcome me like that?"

"One with a background in mud wrestling?" Garik suggested.

Yvonne chuckled huskily, and relaxed again.

Garik poured her a glass of ice water, helped her sit up, and gave her a sip. "Better?" he asked.

"Yes. Thank you. The meds are giving me dry mouth

and talking about the . . . the attack is making me . . . I'm hyperventilating a little."

"That's completely understandable. Elizabeth, would you go wet a washcloth so we can help Yvonne freshen up a little?" Garik never glanced at Elizabeth; all his attention remained on Yvonne.

Elizabeth went in the bathroom to do as he asked, and as she returned she heard him say, "It's tough being a nurse, isn't it? You always know exactly what's wrong with you."

"It's true," Yvonne said.

Elizabeth dabbed at Yvonne's swollen lips, and stroked the cool cloth across her cheek.

Yvonne closed her eye. "That feels good," she said. But she mumbled.

"She's getting tired," Elizabeth whispered to Garik.

He waved the cloth away, and leaned closer to Yvonne. Very quietly, he said, "We're almost done now. Just a couple of more questions. Can you do that?"

Yvonne didn't open her eyes, but she nodded.

"How about his skin?" Garik asked. "What did you see?"

"He was completely covered. Dark leather bomber jacket—the collar was worn almost white. Jeans, I think. Boots. Leather gloves. The ski mask."

"Did you catch any glimpse of him at all? Just an impression."

Elizabeth kept absolutely still, enthralled and desperate not to interrupt.

"White. He was white. And his eyes." Yvonne's voice got breathy. "I saw his eyes. Through the holes. In the mask. They burned. He was . . . crazy, I think. Not like our patients when they have dementia, but livid, focused . . . his eyes burned. I don't know another way to say that."

She clutched the sheet and pulled it up to her neck. "I would recognize his eyes anywhere."

"It's okay," Garik said softly. "He can't get you here."

Yvonne began to shiver. "I know. I'm safe here."

Elizabeth pulled the blanket at the foot of the bed over the top of her and tucked it in.

Garik nodded his thanks, and still spoke to Yvonne. "Yes, you're safe here."

His assurance seemed to comfort Yvonne.

"Did you tell Sheriff Foster what you told me about your assailant's eyes?" Garik asked.

"No. Sheriff Foster was impatient, in a hurry, and the memory was too . . . creepy." Yvonne shivered again.

"You did exactly right." Garik gently put his hand on her shoulder. "Just promise me you won't tell anyone else about the eyes."

"I won't. I haven't told anyone at all, excerpt you . . . and that reporter."

Garik froze. "Reporter?"

"That nice young man." Yvonne smiled, and at last relaxed. "What's his name? Noah. Noah Griffin."

CHAPTER SIXTY-THREE

"I know the reporter. I met him. Noah Griffin is a pleasant man, and if I ask him not to publish his report, I'm sure he'll do as I ask." Elizabeth wasn't at all sure, but Garik looked so grim, so worried, she was moved to reassure him.

Garik drove into Virtue Falls, slowing for the ever-increasing stream of pedestrians. "Have you ever had dealings with the press?" Sarcasm dripped from his tone.

"Of course I have." She thought back on the past. "And not good ones. I still say Noah Griffin's not a bad man."

"He's already sent the story."

"Maybe. That depends on whether he has a stable Internet connection, though, so if we can catch him . . ." A thought niggled at her. "When did you have dealings with the press?"

"My expulsion from the FBI could possibly be blamed on the press." He slid a glance toward her. "But mostly the fault is mine. As I told you . . . I turned into my father."

"Stop being mysterious. Tell me what you did."

"I'm not being mysterious!"

"Then tell me what you did."

"I will." As the number of people on foot became a crowd, he slowed more. "But not here. Not now . . . What is going on?"

She stared at the pedestrians toward the center of town. "The circus has come to town?"

They turned the corner toward the square. "Apparently you're right." Seated high in the truck, he and Elizabeth could see what was causing the commotion.

In the intersection, on the pavement, a large commercial helicopter rested on its struts. The blades slowly rotated. A man and a woman, both dressed in fashionable black, stood outside the open cargo doors, handing out plastic gallons of water and brown paper bags filled with . . . Elizabeth didn't know what. Something that convinced all of Virtue Falls' population they should stand in line to receive it.

"It's Bradley and Vivian Hoff," Elizabeth said.

Garik's eyes narrowed. "Of course. I haven't seen

them in years, but trendy folks that they are, I should have recognized them." He looked Bradley Hoff over, sizing him up as Misty's possible lover—and killer. Both were certainly possible. The guy was handsome in a polished, actor kind of way. He was decently tall, about five-ten, and slender; he wore clothes well. But he was toned, too, for his expensive golf shirt bared arms that bulged with muscle. If Garik remembered correctly, his hair used to be brown. Now it was black, and was cut in a boyishly tousled style that took an entire can of hairspray to achieve.

But Garik was being cynical. He didn't like Hoff for the same reasons the critics hated him; he was slick in his pursuit of success, kissing babies and old women to sell paintings and coffee table books. That didn't mean he was a killer, and personally, Garik thought the guy was too scared of his wife to cheat on her.

At least, if he was smart, he was scared. Vivian Hoff didn't look as if she kissed babies. She looked as if she made babies cry . . . with a single smile.

"They swooped in . . . in a helicopter?" Elizabeth was half-amused, half-appalled. "They brought supplies like you did, and nobody noticed you, but everyone worships them?"

"Bradley Hoff is Nature's Artist. He's the town's golden boy—and I'm not. Beside, look." Garik indicated the pretty young woman flitting around the Hoffs, taking artfully posed photos. "They brought their own photographer. I failed to do that."

"Wow. That's . . . shrewd and . . . weird."

"They're brilliant." The crowds made it impossible to safely keep the truck in motion, so he parked at the curb. "They'll get national publicity for this. And that's what they care about, isn't it?"

"They might care about the people in town."

He stared at her, eyebrows raised.

"It is great publicity," she admitted.

Garik got out, walked around, and helped her out.

Rainbow slipped through the crowd to stand next to Elizabeth. "So even you came in to see what was going on."

Elizabeth glanced at the paper bag in Rainbow's hand. "And even you got a bag of whatever they're distributing."

Rainbow opened the bag. "Toilet paper. A can of tuna. Dried beans. Tampons. Flashlight. Fresh batteries. Hershey bars. Some other stuff."

Elizabeth turned to Garik. "There's where you went wrong. You didn't bring tampons. Or Hershey bars."

For the first time since they had left the hospital, he grinned. "My mistake."

"We missed their arrival." Elizabeth nodded toward the square. "What happened?"

"It was spectacular. About two hours ago, the helicopter made its first pass. It swooped low over the town, made a run down the canyon, pretty well rousted everyone in the area out of their lethargy, then landed right there like they had every right." Rainbow's eyes sparkled; obviously she was one of the people rousted out of her lethargy.

Garik chortled. "I'll bet Foster was pissed."

"You bet. By the time the sheriff got here, ready to arrest whoever was buzzing his town without a permit, the Hoffs were handing out bags filled with necessities, and he slinked away." Rainbow did her imitation of slinking.

"No, he didn't," Garik said. "He's right over on the courthouse steps."

"You're kidding." Rainbow climbed onto the running board of Garik's truck and got a look at Sheriff Foster. "Look at him glower. After the days and nights he's had, you'd think he'd go home to bed. Probably he's afraid to go to sleep in that house. Probably he's afraid his mother will haunt him."

"There are no such thing as ghosts." Elizabeth felt as if she had pointed this out all too often lately, and to people who should know better.

"That old bitch. I think she will haunt him until the day he dies. She had her claws so deep into that boy . . ." Rainbow climbed back down and rubbed her arms as if she felt a chill. "Foster doesn't look like he's slept in days. You did hear about the Suns' house burning down, right?"

Both Garik and Elizabeth turned on her. "What?" "What?"

"Yeah. Last night!" Rainbow looked in equal parts thrilled to break the news and horrified at another tragedy. "No one knows how it started, but their place is on a country road, there's not a hydrant out there, and there wasn't enough water in the volunteer fire truck to fight it. Plus the fire burned fast and hard. We were all scared to death Mike and Courtney were inside, but one of their cars is gone and the fire chief said he was pretty sure there were no human remains inside. I sure hope not. I liked them both."

Elizabeth began, "They were just at—"

Garik put his hand on her shoulder and pressed warningly. "That's a damned shame about their house. But I'm sure they're fine."

Rainbow observed them. "You guys know something."

"I know Foster's going to say the Suns burned their

own house, and I know they didn't." Garik fixed his gaze on the helicopter pilot, now lingering impatiently beside the pilot's door. "I just remembered something I need to do. Elizabeth, hang here with Rainbow until I get back, okay?"

Elizabeth watched him reach into the truck and pull out a Priority Mail box, and head toward the helicopter.

Mail? He wanted to mail a package? Now?

She climbed on the running board to watch.

Meanwhile, Rainbow chatted. "Look! The Hoffs' photographer is taking video now. Wouldn't you know it? The first person to stick her face in there is Cameron Hardwick. Pull out a camera and that girl arrives like the coyote chasing the Acme truck. I wonder if she'll offer to sing a song for the Hoffs. She fancies herself one of America's Top Talents. She wants to go try out, but her father keeps nixing the trip. Seize the day, kid!"

Elizabeth paid no attention. She kept her gaze on Garik. Garik, who approached the pilot, spoke to him, and offered the box.

The pilot shook his head and backed away.

Garik dug in his pocket and flashed his badge.

In all the time Elizabeth had spent with Garik, she had never seen him flash his badge.

The pilot examined it, hesitated, grimaced, and took the package.

Elizabeth climbed down. *How interesting.*

Noah Griffin worked his way through the crowd to her side. "Who's your boyfriend? The one with the badge?"

"Oh. Garik." Elizabeth looked; Garik was speaking intensely to the now-fidgeting pilot. "He's not my boyfriend. He's my ex-husband."

Rainbow butted right in. "He's an FBI agent. Local boy made good in big-time law enforcement."

"Really?" Noah pulled out his phone. "How do you spell his last name?"

Elizabeth took Noah's arm firmly in her grasp. "I'll tell you, but first I want to talk."

"About what?" Noah asked.

"Yeah, about what?" Rainbow asked.

"A private matter," Elizabeth told Rainbow firmly. Then she steered Noah toward the back of the truck. "You interviewed Yvonne Rudda."

"I did." In a characteristic gesture, Noah ran his fingers through his blond-tipped brown hair. "You've got some freaky stuff going on in this town."

Elizabeth didn't care what he thought. She only knew what she wanted. "Hold the story."

"What? Are you kidding? Why?" He had the guts to sound affronted.

"Because Yvonne said she told you she'd recognize the guy by his eyes, and since the guy got away, that could be dangerous for her."

"Um . . . I already transmitted the story."

"And you said that? About the guy's eyes?"

"Sure."

Elizabeth couldn't believe his carelessness. "Did you not think of the danger this could present for Yvonne?" She turned away in disgust.

"C'mon, don't be that way." Noah caught her arm. "You don't have to worry. Yvonne Rudda's not a famous name. I'm not even officially employed by a news agency anymore. Probably no online site will pick up the story."

"You'd better hope not," Elizabeth said, "and if someone does, you'd better hope nothing happens to Yvonne. I mean—I assume you would feel guilty if something did."

"Of course!"

She didn't know whether to believe him. "That's good, because I stood up for you to Garik, and I would hate to think I'm mistaken about your character. I would also hate to think what would happen to you, stuck in this little town, if one of the most beloved nursing professionals we have is killed because of your callousness."

Noah looked astonished. "Are you threatening me?"

"I'm merely pointing out that this part of the world retains a little of the wild, we own a lot of guns, and as we're more and more cut off from civilization, justice could become something less politically correct, and more savage." Where had she learned such intimidating tactics?

From Garik, of course, and—

Andrew Marrero's voice called, "You! There! Reporter! Hold on. You misunderstood. Elizabeth and I—we are ready to release the tsunami video, and we're giving you the exclusive!"

CHAPTER SIXTY-FOUR

"All right, Mr. Jacobsen, I'll do it." The helicopter pilot was not pleased. "But if I took a package from every person here who had an emergency shipment, I couldn't get this helicopter off the ground."

"If you took a package from every person shipping to the FBI, you'd fly without fuel," Garik retorted.

"Yeah. Yeah." The helicopter pilot opened the door and flung the package inside.

Garik stared evenly at him.

"The post office will treat it a lot worse than that," the pilot said.

"Give me your card."

"My card?"

"Your business card." As the pilot dug through his wallet, Garik added, "Get the package mailed ASAP, or I'll find out why." He took the card and turned to face the crowd.

The people who waited in line were closely observing him.

In return, he scanned the crowd.

The Hoffs were both on camera, filming with the Virtue Falls mayor, who was at his most fulsome. In the background of the shot was a large, sparkling oil painting of the sun smiling on the ocean and a long stretch of coast. Without a doubt, one of Bradley's. They were holding up tickets . . . It didn't take a genius to figure out their strategy. They were running a raffle for the painting, one to raise money for Virtue Falls. And it would raise money, Garik was sure. Lots and lots of money.

Rainbow stood alone, looking miffed.

Hand on his revolver, Foster watched Garik.

Noah Griffin stood talking to . . . Elizabeth and Andrew Marrero.

"Shit." Garik could not believe it. He'd been gone ten minutes, and she'd managed to get caught by the reporter and her asshat of a boss.

He headed in their direction, then veered toward Rainbow. "What's up?"

"I don't know." Rainbow was snippy. "She wanted to have a private conversation with her reporter."

Garik sternly looked down his nose at her.

Rainbow stared back defiantly. Then her indignation faded. "All right. She was having her private moment with Noah—it looked like a fight to me—when Marrero came running up saying Noah misunderstood and he and Elizabeth wanted to release the tsunami video together. Marrero's bound and determined to grab credit one way or another, I imagine as Elizabeth's supervisor."

Garik *really* didn't like that guy. In fact, Garik would give him the inside track as Misty's killer, except for a couple of things.

He did not believe the Suns' house had burned by accident; Foster was the suspect for that.

And he knew better than to think that because a guy was annoying, he was also lethal. Marrero could very well be nothing but a big bag of gas without a sincere bone in his body.

Was he a killer, too? God only knew, and before it was over, Garik would know, too.

"Let me see what I can do to derail his schemes," he said.

"You do that," Rainbow answered.

Garik didn't really have a plan, so he walked over and stood beside the reporter, silent and unsmiling. In his experience, a grim, silent, muscular man made people nervous, and people who were nervous did one of three things: retreat, babble, or get aggressive.

The response always revealed more to Garik than an interrogation.

Elizabeth glanced at him in annoyance.

Noah stepped away.

Marrero said, "Do you mind? We're giving an interview here."

Fists clenched, Garik crossed his arms high over his chest and stared, gaze level, eyes expressionless. Yes, each one had revealed something about their personalities.

Noah watched him out of the corners of his eyes, but he spoke to Marrero. "So you're Elizabeth Banner's mentor?"

"Yes. Of course. Who else could be?"

Garik barely contained his amusement; Marrero really needed to learn not to show his irritation so openly during an interview. The reporter always had the last word.

Noah consulted his phone. "In my notes, it says she was an accomplished geologist before she took this position."

Marrero's face flushed a deep, livid shade of burgundy.

"And when I interviewed you in Tahoe," Noah continued, "you yourself said she was the best applicant for the job."

Elizabeth could scarcely contain her exasperation with Marrero and with Noah. "There is no substitute for experience, and while it's true I had the educational credentials, experience is what I've received while on this dig."

"So you're saying Andrew Marrero is your mentor? That your father is not?"

Garik noted that although the question was sharp, Noah's voice softened as he spoke to Elizabeth.

How did she do it? The guy was half in love with her, and as always, she was clueless.

"My father and I had no contact between the time I was four and twenty-six, so I think it's safe to say my father has had minimal influence on my knowledge of geology." The word *obviously* was unspoken.

"Yet you did follow the exact same profession he did," Noah said, "even going so far as to return to the project he started."

"I do have a certain sterling reputation as the leader

of the project." Marrero struggled to insert himself into the discussion. "Do you want to see the tsunami video?"

"I've seen it," Noah said impatiently. "You know that. In accordance with Miss Banner's wishes, I will send the video to the Geological Society of America. I have contacts with the Discovery Channel, so it's also going there."

"That's good," Marrero said. "Very good."

Garik watched Marrero ruminate, trying to figure out an angle that would bring attention to him.

And he did. "Who's your contact at the Discovery Channel?" Marrero asked Noah. "I'll send a background report on the project and suggest they come here to film footage."

"Yeah, that's a good idea." Noah had Marrero figured out, too, and his tone couldn't have been more cynically insulting.

Marrero's color started to climb again.

Elizabeth pinched Noah. Hard.

He jumped and straightened. "Mr. Marrero, I'll get you that name right away, and tell him you're sending in the report."

"Good." Marrero had accomplished his mission. "I'm going back to work, then." Turning to Elizabeth, he said with exquisite sarcasm, "Do you plan on returning to the dig any time soon?"

Before Garik could say a word, she answered, "I'll be there this afternoon."

"How good of you." Marrero headed around the truck. Garik heard him stumble against the side panel and shout, "Damn it, woman!"

Stepping around, Garik saw Marrero storming toward the canyon, and Rainbow dusting herself off.

She looked up and shrugged, unabashed at being caught eavesdropping, and wandered off after Marrero.

At the back of the truck, like a bully on the playground, Elizabeth pushed Noah backward. "What's wrong with you? Are you trying to make my life miserable? We—all of us guys who work for Andrew—make sure his ego is well stoked at all times. It's the only way to keep him halfway pleasant!"

Noah let her push. "He really has it in for you, doesn't he?"

She stopped pushing and stood stock-still. "Garik says Andrew Marrero has issues about living in the shadow of my father's genius."

Garik spoke for the first time. "And your genius, too."

"I got all that figured out," Noah said.

She pushed again. "You won't put that in your report."

"God, no. That gets into possible slander." Noah sat on the truck's bumper.

"Get off my truck," Garik said.

Noah stood up hastily, but kept his focus on Elizabeth. "Really? Charles Banner had no influence on your decision to become a geologist?"

"Probably he did in that I'm intrinsically good at it," she said.

"Genetics at work," Noah suggested.

Elizabeth inclined her head. "Yes, I believe so."

"What about your decision to move here . . . I don't believe for a second you merely wanted to be mentored by Andrew Marrero." Noah was fishing.

Elizabeth, of course, swallowed the bait. "He's very capable. But—"

Garik put his hand on her arm.

Abruptly, she stopped talking.

"Look," Noah said to Garik. "No reporter sticks to

'Just the facts, ma'am' anymore. If she doesn't tell me, I'll speculate, and probably sell it for a lot more than I can get for the truth."

"I could crush you like a bug," Garik told him.

Noah grinned. "Haven't you heard? Reporters are like cockroaches. Kill one, and a million take its place."

Garik took a step toward him.

Noah held up his hands. "I'm one of the good guys. I'm on Elizabeth's side, and I'll stick to the truth, pretty much. And you don't want me out there in the real world where Internet is cheap and easy and I can do a buttload of damage to the Banner project because I didn't feel welcome."

Garik was within a breath of saying he didn't give a crap about the Banner project. But one glance at Elizabeth's face made him shut up.

"It's a good project," she told him.

Unfair. What good did it do him to keep his mouth shut if she could read his mind?

"I don't understand why you're here," Garik said to Noah. "Now that the tsunami and the earthquake are becoming distant memories, for the news, anyway, and it looks like the Hoffs will get the recovery moving along, there's no story. So why are you hanging around?"

"Why does any reporter leave civilization, go off to a tiny town on the coast, and hang around colorful characters?" Noah smiled, sort of cynically, with one side of his mouth. "I'm writing a book."

Garik was pretty sure Noah was laughing at himself.

Elizabeth did laugh. "Really? That's great. When will it be published?"

Noah sighed. "The correct question is, when will it be finished? I'm having more trouble than I expected getting past writing chapter one."

"You don't know what to write after the first chapter?" Elizabeth asked.

"No. I mean . . . those two words. *Chapter One*." Noah seemed completely serious. "In the meantime, I'm supporting myself with freelance reporting. Which is why I'm trying to find out whether you came to Virtue Falls for your father."

Garik shook his head at Elizabeth.

Noah glared.

Elizabeth ignored Garik and answered. "Yes. I wished to get to know my father before the Alzheimer's took him away forever."

"Did you recognize him when you saw him?" Noah pressed her eagerly, as if afraid Garik would interrupt him. Or stomp him.

"From the photos, yes. But not from my childhood." She said that quite firmly.

"Did you recognize Virtue Falls when you arrived?" Noah asked.

"Not at all."

"Did you recognize your house?"

"No."

Noah's eyes lit. "So you went to your house?"

Damn it. She'd fallen for the reporter's ruse. And even worse—Noah had thought to ask a question that had never occurred to Garik. *Damn it.*

If Elizabeth knew she'd been tricked, she gave no indication. She answered the question without emotion, with apparent frankness. "When I first got here, even before I went to visit my father, I was curious, so I went out to see the house where I'd spent my first years."

"Where *it* happened?" Not even Noah had the nerve to elucidate exactly what had happened. "That must have been creepy."

"No. No, it was sad. I had thought if I went back, my recollection would return. But I didn't remember it at all. The house was boarded up, a decrepit wreck sitting out in the middle of nothing, empty of everything . . . even memories." She sighed, then smiled. "Now, if you gentlemen will excuse me, I want to go stand in line for my free bag of supplies, and after that—I need to go to work."

CHAPTER SIXTY-FIVE

By the time Elizabeth got in the line to pick up her foodstuffs and paper products, the line had shrunk to about twenty people, all of them looking a little ragged, a little tired, but all avidly watched Bradley and Vivian Hoff speaking with the mayor of Virtue Falls in front of the camera.

"What are they talking about?" Elizabeth asked the woman in front of her.

"From what I've heard, the mayor is telling them that Virtue Falls has received no attention from Washington State officials, that we don't have the basic amenities, and he's hinting we're all going to turn Republican if they don't fix the roads." The woman laughed, but without humor.

"So they're going to get it on the news?" Elizabeth asked.

"The Hoffs have a lot of influence," the next woman up said. "So the interview should get us some action."

"It better," the first woman said, "I'm tired of taking cold showers and eating cold meals."

"I'm here for flashlight and batteries." Elizabeth pulled her old, battered flashlight out of her bag and showed them the cracked lens. "Geologists are tough on flashlights."

From behind her, Garik said, "I'm here for the toilet paper."

Elizabeth turned to face him, and frowned.

"Hey, toilet paper is important, especially if you don't have it." He looked innocent, not at all as if he was stalking her—for her own safety, of course.

"Hello, Garik, good to see you back in town," the woman in front of Elizabeth said.

"Hello, Mrs. Ubach. Good thing this happened when the kids were out for the summer, huh? How did the high school come through?"

"It's not too bad. That's where I'm living now—in the gym." Mrs. Ubach smiled painfully.

"I want to flush the toilet . . . and have it flush," said the woman two up from Elizabeth. "With water I don't have to pour from a bucket."

"I want to flip a switch and have the light come on," the woman three up said.

"I want to go through *one day* and not get shaken out of bed by an aftershock," the woman in front of her said.

Everybody nodded about that, and shuffled forward in line.

"I want to go home," Mrs. Ubach said. "I want to be able to hire a contractor to take the tree off the roof, and to replace the garage and the windows. I want to cook in my own kitchen, sleep in my own bed, drink my own coffee. I want to be alone, without listening to fifty adults and twenty kids at the shelter, all talking or snoring or crying or fighting . . ." Her voice trailed off. "I should be grateful to be alive. And I am. But I just want . . . to go home."

The litany was all the more heartfelt for being so obviously unrehearsed.

The lady in front hugged her.

As always when faced with such raw human emotions, Elizabeth felt helpless and incompetent. But she patted Mrs. Ubach's arm. "I am very lucky to be staying at the resort, but I do understand. I lost everything except what I had in my bag, and the photo album Peyton Bailey got for me."

Everyone within earshot nodded.

Elizabeth continued, "I keep reaching for my hairbrush, or my bra, or thinking that I want my good running shoes, and everything I've got is someone else's. I'm grateful to have anything. Really, I am. But it's very odd to have lost almost everything. You know?"

Mrs. Ubach stared at her. "You're a nice girl for a geologist."

The line shuffled forward.

When Elizabeth got to the front, Bradley Hoff smiled with perfunctory interest and passed her a paper bag full of supplies. His blue eyes expressed the proper consideration as he said, "I hope this helps ease your difficulties in these tough times."

"Thank you—this is very generous of you," Elizabeth said.

"She's perfect," the photographer called and lifted her camera. "Good profile, and she's pretty. Let's take some pictures."

"Good choice, Loring." Bradley's smile became more personal, and he scrutinized Elizabeth. He looked startled. "Wait. You're Misty's daughter. I knew your mother."

"I know. You . . . you've told me." Several times over the last few months, once he managed to figure out who she was.

"Yes. Of course. We've talked before." He frowned as he searched his mind for information. "You're here working on the Banner geological project. I imagine the earthquake was everything you'd ever hoped for."

"It was great."

The photographer clicked a few shots, then pulled out her video camera.

Vivian stepped between Loring and Elizabeth. "Bradley brings up a point. Elizabeth Banner's got a background. If we do that, *she'll* become the story, rather than the story being our generosity. Eye on the prize, ladies and gentlemen. Eye on the prize." Turning to Elizabeth, she said, "Sorry, dear."

Elizabeth caught a glimpse of the photographer, who looked disgusted and put the lens cover back on the camera.

But Bradley easily yielded to his wife's dictates. He shook Elizabeth's hand again, then turned his attention to the next guy in line. To Garik. "Good to see you. Local boy, right? Garik, isn't it? You're back in town? Visiting and got caught by the earthquake?"

"Something like that." Garik took his bag of supplies and pushed Elizabeth forward, into the middle of the square.

Next in line was an eight-year-old boy.

Bradley's eyes lit up.

The camera started clicking.

"We have a very special package for youngsters." He reached behind him into the helicopter and brought out a colorful bag. "Here you go. Inside, there's Hobbit LEGOs."

"Cool," the boy said.

As Garik and Elizabeth moved away from the helicopter, she said, "Bradley Hoff has met me four times, and doesn't ever remember me. I look enough like my mother that you'd think that if he was her lover, he'd get a clue."

"Could be an act."

"Could be that he meets so many people on his art tours he doesn't remember anybody."

"Sure. Anything's possible. Certainly he's vastly interested in his image, and so's his wife." Garik looked over her shoulder to someone behind her. "Hello, Foster, you're looking a little worn around the edges."

Elizabeth turned to see the sheriff.

Weariness had worn grooves into the sides of Foster's mouth and put bags under his eyes. His hair was greasy. His hat was dirty. His tan uniform showed grime at the collar and cuffs, and what looked like soot dusted his shoulders.

Elizabeth didn't stop to think; she leaned into him and took a breath. "You smell like smoke," she said.

"In case you didn't hear, the Suns' house burned last night," Foster said. "I was there with the fire department trying to put it out."

"You also smell a little like gasoline. Or something." The memory of Yvonne's words sprang into Elizabeth's mind. *He smelled clean, like soap. Maybe a little smoky . . . Smoky, and like some kind of fuel.* Elizabeth started to blurt out an accusation.

Garik's hand clamped onto her shoulder, and he spoke before she could. "Go home and take a shower, Foster."

Garik was right. She couldn't accuse Sheriff Foster of setting fire to the Suns' house. Not here and now, with outside communication so limited and the sheriff so hostile to them both. But what a coincidence that Yvonne's description also noted that smell . . .

"I'm clean. I took a shower at the jail," Foster snapped. "It's my uniform that's dirty. One of my deputies is fetching a fresh one from my house."

"Good planning," Garik said. "Try and get some rest."

Foster looked down at the street, then back up at Garik and Elizabeth, and his eyes burned. "Sure. Like that's going to happen with a drug addict attacking nurses, houses burning down, and our coroner vanished. You wouldn't happen to know where Mike went, do you, Garik?"

"No . . . are you sure he's gone? Because if he is, that's a lucky break for him and Courtney. If they'd been in the house, they might have been overcome by smoke before they could escape, and that would be a tragedy that would haunt us all." Garik didn't soften his tone. He stood unsmiling, stern. He was harassing Sheriff Foster, snapping at his heels.

Foster put his hand on his pistol, took audible breaths, and looked as if he was inches away from pulling his weapon.

So Elizabeth said, "I liked Mike and Courtney very much." She thought that would cool the heated emotions.

Instead Foster bent those red-rimmed manic eyes on her. "When did *you* meet them?"

She knew Garik would not want her to say Mike and Courtney had visited the inn the day before. So she said, "I've met a lot of people in Virtue Falls. Soon I'll have lived here a year."

"Right." Sheriff Foster dropped his hand away from his gun.

He looked so belligerent and exuded such waves of misery, and seemed so in conflict with himself, she was abruptly convinced that Garik was right; Sheriff Foster was the man who had been her mother's lover. He'd killed her, and now he suffered for his crime. Suffered, and struck out again and again in violence and destruction. That would certainly explain his belligerence toward her.

Yet for all the thoughts tumbling through her head, she still felt sorry for him. Gently she put her hand on his sleeve. "If you don't have time to go home, perhaps you could get some sleep on a cot at the jail. You deserve to rest."

He made to strike her hand away, then stopped himself.

Garik said, "We were sorry to hear about the loss of your mother."

"My *mother*," Sheriff Foster repeated. Lifting his hands, he looked at them as if he'd never seen them before. Then he strode toward the courthouse.

Once again, his grip rested on his weapon.

Elizabeth and Garik watched him disappear into the crowd.

"He burned down the Suns' home." A dreadful thought, but one Elizabeth was convinced was true.

"I think so, yes." Taking her arm, Garik walked her toward his truck. Catching sight of Rainbow loitering by the front bumper, he swerved toward the huge chunk of the courthouse's fallen granite façade. He dusted off a flat spot, sat down, then reached for Elizabeth's hand and pulled her down to sit beside him.

"But why?" Elizabeth asked.

"Mike got me some information I was looking for."

"Sheriff Foster could easily have killed them. Over information?"

"He's a man out of control."

"Yet . . . yet Yvonne said she would recognize her

attacker's eyes anywhere. Sheriff Foster questioned her, and she didn't say anything about it being him."

"It was dark. She saw his eyes behind a ski mask. Witnesses are mistaken about this stuff all the time. They think they know—and they don't." Garik spoke with assurance. "The good thing is—once that story comes out about her recognizing him by his eyes, if it is Foster, he'll know it's not true."

"So she won't be in danger," Elizabeth said hopefully.

"I didn't say that. He *is* a man out of control." Garik took her hand. "Promise me you will be careful not to be alone with him."

"I promise. I'm not going to be alone at all." She looked Garik right in the eyes. "I'm going to go to work in Virtue Falls Canyon, and I'm never going to let Ben, Luke, and Joe out of my sight."

"Why do you need to go to work?" Garik leaned close and murmured in her ear. "Why not take some time off and relax while I get this all cleared up?"

He was trying to seduce her out of a job. "Work is what people do," she informed him. "They get up in the morning. They go to work. They work until it's time to quit. They go home."

Garik leaned back, and his tone had a bite to it. "Not everybody has a family history that could get them killed."

"You have a theory that there's someone out there who wants to kill me. You have no conclusive proof. No one has tried to harm me. I can't hide from a theory." She understood logic, and here she was on solid ground.

He switched gears. "You could *not* talk to reporters."

"You heard Noah Griffin. He said if I didn't answer the questions, he'd make something up."

Garik showed his teeth like a junkyard dog. "Let him make it up!"

"At least this way, I'm controlling what gets printed."

"I don't want anything printed about you and the Banner murder case."

"I don't, either. But don't you get it? That's what he's going to write. In his book, in his articles. After all these years, the Banner case is still good press. It's dramatic. It's bloody. There's a love affair. A beautiful woman is murdered. Her husband is convicted. Maybe there's a grieving lover out there." She cupped her forehead with her hand. "Noah's going to write it anyway. At least this way I can make it clear I don't remember anything. And if your theory is right, that's better than speculation that I do."

"You're right." Garik wrapped his arms around her and pulled her close. "I know you're right. I'm . . . I just got you back, and I'm scared I'm going to lose you again. I'm afraid history is going to somehow repeat itself."

She sighed, and relaxed into his embrace. "You just got me back?"

He swallowed as if he hadn't meant to say that. "For one night, I got to hold you in my arms, and make love to you, and pretend you would be mine forever. I . . . liked that. I would like that to be true."

She took pleasure in what he said. She took pleasure in how he said it. And the memory of the pain that had separated them was fading . . . "I would, too. I would like my father not to have murdered my mother. I would like her killer to confess and be arrested, and to never worry about this again. I would like a lot of things." She cupped his face. "Right now, most of all, I would like to go to work."

He surrendered. "So there's one thing we can get right, right now."

"Yes."

"You'll let me drive you to the canyon?" he asked.

"Of course."

"And pick you up when you're done?" He pulled out his keys.

"Today."

"One day at a time, then." He stood and offered his hand.

She allowed him to pull her to her feet.

They faced the square.

Everyone was watching them. *Everyone*.

"To hell with flushing toilets and electric lights," Elizabeth said. "I want the TV to come back on so this town will have something to watch besides us."

CHAPTER SIXTY-SIX

Elizabeth stormed up the slope of the canyon to the place where Garik paced. "Okay, look. You can't do this. You're making the team nervous. Marrero is snapping at everyone. And you're driving me crazy!"

"I'm not doing anything."

"You're pacing."

"I can stop." Garik halted in his tracks.

"I can hear you breathing."

"Sorry. I can't stop that."

"I can hear you wondering what I'm doing, and why. I can feel you watching Ben, Luke, and Joe, assessing

them as potential dangers. You have . . . to go . . . away."
She was railing at him. She knew she was. But he acted
like he was her only shield against an army of attackers.
Imaginary attackers.

"I'll go away tomorrow." Garik looked at his watch.
"Right now, it's five o'clock. Time to quit."

"I don't want to . . . Wait." She could make a deal. "If
I quit now, will you stay away tomorrow?"

"How far away?"

"Far. At the resort. At least."

He rearranged his face to look pitiful. "I'd be bored. I
don't have anything to do at the resort."

"You don't have anything to do here."

"Marrero could put me to work." Garik's puppy face
looked hopeful.

"No. Because you'd still be breathing and thinking,
and all of it would be too loud."

He took her arm. "Let's go home and we'll talk
about it."

Impatient and distraught, she pulled herself out of his
grasp. "You're not going to work here, and I am. So get
used to it."

He crossed his arms. Stared at her forbiddingly. When
that didn't impress her, he said with apparent amiability,
"Okay. Do you need to get your stuff and say good-bye?"

"Okay, what?" she asked suspiciously.

"Okay, I'm not going to work here. Or breathe or think
here. Come on. Get your stuff and say good-bye."

She didn't budge. "And I am going to work and breathe
and think here."

"I would suppose you are. I don't know how to
stop you."

She did not trust him. "You're giving in too easily."

He put his hands on her shoulders and looked into her

eyes. "I have the greatest respect for your intelligence and your integrity. You know there's a chance that my theory is right and your mother's killer is abroad in this town, and you promised to never let Ben, Luke, and Joe out of your sight. I depend on those two things—your intelligence and your integrity—to keep you safe."

"Hm. Right." She still didn't quite believe him, but what was she supposed to say? He appeared to be yielding, and he appeared to be sincere. "I'll go say good-bye and get my stuff."

"Want some help?"

"No!" When she told the team she was leaving, the guys never said a word. They left that to Andrew Marrero, whose scathing comments about their newfound tsunami video prima donna made her wonder why she had ever hoped to please him about anything.

So when she came back up the slope, she was in a dangerous mood.

Garik, on the other hand, was quiet and mellow . . .

. . . which irritated her even more, and she spent the whole ride clutching her case to her chest and looking out the side window.

At the resort, she jumped out of the truck and hurried up the steps and into the empty great room.

Garik joined her. "Where's Margaret?"

Harold appeared, looking grim. "She's upstairs in bed."

Margaret? In bed? In the daytime? "Is she ill?" Elizabeth asked anxiously.

"You'll have to ask her," Harold said in tones of doom.

Garik and Elizabeth exchanged alarmed glances and headed for the stairs.

Margaret was stretched out on her bed, her eyes closed, a damp cloth on her forehead. Her complexion was blotchy and red, and her mouth was set in annoyance. She looked like what she was—an old, angry Irishwoman.

Garik went to the bed and took her hand.

Margaret opened her eyes a slit.

"What's wrong?" he said.

"She called," Margaret answered.

Garik sighed. "I was afraid that was it."

"What?" Elizabeth charged forward. "Who? What?"

"Patricia called," he told her.

"Patricia?" Elizabeth searched her mind. "Oh! Patricia! Margaret's granddaughter."

"Yes. My granddaughter." Margaret spoke in tones of doleful doom. "She's been ringing my cell phone. I've been pretending she couldn't get through. So she got on the ham radio and waited until I was talking to poor dear Annie Di Luca—"

"Annie Di Luca is now a poor dear?" Garik teased.

Margaret sat up and flung the damp cloth off. It smacked the wall. She glared at him. "Do you have a quarrel with me? Because if you do, bring it on!"

Garik backed away. "Absolutely not. You were on the ham radio with poor dear Annie Di Luca, your enemy for about a hundred years, and Patricia interrupted."

With her hand placed dramatically on her forehead, Margaret again reclined on the stack of pillows. "Patricia says, 'Gram, are you all right? Did the earthquake hurt you?' All solicitousness, you know. And I said, 'No, I wasn't hurt.' And she said, 'Sell the resort, and you could be in Hawaii right now.' And I said, 'Sending me to Hawaii won't stop the earthquakes.' And she said, 'No, but you'll be safe.' And I said, 'Have you never heard of volcanoes? There are about a million of them over there.' " Margaret's Irish accent strengthened with every word. "The conversation went downhill from there."

"She sounds difficult," Elizabeth said.

"Jesus, Mary, and Joseph. Patricia is a barracuda with a wallet. She doesn't care about her heritage. She just wants to sell my home and make a profit. The nasty little bitch." Margaret threw one of her pillows at the wall.

Elizabeth handed her one of the pillows off the couch. She threw it.

Garik went to the sideboard and rummaged around until he found the Tullamore Dew. He splashed some into a glass, lifted it to the light, shook his head, and doubled the amount. He brought it to Margaret and put it in her hand. "You'll eat some dinner with that?" he asked.

"Indeed I will. Then I will take a warm bath. Then I will go to bed and sleep until two A.M. when I will wake up and fume, and wonder what I did to deserve such a selfish, greedy granddaughter." Margaret took a sip of the whiskey. To Garik, she said, "You're a good man. I wish you could live here. You'd make my life so much easier."

"Haven't you heard? I'm a crazy man."

"I know. Your craziness has saved my life." She offered her cheek. "Now good night, children. Go have dinner and leave me to brood."

"We will." Garik leaned his hands on the mattress. "I am going to tell Elizabeth why they threw me out of the FBI."

Margaret patted his cheek. "You worry too much. She'll understand."

"She will, I know." Garik turned his head and looked at Elizabeth. "But will I ever forgive myself?"

CHAPTER SIXTY-SEVEN

Garik and Elizabeth took dinner on trays in their suite. They put their plates on trays, and put the trays in the corridor. Then, as the sun sank, they went out on the deck overlooking the ocean.

Garik sat in the swing.

Elizabeth sat in the wicker rocking chair.

In late August on the Pacific coast, the sun set at eight. With no electricity to ruin the night with light pollution, the stars shone hard, pale, and bright, fragments of light against a black velvet sky. The ocean crashed ceaselessly against the jagged, rocky cliffs, and the onshore breeze smelled of salt, seaweed, and fish. The earth trembled; Elizabeth could barely recall a time when it hadn't.

Somehow it seemed as if the earth knew the cataclysmic events it had set in motion. Because of the quake, Virtue Falls had been isolated from the world, bringing Elizabeth into the community in ways she had never imagined. Because of the quake, she had been reunited with her father, and learned who he was, what he remembered . . . and she had come to doubt his guilt.

Because of the quake, Garik had come back into her life.

He was thinner, yes, but more than that, when he sat alone, the expression he wore made her realize he was not that same cocky young man who had swept her off her feet and into an ill-advised marriage. Now he was quieter, more thoughtful, less quick to smile and more likely to care. Something had hurt him, something desperate and horrible, and because of it, she felt sure he would never be young again.

That young man had hurt her . . . but she missed him, too.

Garik took a breath, as if the night air refreshed him, then without any prompting, he said, "I lost my temper and beat up a guy who'd been abusing his three-year-old son."

She was startled. Had he thought she wouldn't approve? "Good for you!"

"Attacking a citizen of this country, no matter what kind of bastard he is, is illegal. And it couldn't have been worse—I beat the shit out of Walker in full view of his neighbors. The only reason I didn't kill him was the other agents pulled me off of him, and one of the neighbors filmed the whole thing and took it to the press. So it was bad." Garik pushed the swing with his foot, a violent rocking. "The whole case turned into a media nightmare. Nightly news, public indignation about the violent, savage FBI agent, calls for my arrest. I turned myself in, of course. Went to jail, posted bail, eventually went to trial." He took a breath. "I could live with all that. What I did was bad. Stupid. A wake-up call to me that I needed to take a breath and regain control."

"Yes . . ." What he'd told her wasn't what made his voice quiver and break. There was more, and her heart caught as she waited.

"What happened next . . . was . . . that Waylon Walker got out of the hospital, and to teach me a lesson, he went home and beat his son to death." In the dark, she couldn't see Garik's face, but she heard the weariness in his voice, his longing to turn back the clock, and the finality of his pronouncement.

"Oh, no." Her own voice was barely a whisper.

"I knew punching the crap out of Walker wasn't going

to help that little boy. No one learns from a fist in the face." Another violent push of the swing.

"No." She remembered what he'd said about his father, the abuse, the blame and the horror. Although she didn't want to, she understood his self-loathing.

"My first priority should have been to get the child removed to protective custody. It wasn't. So the boy died."

"No. Oh, no."

"His name . . . his name was Liam. A good-looking boy, with big brown eyes in a thin face. But he didn't smile. I never got him to smile. He'd been hurt so many times before. The x-rays showed bones broken almost from the day he was born. He cried when he walked, and he limped." Garik's voice caught, then steadied. "All that, and it never occurred to me that his father would treat his son like a chip in a poker game, disposable and easily bet."

"No." She'd been saying the same thing for five minutes straight. Just *no. No.*

"How could I *not* have known? How could I have come so far from my childhood that I forgot there were men like that in the world? Other FBI agents—the ones who had normal home lives—they have the right to screw that up, but not me. That kid was me." The rocking stopped. She thought he put his face in his hands.

"I'm sorry." Inadequate. "No wonder you hate the press." Even more inadequate.

"I don't hate them. I don't have any illusions about them, that's all. They told the story, but I gave it to them. I was pissed at the world. I let my temper take over and never thought of the consequences. I am guilty of that child's death." Garik choked; he was crying.

Yes. That was right. A child had died, and he blamed

himself. He should cry for the child. The way she felt, as if she couldn't quite catch her breath . . . she would cry, too. She would cry soon.

But Garik was still talking. "Liam's death is . . . a sin I'll carry on my soul . . . forever, a pain in my heart I feel . . . every moment. There is no absolution for me. All I can do is vow to never be that maniac again. I *will* think before I take action. I *will* help other kids who are in need. I *will* be the kind of man I set out to be when I joined the FBI. I will always do my best to be the good guy."

What could she say? She had been shocked when he confessed to being a childhood victim of his father's beatings. She had thought they'd reached the truth that had stripped the weight from his bones, turned the expression in his eyes sad and disillusioned.

But no—it was his own actions that broke his heart and his spirit.

She got out of her rocking chair, dusted off her work jeans, wished she had bathed and made herself pretty before they had this conversation.

But she hadn't, and he needed her. Going to the swing, she slid into his lap.

The move did not come easily to her. She felt vaguely silly and much like a bad actress making a play for a Hollywood producer. She did it anyway. For Garik. She wrapped her arms around his neck and whispered in his ear. "You are the good guy. You are the best guy."

"I killed that child." Grief weighed every word.

"No, you didn't. His father killed Liam Walker. But you remember Liam. You take responsibility for Liam. You mourn Liam. Is there anyone else in this world who cares about that little boy's death?"

"His mother is dead, too, found in a Dumpster, beaten

to death under unexplained circumstances." Garik sounded broken.

"I know you. I know when you go to church, you say a prayer and light a candle for Liam's soul."

"I would. But I don't dare go to church. I don't dare show my face to God."

That shocked her. Garik had never been the man who went to mass every Sunday. But he went often enough: when he needed comfort, or felt he'd done wrong. He always came back relieved and healed. Now . . . he was afraid of God?

She chose her words carefully. "But why? Liam's death has made you a better man."

"It shouldn't have taken a little boy's death."

"No. And it shouldn't have taken an earthquake to teach me to love my father. But some of us don't learn our lessons the easy way." She fumbled to put the matter in a way Garik would comprehend. "If you believe in God, in these instances, you will see His will at work."

Garik leaned his forehead against her cheek. His tears dripped on her shoulder. "Thank you," he whispered.

She kissed his cheek, and stroked his hair.

He rocked the swing again, slowly, hypnotically, the motion easing and relieving the turmoil of their broken spirits.

Gradually they relaxed into each other.

She put her arms around his shoulders.

He stroked his hand up and down her spine.

The remembrance of his previous concerns stirred in her mind, and she said, "I want you to know I'm not sitting here because I feel sorry for you."

"No?"

"No. I'm sitting here because I like you, you make me happy, and I wish you to be happy."

"I am . . . happy." He sounded surprised. "Or at least . . . no longer unhappy."

"Good. Also, I wish that we could make love again tonight."

"I could manage that." He hugged her tighter. "I would like that."

"Good. Shall we go in?"

"No. No, I don't think that's necessary." His hand came to rest on her buttons.

"Well . . . I suppose . . . it is dark out here."

"So it is. For the last year, every moment of my life has been lived in the darkest dungeon, chained by guilt. But look." He pointed far out to sea where a shard of silver light was reflected on the face of the ocean swells. "To the east, the moon is rising. To the west, we see the first signs of its illumination. The night is less grim, and with you, the loneliness is broken." He kissed her mouth, a long, slow sharing of breath, of lips against lips, of taste and scent and joy. "Let's stay out here. Let's share the light together."

CHAPTER SIXTY-EIGHT

The chop-chop of helicopters woke Garik. Reluctantly he eased himself out of bed, pulled on his boxers, grabbed the binoculars, and walked out onto the deck. The three helicopters flew north along the coast, then turned inland over Virtue Falls.

Elizabeth stepped out into the sunshine, clad in a man's white shirt, buttoned once at the chest. She yawned and rubbed her fingers through her tousled blond hair. "What is it?"

He glanced at her, then back at the helicopters, and wondered if anyone there had zeroed in on the resort, and her. None of the copters went into a nosedive, so he supposed they were actually surveying the damage rather than his mostly naked ex-wife. Or else they were female helicopter pilots . . . "Looks like the Hoff plan to put Virtue Falls in the spotlight worked. We've got the governor and two news copters headed in." He turned to her with a grin. "The circus really did come to town."

She tugged at his arm. "If we hurry, we can slip over and see my father, then check in with Rainbow and find out what the gossip is." She stood up on her tiptoes, looked into his face, and said, "Then I can go to work."

"I'll take you."

"No, you won't."

"I didn't promise I wouldn't take you."

She took a long breath.

"All right. I'll take you into town and pick you up there. How's that?"

She stepped back and looked him over. "Is that what you call a compromise?"

"Since I want to stand over you with a shotgun, yes."

"Aren't you taking this a little seriously?"

"Since Yvonne got attacked . . . yes."

She took another long breath.

He stopped her before she could get rolling. "Look. If nothing else happens, we'll assume that whoever it was has moved on, although God knows where or how. But right now, even if that attack had nothing to do with your father and mother, there's a nutcase somewhere out there with a knife. You, my dear, are a beautiful blonde, and that makes you a target for nutcases." He took a handful of the pale strands of her hair and rubbed them between his fingers. "So I'll drop you off and pick you up in town. That's my offer. Take it or leave it."

She sighed. "You do know I'm not helpless. I carry one great pocket knife, with lots of blades, for my work. And you taught me some self-defense."

"Have you practiced since I taught you?"

"No."

"Maybe we ought to start."

She grimaced. "I hate when you attack me. I get bruises."

"Or I could ferry you back and forth to the canyon and wait for you there."

"I'll practice with you. Okay. Let's go." She unbuttoned the one button, dropped the shirt and headed into the suite.

He admired the view, then rushed forward to pick her up from behind and whisper, "Have I told you about my three-minute, three-hour, and three-day plan? It's an offer I'm making only to you."

She tilted her head and let him nuzzle her neck. "Sounds intriguing. How does this plan work?"

"We can have sex for three minutes, three hours, and three days. Consecutively."

She laughed and wiggled free. "Since we just enjoyed the three hour plan, and the three day plan is up next, and I have to get to work, I'm going to say . . . later, baby." She skipped out of reach and into her bedroom, and locked the door.

Life was easier this morning. Less weighty, as if Garik had heard Elizabeth's assurance, *You are a good guy, the best guy,* and taken it to heart. As if he needed this kind of investigation to gather all the pieces of himself together. As if the court-ordered psychiatrist was right, and his divorce had destroyed him in ways he hadn't imagined, and only now was he getting back to normal . . . As if he could go to church, and face God, light a candle for Liam Walker, and know that it would help the little boy find his way to a better place.

The pain would always be there, and the guilt, but at least now Garik wanted to live.

He had reasons, more than one, to live and love, work and pray, and he would do his best. He was, as Elizabeth said, a better man.

He went into his bedroom to find some clothes.

The next time he saw Elizabeth, she wore a oversized brown khaki shirt tied at the waist, a pair of oversized jeans she kept cinched at the waist with a men's brown leather belt, and an almost pristine pair of hiking boots.

She looked delectable, and happy, and she chatted about the previous day's work all the way to the Honor Mountain Memory Care Facility, where she once again introduced herself to her father, and where she once again chatted about the previous day's work.

But today, Charles seemed sad, tired, and abstracted. He sat with his head tilted, as if listening for someone, and his gaze searched the corners of his room.

When they left, Garik said, "He's missing your mother."

Elizabeth took a breath to explain her mother had never been there. Then she let it out and said, "Yes. Even since yesterday morning, he seems to have lost ground."

"I thought that, too. The next time we see Dr. Frownfelter, we should ask if that's directly related to the seizures, and if Charles is having a lot of them." He slowed as they approached town. "I thought he had one today while we were there."

"When I was showing him the video and he didn't exclaim about the first wave? I thought that, too." She put her hand on his knee. "I'm glad we're going to visit every morning."

"Me, too." He kept his worry to himself. What was the use of railing on about the chances that her mother's killer would view her attention to her father as a threat? The time spent with Charles Banner was almost visibly slipping away from them; there would be no later. These visits had to be now.

Driving into town was even more difficult today than yesterday, so Garik parked on the outskirts and they walked in, holding hands, intent on getting the scoop from Rainbow.

Instead, when they walked into the Oceanview Café, they were blinded by a barrage of flashes.

Elizabeth lifted her hand to protect her eyes.

"What the hell?" Garik asked.

"There's Elizabeth," Bradley announced in an expansive tone, and walked toward her, smiling.

She looked dumbfounded.

Taking her hand, Bradley turned her to face the crowded table in the middle of the café. "Here's Elizabeth Banner, Virtue Falls' newest media star, and a woman I'm proud to call my friend."

Another barrage of flashbulbs.

Garik recognized the governor, his aides, and at least two TV newscasters. Someone was shooting video—wait, it was that girl photographer from yesterday, Loring.

Vivian Hoff stood beside her, wordlessly directing her.

Garik moved closer to listen.

For the video, Loring was saying, "Elizabeth Banner is a child prodigy who put herself through college and grad school by modeling women's shoes. She followed in her father's footsteps to become one of the world's foremost geologists, and she is the woman who shot the now famous tsunami video for the Geological Society of America. The video took the Internet by storm, posting yesterday afternoon and going viral almost at once, with people watching in amazement as she filmed the big waves at considerable risk to herself. Elizabeth Banner's other claim to fame, of course, is that she's the girl who saw her father kill her mother with the scissors. Yet despite her past, or perhaps because of it, famed American artist Bradley Hoff has long been a fan of her blossoming talent and scientific genius."

Considering that yesterday Bradley couldn't quite remember Elizabeth, Garik considered this news nothing less than astonishing.

Bradley herded Elizabeth from one dignitary and newscaster to another, introducing her and claiming friendship.

Rainbow moved in and out, serving coffee and distributing donuts . . . The governor must have brought them.

Garik crossed his arms and leaned against the wall, and waited.

As the moments ticked away, Elizabeth spoke, she smiled, she shook hands, but her chin jutted, her eyes darted, and her complexion turned red and blotchy.

Bradley was so busy garnering attention, the fool didn't recognize the warning signs.

So Elizabeth's sudden outflung arms caught him by surprise, and slapped him in the chest. "I have to go to work," she declared.

Garik straightened away from the wall, walked to the door, and waited.

"Thank you for your kind words." She stared at the governor, at the news reporters. "But the Banner geological study needs as much time as possible in these . . . these fraught days after the earthquake and tsunami. If you would excuse me."

Garik opened the door.

She fled as if avoiding the gallows.

"And there you have it," Bradley said. "That dedication to work is what has made Elizabeth Banner the foremost geological expert in the world."

Polite applause and approving murmurs swept the Oceanview Café.

Vivian Hoff touched Loring's arm. "Stop filming."

"No kidding." Loring put down the camera.

Vivian swept toward the open door, her heels clicking on the shattered linoleum.

Garik waited for her to pass, then stepped out in time to hear Vivian say, "Elizabeth Banner, halt." She spoke softly.

But Elizabeth heard her, and twirled to face her. "What do you want?" She exuded hostility.

"I want to talk to you about Bradley, all the attention you're receiving, and are going to receive." Still that soft voice, the deadly tone.

"I don't want—"

Vivian advanced. "You have to understand that Bradley is the reason Virtue Falls is in the national spotlight."

"I know that, but—"

"It's because of his kindness that your name is now on everyone's lips."

With her usual pedantic fairness, Elizabeth said, "That's not strictly true. I took the video. It is a very good video. And Noah Griffin is the reporter who placed it—"

"I know it's intoxicating to realize you're a celebrity, but"—Vivian stuck her face into Elizabeth's—"don't try to overshadow the talent. Do . . . you . . . understand . . . me?"

Elizabeth stared at her, wide-eyed with shock. "I believe I do. You want me to make sure I don't take anything away from Bradley Hoff and his stardom."

"You can't take anything away from Bradley Hoff. I want you to make sure you don't try, because I would make you sorry."

"Okay."

"Remember." Vivian turned and marched toward the door.

Garik opened it for her.

She strode inside.

Elizabeth turned to him in astonishment "Did she *threaten* me?"

"I think she did." If he hadn't been here to see the event, he didn't know if he would have believed it. "That woman is scary."

Elizabeth nodded. "Very odd."

They stared through the broken windows into the Oceanview Café.

People were starting to look back. People like the network cameramen. People like the governor.

"Want me to take you to work today?" Garik offered.

"Yes." She walked to the truck and got in, and on the ten-minute drive to the canyon, Garik noted that ruddy color rose and fell in her cheeks, ebbing and flowing like the tides, and several times she closed her eyes and her mouth moved, although she said nothing.

They got to the plateau above the canyon. He pulled off the road, close to the path that led through knee-length grass and to a different world, where science reigned supreme and Elizabeth felt at home. In fact, he could almost watch her relax.

She took off her seatbelt. "They won't find me here."

"I wouldn't depend on that. If the governor wants a tour, he'll get one."

She dropped her head into her hands.

Garik continued, enjoying himself just a little. "They'll bring their cameras. Your new best friend Bradley Hoff will pretend to be interested in your work. Andrew Marrero will glare from the background."

Elizabeth groaned.

"It *is* a circus, and you're in one of the rings as a big deal. Elizabeth, you're famous!"

Elizabeth lifted her head. She opened the door. She turned on him and glared. "They all took pictures of me. They all took video of me. I was on camera. I'm going to be on the news. And I didn't. Even. Have. Any. Makeup on!"

Garik grinned and watched her stride toward the canyon.

Sometimes he forgot how very girly she could be.

Glancing in his rearview mirror, he saw the caravan of cars headed this way.

The governor had demanded his tour.

Today, at least, Garik didn't have to worry about Elizabeth's safety. She was going to have a lot of company.

CHAPTER SIXTY-NINE

No one knew where the fog hid. Sometimes it was gone, vanquished by summer, heat, green growing grass, sweat, and the smell of Coppertone. Sometimes it hung at the edge of the horizon, a pale greasy gray line glistening in the sunshine. And when autumn began to sniff around the coast, fog would roll in like a tsunami, rising higher and higher, a silent menace that broke over the land. Fog muffled every noise, changed tree stumps into stalkers and car headlights into monster eyeballs. Fog moved in without warning, without sound, swallowing the sun and surprising the unwary.

When Elizabeth's phone bleated and shook her out of her concentration, she blinked and sat back on her heels. She dug in her bag and looked. The screen was lit. But no text. No call. Only a number she didn't recognize from an area code she didn't know.

Weird.

Did somebody try to call and it failed? Did the cell tower have a power surge? Maybe the attention Bradley Hoff had brought Virtue Falls had made the phone companies move toward fixing the blackout. If everyone had a way to connect with the outside world, the tensions in town would ease.

Her phone went black.

She rubbed her back and looked around.

At some point while she had been crouched over four square feet of soil and debris deposited by the tsunami, fog had moved in, blotting out the sun.

But at least she had cataloged and photographed every twig, every rock, every expired sea creature. It had been a good day's work. And best of all, for the first time in four days, she was alone. No governor, no state senators, no news reporters, no Loring the photographer. They had all flown away . . .

No Andrew Marrero, no Ben, Luke, and Joe. No Garik.

Uh-oh.

She stripped off her gloves. "Luke?" she called. "Hey, Luke, where are you?"

No answer.

"Andrew? Joe? Ben? . . . Anybody?"

No answer.

Not surprising that they had abandoned her; they were not happy with her. She had witnessed the earthquake. She had taken the tsunami video. She was getting publicity. Lots of publicity.

True to her promise to Garik, she had been carefully tagging after her team.

Today, she'd been absorbed in work, and they had seen their chance and escaped her.

"Damn it," she whispered. Garik was going to be pissed. Standing, she dusted off her knees and called, "Hello! Hey, guys, where are you?"

Had they left for the day?

She checked her cell for the time. It was only four thirty, so probably not. For all that Ben, Luke, and Joe were Marrero's sycophants, they were solid workmen. They had slipped away to work other spots. In fairness, they didn't know she was supposed to keep close to them. They didn't imagine, as Garik did, that evil lurked around every boulder, waiting for its chance to take her out.

She sighed. No use wondering if he was right. No use getting psychotic over a little spooky atmosphere. She'd walk back to town as quickly as possible and hopefully Garik would never find out.

Except, damn it, he could always tell when she lied.

Slinging the bag over her shoulder, she started up the canyon slope.

Guilt made her alternately defiant and worried, because she knew she should have been paying attention. She shouldn't have let the fog catch her unaware. Moreover, she knew Garik was right; there was a chance that

the man who had attacked Yvonne wanted into the care
facility to harm her father, and would also like to harm
her. She shouldn't be alone. And yet here she was, at the
top of the canyon, preparing to walk back to town . . .

She did the intelligent thing. She used her phone and
called Garik.

Immediately his voice mail picked up. So his phone
was still dead.

She called Margaret.

Margaret answered in two rings.

"Is Garik there?" Elizabeth asked.

"He left a good three hours ago. Why? Do you need
him?"

"No, I was going to tell him I'm on my way back to
town."

"By *yourself*?" Margaret's voice rose.

"I know. I shouldn't be alone. But I am. I can't find
the guys, and this is my smartest move. Going to town.
Don't you think?"

"Yes. Yes. Go to town. Can you find your way?"

"Don't fret. In the winter, I find my way in the dark."
Elizabeth looked up at the yellow-glazed blob of sun
hanging in the western sky. "Garik's going to yell at me,
though."

"As will I when you get here!" Margaret sounded
irked—and worried.

"No one could find me out here." Elizabeth heard a
sound off to her left, like the scuffle of a small animal in
the brush . . . or a shoe dragged through dirt. Her heart
jumped. "I've got to go. I need to get to the road, then
into town. Just tell Garik where I am, okay?"

"I will. I'll send him for you. Be quiet and careful."
Margaret hung up.

Elizabeth did the same. She stuck her phone into her

pocket and walked toward the road. At least . . . she thought she walked toward the road. Who could tell in this fog?

She moved through the tall summer grass, straining to listen, to hear something more . . .

Stupid of her to imagine that because fog hung on the air, pale and damp, and because she was alone, that someone was hunting her.

Yet she kept hearing things: twigs snapping, grass swishing, the thud of feet against the cool ground.

She forced herself to stop and listen.

She heard nothing but the distant thunder of the ocean. "Foolishness," she whispered to herself.

She took the long way around to the road, hoping to shake her uneasiness, and when her foot touched the pavement, she laughed softly and picked up the pace. She would be in town in twenty minutes. When Garik arrived, she'd hustle him out of the diner and she would never have to tell him she'd lost track of the guys. Confession might be good for the soul, but—

Her phone bleated again.

She pulled it out of her pocket and looked. It was lit again, same number with some area code she didn't recognize. She'd never heard her phone make that sound before. Was this a text? An aborted call? Was the phone company running tests?

Was it a way for the killer to target her?

No. Oh, God, please, no.

She shoved her phone into her pocket. Heard the rush of sound from behind. Turned and jumped off the pavement.

The fog-shrouded figure hit her left side, caught her arm, and almost yanked it out of the socket.

She screamed.

It swung her around, shoved her.

She landed on her face, mouth open, in the dirt.

It punched her on the back of the head.

Her face bounced into the ground.

Grass. Seeds. Soil.

She choked. *Coughed.*

It rolled her onto her back and pressed a knee to her chest and a knife to her neck.

Male? Female? Elizabeth couldn't tell. She only knew her attacker wore a leather jacket, a ski mask, and black gloves.

It spoke in a gravelly voice, yet its tone was kind, gentle, . . . almost soothing . . . yet with an underlying greed and anticipation. "Let's cut off your pretty hair. We don't want to get blood in it."

Terror rose in her throat. She choked again, hacked, gasped.

"What's wrong?" it whispered.

She clawed, coughed, tears streaming from her eyes, unable to dislodge the debris in her throat.

"Stop it!" Its voice was louder, indignant. It grabbed her cheeks between its fingers, and squeezed. The eyes behind the ski mask blazed. "Stop it. You're ruining it!"

She couldn't *breathe.*

She saw a blur from the side. Something kicked her assailant. Once. Twice.

The creature grunted and tumbled away into the darkness.

She rolled onto her knees, and coughed, and coughed, eyes streaming, unable to do anything except try desperately to recover her breath.

Nearby, but out of sight, she heard the impact of flesh

and bone. Again. And again. Finally, a yelp of pain, and the thud of footsteps.

She spit up the last of the debris. She knelt, head down, gasping.

She listened.

Close at hand, she heard a man's panting breath.

She came to her feet, ready to run.

Garik staggered out of the fog. "Call the cops," he said.

"Oh, my God!" She leaped at him, hugged him, buried her head in his chest. "It was you. I should have known it was you." Her voice scratched at her throat. "How did you know? How did you know he was there?"

"I didn't. I wait for you every night, watch for you to come out of the canyon. Tonight I couldn't see you. Not until your phone went off. Then . . . then he got to you first." Gently, Garik pushed her away. "Elizabeth, call the cops."

"Yes. Of course. Yes." She stepped back, fumbled for her phone, dialed 911.

And watched as Garik collapsed at her feet.

She dropped the phone, knelt beside him. "Garik?"

"Stabbed me in the right side. But I got him, too. I got him." His voice slid into a whisper. "I got him."

CHAPTER SEVENTY

Garik was bleeding. He was bleeding.

There was blood.

Blood spreading across his chest . . .

She stifled a sob. "Garik."

His eyes opened, and closed. "Did you call nine-one-one?"

"Yes! Wait." She crawled around until she found her phone.

Someone was talking, asking for her problem, her location.

"My husband . . . he's hurt, he's bleeding, he needs to go to the hospital. Now."

"Can you tell me why he's bleeding?" the dispatcher asked.

"He was attacked. He was stabbed!"

"What's your location?"

"On the road outside of Virtue Falls by the path that leads to the canyon."

"Who is this?"

"Elizabeth Banner. Send someone now!" Elizabeth hung up, spoke to Garik. "Where's the truck?"

"Down the road." He pointed.

She ran.

The keys were in the ignition. She started the engine, put it in gear, and drove three hundred feet down the road to Garik's prostrate body. She parked, got out, dug around behind the seat. She found a thin travel blanket, folded neatly in the pocket behind the seat. She pulled it out, ran to Garik.

He was bleeding. *Bleeding.*

There was blood.

She slid the blanket underneath him, wrapped it around his chest, tied the ends.

He smiled. "Good job. That'll help."

In the distance, she heard the wail of a siren. "That was fast," she said.

"It's Foster." Garik struggled to stand. "Early to the crime scene, as usual."

"You don't think he's the one that—"

"Don't know. Get me in the truck. In the truck!" Garik's eyes were wild, determined.

She put her arm around him and helped him get to his feet.

He was standing when the police car drove up.

Garik was wounded. He was weak. But he didn't want to show Foster. He didn't dare show Foster. If Foster was the one who had attacked her . . .

"He's got a gun." She tried to help Garik into the tall truck.

"I know. So let's put on a show of strength." But when he reached up to lift himself up, he groaned and fell back.

Sheriff Foster got out of the car. "Put him in here!" he shouted, and pointed to his patrol car. "In the back!"

"I'll drive him," she shouted back. "Help me!"

Sheriff Foster strolled to the truck. He stood with his hand on his weapon. He sneered. He was going to kill them, shove them off into the canyon, and leave them to rot.

She stepped in front of Garik.

She wasn't brave; her heart beat so hard and fast she could hear it in her brain. Her chin trembled, and her knees shook.

But she didn't have a choice. Garik was *bleeding*.

Her gaze met Foster's. She stared at him. *Glared* at him.

Then, by God, Sheriff Foster dropped his gaze. He opened the truck's passenger door and helped hoist Garik inside. He shut the door behind Garik, then he turned to her. "I assume you didn't do this."

"*What?*" She turned on him with fury and vigor.

"Who attacked him?"

"I was attacked. Garik saved me. My assailant ran

away." She ran around to the driver's door and got in. "Did you think *I* stabbed him?"

"Yes. It's usually the spouse, and you . . ." He left the words unspoken, but she heard them anyway.

You're the girl who saw your father kill your mother with the scissors, so you're probably like him.

"Asshole," she muttered.

"Take him to the hospital. I'll be behind you all the way." Sheriff Foster flipped on his emergency lights.

"Bastard loves those lights," Garik muttered.

She didn't care. She put the truck in gear and drove.

Garik reached, and reached, and finally snagged his seatbelt and pulled it over his chest. It took long moments before he got it clicked into place. "Are you hurt?" he asked.

"No. Yes. My arm." It ached. "He about yanked it off. And my throat hurts from coughing. But he didn't cut me. What did he do to you?"

"Tried to knife me in the heart. Didn't make it."

She glanced over to see him exploring the left side of his ribs.

"He sliced me pretty good, though. Not one long slice, sort of here and there and jagged. I don't think his knife was sharp. Hurts worse that way, makes the wounds less serious." He half-smiled. "I'm okay. Blood loss will be a problem. Shock. All that shit. I'll be sore. But I'm fine."

She wanted to believe him, and the terrible tightness around her chest loosened a little.

"Who was it?" he asked.

"I don't know. The guy . . . the, the *person* who attacked Yvonne. Ski mask, leather jacket." She swallowed. "You didn't see him . . . it, either?"

"No, but I kicked the shit out of him. I couldn't see well enough to kick his head, so I kicked his ribs." Garik leaned his head against the back of the seat, and muttered, "It had to be a man."

"Did it?"

"I dunno."

"Maybe he'll have to go to the hospital."

"Maybe . . . maybe he's one of those hermits who live in the woods, and we'll never figure out who he is." Garik sounded tired.

"That's true. But he attacked me, and he attacked Yvonne to get into the care facility. So I think we can say you were right. This guy has something to do with my mother's murder."

"So many possibilities . . ." Garik's voice faded. He slumped in the seat.

Blood stained the blanket over his chest.

Blood will be the problem . . .

She drove inland like a bat out of hell, through fog, over crumpled roads, desperate to arrive before the sun drifted to the west and below the horizon. She drove toward darkness and cold stars, and found herself praying to a god in which she didn't believe.

Sheriff Foster followed her all the way, lights flashing. He had called ahead; the hospital was expecting them.

The medical staff put Garik on a gurney, got him into ER, sewed him up, and gave him a unit of blood.

She sat on a hard chair, unable to look away from the stitching and the IVs. But she didn't faint. She didn't even feel like fainting. Her fury kept her upright.

Someone had attacked her. Garik had come to her rescue. And then the assailant attacked Garik. Stabbed Garik. Tried to murder Garik.

Never in her life had she known that she could kill someone, but if she found the man, or the woman, who had assaulted them, Elizabeth would gladly take them out. Sitting there, she planned first one attack, then another, using a variety of weapons and a variety of moves.

Apparently the only way to get over being squeamish was to be vengeful and bloodthirsty.

When they took Garik away to put him into a private room, Sheriff Foster questioned her. Did she recognize her assailant? How big was he? What did he smell like?

She recognized the questions; they were essentially the same as the ones Garik had asked Yvonne, and Elizabeth knew just as little. "I didn't see him. I was coughing," she said impatiently and for the third time.

"You were coughing." Sheriff Foster said it as if he could not believe her.

"It's August. When he slammed my head into the grass, I swallowed seeds, they got stuck in my throat, and I thought I was going to choke to death."

"And he seemed unhappy with you because you were coughing." Sheriff Foster clicked his pen.

"He said, 'You're spoiling it.' No, wait." She remembered that voice. " 'You're ruining it.' Like putting a knife to my throat was something he'd imagined, and I wasn't reacting like I was supposed to." She looked down at her hands. Her fingers were trembling.

"Huh. Well. Interesting." Sheriff Foster clicked the pen again. "If you think of anything else, give me a call. If your phone works. Which it does since you said it squawked and that was what gave him his target. Let me see the number."

She showed him. "I don't know it."

He wrote it down. "It's probably a burn phone. Anyone can buy one with a preset number of minutes. Very useful if you forgot your phone, or if you're a criminal." He clicked the pen again, twice more.

She watched him. Nervous habit. Sheriff Foster was almost twitching with guilt.

He clicked the pen one more time, then stuck it in his pocket. "I'll come back tomorrow to interview Garik. You look like hell. Get some sleep."

Since the bags beneath his bloodshot eyes were big enough to take a two-week vacation, she thought that was the pot calling the kettle black.

The medical staff wanted to x-ray her shoulder, but she wanted to be with Garik. She *needed* to be with Garik. So she took the aspirin they offered, and hung over him until he began to breathe easily. Then she went into the bathroom and looked in the mirror, realized that not only was Sheriff Foster right, but she also had grass stains on her forehead.

No wonder he had believed her about the coughing.

She washed her face, and when she came out, a cot had appeared in the room. Two minutes, she was asleep, and she stayed that way until two A.M., when Dr. Frownfelter walked in the room.

CHAPTER SEVENTY-ONE

Garik came wide awake when Dr. Frownfelter shambled in, a big bear of a man in a white coat and two days' growth of salt-and-pepper beard.

The doctor walked over to the cot where Elizabeth slept, stood over her, and stared with the most peculiar expression on his face, almost as if he was trying to open the portal to the past, and move her into place.

Garik disliked seeing him hover there, so he called softly, "Doctor."

For a man as tall and big-bellied as he was, Frownfelter walked swiftly and silently to Garik's side. Picking up his wrist, he took his pulse. "How do you feel?"

"Good. For a guy who's been stabbed, real good." With slight motions, Garik tested his shoulders, his ribs.

"Give it a couple of days. The pain is waiting to pounce." Frownfelter listened to Garik's heart. "Mind if I peel back the dressing and look at the wound?"

"If you promise not to pull off any hair." Garik had had quite enough of that for one day.

"I hear women these days like hairless guys. Look at it as a free wax job." But Frownfelter eased off the bandages with an expert touch.

"I don't like the price I had to pay for it." Garik craned his neck to take a look. "What do you think?"

"Dr. Salas did this? She does good work. But the wounds . . ." He shook his head. "They look like the guy was trying to do SOS in Morse code. Dot dash dot . . . The dash looks bad. Ragged."

"Lousy knife work. For someone who's going around attacking people, this guy isn't very good at it."

"This wasn't done with a knife or a sharp point. This was probably scissors."

Dr. Frownfelter's declaration sent a chill up Garik's spine. "That's a positive ID."

"You see all kinds of things in med school." Frownfelter taped the bandages back over Garik's ribs. "And maybe, since you found Misty's body, scissors are on my mind."

Maybe it was euphoria from the painkillers. But Garik felt well enough to handle a straight-on confrontation with Frownfelter. He pressed the button to move the bed into the sitting position. "You know, Doctor, I had you pegged for a suspect in the Misty Banner murder case."

Dr. Frownfelter pushed his glasses up on the top of his head and wearily rubbed his eyes. "I know."

That gave Garik a jolt. "Why do you know? Why do you know I'm even revisiting the case?"

"How could you not? For anyone with a lick of sense, Charles Banner never could have been the murderer." Frownfelter pulled his glasses back down, placed them on his nose, and looked over the top of them. "You have more than one lick of sense."

"I do. You're right."

"What made you decide I wasn't a suspect?"

"When that guy attacked Yvonne in the parking lot and wanted her keys to the facility I thought—*No, Frownfelter could get in anytime he wants.*"

"You think that attack and the one today are connected to the Banner case?"

"I suspected it before. This assault on Elizabeth sort of cinched it." Garik looked him right in the eyes. "But nothing about you adds up, which is why I'm wondering—during the trial, why didn't you stick up for Charles Banner? I've looked at the evidence. You didn't say one word to support him. You must have been his friend. You followed him from Virtue Falls to prison and back again, but you never presented yourself as a character witness."

"At the time, I wasn't sure he hadn't done it."

"You just said that anyone with a lick of sense knew Charles Banner could never have been the murderer."

The visitor chair was shoved against the wall; Dr. Frownfelter pulled it up to the bed. He sat heavily, as if the weight of the world was on his stooped shoulders. "I was . . . relating."

Garik wondered if the pain killers were messing with his head. "Relating to what?"

"I was Misty Banner's doctor. I prescribed her prenatal vitamins. Delivered her baby. Did her postpartum examinations."

Garik's suspicions rose again. "You were in love with her."

"No. God, no. I was in love with my wife." Dr. Frownfelter observed Garik shrewdly. "You don't seem surprised to hear I had a wife."

"Margaret told me."

"Of course she did. The thing about being a small-town family physician is that you get to deal with everything. Spousal abuse, alcoholism, bipolar disease, flu epidemics, erectile dysfunction, deafness, old age, dying. It's an interesting life, because there's such variety. It takes all your time, and all your energy, and sometimes you win, and sometimes . . . you lose." Dr. Frownfelter rubbed his neck as if even the memories weighed him down. "In her hour of need, Misty came to me and told me that she was having an affair."

Garik's spine snapped to attention. "So it's not a rumor. She really was having an affair."

"Most definitely. I asked her why, when she had a husband like Charles who worshiped her, she would betray him. She said . . . she said that her lover was exciting, fascinating, different. That her lover made her forget the pain she felt when she thought of her mother, of her sister, about her terrible, dysfunctional family." Dr. Frownfelter tilted his head against the back of the chair. "But she said her lover was intense, almost frightening, and she asked what to do. She asked me because I was her doctor, and kind, and smarter than her."

Garik could see disaster coming a mile away. "What did you say?"

"She . . . her timing was bad." Dr. Frownfelter rummaged around in his capacious pockets and pulled out a bottle of Tums. He popped a couple and put the bottle back. "The day before, my wife had told me she wanted a divorce. She wanted to live somewhere besides Virtue Falls. Anywhere besides Virtue Falls. So she'd gone to the city, found a doctor at Seattle Children's Hospital, and they made each other very happy."

"I thought she divorced you for infidelity?"

"I let her put that on the papers. This way at least I didn't have to admit my wife was screwing around behind my back." Dr. Frownfelter's heavy lids drooped over his eyes. "Say what you like, but a man's got his pride."

"All right. I get that. What did you say to Misty?" Garik asked again.

Dr. Frownfelter looked straight at him. "I told her she should be ashamed, playing around behind Charles's back, making that good man look like a fool. I told her everyone in town knew what was going on—I had *just* heard rumors—and asked if she'd even *thought* about the consequences to her impressionable child. I told her to break it off, and when she tried to tell me she was frightened, I told her she deserved to be afraid. I was furious. I lashed out at her, then ordered her out of my office." He lifted a shaking hand to his forehead. "The next thing I knew, she was dead. Murdered. Blood all over that house. Everyone said Charles had done it. I was so angry at my wife, I could have killed her, so I thought that was possible. Probable, even. But I wasn't quite sure . . . Misty had said she was afraid of her lover. She acted frightened. And I made her break it off. I did that."

"You felt guilty."

"I didn't *feel* guilty. I *am* guilty."

Garik understood that. He understood that far too well.

Dr. Frownfelter continued, "I'm a doctor. Do no harm, and all that Hippocratic oath stuff. So I stalked Charles Banner, followed him to prison. I wanted to believe he'd done it, that he really had killed his wife. It would have relieved some of my heartburn." Dr. Frownfelter lifted the bottle of Tums out of his pocket again, and showed Garik, then dropped it back in.

"And?"

"Charles isn't like me. He doesn't carry a grudge. He doesn't hate the past. He can forgive his wife. Me? Not a chance. I don't want to kill my ex-wife anymore, but when her hotshot Seattle doctor divorced her, I did a happy dance. Which with my figure, was something to see." Dr. Frownfelter patted his belly. "Once I was convinced Charles hadn't done it, I did do everything I could to get him released from prison. But it was too late. The damage had been done."

"If you're not the one who killed Misty Banner, and Charles isn't the one who killed her, who does it leave?"

"A whole helluva lot of men." Dr. Frownfelter glanced at Elizabeth, still asleep on the cot. "Every straight guy in town wanted Misty Banner."

"That's exactly what Margaret said."

"Margaret's shrewd, and she's right. If you're investigating the crime, you're going to have to look at every guy who lived here then." Dr. Frownfelter stood. "And a few of the women."

"Who's your top candidate?" Garik was very interested in the answer.

But Dr. Frownfelter shook his head. "Look, kid. I got

someone killed for saying the wrong thing. I learn from my lessons. I'm keeping my mouth shut."

Garik put pressure on. "People are getting hurt. Me. Elizabeth. Yvonne Rudda."

"You're an FBI agent. Be more careful with yourself, and with Elizabeth."

"What about Yvonne?"

"All kinds of people are always in and out of hospitals. There's not much security to speak of, not in a regional hospital like this, not during this kind of crisis. So when Yvonne was here, I watched over her, made sure she was safe."

Garik sat up straight and fast, then winced at the tug of pain. "What do mean, *when she was here*?"

"She went home this morning."

"Home? By herself?"

Dr. Frownfelter gently pushed Garik back on the pillows. "Sheila's staying with her."

"Two women staying in an isolated house when there's a killer loose?" Were they out of their minds?

Dr. Frownfelter lifted his hands, and let them fall. "The hospital's full. We're still getting injuries from the earthquake. We've got three beds per room. Yvonne couldn't stay. And she would not go to the shelter."

"She could stay with Sheila." Obvious solution.

"Sheila's got problems at home—unemployed husband, troubled kids from her first marriage. Yvonne and Sheila are smart women. They deal with difficult patients every day, and sometimes violence. We're going to have to trust they'll play it safe."

"Yeah. Sure." Garik wasn't so sanguine about the situation, but then, Dr. Frownfelter didn't know everything he knew. "I did kick the son-of-a-bitch, and got in a few good punches. Has anybody come in with broken ribs, contusions?"

Dr. Frownfelter scratched his head. "We had Big Blake Daniels come in looking pretty bad, but I don't think that's who you want."

"Why not?"

"His wife beat him up—again." Dr. Frownfelter patted Garik's shoulder. "Look, I have to go. I'm supposed to be catching some Zs, not chatting with you. You've got a lot to think about, but try to get some rest. You're going to feel those incisions in the morning." He shambled out.

Elizabeth slowly rolled over. She looked at Garik. "Whoa," she whispered.

"You were awake the whole time?" Garik wasn't surprised.

"Having someone stand over the top of me is not conducive to sleep. Not after . . . what happened this afternoon." Elizabeth clumsily pushed her blanket aside. "My mother definitely had an affair."

"So it would appear."

"And we have another person who doesn't believe my father did it." Abruptly she said, "It's not Sheriff Foster."

"Why not? He showed up right away."

"Yes, and he helped you into the truck, interviewed me about the attack, and he was not injured." She had a point.

But Garik hated to give up on Foster. "He's probably got narcotics in his car. He could have dosed himself to cover his injuries, then come for us. Was he weird during the interview?"

"How could I tell?" Elizabeth asked in exasperation. "It's Sheriff Foster!"

"Yeah." Garik observed her as she tried to get to her feet. "What's wrong? Why are you cradling your arm like that?"

"My shoulder hurts."

"He—the assailant—swung you around by the arm and now your shoulder hurts?" Garik pushed the call button. "If I'd been with it a little earlier, I would have known you were in trouble."

"I'm not in trouble."

"You've got torn ligaments. Bet you."

Elizabeth looked alarmed. "I had two aspirin."

"Aspirin is great stuff. But if you think it's going to fix your shoulder, you're crazy."

One of the nurses walked in.

Garik recognized her, an old girlfriend. "Hi, Gloria, good to see you. This is my ex-wife, Elizabeth Banner, and she needs to go to get an x-ray."

The next morning, three things happened.

Sheriff Foster came back to interview Garik. In less than thirty minutes, Foster managed to sneer about Garik's suspension from the FBI, and Garik managed to insult Foster about last night's investigation. They both asked questions, and they both, reluctantly, answered them.

Garik worked his charms on his ex-girlfriend Gloria so successfully he wrangled an early release out of the hospital for himself and Elizabeth before any nosy visitors showed up from town.

And Noah Griffin's story hit the Internet.

CHAPTER SEVENTY-TWO

As soon as Garik and Elizabeth walked into the resort, they greeted Margaret and the anxious staff, assured everyone that except for Garik's stitches and Elizabeth's torn ligaments, they were fine, and Elizabeth went upstairs to take a nap.

Garik insisted he was fine, stretched out on the couch in the great room, and fell asleep. He woke up to the smell of chicken soup wafting from the kitchen, and made it to the table in time to enjoy a bowl served with crusty bread. Then he told Margaret he had work to do, and he headed up to their suite.

Elizabeth had taken a painkiller and was still asleep.

That suited him just fine.

He took Elizabeth's phone and set up his Wi-Fi.

He logged on, and immediately a message popped up from Tom Perez that read, *Your ex got attacked last night?*

"Son of a goddamn bitch!" His two typing fingers flew. *How do you know that?*

The next message contained a link to *USA Today*.

Garik clicked it and skimmed the article by Noah Griffin, announcing media darling Elizabeth Banner had been attacked as she worked, the second attack in a week for the earthquake-devastated town of Virtue Falls. The first attack had been on beloved nurse Yvonne Rudda, who described her attacker as, "Crazy . . . His eyes burned. I would recognize his eyes anywhere."

"Oh, my God." Garik looked at the time. Too late to go out to Yvonne's tonight.

From Tom: Looks like you might be on to something with your suspicions about the Banner case.

Looks like. Did you get the package I sent?

With the scissors? Not yet.

I am going to make that helicopter pilot sorry. Because if that worthless little shit had tossed an irreplaceable piece of evidence, Garik would kill him.

The scissors? You sent them with a helicopter pilot?

Put the package *with correct postage* into his hands and told him to mail it.

Got his name and address? I can send an agent to get it from him, and scare the shit out of him at the same time.

I'd like that. As Garik pulled out the pilot's business card and typed it in, he could almost see Tom rubbing his hands in anticipation. He sent the info.

From Tom: I'll get the package. How come you didn't kill the guy who attacked your ex?

I'm not allowed to carry a firearm, remember?

I remember. I also remember you're supposed to be good at self-defense. So you always told me.

So's he. Garik kept quiet about their suspicions that the assailant might be a she.

So you got your butt whupped, huh?

And my ribs sliced.

He had a knife?

Doc says scissors.

A long pause. *What have you got yourself into?*

Makes you wonder. I kicked his ribs, got in a few body punches. It's a small town. Not easy to get away from. I'll be watching for the guy who's hurt.

You do that. I'll let you know when I receive the scissors.

CHAPTER SEVENTY-THREE

The next morning, at the Honor Mountain Memory Care Facility, Charles took one look at Elizabeth with her arm strapped to her side, and his eyes filled with tears. He was convinced she had been attacked by the other prisoners, and his distress was so pervasive not even the tsunami video would deflect it.

So Garik and Elizabeth cut their visit short in hopes that Charles would quickly forget them, and his unhappiness.

In the truck, Elizabeth sighed and leaned her head back against the seat. "He's slipping away faster every day."

"Yes." An added pressure on Garik to solve this case. "I'm going to take you back to the resort."

"Where are *you* going?"

"To check on Yvonne. Since that pipsqueak Noah Griffin got his piece on the news"—making matters so much worse—"I figure we don't have a lot of time to figure this out before something else happens."

"Want me to go with you?" she offered.

"You don't look so hot."

"Neither do you."

True to Dr. Frownfelter's prophesy, Garik's cuts hurt like a son-of-a-bitch, so he didn't argue. "Go back and catch a nap." Because the attack had left her fragile and frightened.

"But what if there's trouble out there?" Elizabeth asked.

"I don't expect trouble, but just in case"—he lifted the

top of the console—"I borrowed one of Margaret's pistols. Don't tell anybody. I'm prohibited from carrying it."

Comforted, Elizabeth smiled. "I won't call Sheriff Foster, then."

Garik twice got lost looking for Yvonne's house, and finally found it at the end of a long gravel driveway off a tiny side road.

That was good, because the killer would have the same problems. And bad because Garik would be a lot happier if she had some neighbors to check on her.

Semi truck parts littered the side yard; a trailer, wheels with blown retreads, some connections he didn't recognize.

A dog rose, growling, from its place on the front porch. A big dog, some kind of Chow/German shepherd/Rottweiler mix, with a healthy mouthful of teeth and brown eyes that narrowed to menacing slits.

Cautiously, Garik eased out of the driver's seat, and left his door open in case he had to make a run for it.

The well-kept single-level house had been built in the fifties and had a low-pitched roof, but the earthquake had done sobering damage: broken windows, a large tree down in the front yard with branches that had removed strips of aluminum siding.

As he stepped around the front of the truck, Yvonne rose from weeding the nasturtiums and waved.

The dog's growling lowered to a rumble.

Garik refrained from wiping his brow in relief; it was too early for that. "Yvonne! I didn't see you there."

"I didn't recognize the car, so I figured I'd stay still until I knew who it was." She stuck her trowel into the dirt and stripped off her gardening gloves. "Come on in.

I've got coffee in the pot." As she headed around the side of the house, the dog joined her.

"Guard dog?" Garik asked.

"Yes. This is Glock." She stopped. "Offer your hand. Let him check you out."

Garik did as instructed, and considered himself lucky when that huge muzzle thoroughly sniffed his fingers, and left them all intact.

"Okay. He knows you're a friend now. He won't, um . . ."

"Rip my leg off?"

"Right." As she rounded the corner into the backyard and flung open the sliding glass door, the dog kept close at her side. "Make yourself at home," she said. "Sorry about the mess. I cleaned up some before I got hurt, and Sheila cleaned up some when she brought me home, but what we really need is repair and construction." She poured him coffee from the well-used Mr. Coffee coffee-maker. "Sugar? Cream?"

He pulled out a stool from the breakfast bar and took a seat. "No, thanks. I like it hot and strong."

The dog snorted and lowered himself onto the mat by the door, where he could keep his cold brown eyes fixed on his mistress and the stranger who had intruded on them.

Yvonne put a red Peterbilt mug in front of Garik, poured one for herself, and leaned against the counter.

He inspected her. "You look good."

"Now that I've got that giant bandage off my head, you mean?" She touched tape and gauze that still covered the wound. "I'm glad to have the use of two eyes again. How are you?"

"Good." Garik took a sip of coffee, and barely stopped

himself from grimacing. No wonder the dog snorted. Glock knew what he was talking about. She must have had this brewing for days; this stuff could sterilize living tissue. "I've got some stitches, a few bruises . . . but you should see the other guy."

She didn't laugh, and her body language sucked rocks. She was folded in on herself, shoulders hunched, one arm crossed over her belly, the other holding her mug. "Did you catch him?"

"No. He can fight, and he had a knife. Well, I thought he had a knife. Dr. Frownfelter disagreed with me. He said it was scissors."

She touched her bandage again. "That would explain the damage to my face. I'll always be scarred from that attack." She sipped the coffee. "Almost thirty years working with dementia, and I get hurt by some drug addict looking for a fix."

"If that's the truth, why did he attack Elizabeth?" Garik sipped again, cautiously. Still strong. And caffeinated. He'd never sleep again.

"I . . . I don't know."

"I'm thinking it's somebody local, somebody we know."

"Who? And why?"

He didn't want to bring up the Banner case. She would probably point out, and rightly, that that had happened twenty-three years ago, and the town had been peaceful since. If he said Charles's return and Elizabeth's residence here had triggered the incidents, she would say that Charles had been here for over a year and Elizabeth was closing in on her first anniversary, and nothing had happened before. If he said it took the two of them getting together to cause the problem, she would say that was far-fetched, and it was. Except that it was happening. With scissors.

"I wish I knew who it was, and why it was happening. It would make my life a lot easier." Garik looked around. "Where's Sheila? I heard she was out here with you."

"Her husband's fighting with her kids and she had to go home. When I start feeling sorry for myself, I think about the mess she has and decide I've got it pretty good. Living alone for long stretches of time has its advantages." She toasted him with her mug.

"I don't like you being alone."

"No. Right now, I don't like being alone, either." She poured the dregs of her coffee into the sink and rinsed the cup.

Garik took that as a sign that he could stop drinking the drain cleaner she called coffee. He pushed his mug away, and glanced at Glock.

How did a dog manage to appear cynically amused?

"I'm not moving to a shelter," she said.

"How about moving to the resort?"

Glock lifted his head and looked at Yvonne.

"Wow. That would be cool. I've never stayed there—can't afford it." Yvonne took Garik's cup. "Want it heated up?"

"No, thanks." He didn't dare glance at Glock. "I'm cutting back."

Yvonne washed the mug and slowly dried it. With a sigh, she said, "No. I just can't. Bradley Hoff got us on the news, and the big fuss has got the state and the feds moving their lazy butts to fix the highway. I know my husband. John's going to be the first in line to drive it, and I want to be home when he gets here."

"Have you been able to talk to him?"

"On and off. The home line is nothing but static, but he's reached me by cell three times." She touched her bandage again. "This attack—he's frantic. I need to be here."

"You shouldn't be alone. Not if I'm right about the guy who attacked you." Garik tacked on, "John would agree with me."

Her eyes were dark, but she smiled a little bit and opened the drawer beside her. She pulled out a pistol, a Glock. It shone; it was well-cared-for. "John's a collector, and I know how to shoot. I know how to shoot really well. This is loaded. I've got pistols stashed all over the house, and they're all loaded. I've got a rifle in the bedroom, and one in the garage." She opened up her gardening vest and showed him her firearm.

He recognized it right away: a Walther PPK. "Wow. Just like James Bond." And he'd been so proud of carrying Margaret's firearm. It hardly compared.

"That's right. I've got this little darling with me at all times. It's tiny, but it's powerful. Before I was attacked, I might have hesitated to shoot a man. But not now."

"I guess showing up like I did, I'm lucky you didn't finish the job the assailant started." Between the dog and the firepower, Garik figured he had narrowly escaped death.

"You're safe. Other than John and Sheila, you're the only person I really trust right now." She shut her vest. She put the Glock back in the drawer and shut it. "I figure you couldn't have attacked yourself."

"Elizabeth's one of the good guys, too." He made a last appeal. "The resort's nice. Until we run out of propane, we've got a generator, so we've got water and electricity."

She laughed out loud. "I've got a generator. I've got electricity and water. I've got a full pantry, and my vegetable garden is the envy of Virtue Falls. We're out here in the country, so we've got to have those things."

"We've got a chef," he offered. "You wouldn't have to cook."

"It sounds good, it really does, and I thank you. But you don't have John, so I'm staying put."

"As soon as we hear he's on his way, I'll bring you back here." But Garik could see he wasn't going to win. Yvonne was an adult; he couldn't force her, and she had been hurt, both mentally and physically. She needed the security of her own home.

Plus, he believed her when she said she would shoot an intruder, and he believed the dog would mop up whatever remained. "Okay," Garik said, "promise you'll call me if you need anything."

"If I can get through."

"Damn cell phones. I keep forgetting."

"We all keep forgetting."

"Then promise me you'll be suspicious of everybody, I don't care who it is. Don't open your door to anybody. Be prepared to shoot or run away, or both, and let Glock tear the nuts off any guy who tries to come up the front walk."

She nodded. "I know. You don't know how scared I was." Her voice trembled. "I'm going to be careful, I promise."

"That'll have to do, then." Garik rose and started to go into the kitchen to hug her.

Glock rose to his feet, growling deep in his chest.

Garik froze in his tracks, and slowly backed away. "It was good to see you, Yvonne. Take care. Take a lot of care."

Late that afternoon, while Yvonne scrubbed new potatoes and snapped green beans, Glock rose to his feet, teeth bared, growling. "Who is it this time?" she asked him. Not Garik—Glock wouldn't react with such hostility to someone he had already met.

No, this was a stranger, so Yvonne rinsed her hands and dried them, and tucked her Walther pistol into her waistband at the back of her jeans. Quietly, she walked through the living room, and stood behind the curtains and looked out.

"My God!" She couldn't believe it. She shushed Glock's growling, hurried to the front door, and opened it. "I never expected to see you out this far," she said. "Come in!"

CHAPTER SEVENTY-FOUR

Inside herself, Kateri floated through black water, empty of everything but monsters and glowing eyes. The dark pressed on her crumpled body, sat on her chest, made each breath an agony.

Inevitably, she ascended. The water was blue now, midnight blue, clear of life, of noise, of sensation. She wanted to stay.

But once again she ascended, past dark green seaweed waving its sticky tendrils, past mermaids and frogs and beasts she had only imagined.

Up. Up.

Pain was building.

But inevitably, as she rose, she was waking.

The water was pale, almost clear.

She could hear noise—monitors beeping, people talking.

She could something burning in her gut, something slashing at her hips. Her skin had been scrubbed off. She felt her muscles, nerves, bones were exposed. She knew she would never again recognize herself.

She couldn't face it. She could not face it. She tried to sink.

Instead she bobbed to the surface.

She opened her eyes.

She saw morning sunlight streaming in the hospital window.

She saw machines, faces covered by masks, eyes staring.

She took her first spontaneous breath—and screamed. And writhed. And fought.

At nine seventeen A.M., at the edge of the continental shelf, the stresses from the earthquake and the aftershocks had increased beyond the earth's bearing. A fault, different from the first, ruptured. One side rose and slid north toward Alaska, the other sank and slid south toward California.

The earthquake measured six-point-seven on the Richter scale.

The shaking hit the Washington coast hard and fast, lasted eighty-five seconds, knocked everyone in Virtue Falls off their feet, and broke everything that wasn't already broken.

At the resort, the earthquake trapped Margaret on her bed under her canopy. The earthquake knocked Harold down the stairs. Margaret had to fight her way out from under velvet bed curtains. Harold's prosthetic leg was broken.

At the Honor Mountain Memory Care Facility, the earthquake panicked the patients. Charles Banner froze in a prolonged seizure, which the overwhelmed medical staff failed to realize until afterward.

A tsunami rose in a swell on the ocean, but the primary energy headed west, across the ocean toward Hawaii and Japan. Only a few minor tsunamis washed into the Washington coast.

Although the country waited anxiously for new video, Elizabeth Banner failed to film these waves, and the people had to be satisfied with her written eyewitness account.

And all the progress that had been made in restoring utilities, roads, and services was destroyed. Cell service vanished, and Virtue Falls was cut off once more.

CHAPTER SEVENTY-FIVE

Mona Coleman from the sheriff's office stopped by the back table in the Oceanview Café, and she said, "You're the earthquake expert, Elizabeth. So tell me—how come this earthquake ranked so much lower on the Richter scale than the last one, but I got hurt?" Her nasty smirk was ruined by her split lip.

In the last three days, Garik had heard the explanation for like a hundred times.

But Elizabeth patiently explained, "There are different kinds of fault lines, creating different kinds of earthquakes. In the first earthquake, the motion was essentially up and down, like when you shake out a sheet. The second earthquake was a sideways motion, like a bellydancer shimmying."

"That's just repulsive," Mona snapped, and headed toward the counter where she slapped her hand on the Formica. "I'd like a cappuccino here!"

"I don't know whether she means earthquakes are repulsive, or bellydancers," Garik said.

"It doesn't make sense to say earthquakes are repulsive," Elizabeth said. "They're a force of nature."

"It doesn't make sense to call bellydancers repulsive, either." He watched Mona harangue Dax, the cook, about the lousy service. "Mona's holding her side like it hurts. She qualifies as your attacker."

"She's certainly mean enough. If only she had the body mass we'd have this crime solved."

Garik laughed.

Elizabeth looked serious.

He sighed.

After three days of sitting in the Oceanview Café, he knew the restaurant's cycles. Right now, after lunch, folks dropped in for drinks and sometimes a cheese sandwich to go. Later there would be a minor rush for dinner—more cheese sandwiches—then in the evening, more folks came in with a flask in their pocket, and shared a drink or two. As long as they were discreet, nobody cared. Who was going to tell the state liquor commission? Maybe the bar down the street, but since the latest earthquake, no one had a working phone, so it wasn't a worry.

During these three days, Garik had made several interesting discoveries.

Rainbow was behaving oddly, skipping shifts and

showing up to waitress only when she felt like it. She claimed that during the most recent earthquake, she had hurt her back. But except for a puffy lip that looked as if she—or someone—had bitten it, she seemed fine.

Bradley and Vivian Hoff had been in. When the earthquake hit, Vivian had been driving, the road had shifted sideways in front of them, and they had gone into a ditch. They both limped dramatically and made clear their incredible generosity in remaining in Virtue Falls when they could have flown to a safer location.

Some gullible townspeople thanked them.

Three days, and all the useful information Garik could uncover was that Virtue Falls was isolated again, and half the town was running out of toilet paper.

Three days, and no other woman had been attacked, his stitches were itching, and Elizabeth had cautiously begun to use her arm. Three days, and he really needed to figure out who Misty's killer was before someone else got hurt.

Elizabeth threw her fist into the air so suddenly she startled him. "I wish we had a way to connect to the Internet!"

"Me, too." Because he hadn't heard a word from Tom about those scissors.

"I want to cite the tiniest fact, and I can't. I can't see it because there's no Internet!"

Leaning over, he looked at her computer screen. "What are you writing?"

"Before we lost contact with the outside world, the Geological Society of America asked me to write up my report for their magazine. I'm adding information on the second earthquake, since I'm sure they're going to figure any quakes that occur this year as one cosmic event."

"It's very prestigious to be asked, right?"

"It is, yes."

"They didn't ask Andrew Marrero, right?"

"No, I don't believe so." She smiled smugly. Then her smile faded. "But I don't know for sure. No one has seen him in days."

"Yeah . . ." Garik leaned back in his chair. "Then he's hurt and he's hiding, so he's our guilty party."

"Unless *he's* been murdered."

"By who?"

"Ben, Luke, and Joe? They are *really* annoyed with him."

"Seems unlikely." Garik lowered his voice. "He's not home. I went to check on him. When he didn't answer the door, I picked the lock and went in. The place was empty. It doesn't do me any good to think Marrero is our killer if I can't find him."

"I hope he's okay."

"Because you feel guilty because you usurped all the attention about the earthquake and tsunami?"

She considered that, then nodded. "Yes. You're right. That is why."

Invariably honest. That was his Elizabeth. "We've still got Sheriff Foster. Mona claims he keeps going down to the morgue where his mother's body still rests, and he talks to Mother Dearest." He watched Mona march out of the door with her cappuccino and across the street. "If this is a crime of madness, he's way ahead in the polls."

"I know." Elizabeth shivered. "That guy scares me. It's like he's on a timer, and he's going to explode."

"And he's got a gun."

"So do you," she said with satisfaction.

"I gave it back to Margaret."

Elizabeth sputtered. B . . . but why?"

"Because it's Margaret's pistol. She handles it well."
He hated to alarm Elizabeth, but he had to tell her the
truth. "I'm afraid she might need to protect herself."

"What do you think? That the townspeople will
storm the resort for the store of toilet paper?" She was
joking . . . and she was frowning.

"It's a possibility. This last earthquake has made everyone a little nuts." Certainly every time Mona came in,
Dax got more wild-eyed. "But no, it's Foster I'm worried
about. I would put money on him being the arsonist
behind the fire at the Suns' house."

Elizabeth shut her computer with a definite click.
"You think Sheriff Foster will try to burn the resort?
And Margaret would shoot him?"

"Harold knows his way around a gun, but he's only
got one leg. The other staff . . . I dunno what they're
good for when it comes to self-defense. But I do know if
Foster tried to do anything to her resort, Margaret would
gladly kill him." Garik glanced at his watch. "Come on.
We need to leave now if we're going to get to our doctors' appointments."

Elizabeth slid her computer into her bag. "Then I
guess I'm glad you gave Margaret her pistol back. But
what if my mother's killer gets a gun? What if he shoots
you?"

"Always a possibility, but he seems to have a thing for
scissors, and guys like that tend to run to type." He slung
her bag over his shoulder. "Which is why I also like to
keep an eye on the Hoffs."

"As killers? Both of them?" She headed for the
door.

Garik followed close behind, and when they stepped

out on the street, he scanned the few sullen citizens loitering on the corners. "When that woman threatened you, told you not to step between Bradley and the press, I realized—she's ruthless and controlling. If Bradley Hoff had been your mother's lover, and Vivian told him to kill Misty, he would have done what he was told."

"So you think she's the power behind the throne?" Elizabeth remembered, and shivered. "Maybe so, but whoever attacked Yvonne and me—he was into it. I mean, unless it was Rainbow. Then *she* was into it."

"I don't think it's Rainbow. But then, I may have landed a punch on that guy's face, and she's got that fat lip." He opened the truck door for Elizabeth and watched her climb in, admiring her fine ass and glad the two of them were healing, because it had been a very, very long time since his confession on the deck, and her exceptional efforts to comfort him.

She looked down at him. "In regards to my mother's murder, we're still where we were when we started."

"No, you believe in your father's innocence. And we've eliminated one prime suspect, Dr. Frownfelter." Garik stepped up on the running board and kissed her, a slow, warm, reassuring kiss. "Tensions are running high in this town. My gut is rumbling. Trouble's going to break soon."

She kissed him back, but that didn't stop her from saying in exasperation, "You're talking about instinct. That doesn't make sense. There's no logic in believing your gut has a valuable opinion."

"Maybe not." But he knew he was right.

He would give a lot to be able to reach Tom Perez. They latest earthquake had destroyed even Elizabeth's cell service, and Garik wanted, *needed* to know—had

Tom received the scissors? And what fingerprints did the lab lift off the handles?

When he knew that, this crime would take a whole new turn. And yes, his gut told him that, too.

CHAPTER SEVENTY-SIX

That night after dinner, Elizabeth rose from her chair. "If you don't mind, I'm going up. I haven't been sleeping well. The doctor says my shoulder is much better, but between the pain and the nightmares, I'm a zombie."

"I don't care if you're a zombie, we're not serving brains tomorrow night," Margaret said.

Surprised, Elizabeth laughed.

Margaret offered her cheek. "Good night, dear."

Elizabeth kissed her and wandered up to the suite, knowing Garik would not be far behind. She showered and put on shorts and a T-shirt.

When he joined her, she was out on the deck, in the wicker rocking chair, one leg tucked under, smiling as she watched the sun set. He sat next to her, a handsome, brave man whom she loved and admired. For right now, that was enough.

A few long, thin clouds clung to the horizon, blushing pink, then orange. The waves danced with the colors, plaiting patterns that rose and vanished in a second, yet wove themselves forever on the heart.

The earthquakes, the sorrows, the relationships that changed and moved in and slipped away, the awareness that life was transient and easily ended . . . All that made

Elizabeth appreciate the moments of beauty as she never had before.

As the sun flashed its last beam across the continent, she reached out a hand.

Garik grasped it, entwined his fingers with hers, and together they watched the first bold stars poke their heads through a rapidly darkening sky.

She took in a deep breath, and said it. "I'm going to work tomorrow."

He claimed concern for her health. "You shouldn't strain your shoulder yet."

"I won't do anything to strain my shoulder. The heaviest thing I'll lift is a brush and a pencil." That was an easy promise to make. The shoulder was better, but not healed.

"It's rough terrain. You might fall."

"If I do, I promise not to catch myself with my bad arm."

He took a long breath, and blurted, "Why? Why do you want to go to work? I've never understood your fascination with digging in the dirt."

She felt as if she'd said it a hundred times during their marriage, but she said it again. "It's not digging in the dirt. It's discovery. It's finding the roots of the world. It's . . . geology." She braced herself for argument.

Instead he said, "Can you explain it to me?"

He had never asked that before.

She looked at him, trying to see his face.

But they sat on the edge of the continent. Light had fled to Hawaii, and the orient, and he was only a stark outline and a deep voice. She pointed to the sky. "When we look at the stars, we're looking at the history of the universe. When I hold a rock in my hand, I'm holding a window to the past. The sweep and grandeur of a rock holds the same promise of eternity as a star."

"Oh. That's cool."

"I think so." She squeezed his fingers. "When I break a rock open with my pick, I'm a prophet. I see the past. I see the future. I know where the world is going, and where it's been. And I always, always want to know more."

"I, um, don't have that kind of job." He sounded vaguely perplexed.

"No. You don't worry about the past that stretches back to infinity or the future that could end tomorrow." She was very aware of the schism that divided their jobs. She'd always been aware. "You have a real job, involving real people. You save lives. You make a difference, right here and right now. Everything you do has an influence on the world today." But for the first time, she got to say with satisfaction, "But you know what?"

"What?"

"My father said, 'Virtue Falls is a place on the coast where the tsunamis sweep in high and fast, sometimes without warning.' Some people believed him, and when I said it again, they believed me. They didn't believe the Native American legend because they thought that was superstition. But they believed us because we're scientists." Proudly she said, "So I save lives, too. That's nice."

Garik was silent so long she first wondered if he was trying to contain his laughter, then whether she'd put him to sleep.

For the first time, she noticed that the breeze off the ocean was cool. She slid her hand out of his, and crossed her arms over her chest, trying belatedly to gather the pieces of her soul that she had so lovingly laid out for him to inspect.

After a thoughtful interlude that seemed to stretch as

far as the horizon itself, he got out of his swing, and knelt at her feet, and found her fingers and kissed them. "You are an amazing woman." Standing, he pulled her to her feet and into his arms. He held her, and rocked her. "You see eternity, and you save lives. That's so far above the dirt-dog common shit of life I dig around in."

His praise, his affection, was so unexpected, she didn't know what to do, what to say.

The scent of him was warm and rich, a familiar comfort and a new memory. His body heated her, banishing the chill of the ocean breeze, of her long isolation. "You never liked what I did," she said.

"But I always liked *you*." He took her jaw in one hand, tilted her head back, and kissed her neck, her shoulder, and for one moment, rested his head against her in a gesture of love and homage.

Lifting her arms, she wrapped them around his shoulders, opening her body to him. "I like you, too," she said. "I love you."

He straightened and pulled her closer, bringing their bodies together in a heated promise of later delights. Sliding his hands under her T-shirt, he found her breasts. He weighed them in his hands. Softly he pinched her nipples, using a slow rhythm that made her breath grow deeper, more vital.

Sex. He wanted sex. Thank God. Because so did she.

"Let me talk love words that you will understand." He dipped his head. He spoke intimately in her ear. "You remind of a volcano—Vesuvius comes to mind—a snow-capped peak which explodes with no warning, with fire and smoke and heat that encompasses everything around."

"Oh . . ." she said huskily. She liked his almost-lyrical turn of phrase . . . and the way one of his hands moved from her breast to the inside of her thigh. His fingers skimmed across her skin under the hem of her shorts. His thumb lifted her panties, slid beneath.

She held her breath.

He said, "I'm lucky enough to be the man who dies a little every time you . . . blow."

She gave an explosive snort of laughter. "I love it when you talk dirty." She wrapped her leg around his thigh to ease his access, to bring them closer.

He found her clitoris and stroked softly. "I love your hot lava."

"I love . . ." She caught her breath, then gathered her wits and said, "I love your pyroclastic flows."

His finger stilled. "If I knew what that meant, I would answer with equal wit."

Without even thinking, she said, "A pyroclastic flow is when a volcano suddenly lets off a blast of hot mud and gasses which race down the side of the mountain, incinerating everything in its path. The speed of a pyroclastic flow is determined by—"

He put his mouth on hers, and shut her up in the most primitive way possible.

And before the hour was over, she remembered what it was to be caught in a blistering heat that burned away the flesh and left only two spirits, fused into one.

CHAPTER SEVENTY-SEVEN

Sheriff Dennis Foster sat by the ham radio in the courthouse and listened to John Rudda cry.

In between sobs, John said over and over, "I should have left the truck at the truck stop. I should have come home. But I won . . . I won a bundle at poker and I thought . . . I thought I would take Yvonne to Reno. You know, to gamble and watch some shows. Give her a break from all those crazy people she works with. She never complained, but God . . . God . . . God. Are you sure it's her?"

"I'm sorry, John. Yes. It's a positive ID." This morning at dawn, two of Sophie Ciccolella's dogs had found Yvonne's body up in a tree by Beggar's Creek. She'd been washed up there by the second bunch of tsunami waves. Her throat had been slashed, her hair cut, and her eyes removed.

But it was still Yvonne.

For twenty-three years, Dennis Foster had pretended that he'd done the right thing when he investigated Misty Banner's murder. He had convinced himself, almost, that he had done everything possible to convict the man who murdered her.

But he couldn't fool himself anymore. That little pipsqueak Garik Jacobsen was right. Dennis Foster was guilty, at the very least, of conspiracy to conceal evidence. He'd thrown away the FBI flyer, but he knew what it said. And he knew what Yvonne's murder meant.

The killer wasn't in San Francisco; or San Diego; or

Vancouver, British Columbia The killer was in Virtue Falls.

He looked down at his own hands.

He wasn't sure the killer wasn't sitting in this chair.

Garik walked out of the resort's front door, and there Elizabeth was, sitting in his truck, rummaging through her bag, humming as she riffled through the stuff she always carried to the dig. She looked so pleased with herself, so confident, so happy, that he finally yielded to the inevitable.

She loved geology as much as she loved him, and he might as well figure she was going to work every day whether he liked it or not. And he might as well get enthused about that branch of the sciences, because it would be part of his life forever. And he had better figure out what he was going to do for a living, because he was going to be living in Virtue Falls . . . with Elizabeth.

This was no one-way street. She had wholeheartedly joined in his hunt for her mother's killer, following him through his initial instincts when with her logical mind and his lack of evidence, she must have been convinced he was overreacting.

Now, she looked up, saw him, and smiled.

No, she didn't merely smile. She *glowed*. Because he was near.

How cool was that?

Somehow, the two of them had become the world's most unlikely couple. In the future, they would fight, laugh, talk, love—but they would always, always be together.

He smiled back. *Glowed* back. He walked across the sunny parking lot toward the driver's door, intent on kissing her, telling her what he had realized their life would be, when something happened that hadn't happened for far too long; his pocket vibrated. For a moment, he wondered what it was. Then he pulled out his cell phone and stared at the screen. It showed an incoming call. From the county.

He had service. "I have service," he said. Then he shouted, "I have cell service!"

Elizabeth grinned at him. "I do, too," she called through the open window. Then, "Are you going to answer it?"

"Right." He did. "Hello?"

"It's, um, Sheriff Foster." Pause.

Garik's grin faded. "Yes?"

"I'd like to see you ASAP." Pause. "I'm at the courthouse."

"I'll get there as soon as I can." He hung up.

Dennis Foster sounded as if he had finally, really, completely flipped out.

Garik would go in prepared for an ambush.

As he stared at the phone in his hand, texts crowded the screen of his phone, the first one from the day he put his gun in his mouth. The numbers mounted up, he felt an absolute sense of WTF. Then he laughed at himself. He'd wanted to be connected again. *This* was his punishment.

He walked to the passenger door. "I have to check in with my supervisor at the FBI, and I need to do it while I've got service. Can you wait?"

Elizabeth hopped out of the truck with her bag over her shoulder. With that same happy, I'm-going-to-work smile, she announced, "While I have greatly enjoyed having you haul me all over Virtue Falls, this time I'll drive myself."

Oh, no. "What? Where? How?"

"First, I'm going to go to see my father. Then I'm going to go to the Oceanview Café and get a coffee. Then I'm going to go to work. And I'm going in *my own* car." He was appalled, and she knew it, because she viewed him with a mixture of humor and displeasure. She pulled her car keys out of her bag and dangled them in front of his face. "I *can* drive, you know, and very well. I'm from California, where only the swift and agile survive."

"I know that. It's the—"

"I know. It's the danger." She stepped closer, body to body. "There's a killer on the loose. Don't worry. I've got a phone. You've got a phone. We've got service, which means someone out there in the great big world is actually fixing something."

"Like I have faith in that!"

"I'll check in. You check in. We'll be in contact all the time. I will be careful, I promise." Standing on her toes, she kissed his lips.

He wrapped his arm around her waist, held her as if he could never let her go, and kissed her back.

Then he let her go.

She said, "I have promised to be careful. Now—you promise to be careful, too." She smiled, but her eyes were anxious.

"I will." He watched her walk to her car, get in, and drive away.

Standing there in the middle of the parking lot, he called Tom Perez. Because he damned well needed to get this case wrapped up, and fast, before Elizabeth got hurt.

The call wouldn't go through.

He swore, viciously and fluently.

But the phone showed three bars. He had a connection, and he needed Tom Perez.

He opened his e-mail to see if Tom had tried to contact him.

He had.

The first e-mail was from the morning of the earthquake, and had "Scissors" in the subject line. Tom Perez said, *I sent out an agent to this helicopter guy's house and caught him as he was leaving on a job. Agent scared the guy . . .*

"Good," Garik muttered.

. . . Guy claimed he'd mailed the package the night before, dropped it at a box at the post office. Agent told him he was in trouble if he was lying. Guy insisted he was telling the truth. So now we wait for the USPS to work their magic.

One from yesterday. *Got the scissors. Told the lab which case we were reviewing. Scissors got bumped to the front of the line. Tech said, it's like having the Shroud of Turin in my lab.*

This morning: *Scissors have fingerprints on the handles in the murder grip. Fingerprints not Charles Banner's. Fingerprint is unknown, but it matches a partial at a murder in San Francisco.*

Garik replied, *Urgently need FBI secure network on my phone.*

The software appeared. He logged in with another trick password. And he typed, *What murder?*

The latest Edward Scissorhands.

Thumbs suspended above the keyboard, Garik stared at the screen. Then: *What in the fuck are you talking about? Are you saying Misty Banner's murderer is a serial killer who slaughters . . .* His brain put the pieces together, and every one of them snapped into place. *Of course. Edward Scissorhands, who slaughters blond mothers and their children, then mutilates the children.*

Tom messaged: *He cuts the children's eyes out.*

Garik's mind worked feverishly. *Yes. The children . . . can't see what he did if they have no eyes.*

Tom agreed. *If you're one sick bastard, that is the way you would think.*

This all comes back to Misty Banner's murder. Garik sprinted toward his truck.

He didn't see Tom Perez's last message: *Keep me in the loop. I'm ready to send agents into Virtue Falls.*

CHAPTER SEVENTY-EIGHT

Everyday when the sun shone, the Honor Mountain Memory Care Facility residents were encouraged to come outside. Supervised by the medical staff, they wandered the paths of the small garden at the front to the side of the building. It was there Elizabeth found Charles, sitting on a bench, smiling at an exuberant climbing rose.

"Hey." She dropped a kiss on the top of his head.

He stared at her, as he always did, as he tried to place her. Then his face lit up. "Elizabeth! How good to see you."

She beamed. Any day when he recognized her was a good day. She seated herself beside him on the bench. "Do you want to see the tsunami video?"

"Not today, dear." Apparently he recalled it from the dozen times he'd viewed it before. "I was wondering how the work was progressing après tsunami."

"In the canyon?" Her enthusiasm bubbled over. "There's so many exciting discoveries. When we can get marine biologists in to view the remains of some of the creatures the ocean brought up from the depths, I think we'll have a whole new branch of science buzzing with excitement."

"What have you seen?" He faced her, and his blue eyes sparkled.

"The last time I was at the dig"—the day she was attacked—"I found a shrimp which I swear has only been recorded off the coast of Japan. Here." She brought out her laptop and showed him photos.

He frowned. "I can't quite see . . ."

"The fog rolled in. The light was bad. I wasn't paying attention . . ." She pulled out her notebook and pencil. "The swimmerets on the abdomen didn't have the same joints as the common shrimp we see off the Washington coast. They looked more like this." She sketched them and frowned. "That's not good. It was more like this." She sketched again. "Well, that's not good, either. They had an extra joint right here . . ." She strained to get it right.

Charles laughed. "I know where you got your artistic talent from."

She looked at him inquiringly.

"Me." He tapped his chest.

"You? But when I was young, the drawings you did were very good."

"Not mine." He laughed again.

"Yes." She knew what she was talking about. "You took an art class from Bradley Hoff."

"Your mother got good. I was terrible." He seemed to think he knew what he was talking about.

"No, really. Look." Pulling out her album, she flipped

to the drawings. "There's the one that Mama drew of me. I look a little lopsided, and one of my eyes is higher than the other, but I like it." Her fingers lingered on the edges of the vellum. Then she turned the page. "Here's the one you drew of Mama. It's just a pencil sketch, but so life-like. It's as if you captured her essence, a happy smile that masked a tinge of sadness. She looks . . . kind. Loving."

Charles's hand hovered over the drawing, and his fingers trembled. "That is Misty. It is." He withdrew his hand. "But I have never seen that drawing before. And I didn't do it."

"Who else would have done it?"

Charles stared at the drawing, and everything about his expression was dry, brittle, like leaves that had fallen and waited for winter to turn to dust.

She insisted, "Who else would have drawn that?"

Charles looked up, then away. "One of the other students."

"That's ridiculous. None of the other students would draw a picture like that of my mother. Not one so . . . so complete. So thoughtful. It had to be you." *It had to be.*

"Everyone loved her," he said.

Elizabeth nodded. "Of course. That's what I've heard so often."

Maybe Charles couldn't create that drawing now. But he had Alzheimer's. He had reverted. He had forgotten.

Her father *had* created this drawing.

He had to have. Because . . . who else could it be?

CHAPTER SEVENTY-NINE

Garik strode into the Virtue Falls City Hall like the meanest, maddest agent of justice since Clint Eastwood in *The Good, the Bad, and the Ugly*.

Foster must have recognized Garik's attitude, because when he saw Garik making his way across the floor, around and through the rubble, he got to his feet.

Garik walked up to him, chest to chest. "We need to go someplace private where we can talk."

Foster glanced at Mona. He jerked his thumb toward the back. "Evidence room." As they walked, he asked, "You know your way around there, don't you?"

Garik's temper simmered. "No. But Mike did. You remember Mike Sun. You burned his house."

Foster flung himself around and shouted, "Shut up. You shut up!"

The chatter in the big room died. Everyone stared.

Foster glanced around, then headed toward the back again.

He unlocked the narrow door and stepped aside to let Garik in.

"After you," Garik said.

Foster sneered, but he led the way.

The cramped evidence room smelled musty; the lack of air conditioning encouraged the humid ocean air to do its damage. The shelves were full, but one white box was on the floor, open and empty. The box was marked BANNER MURDER.

Garik kept his hands free and stood ready to attack.

Foster just looked at him out of those bloodshot,

hopeless eyes. "You probably wonder why I called *you*, of all people."

Garik's temper exploded. "I don't give a fuck why you called me. You know that Mike took the evidence for the Banner case. I sent those scissors to the FBI for testing. Those unknown fingerprints, the ones the killer put on the scissors? They match a print in San Francisco, one from the serial killer called Edward Scissorhands."

Foster's dull eyes didn't even flicker. He did not say a word.

"You . . . knew." Garik was incredulous—and angry. "You *knew*."

"I didn't know. I suspected." Foster looked down. "Yvonne Rudda's body washed up at Beggar's Creek."

Garik staggered backward. "God. Yvonne. I told her . . . she had that dog. And her guns. How . . . ?"

"I don't know."

"Someone she knew."

"Yes."

Garik's fists flexed. "We have a serial killer loose in Virtue Falls, a guy who's killed dozens of women and children, a serial killer who's after Charles Banner and his daughter, and takes any woman who gets in his way—and you didn't care."

"I care."

"You care about your reputation more."

Foster licked his lips. "It's worse than that. I'm not sure it's not me."

That made Garik take a step forward. "What are you talking about?"

"Wherever the murders take place, I'm there." Foster took a moment to swallow. "I'm close enough to get to those women, kill them and their kids, and get back to my law enforcement conference without anybody ever knowing."

"But you know you didn't do it."

Foster's eyes flickered. "I don't remember. I go to sleep, you know, and I dream, and I wake up and a few days or weeks later, I hear another woman's been killed."

"You're not making sense." Which was, Garik knew, the definition of madness. But was this craziness? Or was this Dennis Foster making excuses for himself?

"I don't like women. Okay? I've never liked women. Those high-pitched voices and those soft bodies they fling around to entrap men." Foster's lips curled as he was nauseated. "Women are evil, created by God to ruin men. We should treat them like cattle. Instead, we exalt them." He looked at his hands. "So I could have done it. I could have done all of it."

"Show me your ribs," Garik said.

"What?"

"Show me your ribs."

For one moment, Foster looked as if he was going to refuse. Then his face crumpled. He pulled his shirt out from under his belt, lifted it, and revealed pale, unmarked skin.

"I kicked the shit out of the killer," Garik said. "Don't flatter yourself, You're not the guy. You don't have what it takes to be a good cop, and you don't have what it takes to be a serial killer."

At last Foster sparked to life. He reached for his gun.

Garik took him out with an uppercut that snapped Foster's head back and sent him careening with a clang into the metal shelving. White boxes fell. Foster tripped on the shower of evidence and landed on his ass.

Garik leaned over and took Foster by the collar. He

jerked his head and shoulders off the floor, and spoke right into his face. "Don't try and build yourself up in your own mind. You killed your mother. You burned down the Suns' house. You're responsible for withholding the evidence that got all those women and their little kids murdered most horribly. That's enough. That's plenty. Live with that."

CHAPTER EIGHTY

Elizabeth stood at the counter, holding her coffee in both hands and shaking her head in disbelief. "How was she killed?"

"The way I understand it," Mrs. Ubach said, "she got caught by that second round of tsunamis and drowned."

"You keep believing that, Pollyanna. I heard she had her throat cut and her eyes gouged out." Mrs. Branyon smirked. "I wonder who would do that . . . Elizabeth Banner?"

Elizabeth comprehended; this old woman was calling her a killer, a woman who would murder a friend and mutilate the body. Fury roared through her; nothing she had done deserved that insinuation. With a snap quite unlike her usual calm manner, Elizabeth said, "Yvonne Rudda was my father's nurse, and my friend, and if she is really dead, I will mourn her in the fullness of my heart. So let us not make her possible death fodder for gossip."

"You tell her, sister," Mrs. Branyon's daughter said.

Mrs. Branyon whipped around and glared. "Frances!"

"Mother, that was mean. And today, with Yvonne gone, it's . . . just . . ." Frances dug a shredded tissue out of her pocket and wiped her nose. "Really mean."

The Oceanview Café was packed with people gathered here to share their shock and grief. They sat with their phones out, staring blankly, typing, staring some more. Conversation came in fits and starts, words spoken in low voices by friends who didn't know, didn't believe, couldn't bear to think it was true.

Noah Griffin was nowhere to be seen.

Smart guy, since he had been the reporter who put Yvonne's name out there for a killer. Sooner or later, someone was going to rightly blame him.

Bradley Hoff sat on a stool at the end of the counter, picking at a stale cheese sandwich. He looked up now, and in a firm voice said, "I'm sure the first report, that she was drowned by the tsunami, is the right report. The other report, that she was murdered, is unconfirmed. So let's remember that here in Virtue Falls, even in the best of times, we're almost completely cut off from the world, and we need to treat each other like family."

Heads nodded all around. In this town, Bradley Hoff got a lot of respect.

Elizabeth was grateful for his support. He shut Mrs. Branyon down as no one else could, and now the old lady stirred her coffee and muttered disparagingly, but quietly.

The heat in Elizabeth's face faded. Her bag sat on a stool beside her; she reached in and pulled out her phone.

She still had cell service. For some reason, that made her feel secure, as if as long as she could reach out to someone in the wide, wide world, she would be able to survive the bitter grief that threatened to take the sunshine away from this day.

Then Garik walked in, and he brought the sunshine

with him. But he looked sober, and he massaged his knuckles as if they hurt.

Elizabeth put down her coffee and went to him. "Is it true?" she asked softly. "Is she dead? Was she murdered?"

Speaking to her only, he said, "And mutilated. I got the details out of Mona the Mouth."

Old Mrs. Branyon butted right in. Her voice focused all attention on Garik and Elizabeth. "We've got a right to know, young man. Did someone murder Yvonne Rudda?"

He nodded. "Everyone needs to be very careful. We have a killer in town."

The café grew silent. People who were standing, sat. People who were sitting, stood.

Soberly, Garik said, "He—or she—is vicious and crafty. I spoke to Yvonne, and she was armed, good with a firearm, and she had a dog. Yet she was taken and cruelly murdered. I cannot say this strongly enough. Women, especially, watch out for yourselves. We can't fool ourselves about this. It's not a stranger. It's someone we know."

Everyone looked around as if they could spot the evil in another's heart.

"Was she . . . ? Were her eyes . . . ?" Frances stammered to a halt.

Mrs. Branyon asked bluntly, "Were her eyes gouged out?"

Garik said, "Yes." That was all. Just yes. But that single word confirmed every fear.

"What can we do to help each other?" Bradley Hoff asked.

"Network. Check on your neighbors. Keep in contact." Garik lifted his cell phone for all to see. "Has everybody got cell service back?"

A variety of answers came back at him. "Most of the time." "No." "Sometimes." "It's been steady since this morning."

"Mostly good news for us, then," Garik said. "Things are improving. We're not so cut off. We can get this bastard."

As Garik encouraged the citizens of Virtue Falls, Elizabeth felt a tremendous upwelling of admiration. Garik was a good man, one who learned from the past. People looked to him for leadership, and he led them effortlessly. Elizabeth respected his strength and character, and more than that—she loved him. So much.

Bradley slid off his stool. "Garik, can I get your cell number? I'm pretty good with reading faces—it's an occupational hazard. I'll keep watch and let you know if I see anything suspicious."

Head tilted and half-turned, Garik studied him.

Elizabeth knew what he hoped to see. Bradley was one of their prime suspects. Yet . . . what harm could come from taking him up on his offer? If Bradley incriminated an innocent man, it would be easy enough to prove him wrong, and that would be a clue, too. And if Bradley really could see the evil beneath the façade, what a help that would be.

"Elizabeth, have you got paper in that bag of yours?" Garik asked.

She brought out her battered spiral notebook and a pen, and handed them to him.

Garik scribbled his name and phone number, tore off the sheet, and offered it to Bradley.

"Can I have your number, too?" Frances asked. "Just in case?"

"Sure." Garik wrote his number down and handed it to Frances.

Dax leaned his elbows on the counter. "I'd take it. I see all kinds of things come through this café. I might see something of interest."

"Good idea," Garik said.

Poor Garik. Everybody knew him. Everybody trusted him.

Bradley looked abashed. "I've started something. Here—I'll copy your number and tear them off to give to anyone who wants it."

"That's great. Thank you." Garik gave him the notebook and pen. He started to turn away, then turned back. "Where's your wife? Where's Vivian?"

"She's at home, in the studio, preparing promo for Virtue Falls." Bradley scribbled Garik's number on the paper, tore it off, and handed it to Dax.

"It might be worth your time to check on her, tell her what's going on," Garik said. "She's a woman alone."

Bradley look startled, then almost amused. "Unless the killer is smarter and swifter and stronger than Vivian, I'd put my money on her."

"Forewarned is forearmed." Frances's eyes swam with tears, and gently she placed her hand on Bradley's forearm. "I went to school with Yvonne. And think about it. Stabbed and . . . and . . . her eyes . . ."

"You're right." Bradley put his hand over hers. "I'll call Vivian as soon as I'm done here."

Garik took Elizabeth's arm. "Come on. I need to talk."

Bradley held up the notebook. "Elizabeth, if you don't mind, I'll keep this until I've written out Garik's number and handed it around to whoever wants it?"

"Yes, of course. I'll come back and get it." She left her bag on the stool.

Garik led her outside.

"Is all of it true?" Elizabeth asked. "About Yvonne? It wasn't the tsunami that swept her away?"

"He killed her, dropped her into the ocean, then the tsunami brought her back. I can't imagine he planned on the second earthquake and having her body wash up in a tree."

"Oh, God." Elizabeth felt sick.

"I don't know how he did it. She had a dog. She had a gun." Garik glanced back into the café where the people crowded the seats. "She knew her attacker. She had to. Where's Rainbow?"

"She's not working today."

"Anybody seen Marrero?"

"No. Not a sign of him." She lowered her voice as if the empty street could hear them. "What about Bradley Hoff? If he did the deed, he's pretty bold to show his face and offer to help."

"If he did it, then he's enjoying himself." Garik's face was sculpted of oak and stone. "Killers love to observe the aftermath of their crimes."

Chilled, she rubbed her arms and glanced through the window.

Bradley Hoff watched her.

She didn't like him, she decided. She didn't like him at all. And the things her father had said . . . if she believed them . . .

"There's more." Garik put his hand on her shoulder, and told her how Mike had stolen the evidence for him. He told her how he had managed to ship the scissors out of Virtue Falls via the Hoffs' helicopter pilot, and how the FBI had run all the fingerprints. And he told her a partial fingerprint in a San Francisco killing matched a fingerprint on those scissors.

"What do you mean?" she asked. "The guy who murdered my mother was in San Francisco? And is now here?"

"The partial belongs to a serial killer called Edward Scissorhands."

She tried to comprehend. "A serial killer? My mother was murdered by a serial killer?"

"If I'm reading the profile right—she was his first kill. She set him off. Now he kills blond women, mothers of young children—and their children." Gently, Garik put his arm around Elizabeth's shoulders and held her as if he wished to brace her for the last blast of news. "The children . . . after they're dead, he mutilates them. He cuts out their eyes . . . Elizabeth, this guy not only has the right fingerprint, but he fits the profile as Misty Banner's killer. And it's clear that he wants . . . that he regrets he didn't kill *you*. Do you understand? After twenty-three years, he still wants to kill *you* so you can't bear witness to your mother's murder."

Elizabeth stood there, on a sidewalk in Virtue Falls, and tried to comprehend what this meant to her.

Everything about the case was horrible, yet out of all the things Garik had told her, the most important thing she heard was . . . her father was innocent. Not merely innocent by someone's opinion—the nurses', Dr. Frownfelter's, Garik's, hers—but innocent by reason of hard, incontestable evidence.

Elizabeth had seen her mother killed, but the label that had been slapped on her since she was four years old was *not* true. She was not the girl who saw her father kill her mother with the scissors.

And in a tiny, selfish portion of her mind, she was glad.

Except . . . now a serial killer murdered because of her and her mother.

She felt oddly ill, as if she carried responsibility for those deaths.

"How many has he killed?" she asked.

"Law enforcement is unsure of the exact number." Still with his arm around her, Garik led her farther away from the café. "More than a dozen women. More than a dozen children. And a few people who got in the way."

"Do you think it is safe for me to go to work?" she asked.

Immediately Garik snapped, "Hell, no!" He took a breath and tried for a more equitable tone. "I don't think it's safe for you to be anywhere. I would bring in a helicopter and send you out of town if I thought you would be secure elsewhere. But I can't go with you—I need to find this guy. If I sent you away, he might follow. In fact, I know he would. He has you in his sights." Garik contemplated her. He looked back at the café. He looked up the street, and down the street. "We should have done some catching up on your self-defense skills."

"We were both a little wounded. Still are." She put her hand to his ribs, felt the bandage, knew the stitches still hadn't come out. And her shoulder ached; would ache for weeks, the doctor told her. "I *need* to work. I *need* something to occupy my mind. Writing the article's not going to do it. I know you're going to say that last time I lost track of the guys and almost got myself killed. But this time, I'm going to hang with them every minute." She waved her hand toward the sky. "The sun is shining."

"Fog comes in fast."

"I won't stay out past four. I've got a great pocket knife." She groped for her bag, realized it was still inside. "I need to get my stuff."

Together they headed back into the café.

The low buzz of conversation paused. All heads turned their way.

Bradley was on the phone, speaking portentously to his wife. Without pausing, he lifted Elizabeth's bag and offered it to her.

She took it with thanks. A glance inside showed her notebook had been tucked neatly into the proper pocket. Obviously, an artist understood the need for pen and paper.

"Are we set?" Garik asked the crowd in the restaurant. "Have you spread the word of warning to everyone who is vulnerable?"

Heads nodded.

"All right, then. Keep a watchful eye on each other. It's the best way to stay safe." He gave a wave.

Garik and Elizabeth walked out the door and toward his truck.

Garik helped her into the passenger side. "Now show me the knife," he said.

She pulled it out of her bag. "It's strong and it's sharp. I use it to cut rope and brush."

"Would you kill a man with it?" Garik focused on her intently.

"A man who wanted to cut out my eyes? Yes!"

"Good girl." Garik patted her knee.

She caught his hand with hers and pressed it down, wanting to connect with him, to make him understand. "I need to go to work because I need something to keep me busy. I need to think."

"Think about what?"

"Everything. Stuff my father said today." In her mind's eye, she saw again Charles's trembling fingers hover over the drawing of her mother. "He's good today. He's talking. *He knew me.*"

"Good, because I want to go talk to him. Somewhere in his mind, he knows something. I've got to get this right the first time, so before I accuse anyone of anything, I want to hear what Charles Banner remembers."

"I'm like him." For the first time in her life, she wasn't afraid to say that. "There's so much hovering right at the edges of my thoughts."

"How will going to work help?" Garik watched her with pleading, puppy-dog eyes, trying to get her to change her mind.

"It's my subconscious we're trying to break wide open, and pounding at it doesn't work. Trust me, Aunt Sandy tried. I need to be distracted, to put the pieces together intuitively." Anger stirred in her. "Because if I'm going to be killed for what I remember—I do want to remember it."

CHAPTER EIGHTY-ONE

Sheriff Dennis Foster stood in the courthouse and stared across the square. Through the big window at the Oceanview Café, he had seen Garik Jacobsen talking to the people of Virtue Falls, and those people gathered around as if he was the second coming.

Garik had been a troublemaker from the day Margaret Smith had adopted him, but everybody here knew him, believed him, trusted him.

And he, Dennis Foster, the boy who'd been born and raised in Virtue Falls, who was elected as sheriff again and again, who served the citizens faithfully as a public

servant . . . they avoided him. No one chatted to Sheriff
Foster unless they got a speeding ticket or had something
stolen. He was a pariah in his own town.

Why? No one knew he had burned Mike Sun's house.
No one knew he had killed his mother. Most of all, no
one knew he was guilty of gross negligence in the Banner
case, that those murdered women and children haunted
his days and his nights. No one except for Garik Jacobsen, anyway.

Sooner or later, Garik would make sure everybody
knew.

Turning away from the sight of Garik Jacobsen and
his sycophants, Sheriff Foster got in his patrol car and
went home.

At last, he went home.

The front door was unlocked. Why not? The windows
were still broken. Knickknacks still covered the floor.
Dust covered everything.

He walked slowly through the living room, remembering years spent sitting on the couch, watching TV and
trying desperately to shut out his mother's voice. He went
into the kitchen, wrecked and reeking of spoiled food,
and looked at the stain on the floor where his mother's
body had rested.

He backed out, then walked into his mother's bedroom. He saw the clutter of crosses and ceramic figures
of Jesus. He smelled the mixture of flowery perfume and
old lady funk. If he squinted his eyes, he could see Mother
sitting on the bed, hear her haranguing him about taking care of her rather than spending all his time out chasing invisible criminals.

Slowly, he pulled his service pistol from its holster.
Clicking off the safety, he pointed it at her picture on the

bureau, and pulled the trigger. The frame and glass exploded. His mother's photograph shredded.

She was dead. Again.

He had killed her. Again.

Then, making sure a fresh round had moved into the chamber, he put the muzzle of the gun under his chin. He took a breath, his last. He pulled the trigger and blew out his own brains.

It was just easier than having to face justice.

CHAPTER EIGHTY-TWO

Garik pulled into the Honor Mountain Memory Care Facility, parked as close as possible to the door, and headed in. Without his usual chitchat and charm, he flashed his ID and did the necessary stuff to quickly get into the nursing home.

He needed to know. He needed to know *now*.

Charles sat slumped in front of his computer, watching Elizabeth's tsunami video online. He watched as if he'd never seen it before. His expression was forlorn; it seemed as if in the last few weeks, since he'd begun having seizures, he was suddenly an old man.

An old man . . . a dying man.

Garik settled into the chair next to Charles's desk. He reached out and grasped Charles's hands.

Charles turned his gaze away from the screen. He examined Garik. At last he said, "You're Elizabeth's husband."

"Yes." Perhaps this would not be a hopeless cause. "I need to talk to you about Misty's murder."

"I didn't do it." Charles looked weary, sounded weary, as if he'd said it a thousand times.

"I believe you."

Charles viewed him cautiously.

"But I don't know who *did* do it. I need to know who killed Misty. Tell me what you saw when you walked into the scene of the crime."

Charles took deep breaths, as if he was insulted. "It wasn't the scene of the crime. It was my home."

"Tell me what you saw."

"It hurts. It hurts to remember."

"Please, sir. I think I can help you. Tell me what you saw."

Charles parked his car in front of the cozy Craftsman-style house, sat with his hands on the steering wheel, and stared at the place that had been his home for the past four years. He loved this spot, and he had thought Misty did, too.

She had painted the house white, the shutters cornflower blue, and she'd worked for days scraping the front door down to the original oak and refinishing it so it glowed with a rich wood patina. She'd found the old-fashioned wicker furniture at a garage sale, cleaned it up and painted it, and sewn blue-and-white striped seat cushions. Flower baskets hung from the top rails on the wide front porch; reds and golds and purples rioted joyously, chaotically.

This house looked like a well-loved seaside home, and inside, he knew, Misty had worked twice as hard to make it comfortable and happy.

Tears filled his eyes. He wiped them away.

Was it all a lie?

Had she done all this work to keep him off guard? So he wouldn't realize why she no longer slept in their bed? For months, ever since she'd returned from her mother's funeral, she had slept in the extra bedroom.

He'd tried to be understanding. He had talked to her, asked what he could do to help, gone to that stupid art class with her, taken her to Seattle to the Sound of Music *sing-along . . . and she had been so sweet, hugging him, kissing him, thanking him. She had admitted she had problems stemming from the finality of her mother's death, begged him for more time to deal with her grief and guilt, talked to him while tears brimmed in her big blue eyes.*

Was it all a sham?

Was it true, what that awful Foster woman said? That Misty and her lover and the whole world were laughing at him?

Charles put his hand on his chest.

His pride hurt. It really did. But he had always known he was too old for Misty, that she should have a younger man.

It wasn't his pride that had broken. It was his heart. If this was true, if all these years Misty had lied to him . . .

Except . . . he didn't believe that of Misty. Perhaps she had made a mistake. Perhaps she had fallen in bed with another man for reasons Charles didn't understand. But he couldn't believe she had never loved him. For over five years, he had known her, lived with her, talked to her, and she was a woman of sincere feelings and gentle depths.

And she loved their baby. She was a wonderful mother,

spending hours with Elizabeth, teaching her, laughing with her, holding her.

He had to remember what he had witnessed in Misty, the joy she had brought him, and go into the house with the attitude that if she was willing, they could work this out.

He got out and slammed the car door.

Usually when he drove up, Misty and Elizabeth came out, and Elizabeth ran to him and hugged him, and Misty kissed his cheek and smiled at him.

Today, although the front door was open and the screen door shut, everything was silent.

Perhaps they'd gone for a walk.

Or perhaps Misty had heard about the scene at the diner, and sat inside waiting to talk to him.

He didn't know what to hope for.

He walked up the stairs, his footsteps reluctant and heavy. He opened the screen door and stepped inside the living room.

The windows were open, the lace curtains blowing in the ocean breeze. But the room was empty.

He took a disappointed breath . . . his home even smelled different to him, bitterly metallic, as if something had spilled and not been wiped up.

Misty had placed a large area rug in the middle of the hardwood floor, and as soon as he stepped on it he knew something had indeed spilled.

The rug squished beneath his shoes.

He looked down in concern. Had the kitchen sink overflowed? Had Elizabeth flushed a toy down the toilet? They would have to call the plumber . . .

He took another few steps.

The rug grew wetter, the moisture squeezing up around his white running shoes . . . it was red. Dark red.

What had happened here?

Even then, with the evidence before his eyes, he didn't understand.

"Misty?" he called. "Elizabeth?"

The house echoed eerily.

If he hadn't had a four-year-old, he probably wouldn't have noticed the sharp, silvery blade tossed carelessly on the wide seat of the Morris chair. But he did have a child, and scissors were a dangerous thing to leave lying around. He picked them up.

They were sticky with red.

He stared at them. Knelt and put his knee on the rug. Saw the red ooze up around and into his faded blue jeans. Put his hand to the floor, then lifted it and stared at his bloody palm.

That's when his mind comprehended.

Bloody scissors. Bloody shoes. Bloody hand. Blood-soaked rug.

And that smell was the smell of blood and fear and death.

He lifted his gaze.

Blood spattered the pale green wall and the framed photo of their family.

Faint with fear, he stumbled as he got to his feet. He wiped his hand on his T-shirt. He thought he screamed their names. "Misty! Elizabeth!"

He ran into the hallway and down to the master bedroom, clutching the scissors, thinking that perhaps the killer was still lurking inside, that he, Charles, could take him out.

No one in the bedroom. No sign of Misty. No sign of Elizabeth.

No sign of blood.

He ran to Elizabeth's little bedroom, decorated with dragons and fairies.

No one inside. No one at all.

No blood.

He stood, trembling, desperate to find them, to save his family from whatever horror had occurred here. And he heard a shuffling sound in the closet, like a mouse. Like a frightened child.

Or someone who was dying.

He flung the door open. It was dark in here, an old-fashioned walk-in closet with hanging rods on two sides, a light bulb dangling from the ceiling, the house's fuse box against the wall. Misty had built shelves at the back and a big chest with a lid so Elizabeth could put her own toys away.

She never did. He always had to coax her, help her, and even now, her dolls and LEGOs and cars were scattered across the floor.

The lid on the toy box was closed.

The perfect place for a small girl to hide.

The perfect coffin where a small girl could die.

"Elizabeth, it's Daddy." He flipped on the light. "Sweetheart, please tell me you're in here." He walked toward the box, making a path, shoving toys aside with his blood-stained shoes. In hope and dread, he lifted the lid.

Elizabeth was there, her blue eyes big, dry, horrified.

No blood. He saw no blood.

He reached in for her.

She cowered, trying to make herself as tiny as possible, and in the reflection of her fear, he saw what she saw.

He was covered in blood. And he still held the scissors.

He didn't know what to do. His joyous, open, happy child had been transformed.

She was afraid of him.

He placed the scissors on the floor. He knelt beside the toy chest. "Are you okay, sweetheart? Are you hurt?"

She shook her head in tiny, jerky motions.

"Do you know where Mommy is?"

She stopped shaking her head, then started again, the motions bigger now.

She was lying. She had seen it. Whatever had happened here today, she had seen it.

"It's okay," he said. God, he was lying to her. It was never going to be okay again. "I'll take care of you. Do you want me to take care of you?"

A hesitation.

Then she scrambled up, into his embrace, throwing her arms around his neck and her legs around his chest, clinging, trying to burrow into him, looking for a hiding place, a safe place.

He rocked her, stroked her face, making crooning noises, trying to give comfort when he knew—he knew—there was none to give.

CHAPTER EIGHTY-THREE

But a sense of lingering danger drove Charles to shift his daughter to one hip. Picking up the scissors again, he got to his feet.

His wife was missing. Someone had killed here today. Someone had been killed. And someone might soon realize a witness remained alive . . .

They had to get out of here.

He hurried to the closet door, stopped, and listened.

Except for the breeze that carried the eternal rhythm of the ocean, the house was silent.

He moved noiselessly to the bedroom door. Out into the hall. Before they stepped into the blood-soaked living room, he whispered to Elizabeth, "Close your eyes, sweetheart. Don't look. Promise you won't look."

She made herself as small as possible, scrunched her eyes shut, and pushed her head against his neck.

He hurried through the living room, trying not to look himself, trying not to remember, wishing he could turn back time, wishing he had come here as soon as that Foster woman had given him the news. While he had gone to think things through, Misty had been . . . murdered.

God. Oh, God.

So much blood. Misty's blood.

As he and Elizabeth stepped out on the porch, he heard the sound of a vehicle approaching. In fear and fury, he looked up the long gravel drive—and it was the mail truck! Thank God, the mail truck.

His postal carrier saw him and slammed on his brakes.

The two men stared at each other.

Then . . . then the son-of-a-bitch of a mailman lifted his camera and took a picture.

Elizabeth looked up, making soundless mewls of terror.

Charles tried to shout for help, but his voice caught in his throat.

Then, as if the demons of hell were after him, the postal carrier backed up, did a three-point turn, and drove off, spitting gravel from his tires.

Charles stood, breathing heavily, unsure what to do next.

Go back in and call the police? Yes. But he couldn't go back in there. He couldn't take Elizabeth back in there.

In a turmoil, he sat heavily on the step and put Eliza-

beth in his lap. "Who did this?" he asked Elizabeth. "Can you tell Daddy who did this?"

While tears spilled down her cheeks and through the blood that had somehow made its way to her face, she shook her head again. And again.

Getting out his handkerchief, he licked the white cotton and wiped at the blood, and realized his hands were still stained with red.

"Daddy has to go inside and call the police."

She flung her arms around his neck again and clung.

"Can you close your eyes so I can go call the police?" he asked.

She nodded.

He stood.

At that moment, in the distance, he heard a siren.

Thank God. Someone—the damned cowardly postal carrier—had called the law. Charles stood, waiting, holding his daughter in his arms, stroking her hair, murmuring hushed words of comfort in her ears, waiting for help . . .

The last thing he remembered from that day was shouting and crying, trying to cling to his daughter . . . as they tore her out of his arms.

After that, nothing mattered.

Not the way they slammed him to the porch, not the way they cuffed his hands behind him, not the way they shoved him into the back of the patrol car.

Nothing mattered except that last glimpse of Elizabeth as she silently wept, and strained to reach him.

Charles sat, hands upturned in his lap, staring at nothing.

Garik wiped his sweating forehead. "Jesus Christ. They didn't listen to you at all? They never searched for another killer?"

"I couldn't hold on to my baby." Charles's voice was dull and soft. "Elizabeth was a little girl. She thought I was invincible. She thought her daddy could do anything. And I couldn't hold on to her. I lost her. She thinks I abandoned her. Of course. That's what any child would think . . ."

Of course. Charles was right. No wonder Elizabeth didn't speak for a year and a half. No wonder she didn't trust. No wonder she demanded logic in her life.

Emotion had failed her. Love had failed her. She had been irrevocably scarred and nothing could change that.

"Listen." Garik leaned his elbows on his knees and looked straight into Charles's eyes. "I need to know the name of Misty's lover. You have to know who he was. Who? Just tell me. Even if you're wrong, I want to know who you suspect."

"I never did know who it could be . . . until this morning when Elizabeth showed me those drawings. She was convinced I had done them, and I . . . I don't remember . . . there's so many blanks in my mind. But I sat in the garden in the sunlight, and I could see . . . and I know I didn't do them." Charles shook his head. "Misty didn't do them. They were too good for that."

"So . . . Bradley Hoff." Garik stood up. "Misty's killer is Bradley Hoff."

"He's after my baby." Charles shuddered. "He wants to kill my baby."

"It's okay. Elizabeth is at the dig. She's got those nerdy science guys with her." Garik was talking, convincing Charles, convincing himself. "She promised she would stay with them until I picked her up." But Garik had to confirm.

He pulled out his cell phone. He had power. He had signal.

He called Elizabeth.

The call went right to voice mail.

He hung up, and turned to run out the door.

Charles grabbed his arm with surprising strength. "You can't leave me here. I have to go with you."

The old guy would be a liability. He would hold Garik up. But fair was fair.

Garik helped Charles stand. He took him by the arm. "Yeah. Yeah, I could use the help."

CHAPTER EIGHTY-FOUR

It was two o'clock before Elizabeth lifted her head from her patch of dirt. "I'm going to take a break," she told Ben.

He lifted a hand in acknowledgment. "Don't go far."

The news about Yvonne had made the rounds fast. Plus Elizabeth was pretty sure her research team was embarrassed that they'd left her alone the night she'd been attacked. They weren't bad guys; she'd just come into an all-boys club and been the outsider, and the one person who could have assisted her to gain entry, Andrew Marrero, had been too much of a bully to help.

Today Ben, Luke, and Joe made sure they stayed close.

Elizabeth walked to one of the biggest boulders deposited by the tsunami, climbed up, and pulled out her bottle of water. The rare, warm, dry August days had turned the mud to dust, and the dust parched her throat. She took a long drink, and looked out over the horizon.

Ben had decided they should work in an area not far from the sea. Marrero hadn't approved the change, but Ben said another earthquake would bring another tsunami, and they needed to catalog as many changes as they could before that happened. Unspoken was the agreement that Marrero would have a fit when he returned. Also unspoken was that no one cared.

Sitting here she heard the constant, low rhythm of the waves, smelled the spicy cypress, and through the loose, hanging branches and dense sprays of dark green foliage, she could see the sunlight on the deep blue ocean.

The work had done what she hoped: freed her mind from anxiety, grief, and worry, and given her thoughts a chance to rattle loose from the depths of her subconscious.

Yes, she might be right. Perhaps her father had learned to draw, and with the Alzheimer's, lost the skill. But when Charles looked at that sketch of Misty, he seemed almost grief-stricken. Heart-sore.

Elizabeth understood.

She didn't want to look at that drawing and think of some man watching her mother so closely that he sketched a masterpiece. Because if that was true, then the picture Elizabeth treasured so much had been drawn by Misty's lover.

She dug her album out of her bag, found the drawing, and pulled it loose. Flipping it over, she searched for a signature.

Nothing.

She turned it over again, and stared at the sketch, created with care and inspiration in pencil and charcoal, and yet . . . not signed.

The watercolor of her mother kneeling in the sand beside a tow-haired child had been signed. She remembered the scrawl in the lower right-hand corner . . .

Elizabeth's hands began to shake. The black-and-white drawing wavered, replaced in her brain by a drawing of luminous pastels. She saw a child's chubby fingers holding that painting, touching that painting. She remembered loving that painting . . .

Or did she? Perhaps this was not a memory, but a dream, the fantasy of a lonely, motherless child. Yet in her mind's eye, she could see it so clearly.

Pulling out her phone, she started to call Garik.

A piece of paper fluttered out of the side pocket.

A note, in Garik's handwriting: *In case we lose cell service again—meet me at your old house at three. By then, I'll have something to show you.*

She didn't believe it. When would he have put that in her bag? Why not just tell her?

She called him.

"Damn it to hell." She didn't have service.

She examined the note again.

No way around it. This was Garik's handwriting: loose, large, distinctive.

She flung her bag over her shoulder. She called down to the guys, "I'm going to walk up to the top of the canyon and see if I can get through to Garik."

Shaken from their concentration, Ben, Luke, and Joe looked up from the work in disgust.

Joe stood. "I'll walk you." To the other two, he said, "I've got to take a leak, anyway."

Elizabeth almost grinned. Relentlessly practical, these

guys—if she was going to tear one of them away from the work, he might as well take the break that refreshes.

Joe and Elizabeth made the climb to the rim of the canyon.

Joe visited the Port-a-Potty.

Elizabeth tried her phone. Nothing. No bars. No service.

Joe came out, adjusting his waistband.

"Can you make a call?" she asked him.

He gave his phone a try, and shook his head. "Nope. Even when we haven't had a couple of sizable earthquakes, this close to the Pacific, service is iffy."

"Yes." She looked down at the note still clutched in her hand. "The thing is, I've got a note from Garik telling me to meet him at my old house."

"Your old house? You mean, where your father—"

She cut Joe off before he could repeat the words she had heard so many times in the past. The words that she now knew were not true. "Yes. That house. Garik says he's got something to show me. So I'm going to go ahead and see what he wants."

Joe put his hands on his hips and tried to look manly, rather than nerdy. "You can't go alone."

She shouldn't. She looked at the note again. She looked at the black-and-white drawing. She thought about the watercolor. And she thought about Garik, waiting for her with news about the killer. "It's not far. There's nothing between here and there. I know what you're thinking— I'm thinking it, too—but logically, I can't see a murderer figuring out that I'm anywhere but at the research site."

She had spoken the magic scientific word. *Logically.*

"That makes sense. But I'll go with you anyway." Joe went to the rim and shouted, "I'm taking Elizabeth to her old house to meet Garik." The two of them started walking. "I *have* to go," he told her. "If by some chance something happened to you and I didn't, Garik would crush me like a bug."

"That is so true." She tried again to grin. She couldn't quite do it. Because she was scared. She was jumpy. She was hopeful. She was intent on their destination, yet she managed to chat as they walked the mile to the empty house on the empty plateau above the sea.

When the house came into sight, they both stopped.

"I heard it was haunted," Joe said. "Now I believe it."

She nodded.

Here her childhood had been destroyed. Here her life had changed forever—and yet to her, now, it looked like an old-fashioned, decrepit, isolated seaside home on a plot of land five miles wide. Here, salt-toughened grasses waved, a few scattered cypresses bowed down to the constant wind, paint peeled off the siding that sagged with weariness. Broken windows showed jagged teeth. The roof was missing shingles. The place was sad. As Joe said, haunted.

"No vehicle in front," Joe said. "What time's he supposed to meet you?"

She glanced at her watch. It was two fifteen. "Three."

"We've got some time then. Come on, let's check it out."

"Yes. Let's check it out."

CHAPTER EIGHTY-FIVE

Garik had no right to take Charles from the Honor Mountain Memory Care Facility. He wasn't a relative. He had no legal justification.

But he walked confidently down the corridor toward the front door, escorting Charles, speaking to everyone they met. The facility was still in shock from the discovery of Yvonne's body, numb with horror and grief. The medical professionals, the other patients . . . no one paid them more than passing heed.

Charles walked beside him exuding a special kind of assurance, as if he understood exactly what was at stake, and in fact as they got closer to the nurses' station, the one that guarded the door, he murmured, "I've always wanted to break out of prison, and this is exactly how I imagined I would do it."

Garik glanced sharply at him.

Did he see the care facility as a prison?

Of course he did. Another prison that confined him and kept him from going out into the world to do his work, visit his daughter . . . seek revenge.

The test for this jail break would come at the nurses' station. Someone had to buzz them out, and Garik had to convince them it was okay. Everyone always saw Garik with Elizabeth, everyone knew Elizabeth was Charles's daughter, and everyone knew they had been married.

Maybe this would work.

This had better work.

Garik and Charles walked up. Garik leaned against the desk and smiled sympathetically at the two female LPNs who stood with red-rimmed eyes, and at Layla, the new nurse who had taken Yvonne's place. "How is everyone doing?" he asked.

They all nodded with varying shades of sorrow.

"I didn't know Yvonne well," said one of the LPNs. "I've never worked the same shift. But this goes beyond friendship into—"

"Horror," Charles said.

"Yes," the LPN agreed.

"Charles is pretty shook up, too," Garik told them, "and in need of some sunshine. Is it okay if I take him out into the garden?"

Layla hesitated.

"I knew Yvonne so well." Charles's voice broke. "She was kind to me and kind to my daughter, and I am so sad."

He sounded sincere.

Garik knew he *was* sincere. "If you're in doubt that this is okay, call Sheila," he said. "She knows me. She's knows I'm an ex-FBI agent. She knows Charles. She'll vouch for us walking outside together." He was pretty sure she would, too.

"Sheila doesn't come on until the night shift. I'm not going to bother her while she's sleeping." With her hand on her shoulder, Layla rotated her neck as if she had a kink in the muscle. "You can go. No more than fifteen minutes. Aurora, you go with them."

The biggest LPN, a massive woman with a Midwestern accent, nodded and came out from behind the desk.

From behind the desk, Layla unlocked the door.

Garik spoke in Charles's ear. "My truck—it's the white Ford F-250. I'm parked close. Angle that direction. Don't run until the last minute. I'll catch up with you."

Charles nodded.

As they exited the building, Garik smiled at Aurora—and gave Charles a push toward the garden. "So," Garik said as Charles wandered toward the row of roses, "Where are you from?"

"Minnesota." Aurora pronounced it with a distinctive lilt. With her gaze on Charles, she asked, "Is it all right for him to go so far on his own?"

"He's old. He's feeble. He's been in prison for years. And he's suffering seizures. I think we're okay." Garik marked every time Charles swerved, turned to look back at his escorts and smile sweetly, leaned over to smell the roses. Yet always he moved toward the parking lot, toward the truck.

Old and feeble and a prisoner and suffering seizures, yes. But the man was brilliant, and Garik felt his respect—and his sense of urgency—escalate.

"Patients will do anything to get away," Aurora said with assurance.

"Where could he go?" Garik gestured toward the forest that surrounded the facility. "It's not like he can find a bar around here and stop for a beer."

Aurora stared at Garik as if he was not too bright. "The patients, they can't think that far ahead. He could get lost in the woods and we wouldn't find him until he was dead of starvation and exposure."

Garik did his best to look abashed. "You're absolutely right. If he takes off, I promise I'll run after him."

The female viewed Garik with narrow-eyed suspicion.

Either Garik was losing his touch, or Aurora was one smart cookie.

And Charles was veering away from the garden.

Garik put his hand on her arm. "I'll catch up with him." He hurried toward Charles.

Aurora hurried after him.

Charles picked up speed, heading toward the truck.

"Hey!" Garik started jogging. "Charles, hold up!" He

gave Aurora a big thumbs-up, and surreptitiously used the remote key to unlock the vehicle. "Charlie, really. Come on. You can't get away."

Charles opened the passenger side and climbed in.

Garik faced Aurora and laughed a little. "Unless he can hotwire my truck, he's reached the end of the line. Relax. I can get him. I'll show him the interior. He really is a good guy."

Aurora slowed. She stopped.

At last Garik yielded to his need to *hurry*. He sprinted to driver's side. He opened the door, slid inside, started the engine.

Charles locked the doors.

Aurora shrieked in fury and roared toward them.

Garik peeled out of the parking lot, burning rubber all the way. "Hang on, amigo, this is going to be a wild ride," he shouted to Charles, and floorboarded the gas pedal.

CHAPTER EIGHTY-SIX

As soon as the Honor Mountain Memory Care Facility vanished in the rearview mirror, Garik called Elizabeth.

The call went right to voice mail.

"Oh, come *on*," he said.

"What's wrong?" Charles asked.

"I can't reach Elizabeth right now." He tried to sound reassuring.

A quick glance at Charles proved he hadn't succeeded.

What next? "I'm going to make another phone call, check in on another suspect." Garik dialed Marrero's number—he'd called it often enough in the past few days—hoping to hell Marrero had showed up at Virtue Falls Canyon and was answering his phone, hoping even more Marrero's stabbed and lifeless body hadn't been carried inland by the tsunami, or worse, carried out to sea, never to be seen again.

Garik jumped when the call clicked through, and without waiting for an answer, he said, "Where are you, you bastard?"

But a woman's voice spoke. "Hang on a minute. Andrew's a little tied up right now. Let me put this to his ear."

Startled, Garik asked, "Who is this?"

But the female was gone, and the next voice was Marrero's. He shouted, "Call the cops! This madwoman has kidnapped me!"

In the background, Garik could hear the woman say, "Now, darling, you're overreacting."

Garik tried to get his breath. "Marrero, who kidnapped you?"

"Rainbow!"

No wonder Andrew Marrero had been absent for so long. No wonder Rainbow looked so smug, and appeared only when she wanted. No wonder she had a puffy mouth . . . Garik sought clarity. "You mean *Rainbow* has taken you prisoner and you can't escape? You can't get away from *Rainbow*?"

"She waited until I was asleep and tied me to the bed!" Marrero was obviously furious.

As alibis went, Garik thought that was very impressive. "Okay."

"This is the most humiliating, horrifying experience of my life!" Marrero sounded as if he was expecting sympathy.

Probably he wouldn't appreciate Garik's rising amusement.

Garik could hear Rainbow croon, "Watch how you are talking, lover. I told you—if I want any lip from you, I'll take it out of my zipper."

"Call the cops!" Rainbow must have taken the phone away from Marrero's ear, for Marrero sounded far away.

"You're a very naughty boy, telling him to do that." Rainbow's voice got fainter. "You deserve to be punished, and I'll have to use my paddle on your plump white ass."

Garik could not hang up fast enough. He was pretty sure that when he'd had the chance to think about it, he would be emotionally scarred.

But right now, what mattered was knowing Marrero and Rainbow were eliminated, once and for all, as suspects in Misty's murder.

Garik glanced worriedly at Charles. Not that he didn't agree with Charles—Bradley Hoff was the killer. But accomplices always added a frightening complication to any case.

Garik called Elizabeth again.

No answer.

He called the Oceanview Café.

Dax answered.

"This is Garik Jacobsen. Is Bradley Hoff there?"

"He left about a half hour ago to check up on his wife." Dax lowered his voice. "Why? Do you think Vivian Hoff is in danger?"

No. Garik thought Vivian Hoff was dead. "Is Elizabeth there?"

"No. She left with you. What—?"

Garik hung up. With a glance at Charles, he said,

"Okay, look. The good news is, we've narrowed our list of suspects to one, and you're right. I can't say for sure it's Bradley Hoff, but that's pretty much merely the caution of a grizzled FBI agent. The bad news is, I'm not getting Elizabeth on the phone. All that probably means is that she doesn't have service. Since the earthquake, that's been a problem for everyone."

"What are we going to do now?" Charles's voice was calm, but in his lap, his hands gripped each other so tightly his knuckles bulged.

"We're going to go to Virtue Falls Canyon and talk to her in person."

"Good." Charles nodded. "Good."

Garik headed to the research site, following the road that paralleled the canyon, watching for signs that the team was working below. He sighed with relief when he saw equipment dumped near the canyon rim close to the ocean. "Stay here," he said. "Let me find her." He turned off the truck, took the keys, and jogged the path. Standing at the top, he scanned the area until he saw them: two guys, working in the dirt.

Hey!" he yelled. "Where's Elizabeth?"

The guys looked up, looked at each other, then Ben stood and yelled back, "She said she'd heard from you, and she left."

Garik's mouth went dry. "The hell she did. What did I say?"

"To meet you at her old house."

Elizabeth had been duped. Somehow, his brilliant, logical scientist had been fooled.

Garik raced back to the truck.

As he opened the door, Ben shouted from the rim of the canyon, "Joe's with her!"

They didn't get it. They thought if they sent one guy

to walk with her, one young scholar to protect her, she would be fine.

In fact, both Elizabeth and Joe were going to die.

Garik got in the truck, started the engine, and roared down the road toward the old Banner house. "Charles," he said. "I'm not going to lie to you. I don't know how, but someone conned her, told her I wanted to meet her at the home where you lived with Misty and Elizabeth." The choice of place sent a chill down his spine.

Charles stared straight through the windshield, his stare vacant, his jaw tight.

Garik continued, "We're going there now. It'll only take about ten minutes."

Charles didn't respond.

"Charles?" Garik put his hand on Charles's shoulder.

Charles fell sideways.

Slamming on his brakes, Garik skidded to a halt, graveling flying off the side of the road.

Charles shuddered violently. His spine arched like a bow. His legs kicked out, once, twice, again.

Seizure.

"No. No. No." Garik opened the console and grabbed a wad of napkins. He folded them into a long, tight stick and forced Charles's mouth open. He thrust them between Charles's teeth. "Don't do this. Don't do this now, Charles."

Charles's eyes stared at him, open wide, frantic and blind.

Maybe he knew what was happening. For sure he would want Garik to save his daughter.

"Right." Garik had done everything he could for Charles.

He put the car back into gear and pressed on the gas.

CHAPTER EIGHTY-SEVEN

As Elizabeth and Joe approached the house from the back, Joe abruptly confessed, "That night, when we left you alone and you were attacked—that made us feel like shit."

Elizabeth looked at him in surprise. "Well . . . good."

He winced, and looked a little like he was going to kick the grass. "We didn't realize there was any danger."

Elizabeth relented. "I know you didn't."

"Let me go in and make sure it's safe."

Elizabeth found her pocket knife tucked in her bag, brought it out, and held it so the longest blade glinted in the sun. Her voice was cool. "You do that."

At work, Joe had seen her use that knife dozens of times before. But now he viewed her as if she was Xena, warrior princess. "You think we'll need that?"

"No. If I thought we needed it, I wouldn't have come. But if this guy who goes around attacking and killing women is in there—then yeah, we need it."

Joe obviously hadn't put it together, that he was doing more than walking with her, that he might have to protect her. His brown eyes got big and scared. "My dad's good with a knife," he said.

"So are you. I've seen you."

"Cutting brush!"

She patted his shoulder. "Don't worry about it. This place feels . . . so abandoned."

But Joe was jumpy now, and went in and came out in a few minutes. "You're right. Nobody's in there. I thought it would be spooky, but it's just old and dirty and beat-up." He seemed almost disappointed.

She was curious to see it again, and more than that, something called to her: the hope of memories. "I'm going in anyway." She slid her knife back in her bag and slung the bag over her shoulder.

He sat down on the steps. "Watch out for wildlife."

Startled, she raised her eyebrows.

"Mice," he said. "There are droppings in there."

Not just droppings, she discovered, but also dust and exposed insulation. The closed-in back porch was filthy, cramped, the wooden floor broken where the washer had shimmied its way through the boards. She recognized the odor—all homes close to the ocean smelled the same, like saltwater doom waiting to happen.

She walked down the hallway and looked into one bedroom. A moldy, queen-sized mattress leaned against the wall. So this had been her parents' room.

She walked to the next door: an old-fashioned bathroom with a pale green sink, a pale green toilet, and a white tub stained with rust.

The next door . . . an empty room, a smaller room, with peeling wallpaper and ragged, faded pink curtains.

A child's room.

Her room.

Sad. She didn't know how else to describe it. Just . . . sad.

A little girl had once hidden in here. Hidden from what she had seen.

Elizabeth didn't remember. Or rather—she remembered only one thing, a drawing that wasn't in her scrapbook, a watercolor of a little girl sorting seashells at the shore while her mother watched over her.

She was almost sure it was real.

Standing in the room, she absorbed the house's atmosphere. "Mommy," she whispered. "Tell me where it is."

Where would a frightened little girl hide her treasure?

She opened the closet door and stepped inside.

A former resident had left winter coats hanging in here, now moth-eaten and mildewed. Chipboard shelves, denuded of paint and empty of toys or clothes, drooped from the humidity. Other than that, the closet was bare. Nothing to see here. Nothing of interest.

Did Elizabeth really expect the watercolor would be conveniently placed for her discovery?

Okay. She had. It seemed to her that if her mind had at last given up one small shard of remembrance, it was only fair she should be able to verify it. But no—life didn't work that way.

She needed to look closer, get down on her knees and run her hands under the bottom set of shelves, look into the places where a little girl would hide a cherished possession. Yet the closet seemed close and airless, too small and getting smaller by the minute. She had longed to absorb the house's atmosphere; well, in here, she wanted to brush at her skin, to take away the sense of evil crawling beneath her clothing.

She flipped the switch beside the door.

The hanging bulb remained stubbornly off.

Beside the switch, the electrical fuse door was rusted shut. Taking the metal ring, she jerked hard.

The ring broke. She staggered backward.

Gingerly she placed her bag on the filthy floor. Pulling her keys out, she tried to pry the door open.

The keys were too wide to get into the narrow gap.

She dropped them back into the bag and located her pocket knife. She opened the longest blade and slid it between the door and the wall. With an audible crack, the door opened a mere inch. Wedging her fingers underneath, she pulled it, the rusty hinges creaking as gradually the interior was revealed: nothing but electrical fuses, their switches leaning the same direction.

Disappointment sighed through her, then irritation.

What had she expected? It was a fuse box, not a treasure chest.

On the inside of the door, affixed with yellowing tape, was a piece of paper with a basic outline of the fuses and what each fuse controlled: kitchen, back porch, living room, bedrooms, bathroom. Pretty basic: most people wanted to know which fuse to flip when the lights blinked out or the hair dryer wouldn't work.

But this was no ordinary, cheap piece of paper. It was vellum, thick, made from cotton, used for blueprints and . . . drawings. Drawings like the ones in her album.

She loosened the tape, took it and her bag, and stepped into the bedroom, into the sunlight. She turned over the paper—and there it was.

The watercolor had been first sketched in pencil, then filled in the palest of pastels. The artist had created a masterpiece of waves, sand, a four-year-old girl with a head of hair so white and fine, it looked like a puff of dandelion seeds . . . and a luminous, curvaceous young woman kneeling beside her, showing her the wonder of a seashell. Above them, a wash of pale blue sky curved down to blend into the horizon.

Elizabeth's breath caught.

This was art. This was inspiration.

This was love.

And the scrawled name at the bottom told her everything she needed to know.

Bradley Hoff.

Bradley Hoff had loved her mother.

Bradley Hoff had killed her mother.

CHAPTER EIGHTY-EIGHT

At the sound of footsteps coming down the hall, Elizabeth lifted her head and called, "Joe?"

But the man who stepped into the door of the bedroom was not Joe.

Of course not.

Bradley Hoff stood there in blue jeans so worn they were faded white, a white T-shirt splattered with pastel shades of oil paints, running shoes . . . and carrying a long pair of shiny scissors like a blade.

Her heart began to thump hard in her chest. "Where's Joe?"

"He's outside." He smiled, a crooked smile of great charm. "He, um, took a blow to the head."

Had she managed to get Joe killed?

"How did you know I would be here?" she asked.

"I put the note in your bag."

"But . . . Garik's handwriting." His distinctive handwriting. She knew it so well.

"I'm an artist." Bradley said simply. "I can create lines. I got Jacobsen's phone number, studied how he made his numbers, then I practiced as I handed it out to the fine, upstanding citizens of Virtue Falls. By the time I wrote the note, I was pretty good. Don't you agree?"

She couldn't believe her own gullibility. "You made me think Garik had written that note. You put it in my bag. You lured me here." She had to ask. She had to hear him say the words. "Why would you do that?"

He looked almost young. He looked fit. And his blue eyes sparkled with anticipation. In a voice saturated with confidence, he said, "Elizabeth, you know the answer."

She did. She had always known the answer. She had feared this moment all her life. "You killed my mother. And you intend to kill me."

"I had to kill your mother. She betrayed me." Bradley's mouth quivered; he looked like a man wounded and deceived.

"Betrayed you." His arrogance staggered Elizabeth. "How?"

"I seduced her. I taught her what it was to love. I kept our affair secret. I let her continue on with her sham of a marriage." As if wiping away a tear, he put his hand to his cheek . . . his dry cheek. "All I required from her was that she be my muse."

"Your muse . . . why would you kill your muse?"

"She phoned me. She said to come here. I did. I imagined all kinds of things. I imagined she was going to say she would leave Charles and you, and come away with me, and I would paint her every day of my life." Bradley sighed with remembered pleasure. Then his smile faded. "Instead, she told me . . . she told me it was over." Twenty-three years later, his eyes flashed with remembered rage.

"So you slit her throat."

"Slit her throat? No!" He made a wide, slashing motion. The silver scissors glinted. "I committed a magnificent crime of passion! I ripped her throat open. I tore her guts out. She tried to crawl away. Tried to crawl toward the front door. I stabbed her in the back, in the heart." He whispered, *She tried to crawl toward the front door.* Do you know why?"

Elizabeth swallowed. She nodded.

"No, you don't." He was indignant. "It took me years before I realized what she tried to do."

"The logic is irrefutable." Elizabeth was proud of her

calm manner. "I was in the bedroom, and she was trying to lead you away from me."

That intense gaze flashed up to hers. "Yes. You're right. She loved you more than me."

"No kidding." Elizabeth held her bag in her left hand. She held the small watercolor clasped between two fingers of her right hand.

"She was going to return to your father, to that milk-sop marriage with a man who was *good* to her. She didn't understand. She was my muse." In an extravagantly romantic motion, he pushed the casual droop of hair off his forehead. "Do you know the kind of work I did while she loved me?"

"I think so." Elizabeth showed him the watercolor, and in a voice imbued with scorn, she said, "This is not some feeble Nature's Artist crap. This is *good.*"

"I don't *ever* paint crap!" He flip-flopped from one emotion to another, from brokenhearted agony to violent rage, from self-righteous smugness to simmering resentment.

No matter what she did, she was in trouble.

Garik didn't know she was here.

Joe was hurt, or worse.

She had to save herself.

Elizabeth had him off-balance. She had to keep him off-balance. "Really?" she said. "What you paint now isn't crap? *Really?*" Her words dripped scorn, and she kept the watercolor turned toward him. "Because when I study this as opposed to that commercial stuff you now do, I can see the difference. You had feelings for the scene, for the subjects. You were obsessed."

He stared at the watercolor, breathing hard.

"You're *still* obsessed. With this subject. But not the pretty watercolors. Not the paintings of Virtue Falls and the beach and the sunsets. You know the difference," she said softly. "You *do*. You see the difference between the passion that permeates this watercolor . . . and that *crap* you paint now."

"Don't call it crap!" he shouted in an explosion of resentment and anger. "People love that crap!"

"Crap! Crap! Crap! Your new paintings are very pretty. Pretty." She paced toward him. *"Pretty! And crap!"*

When she was almost in reach, he grabbed for her.

She jumped back. "If my mother saw what you were painting now, what would she say?"

His lips compressed. His head lowered as if he was a bull ready to attack.

"She would be ashamed of you." Elizabeth pounded at his most vulnerable spot—his ego. "After the earthquake, you wanted to kill my father. You came to Virtue Falls to kill him."

"The online article said you were visiting him, that you were connecting with him. Sooner or later, the two of you would get together and somehow you were going to figure it out. Who I was. What I'd done."

"Why did you care?"

"I'm the smart one. *I'm* in charge."

Surprise! He was a control freak. "For the keys to the facility, you attacked Yvonne in the parking lot. But you did it the night before you arrived. How?"

"You are so astute, Elizabeth." Bradley seemed almost to admire her.

She thought he probably did. If he defeated an intelligent opponent, in his own mind, he was even grander and more important.

This man lived to be important.

He said, "I met a man in Portland at one of my art shows. He bragged about the small, unlicensed helicopter he had built for himself. He bragged that he could fly it low, under the radar, and never got caught. He told me that for one of my paintings, I could rent it. So I did. I rented it, and him, and flew here. The stupid thing leaked fuel all the way here, and all the way back." Bradley wrinkled his nose as he remembered the stench.

"Yes. Yvonne said her attacker smelled like fuel."

"Did she? Good thing I killed her, then."

"God, yes . . . but the pilot knows about you?" Which would be too much to hope for . . .

And was, for Bradley said, "Don't be ridiculous. He knew too much, and I had to kill him."

He made murder sound so simple, so logical.

Keep him talking. Keep him talking. "What does your wife say?"

"My wife? Who? Oh . . . Vivian?" He fingered the tip of his scissors. "Vivian says nothing."

Elizabeth didn't like his tone, his little smile. "What do you mean?"

"Do you remember the legend of Blackbeard's wives? He married many, and one by one they disappeared. Finally he married a smart woman. He gave her the household keys, and told her she could go into any room in his mansion, except one. She couldn't resist. She unlocked that door, and found the heads of all his other wives hanging there, their faces frozen forever in the death grimace."

The story made Elizabeth's skin crawl. "Vivian discovered your stash of . . . heads?"

"Not quite. She broke into the back room of my studio, and saw my souvenirs and my paintings." He laughed a little. "It was so interesting to catch her in there, to coax her into confessing. All these years, I thought she was nothing but a fool, a tool, someone for me to use. But she knew what I was. She knew what I was doing."

"So you killed your wife? Because she knew that you'd killed my mother?"

With deceptive simplicity, he said, "Vivian knew that I killed them all."

Elizabeth froze, held her breath until she was faint, felt the fear spread from her gut to her cool, numb fingertips.

"The women. The blondes. The mothers." Those weird blue eyes blazed with evil delight.

He was admitting to everything. Everything Garik had told her. Everything she had feared.

Elizabeth took a deep breath. She had to remain conscious. She had to be smart. She had to survive. She pretended not to know. "You've been killing blond mothers?"

"And their children."

"You've been killing *me*." Garik had told her. She knew the truth. But she hadn't understood. Not until now, when she could see Bradley's pleasure, and his determination.

With chilling precision, he said, "That day, twenty-three years ago, I left you alive. I have never made the same mistake again."

"The children. You're killing . . . little children?" Tears leaked from the corners of Elizabeth's eyes. Tears of grief. Tears of fear. "Because . . . because you didn't kill me?"

"You saw me. You saw me when I was talking to your mother, kissing her, seducing her." His lips curled back from his teeth. "Wretched little girl, always there at the worst times. Misty finally, *finally* took you to play group twice a week so we could make love, and so I could paint her. Then, that day, when she was telling me it was over, I saw you peeking around the corner. You wretched, nosy kid . . ."

"I did see you kill my mother." The knowledge made

her stagger. She had actually seen him kill her mother. Yet still . . . she didn't remember.

She looked at the watercolor. This fragment of memory was all she had.

"Yes. But in the heat of action, I forgot about you. Because I had to kill her, because I grieved at what I had to do." As if a tear would make his viciousness acceptable, Bradley cried a single, real tear. Then in a prosaic tone, he added, "Because I had to get rid of her body first."

Elizabeth could see the moment in her mind. "When you came back to get me, it was too late. Daddy had already found me. The police were already here. It was too late."

"It didn't matter. Nothing mattered. She was dead. Misty was dead. My muse . . . was dead." Now real grief twisted Bradley's face.

"You're missing the point. You *murdered* her."

"I did what I had to do!"

"You killed my mother . . . and your paintings were never the same." Elizabeth allowed the watercolor to drop.

As if he couldn't take his gaze away, he watched it flutter to the floor.

She slid her hand into her bag and brought out her knife.

In a mournful tone, he said, "After all this is over, never again will I perform work worthy of my genius."

"Oh, how you mourn your genius." She allowed her sarcasm to overflow.

He yanked his gaze up to hers.

"You killed my mother for your paintings. You killed blond women because they remind you of my mother. You killed children because"—in a burst of fury, Elizabeth yelled—"you're a fucking coward who destroys people who are smaller and weaker than you."

Bradley shook as if an earthquake rattled him from

the inside out. Those blue eyes grew blindly manic. Lifting the scissors, he rushed at her fast and hard.

She swung aside, slammed her bag into his throat, and thrust her knife into his belly.

"Bitch!" Bradley shouted.

She dropped her bag, left her knife in his gut, and ran.

CHAPTER EIGHTY-NINE

Moving fast, Elizabeth rounded the corner into the living room—and Bradley tackled her from behind. She screamed as she went down, then hit flat and hard on the bare chipboard floor.

Her lips split. Her breath slammed out of her lungs.

He landed on top of her.

She put her hands down to push herself up.

His hand slashed down over top of hers.

Agony.

A pair of scissors pinned her to the floor. His pair of scissors . . . through her palm.

Blood rose from the wound. Blood pooled on the floor.

She couldn't believe—this was wrong. Impossible. Her nightmares come to life. She was helpless against the man who had slaughtered her mother.

She screamed and scrambled to reach for the handles.

He slammed her to the floor again, his knee against her back. He grabbed her jaw, twisted it around until he wrenched her neck, until she could see him out of the corners of her eyes. Said, "I've been waiting for twenty-three years to do this."

No. He would not kill her. She wouldn't allow it.

He yanked the scissors out of her hand.

Agony. She screamed again.

He repeated the words he'd said to her once before, "Let's cut off your pretty hair. We don't want to get blood in it."

She felt a snip close to her ear. Blond strands drifted to the floor.

He placed the points of the scissors against her eye.

And with her bloody hand, she reached behind her, grabbed his hair, and slammed his head forward and her head back.

She felt it; his face broke against her skull.

Now *he* screamed.

Driven by pain, by desperation, she bucked like a wild horse, throwing him off. She flipped over, and smacked the side of his head, over his ear, with her flat of her palm, driving air into his ear canal.

For one moment, his face went slack. He fell backward.

She rolled, got halfway to her feet.

He kicked her leg out from underneath her.

She caught a glimpse of his bloody face, of his eyes, insane with fury.

Insane. Yes. And livid.

Then, from the side, she heard a roar.

A male body crashed into Bradley, knocking him away and tumbling him across the room.

Elizabeth caught a glimpse of Garik as he slammed Bradley against the wall. Garik punched him, fast and hard, in the face, the chest, the belly.

But hurt as he was, Bradley still fought.

Insane.

His insanity gave him strength and cunning—and he

still held the scissors. He knew Garik's weakness, the ribs still unhealed, and he dodged and slashed, going for Garik's side again and again.

Every time he did, Garik fell back, gasping.

Every time Garik faltered, he returned to fight again.

Never taking her gaze from the two men, she tried to stand.

Her knee collapsed.

She crawled her way to the wall, used it to support herself as she inched to her feet. She was bleeding. From her hand, from her face. Blood slid down the back of her neck.

She looked around, found a two-by-four torn from a boarded-up window. Picking it up was torment. Lifting it over her head, she turned—in time to see Bradley rush Garik. Like a bullfighter, Garik stepped aside, gave him a push, and slammed him into the wall.

The scissors clanged to the floor.

Bradley crumpled, unconscious.

Elizabeth dropped the two-by-four. She slid to her knees in relief.

Garik checked Bradley for a pulse. "He's still alive. Damn it." He stood over him, fists clenched, jaw clenched, expression tight with wrath and frustration. "I ought to finish the job."

"No. You can't. You really can't." Elizabeth started crying—from pain, from relief, from a frantic worry that would not ease as long as Bradley Hoff breathed free. "If you do that, you'd never work for the FBI again."

"I don't care about that. That's over, anyway. And someone's got to kill him. He's evil, and he deserves to die." With his foot, Garik pushed at Bradley's limp body. He sighed in disgust, and turned away. Coming to Elizabeth, he knelt in front of her, and took her in his arms. "But you're right. I can't do it. No matter what kind of garbage he is, I can't kill an unconscious man."

Elizabeth cried on Garik's chest.

He murmured softly to her as he dug out his phone. "I'm calling nine-one-one and telling them to send an ambulance. You've got blood all over you."

"You're bleeding, too."

"He opened some of the stitches. What did he do to you?" Lifting her chin, he looked at her face. "You must have hit your face, and that looks painful. But where is the blood coming from?"

She held up her mutilated hand.

He took it in his. His horror was palpable. "This is . . . my God, Elizabeth. This is barbaric. I *can* kill him, because he so deserves to die." Garik half-turned toward Bradley's body.

But the body was gone.

Bradley was on his feet, bloody, vicious, the two-by-four clutched in his hand, his malicious gaze fixed on Garik.

Elizabeth yelled a warning.

Garik lifted his arm barely in time.

Bradley swung the two-by-four.

Garik took the blow on his forearm and forehead.

Elizabeth heard bone crack. "Garik!"

Garik fell to the floor, unconscious.

She lunged for him. Dead? Was Garik dead?

Bradley grabbed her hair in his fist and forced her to the floor.

She screamed in pain and panic.

He dragged her across the splintered boards to the scissors. He picked them up. Through blood and gore and malice, he smiled.

He thought he had won.

But she now understood him all too well. She knew what he feared.

Grabbing his wrist, she held it, fighting to control him. "Look around you," she said. "Do you see the blood? Some of it is yours. Some of it is mine. Some of it is Garik's. But *you* caused it all. You're bruised. You're broken. You've had a knife in your belly. DNA tests will ID you. Your fingerprints will ID you. And everyone will know. You're caught. You're dead. Even if you kill Garik, even if you kill me, even if you get rid of our bodies, they'll catch you. They'll put you in prison. They'll fry you."

Bradley looked. He saw. "I can get away."

"No. You're caught in your own trap."

She saw the knowledge dawn in his eyes—the knowledge that she was right. Finally, at last, he would face justice.

For one moment, hope burned in her heart.

Then he put his scissors to her face. "I don't care. Ever since I killed Misty, ever since I realized I had left a witness, I've been planning how I would cut out your eyes. How here, in this place, I would finish what I started. Now, at last, my dreams will come true. Misty was my first kill . . . and you will be my last. *Perfect.*"

Wild with terror, she fought him.

The scissors came closer. Closer.

His wrist flexed against her palm.

The scissors touched the corner of her eye.

She couldn't look away from him, from that madness that twisted his face.

The last thing she would ever see . . .

Suddenly . . . he jerked as if something had hit him. His eyes grew wide and astonished. His mouth dropped open . . . and blood trickled out.

What . . . ? How . . . ?

She looked beyond him, over his shoulder.

Her father stood behind Bradley.

She looked back at Bradley.

The point of her knife protruded from his throat.

Charles twisted the blade. Yanked it free. Grabbing Bradley by the shoulder, he threw him away from her.

Bradley staggered, his knees weak. He turned and stared at Charles without comprehension. His lips moved, but Elizabeth heard only a horrible gurgling. He fell to his knees.

Her father kicked his chest.

Bradley collapsed backward, his legs at awkward angles, his hands flopping.

Coolly, deliberately, Charles knelt on him, knee on his chest, and plunged the knife into Bradley's heart.

When Bradley's twitching stopped and his eyes went cold and blank, Charles looked out the broken window at the sky. "There, Misty," he said, "I did what I promised. I saved our daughter. I saved Elizabeth."

CHAPTER NINETY

It was midnight when Sheila let Elizabeth and Garik into the Honor Mountain Memory Care Facility. In a low voice, as she led them down the corridor, she said, "He's been waiting for you. He wouldn't go to sleep until you got here."

"He was a hero today." Garik was euphoric. "If I

hadn't taken him, we'd have both died. And Joe, too, poor guy. He's still in the hospital, glad to be alive."

"Let's not make a habit of stealing our patients, though, hm? And don't keep Charles up too late. He's . . . fragile." Sheila stopped in the doorway of Charles's room. "Here they are, Mr. Banner, safe and sound."

Charles was resting on the pillows, the nightlight dim above his head, and when he saw them, his face lit up with joy. "Children. I was so worried."

Elizabeth ran to him, hugged him, pressed her face into his shoulder, and wept.

Garik didn't blame her. After today, he was feeling pretty sentimental himself.

"Now, dear." Charles patted her back. "How are you? Are you hurt?"

She couldn't answer, so Garik said, "We're fine. A little battered"—an understatement—"and Elizabeth had to get a haircut."

"I see that." Charles smoothed her head. "It's very attractive."

Elizabeth touched the short, cropped cut and cried harder.

"She has to go into Seattle for surgery on her hand," Garik said.

Elizabeth sat up, sniffled, and blew her nose. She held up her palm completely encased in gauze and tape, her fingers sticking out, swollen and bruised. "And Garik's left arm is broken in two places."

Garik lifted his cast.

Elizabeth continued, "But thanks to you, we survived."

"Garik did his part." Charles offered his hand.

Garik shook it. "*You* killed him."

Charles's amiable expression faded. "I owed him."

"I understand that." Garik had never understood anything so well in his life. "Is Misty happy about this?"

"I haven't seen her lately," Charles said. "Not since my first seizure."

Garik and Elizabeth exchanged glances.

Garik hadn't realized Charles knew he had seizures.

"She'll be back, I'm sure," Elizabeth said, then looked confused and concerned, a woman who steadfastly didn't believe in ghosts and had just reassured her father he would be visited again.

"I don't think so. Not in this lifetime, anyway. She had to move on sometime, you know." Charles tried to smile, but his voice echoed with loneliness.

"The next time we come, we'll bring a reporter, name of Noah Griffin. You can tell him the story of you and Misty," Garik said. "He wants to write a book."

"No, don't bother." Charles reclined against the pillows, and he closed his eyes, rejecting the idea.

"But you'll be a hero," Elizabeth said.

"I never wanted to be a hero." Charles gaze opened his eyes to gaze at her. "I wanted to be a good husband and a good father." With one finger, he stroked Elizabeth's cheek. "I missed out on most of that, but I'm proud of the wonderful young woman you've grown up to be."

"I'm proud of you, too, Daddy." Elizabeth's voice grew hoarse from tears and emotion. So much deep-felt, never-before-experienced emotion.

"Will you be wearing a wedding ring again soon?" Charles asked.

"As soon as possible," Garik said firmly. "Although I imagine this time Margaret will want to host the wedding at the resort, invite the whole town, make it a big event with all the trimmings."

Elizabeth's spine straightened. "I can't do that. I don't have time. I've got a tsunami to research!"

"You tell a ninety-one-year-old woman that," Garik said.

"And break her heart," Charles added.

The men grinned as they watched Elizabeth reach the obvious conclusion—she was stuck.

The room eased into silence, into the quiet camaraderie of people who had together fought a battle, and won.

Then, in the doorway, Sheila said, "It's late, and it's been a very exciting day for Mr. Banner. Garik and Elizabeth, why don't you two come back in the morning after he's had a good night's sleep?"

"Of course." Elizabeth rose from her place on the bed, and pressed a kiss on Charles's cheek. "Good night. Sweet dreams."

"You, too, my darling girl." Charles smiled tremulously into her face. "Your mother said that after you were born, I would think you were even more beautiful than her. No one could be more beautiful than Misty, but like her, you have a spirit that shines from inside, and I love you dearly."

Elizabeth cried again—she didn't seem to be able to contain herself tonight—and kissed him. "I love you, too, Daddy."

Garik shook Charles's hand again. "Good night, Charles. We fought the good fight today. Now it's time for the wounded warriors to enjoy a good night's sleep."

"Wounded warriors." Charles's smile blossomed. "Yes. I like that. That describes us all perfectly."

Elizabeth hugged him again.

Garik shook his hand again.

Sheila escorted them out the door and toward the exit. Garik and Elizabeth slid their arms around each other's waists, taking care not to hurt each other more, and both staggered with weariness as they crossed the parking lot to his truck.

Tonight, the resort seemed exactly like home.

In his room, Charles sighed with happiness and closed his eyes.

Today had been the day he had never dared imagine could happen. He had served justice on the man who had killed Misty.

That seizure today in Garik's truck . . . had been the worst ever. Charles had been frozen, aware and yet helpless. In the prison of his brain, he knew that this was his only chance to take revenge on the man who had hurt Misty, who had destroyed their family—and he could not move.

Then, thank God, the seizure had ended. He'd been released. He could move. He had eased himself out of the truck, pushed open the front door, and seen Bradley Hoff holding a pair of scissors to Elizabeth's face.

A cold, clear rage had possessed Charles.

Remembering that moment, he laughed a little to himself. Who knew that in all those prison years, he had actually learned a few things about how to handle a knife? Yet he had, for he scooped up the pocket knife that glinted on the floor and with a panache that surprised even him, he—

Charles caught his breath.

His fists clenched.

His spine arched.

No. He fought. *Not another seizure.* Not tonight. Not so soon.

Pain. Pressure. His feet kicked at the covers. His body spasmed . . .

A burst of light.

The symptoms disappeared. Just like that, they were gone. No more pain. No more pressure. He relaxed and opened his eyes.

And there she was, his Misty, standing next to the bed and smiling at him with such delight. "You did it."

"I know. I killed him. He deserved it for what he did to you, and for what he wanted to do to Elizabeth."

"Yes . . ." She took his hand in hers. "That's what you were sent back to Virtue Falls to do."

"Was it? Then I'm glad I was a success in that, at least."

"You are the man I have always loved."

"Then I want nothing else from life."

"Do you remember our wedding? We promised each other eternity." She waved an arm, and he realized he had left his room.

He stood on a wide plateau. The sun shone on his skin, but there was no sun. The green grass waved in the wind, but there was no breeze. Flowers grew in colors that saturated his senses. Nearby was a clump of trees, and they murmured of the land, the water, the light. The scent of Misty filled him to the brim with joy.

Taking her in his arms, he looked down at her, his kind, gentle, loving wife, and he said, "Only eternity? Is that all the time I have with you?"

Misty laughed, a chime of happiness.

And they were beyond.

CHAPTER NINETY-ONE

On the day they buried Charles and Misty Banner, in a fitting tribute, the earth shook so hard Garik and Elizabeth had to hold onto each other to stand erect beside the gravesites.

Despite the solemnity of the occasion, they laughed.

CHAPTER NINETY-TWO

When Garik, Tom Perez, and the FBI agents broke through the locked door at the back of Bradley's studio, they found a long, narrow, windowless room, lined with paintings of Bradley's victims. He had rendered each portrait with chilling skill, creating a visual rendition of a murderer's pleasure and a victim's growing pain and terror—and attached to each canvas with glue and paint was the lock of blond hair Bradley had collected.

As experienced with murder as the agents were, still those paintings shattered them with horror.

The paintings of Misty were glorious, breathtaking, classics. In one, Bradley Hoff delineated a beautiful woman at the height of her seductive power, looking with longing at a hazy horizon at the far end of the ocean.

Only on Misty's portrait was the hair bloodstained.

Bradley's work as Nature's Artist would soon fade, but these works of exquisite terror spoke to everyone who saw them, and they would hang in the world's finest museums forever.

Bradley would be famous for all eternity.

As Margaret pithily put it, "Too bad for him he's going to burn in hell for exactly that long, too."

CHAPTER NINETY-THREE

On the first anniversary of the great Washington earthquake, Lt. JG Luis Sánchez pushed Kateri's wheelchair over a rutted, grassy trail to the top of the highest cliff overlooking the Pacific Ocean. He had tried to convince her to stay in town and mingle with the locals and tourists who had come in for the first annual earthquake celebration, but she had a reason for returning to Virtue Falls today, and it was not to be pitied by her former friends. So she fixed her eyes on Sánchez and ordered him to bring her up here, where the salt breeze would blow away the memory of a year of pain, betrayal, and heartache.

And he, who had so faithfully called, visited, and encouraged, reluctantly agreed to take her away from the festivities. Now he set the brake on the wheelchair and squatted beside her. "Glorious, isn't it?" he said.

To the north, Virtue Falls Harbor was awash in construction cranes as the idiots rebuilt as if the tsunami had never happened. To the south was Virtue Falls Resort, where after the quake Margaret Smith had thrown money around to bring her inn back to its revered excellence, and now did a brisk business. All along the coast, pocket beaches spread out their white sands for the tourists who assured each other another tsunami could not happen so soon.

Here was between.

Out there, in the ocean, islands of stone harbored seals and sea lions who basked in the sun, and waves blasted the great rocks stacked in mighty pillars and arches. Young seabirds rode the warm wind, and wheeled and swooped, exuberant with the joy of their new wings.

For one who had grown far too used to the sterile smell of antiseptic, the salt, dirt, and crushed grass mixed to form a heady perfume.

Kateri breathed, listened, and watched.

Those were functions of living most people took for granted.

She did not. Nor did she take her memories for granted. Too much of this year had blurred into a mess of pain, stress, futile anger, and . . . more pain. Here, she was away from all that. Here, she was home. She told Sánchez, "This place is the reason I fought my way into the Coast Guard and just about killed myself getting through the Academy."

"You got a raw deal." He meant it, too.

She shrugged. "The Coast Guard couldn't keep me, not in the shape I'm in, and especially not after the accusations of incompetence. I can't go back to dealing cards at the casino—funny, but the players want a pretty girl who hasn't been dragged through a glass window, drowned, and broken into little bits." She lifted her arm; her elbow had never set right and her lower arm twisted to the side. Her little finger skewed inward, and pale scars tracked across the skin on the back of her hand. "This is what happens when the doctors are so busy saving your life they consider the shape of your bones to be secondary."

"I think you're beautiful," Sánchez said.

"I think you're full of shit." She didn't give him time to come up with some compliment about her character shining through her face. "My mother always told me, 'Life ain't fair.' She was Native American. She knew what she was talking about."

There wasn't much Sánchez could say about that, so wisely he kept his mouth shut.

Abruptly she said, "Luis, go away."

He looked up at her, his big, brown eyes stricken and worried.

She cupped his cheek; her shattered hand made a horrible contrast to his healthy, tanned skin. "Go away. I promise not to wheel myself over the cliff. I simply want to be alone for as long as it takes me to celebrate a year of life I should never have enjoyed."

He knew she was being sarcastic, and like the generous Latin gentleman he was, he took her hand and kissed it.

She shouldn't pick on him. Just because he was handy didn't mean he deserved a dose of her bitterness. She shifted to fully face him. "Luis, I need some time alone. That's all. Between the doctors and nurses and physical therapists and lawyers, I haven't been alone for a whole year, and to come back here, to the place where it happened—I need a moment of reflection." That sounded good.

Civilized.

Quite the opposite of how she felt.

Sánchez wasn't fooled. He looked her dead in the eyes and said, "You swear on the graves of your ancestors that you won't in any way, shape, or form fling yourself off this cliff and into the ocean?"

"Wow. Pin me down, why don't you? I promise. I simply have something to say and I can't when you're here."

"You're talking to who?"

"The frog god."

"Oh. Okay." Luis rose to his feet. "I'll be back in ten minutes. That's all you get. Ten minutes. You'd better get it all said in that amount of time, because after that we're going down to listen to the art auction."

"Ew." Kateri didn't want to go for more than one reason. "Do we have to? They're auctioning off that ocean painting from Bradley Hoff . . . sick bastard."

"Bidding is expecting to start at one hundred thousand dollars."

"Bradley Hoff wasn't the only sick bastard," she observed.

"True. Who would want one of his paintings in their living room?" Luis started down the hill, and turning back, he shouted, "Ten minutes!"

When he was out of sight, she turned to the ocean. "Ten minutes. How do I express my feelings in ten minutes? How do I ask . . . *what the hell were you thinking?* I'm half Native American. My parents were divorced. My mother drank herself to death. I worked and challenged myself every day of my life. I became the commander of a Coast Guard station. I dedicated myself to the ocean, to knowing the currents, to worshipping the storms, to saving people's lives. It wasn't as if I didn't know suffering, or hard work, or emotional turmoil—I did. Then you dragged me out of my cutter, broke me into pieces, drowned me, revived me, made me live through a rebirth . . . and for what? For what? So Landon Fucking Adams from Snob-ass, New York, could take my place as the commander of my Coast Guard station? So the United States government, which I swore to protect and uphold, could take Landon Fucking Adams's lying, cheating testimony and sue me for incompetence in the loss of my cutter?" She closed her eyes, swallowed, and coughed. Sometimes, when she got excited, she felt as if she was drowning again.

She started again, more slowly, more quietly. "Sure. Witnesses came forward and said he was lying, that he's the reason I couldn't make it through the breakwater before the tsunami hit, and he was covering his ass. I got acquitted of all charges. But the assholes in town say stuff like 'Where there's smoke, there's fire' and 'That Kateri, she's American Indian, and her mother died an alcoholic,' like that has anything to do with me. And the government, who knows Landon Fucking Adams slandered me, has given him my command. *My* command." She put her hand over her heart. "He doesn't know the West Coast. He's going to get somebody killed. He only got the job because his uncle got reelected to Congress. I'm humiliated for myself and afraid for my men. But you don't care, do you? You don't care." Into her mind floated those huge eyes, that gaping mouth coming closer and closer.

She should be afraid to challenge the frog god.

But what was he going to do? Kill her again?

"Care," she whispered. "If you don't care about me, I demand you care about my men."

The earth quivered.

"Yes, you hear me. I know you do." She sat quietly and gathered her thoughts. "My people tell me the frog god has a plan for me. My people think I make the earth shake, and they sort of worship me now. Which is damned uncomfortable, let me tell you. Also, the medical staff in Seattle are afraid of me. Not that the scientific types admit it, but they are. I know this because . . . sometimes

I know things." Up to now, she hadn't even admitted that to herself—and she hated it.

She said, "I'm up to my ass in legal fees. The government would prefer if I bite it so they don't have to pay the cost of my rehabilitation. I've got two new hips, a new partial knee, and a physical therapist who tells me I'll never walk unaided again." She moved the footrests out of the way. She put her feet firmly on the ground. She placed her hands on arms of her wheelchair. Slowly she hoisted herself into the standing position.

She took her first step in a year.

She took her second step. And her third. And her fourth.

She lifted her feet abnormally high. Balance was a challenge. Pain struck in the atrophied muscles.

Strength of will made up for it all.

The wind blew. The waves crashed. The earth quivered.

She braced her feet.

She lifted her fists to the sea, and shouted, "I'm here. I'm alive. I can walk. So tell me the plan. Show me the plan. You wrote the plan. Now I demand to know!"

Read on for an excerpt from Christina Dodd's
next book

OBSESSION FALLS

Available in September 2015 in hardcover from
St. Martin's Press

CHAPTER ONE

The highway from Idaho's Sun Valley travels north into the Sawtooth Mountains with two lanes and strategically located turnouts in case a person needs to change a tire or gawk at the scenery. The road winds past shacks constructed of beer bottles and aluminum siding; past rusty mobile homes and clapboard houses in need of paint. That highway is a drive back in time, to a moment when the West opened its arms to every pioneer and misfit in the world.

Then the National Forest Service moved in.

No one ever said they did it wrong. The world deserves places of wildness, where no one logs trees that have grown since the time of Jesus, where snowmobiles and ATMs can't challenge black bears to battle and take out rare and delicate flowers. Most people want a place where hikers and backpackers can roam the wilderness, and then only in summer months when winter retreats . . . and waits.

But even the National Forest Service can do nothing about Wildrose Valley. Wildrose Valley Road turns off the main highway, and rises up and up in hairpin turns that make flatlanders clutch and cringe. The surface is gravel, full of washboard stretches that beat a woman's teeth together as she drives her rented black Jeep Cherokee toward the place where she had been born.

She tops the summit and there it is—the valley, slung like a hammock between the mountains. Ranchers had settled here in the early twentieth century, carving out tracts of land where they raised cattle and children, grew gardens and alfalfa, fought freezing cold and the Depression and bankruptcy.

But here and now, in August, the valley is wide, yellow with grass, dappled with cattle and antelope. Meadows stretch miles to the far horizon where the mountains close in. The Forest Service likes to think they protect the wilderness; in truth, the Sawtooth Mountains themselves are the sentinels and guardians of the land.

Taylor Summers had spent her first nine years roaming the Sawtooth Mountains in search of a safe place, away from her home, away from her parents' constant, bitter arguments about her father's ranch, her mother's ambitions, and Taylor, who had somehow become the heart of their conflict.

Then, on her tenth birthday, she had moved with her mother to Baltimore, and was never again to see Wildrose Valley . . . until today.

She drove slowly down the steep grade and into the flatlands, absorbing the changes. Where small craftsman-style ranch houses had once stood, mansions now sprawled. Not many mansions, though; rich people bought wide acreages and surrounded themselves with vistas that could not be blocked.

Taylor didn't blame them. Today, when she rolled down her windows, she heard nothing but the wind through the golden grasses and the occasional call of a bird. She recognized a few landmarks: a stand of maple trees where she used to play, the unpainted wreck of a barn where she'd swung in an exhilarating ride on a rope out of the hayloft and through the wide-open doors.

And there! *There* was the turnoff to the Summers ranch, owned by her family for over a hundred years, until her mother forced her father to sell it in the divorce and divide the profits.

Involuntarily, Taylor's foot slipped off the accelerator and the car slowed.

Look! The people who bought the place had put up a phony gate, and they had the guts to put up a sign calling the place SUMMERS FOREVER.

They not only had claimed her heritage, they'd also claimed her name.

The *bastards*.

Taylor rolled up her windows, put her foot back on the gas, and drove through ruts and dust through the flats at the end of the basin toward her goal, where the mountains came together, squeezing the road like a vise.

An hour of driving too fast got her at last to the serenity of mountains. Here was the forest she sought. The air was thin, sharp, fresh with the scents of pine and earth and growth and, yes, surely . . . inspiration.

Taylor had always considered herself a true artist.

Sure, she had gone to college to study graphic design, and sure, she had segued into interior decorating. But for all that she had besmirched her talent with good jobs that made gobs of money, she hugged close a strong sense of superiority. Deep inside, she had believed that if she flung away the trappings of success and became a full-time artist, her talent would change the world.

So to celebrate the crashing destruction of her second engagement, she had flown to Salt Lake City, rented a vehicle, and driven north along the Wasatch Range. She stopped to sketch every vista, expecting that sensitive, brilliant, expressive art would form beneath her fingers . . . . . .

No. Not once. Not a hint of genius, of uplifting emotion or self-knowledge or glory or pain. All these years of believing in herself, and this . . . this was it?

Drawn by the conviction that if she got home, she would rediscover her muse, she drove north, into Idaho. In Sun Valley, she rented a room, spent the night, and now here she was, heart pounding as she pulled into an isolated picnic area. She backed the Cherokee into a parking spot hidden by brush and trees. She grabbed a bottle of water, her waist pack, and her drawing pad, and climbed out. She followed a trail that wound through the trees, looking for the one spot she wished, believed, *hoped,* would reignite her vision.

In less than a mile, the forest ended and a wide, green meadow opened its arms to her, and she recognized this place. *This,* far more than the ranch, was home. Here her father had taught her to camp, to hike, to hunt. Of all her early life, those were the moments she treasured.

Taylor climbed up on one of the smooth, massive black basalt boulders abandoned by the glaciers. To her left and her right, as far as she could see, forbidding and majestic pinnacles pierced the pale blue of the August sky. To capture the grandeur of the Sawtooth Mountains required bold-hued oil paints done on a large canvas by a master.

All they had was her.

But she was here, and she longed to pay tribute to the forces of the earth.

Opening her sketch pad, she took up her charcoal pencil and gave her soul over to the vista before her.

When she had finished, she pulled back and studied her achievement.

In high school, her art teacher had told her anyone could draw a mountain, but a true artist depicted the soul of the mountain and gave the viewer a sense of glorious austerity or forbidding heights or searing cold. A true artist created not art, but feelings: longing, terror, love. Most of all, Taylor's art teacher warned her against making mountains look like ice cream cones.

Taylor could state with great assurance the mountains she had sketched did not look like ice cream cones.

They looked like ingrown toenails.

She rifled through her sketch pad, looking at each and every one of her drawings. How had she reduced the imperious majesty and eternal grandeur of the western mountains to such a disgusting human condition? She had dreamed of and planned for this, imagined her artistic talent would blossom in the place so long cherished in her childhood memories. Instead, she was a failure, such a failure that she was almost relieved when she heard a car bouncing along the washboard gravel road behind her. She shut her drawing tablet, slid off the rock, and headed into a stand of pines.

Not that she needed to hide. She had as much right to be here as anyone. But she was a woman alone. The car probably contained a rancher or some tourists, but wild game attracted out-of-season hunters, old gold claims dotted the creeks, and longtime residents carried guns. Up here, it was better to be safe than sorry.

When a black Mercedes came around the bend, hitting every rut as if it was a personal challenge, she grinned.

Rich tourists. She knew the type, city folks who could not believe that every road in America wasn't paved for their convenience. She wondered how far they would go before the washboards defeated them, or before they destroyed their car's oil pan on a protruding rock.

They passed out of sight behind a boulder as big as a house, where the road cut through the meadow, and there the sound of the engine cut out.

Probably they had a picnic lunch. They'd dine and head back . . .

She glanced at her watch. Two-thirty. Pretty soon, she needed to return to her rental Cherokee, too. It was a good two-plus-hours drive back to town. But first . . . . . . she started walking deeper into the woods, looking for something less imposing to sketch. A tree, maybe. Or a bug.

On the road, two doors slammed.

One man spoke, coldly, clearly: "Get him out of the trunk."

CHAPTER TWO

Taylor stopped.

Him? Out of the trunk?

She didn't like this guy's tone. She didn't like his words.

Who, or what, was in the trunk?

"Do you think this is far enough?" The other man sounded itchy, nervous.

She started walking again. *None of her business* . . . . . .

"How the hell much farther do you want to drive on that miserable crapfest of a trail? Jimmy said to bring him up here, find some place lonely, finish him, and dump the body—"

She froze.

"Isn't this lonely enough for you?"

"I guess—"

A thump.

"Yes!"

Finish him? Dump the body?

She felt disoriented. Birds were twittering. Above her, massive Douglas fir trees wrapped the heavens in their branches and sang a song to the wind.

And someone within her earshot was talking about . . . *dumping the body?*

"Then that's what we're going to do," the first guy said. "You want to argue with Jimmy?"

"No. No," the other guy stammered. "Not that scary bastard."

Some guy named Jimmy had hired these guys to . . . . . .

The trunk latch opened with barely a sound.

A child's scream filled the air.

This could not be happening. Taylor could not be up here, alone in the most peaceful place on earth, trying to get back her artistic mojo, and bear witness to a murder. A child's murder.

The second man said, "Jesus Christ, he hurled all over the trunk. I'm going to have to take this to the car detailers to get it cleaned up."

"No, you're not. How are you going to explain barf in the trunk? Tell them we were hauling a kid in there? Clean it yourself." The first guy had a baritone voice, and when he rolled out the orders, he did it with authority.

Above the voices, the child's wail became sobbing, punctuated by gasps for air.

Taylor did not want to be here.

But she was.

Chills ran up her arms, and she felt like hurling, too.

She left the protection of the trees and moved quietly into place behind the boulder.

She was safe here. She was. The boulder was as big as a house. Dense. Tall. Rolled into place by some ice age glacier.

She was safe.

She was a fool.

With her back against the rough stone, she slid and looked, slid and looked. Finally the car came into view.

And the men.

And the little boy.

And the guns.

Pistols, big pistols, held with casual familiarity in the men's hands.

One guy was bulky and narrow-eyed. He was in charge.

One was thin and muttering. He held the boy by the scruff of the neck and shook him like a terrier with a rat.

The boy . . . the boy was about eight, white-faced, dark-haired, covered with vomit. Terrified.

Taylor was terrified, too. Her hands trembled. Her knees shook. Her heart thundered in her ears.

But she could still hear the casual slap Mr. Skinny gave the boy.

"Shut up," he said.

The boy sobbed more softly.

She looked again. She recognized the big guy. Seamore "Dash" Roberts, running back, Miami Dolphins, big scandal, jail time, a career that barely survived in arena football . . . yeah.

The other guy wasn't anybody. He was just, you know, sweaty.

Both guys wore suits. Up here. In the land of ranchers, Ford trucks, tourists, and the occasional tree-hugger. So these men in the suits were out of place. But they didn't care. Because they were here to kill the boy and get out.

Good. Good. She could ID these guys . . . when she got down to the police department. *After they'd murdered that little boy.*

"Where do you want to do it?" Mr. Skinny asked.

Dash glanced around.

Taylor flattened herself against the rock.

"There, by that tree stump." He pointed. "That way we can prop him up. He'll face the road and when Mc-Manus shows up, he'll see him right away."

"Let him search." Mr. Skinny laughed.

The boy's crying gave a hitch.

She glanced again.

He was terrified. Yes, he was. But he was also eyeing the men, looking around at his surroundings, like he knew he had to make a run for it. Like he knew he had to save himself.

"Christ's sake, think about it." Dash again, snappy and scornful. "There are wild animals up here. Wolves. Coyotes. We hide the body, they'll drag it away and eat it. Jimmy will be furious. He's paying, and he wants the most bang for his buck. Shock. Horror. All that crap."

"He really wants to get this dude's attention, doesn't he?"

"You don't want to get on Jimmy's wrong side. He knows how to handle business."

The child shivered convulsively. He wore a school uniform. A school uniform, for shit's sake, with slacks, a pressed shirt and a tie. He was old enough to know he was going to die, and young enough not really to understand.

Well. Who did understand? She didn't. She wished she could help him. But there was no way. She wasn't carrying a gun. She couldn't just run at these guys, guys who were obviously professional hit men, and save the kid. All she would do was die, too. That wouldn't help the boy. She could do nothing but watch helplessly.

Even as she thought that, she was quietly, relentlessly tearing the sheets out of her drawing tablet. They were eight-by-eleven, good-sized sheets of paper with whipped cream clouds and ingrown toenail mountains.

She didn't have a plan.

Or rather—it was a stupid plan.

But the wind was blowing. The stand of trees was no more than twenty yards away. If she ran fast enough and dodged quickly enough, she could get away. And she couldn't stand to live the rest of her life knowing she didn't make even the most feeble attempt to save a child from murder by two professional killers.

Stupid plan. So stupid. She was going to get herself killed.

She heard her father's voice in her head. *Taylor, you can't outrun a bullet.*

She knew it. She really did. But the boy's crying was getting louder again, the men more silent. They were getting down to business, which was to murder the child and pose him so that guy, McManus, saw him as soon as he drove up the road.

Shock. Horror. All that crap.

When she had freed a dozen sheets of paper, she put the tablet on the ground and stepped on it. Holding three sheets high above her head like unformed paper airplanes, she let the wind catch them, heard them flap, took a breath—and released them.